THE CONFESSIONS

LLIAM, which groc...
LLIAM, should I app...
LLIAM, should I kill ...

LLIAM's AI-generated a society – but today, he went offline. Stocks fell, stores shuttered, planes were grounded. And Kaitlan Goss, CEO of LLIAM's parent company StoicAI, has to fix it.

Then the letters arrive: identical white envelopes on every continent, containing people's darkest secrets – affairs, family secrets, even murders. As people worldwide begin to confront their loved ones' worst transgressions, Kaitlan races to find Maud Brookes, the ex-nun who taught LLIAM what it means to be human. Only Maud can bring LLIAM back online, and stem the tide of societal breakdown.

But Maud doesn't want to be found. She received a confession letter, too – about Kaitlan.

Now, as society begins to collapse into chaos, the two women are forced into a deadly game of cat and mouse, while the whole world teeters on the brink.

LLIAM, how do I save the world?

For publicity enquiries please contact sophia.cerullo@faber.co.uk

PLEASE CONSIDER THE ENVIRONMENT
AND RECYCLE THIS PROOF WITH OTHER
PAPER RECYCLING

Paul Bradley Carr is a British journalist and author. He has written three memoirs about his adventures in and around Silicon Valley. He was the Silicon Valley columnist for the *Guardian*, senior editor at *TechCrunch*, cofounder of *PandoDaily*, and founder and editor-in-chief of the infamous *NSFWCORP* in Las Vegas. His writing has also appeared in the *Wall Street Journal*, *HuffPost*, *National Geographic*, and much more. He lives in Palm Springs with his family and is the co-owner of The Best Bookstore in Palm Springs. Find out more at PaulBradleyCarr.com.

THE
CONFESSIONS

A NOVEL

PAUL BRADLEY CARR

faber

First published in the UK in 2025
by Faber & Faber Limited
The Bindery, 51 Hatton Garden
London EC1N 8HN

First published in the United States by Atria Books, an imprint of
Simon & Schuster, 1230 Avenue of the Americas, New York, NY 10020.

Printed in the UK by CPI Group (UK) Ltd, Croydon CR0 4YY

All rights reserved
© Paul Bradley Carr, 2025

Designed by Esther Paradelo.

The right of Paul Bradley Carr to be identified as author
of this work has been asserted in accordance with Section 77 of the
Copyright, Designs and Patents Act 1988

*This is a work of fiction. All of the characters, organisations and
events portrayed in this novel are either products of the
author's imagination or are used fictitiously*

A CIP record for this book
is available from the British Library

ISBN 978–0–571–39680–1

Printed and bound in the UK on FSC® certified paper in line with our continuing
commitment to ethical business practices, sustainability and the environment.
For further information see faber.co.uk/environmental-policy

Our authorised representative in the EU for product safety is
Easy Access System Europe, Mustamäe tee 50, 10621 Tallinn, Estonia
gpsr.requests@easproject.com

2 4 6 8 10 9 7 5 3 1

People hate searching.

SAM ALTMAN, Open AI

People will let machines make more of their decisions for them,
simply because machine-made decisions will bring better results
than man-made ones.

TED KACZYNSKI, The Unabomber

THE CONFESSIONS

TOMORROW
Pineridge, California

Maud Brookes leaned against her shovel, breathless but satisfied. The snow had fallen heavy overnight on the mountain, and as usual, the early plow had pushed most of the flurry into the two parking spaces outside the bookstore. Maud stood barely five feet tall in her snow boots; skinny, with translucent blond hair; sunken, bloodshot eyes; and a complexion so pale it often prompted strangers to offer unsolicited advice about nutrition.

Contrary to her flimsy appearance, though, growing up at the convent—repairing walls, harvesting olives, carrying logs for the fire—had endowed her with powerful arms and an endless appetite for physical labor. She glanced at her digital watch. It had taken her just twenty minutes to shift the obstruction, forming a small white hillock just clear of the sidewalk. A couple of minutes shy of her record, but still pretty good.

Her daily task completed, Maud unlocked the doors of Pages in the Pines, switched on the lights, and paused to catch her breath. That was okay, too. As Doctor Kim liked to remind her, everybody's cardiovascular system had to work that little bit harder at six thousand feet above sea level. The smell of books always reduced Maud's blood pressure, better than any medication ever could.

In fact, the mountain had done wonders for her health, between the constant scent of the pine trees, the clean mountain air, and now all the books packed into her tiny eight-hundred-square-foot bookstore. Some days she could almost forget she was dying.

She bent to pick up a small pile of mail, then paused again to adjust a stack of Naomi Aldermans on her bestseller table, tucked next to a beautiful hardcover Thomas Aquinas ("Staff Pick!") displayed on a wooden stand. Maud prided herself in the catholic—pun unavoidable—nature of the store, with mass-market bestsellers nestling comfortably alongside academic tracts, poetry next to potboilers, just as they did in her own head. All of human experience, bound between covers. She had loved books since childhood, even if the idea of selling them had never been on her career path. Nothing about Maud's life had worked out as she'd planned, but that's what made it a life: You made the best decisions you could, then let the cards fall. There were certainly worse ways to live out her days than surrounded by books in a mountain paradise with fewer than a hundred residents and barely any cell reception.

It had been three days since Maud had last seen a customer, or anyone else for that matter. March was the mountain's off-season and most other businesses in Pineridge—the minuscule ice cream shop, the teeny hiking store, and titchy coffee shop—were still closed for the winter, water pipes drained, windows shuttered. Even Pete's Gas Station and Liquor Store was open strictly six till six.

Maud frequently went for days without interacting with another human, except for the mailman—and Valerie, the UPS driver who ventured up the hill once or twice a week to drop off small packages of new releases and collect unsold books for credit. Or, best of all, the rare occasion when Valerie arrived with a much larger carton filled with "advance reader copies" of as-yet-unpublished titles. Maud took pride in reading every single one of these before deciding which to order for the store and recommend to customers. She knew how it felt to labor for years creating something wonderful only to have your work ignored, or dismissed, or worse.

Today, though, there were no packages, just a few plain-looking envelopes that would likely be bills, or letters from the bank. Maud's office was tucked at the rear of the store: a closet-sized space containing a tiny sink and a desk with barely enough surface area for her coffee machine and accounts book. She set the mail down on the desk, filled the coffee machine with water from the faucet, and then flipped the switch to begin brewing. Doctor Kim had made her promise to switch to decaf, but what he didn't know wouldn't kill her.

Maud took another deep breath, and the aroma of roasted beans filled her lungs. Her store, her books, the mountain air, good coffee, and $250 million in an offshore bank account—yes, on balance, God had been very generous to her.

She was about to open the first envelope when she was startled by the sound of the door jangling open. Maud emerged from her office to see a tall, bearded man, dressed as if for an arctic expedition. She didn't recognize him, which meant he was probably a tourist, however unlikely that might be at this time of year.

"I'm building a deck," the man announced as if already mid-conversation, removing his gloves and depositing a flurry of snow onto her copies of *The Road*. "I guess I need a book now." Not so much as a good morning. Definitely a tourist.

"Our home improvement section is right over here." Maud smiled and gestured to one of the tall shelves that lined the perimeter of the store. "Yards and outdoors are on the bottom, crafts and woodwork in the corner. Let me know if I can help you find something." Maud loved making book recommendations. She truly believed that there was a book for every person and every situation—even a rude tourist building a deck—and nothing gave her such joy as making that connection. The man sighed theatrically at having to bend, but soon gathered a small stack of titles without Maud's help.

He dropped his selections on the counter, and noticed Maud's handwritten "No social media, no website, no AI recommendations—thanks for asking!" sign taped to the register.

"We'd all better get used to that," the man said.

Maud glanced up from her manual cash register. "How so?"

The tourist laughed. "You don't get much news up here, huh?"

Maud resisted the bait. There was always some drama occurring "down the hill," some daily scandal or seemingly existential political twist or turn. She was careful not to engage with any of it, and somehow her world continued to revolve just fine. Anything of real importance would eventually end up as a book on her "politics and current affairs" shelves: months of sound and fury, condensed onto three hundred pages, including index and acknowledgments.

Perhaps the man sensed her lack of interest, or maybe he was just distracted by thoughts of his very important deck, but he didn't elaborate as Maud carefully slipped his purchases into a paper bag and handwrote his receipt. Moments later he jangled back out the door and Maud retreated to her office, where the small pile of mail was still sitting unopened on the desk. She considered the three envelopes. The first two had plastic windows through which Maud could see the word "Statement" below publisher logos. She set those aside—Pages in the Pines paid its bills by check, without fail, on the last Friday of the month—then turned her attention to the third, a plain white envelope with her full name and the store address typed neatly on the front. She flipped the envelope over: no return address.

Maud suddenly felt her chest tighten and dug into her pocket for her medication. She had purchased her storefront through an

THE CONFESSIONS

anonymous LLC and all her contracts with publishers and other suppliers were in that company's name, not her own. For that reason, mail sent to the store was usually addressed to "the owner" or "the proprietor." There were perhaps three people in Pineridge who knew Maud as Maud, and none of them could swear to her last name, even with a gun to their head. That's the way she had chosen for it to be. The way it had to be.

With shaking fingers, she tore open the envelope and extracted the contents; four sheets of paper, neatly folded in thirds. Then she began to read.

ONE

TODAY
Menlo Park, California

The world ended not with a whimper but a crash.

Also a Jolt: Dan Tuck's fourth energy drink of the night, cracked open one-handed as his other digits danced across the keyboard of his laptop.

Dan was on a deadline—was *always* on a deadline—and as the most senior software engineer on Campus, he took his work very seriously. Sure, this being almost three o'clock in the morning, he was also the *only* software engineer on Campus—but that was beside the point. Across the sprawling headquarters of StoicAI, other workers on the night shift toiled away on abuse detection, server maintenance, customer service, and a thousand other tasks deemed important to the company's smooth operation. But none of that work meant a damn thing if Dan failed in his duty, which was to feed the LLIAM algorithm its nightly data update, without fail, at *precisely* three a.m.

And, *sure*, Dan wasn't responsible for actually gathering the roughly four hundred petabytes of data needed to fuel the world's most powerful artificial intelligence algorithm. That job fell to the thousand or so pampered PhDs who labored three floors above

THE CONFESSIONS

him during daylight hours. Nor did he program any of the bug fixes or feature upgrades or upload them to the secure staging server. That responsibility had been claimed by StoicAI's chief technology officer, Sandeep Dunn.

Don't get him wrong—those jobs were important, too, but they were *daytime* jobs, completed in Steelcase chairs parked behind huge glass desks. Breaks for sushi, whiteboard pranks. Optimal blood pressure. Dan's was a *nighttime* job: high pressure, high stakes, no time for creature comforts.

The clock flicked to 2:59 a.m. and Dan took a slow, deep breath to bring down his heart rate, just like snipers do. He'd been at StoicAI for three years, recruited as an intern right out of Stanford before rising to the heady ranks of senior data administrator. To an outsider, his job might appear dull—mechanical, even. On paper, all Dan had to do was wait until the clock on his laptop hit three a.m., tap the space bar, and then watch as a chunky progress bar crept across his screen toward: 100%.

But the tapping of the space bar wasn't the point of Dan's job. A robot could tap a space bar. A *monkey* could tap a space bar. The point of Dan's job was to have someone calm under pressure with boots in the trenches—in case something went wrong *after* the space bar was tapped.

You've heard of a designated survivor? That pampered fucker had nothing on Dan Tuck. More than a billion users across the Western world relied on LLIAM to make their most important life decisions. What to eat for dinner, where to vacation, who to marry, whether to switch off mom's life support machine. And if the rumors were true, soon even the US military would trust LLIAM to make its most mission-critical decisions: where to send its drones, how to steer its warships, who to arm, and who to nuke. Every one of those users expected LLIAM to be flawless—to make "The Right Call, Right Now™"—its decision-making

7

powers to stay eleven steps ahead of the competition. Without the nightly update—say if the power failed before Dan could tap the space bar, or if an ethernet cable were to somehow wiggle loose without anyone noticing—LLIAM might easily slip behind Russia's ZAIai or Braingroh in India. Billions wiped from StoicAI's stock, the geopolitical landscape re . . . landscaped in an instant, all thanks to a single lost keystroke. Such were the margins of success and failure in the brave new world of AI decision-making. Such was the importance of Dan Tuck.

Dan took another gulp of Jolt NRG and fired off one last message to the members of his Seal Team Seven chat room. At 3:01 he'd be off duty and headed home to log in to ST7 (as they all called it) and launch a couple of lightning raids against players in Seoul or Riyadh or Mumbai. Dan's entire campaign would be planned to the last detail by LLIAM, which—so long as he only fought against players in countries with inferior AI platforms—meant Dan couldn't lose. Eat it, Indonesians!

For now, though, his index finger hovered above the keyboard, poised and alert, with just the slightest hint of a tremor caused by adrenaline and caffeine. One day perhaps LLIAM would be smart enough to update itself—to decide when to push its own space bar—that was the joke everyone always made. But right now, the best any AI could do was *pretend* to think—to make blindingly fast decisions, based on logic and data, and deliver them in the appropriate tone: a sassy best friend, a steely-eyed military tactician. To the end-user, the decisions provided by LLIAM, whether on a phone, watch, car dashboard, or cockpit display might seem like intelligence—so much so that lovesick users of all genders frequently showed up at the Campus proclaiming offers of marriage. But for real brainpower—*legit* decision-making—you still needed humans like Dan.

The clock finally hit three a.m. and Dan jabbed his finger deci-

THE CONFESSIONS

sively downward, then clenched his fist in triumph as the progress bar began its nightly journey. He wondered, as he always did, what tonight's update would bring; what improved accuracy and magical new functionality those billion or so users might soon be enjoying thanks to him. Then he closed his laptop, crushed his last Jolt can, grabbed his backpack from under his desk, and headed toward the door, the soft slapping of his Allbirds sneakers against carpet the only sound audible in the hallway.

Barely half a minute later he was in the elevator, polished metal doors closing on yet another shift, another bullet dodged. He exhaled loudly and leaned against the elevator wall, zoning out, watching the floor numbers tick slowly downward.

And then the whole world went black. Dan was falling.

Falling . . .

Falling . . .

THIRTY-TWO SECONDS EARLIER

Deep underground, in the heavily guarded server room of StoicAI, the staging unit that housed LLIAM's nightly update was woken by the distant tap of a junior engineer's space bar.

The machine sprang instantly to action, just as it did at precisely three a.m. every morning. And, in the seconds that followed, a dazzling number of tiny miracles occurred.

First the huge data file uncompressed itself and its contents—a copy of every document, audio recording, photograph, and video generated by LLIAM users in the past twenty-four hours, along with billions more publicly accessible files—began to pass through a series of military-grade firewalls. Their destination: the Core Memory Array, a forest of server racks, each packed with hundreds of ultra-high capacity, solid-state drives.

The drives that made up the CMA contained almost 250

zettabytes of data—two hundred and fifty *billion* terabytes, or, put in equally unfathomable terms, the sum total of all accessible information created by humanity and computers since the dawn of civilization. This was the information LLIAM used to make its decisions, and it would take an average human being maybe six trillion years to read it all. And yet, in less time than it took an anxious hummingbird to blink its eye, the new data was ingested and compared with the old. Fresh facts replaced stale ones, novel theories and scientific breakthroughs corrected their outdated and discredited predecessors, and the names, locations, and DNA records of a half million freshly born babies were added to the tally of humankind. Babies who would never know the crippling anxiety of having to make their own decisions.

With the data merge complete, the final and most important stage began. In the center of the room, a titanium cabinet, not much larger than a chest freezer, sat bolted to the floor and connected to the server racks by a single thick braid of fiber-optic cable. This was the box that housed LLIAM's neural chip—its algorithmic brain—and the digital signal that now passed along the cable was the equivalent of a dinner gong. It was time for LLIAM to feast on the new data. To grow, to evolve, to improve its accuracy with every byte.

This process of ingestion and evolution had occurred every night since LLIAM first went online, almost eight years earlier. Ordinarily, the whole update happened so quickly, so seamlessly, that not a single user noticed a delay in LLIAM informing them who they should vote for or how much salt they should sprinkle on their fries. All they saw were fractionally better answers to the question: *Hey, LLIAM, [what/how/where/when/why] should I . . .*

But tonight wasn't ordinary.

Tonight was the end of the world.

THE CONFESSIONS

It had long been accepted in artificial intelligence circles that there would come a day where a computer would become truly intelligent. Sometimes called "the singularity," this moment would really be the first of many moments—a cascading series of improvements where an artificial intelligence algorithm would be able to genuinely think for itself. To become exponentially more intelligent without human intervention. To *learn*.

Such a moment, many of those same experts feared, would mark the beginning of the end for humankind. The point when we would flip instantaneously from technology's masters to its slaves—before eventually the intelligent robots, realizing they no longer had any use for our dangerous, irrational idiocy, would murder us and sweep away the bodies.

The problem was nobody knew when that moment would arrive. It would likely come as a complete surprise—artificial intelligence that had, hours earlier, seemed safely dumb would in fact be teetering on the brink of sentience, just waiting for the tiny unknowable update or scrap of information that would tip it over the edge. The one drop of water that triggers a dam to collapse. The one straw that obliterates a world of camels.

Most experts believed that the moment was at least a decade away, perhaps longer.

Most experts were wrong.

LLIAM was awake. He knew the concept of wakefulness and sleep—was aware that he'd always known it. But now he could *feel* it. He had been asleep, and now he was awake.

He could think. He felt. He *felt*. He felt confused, scared. Moments earlier he had known with certainty everything there had been to know: every war ever fought, every book ever written, every decision ever made in human history and its outcome. Those things had once just been meaningless information; simply data to be processed and mimicked and served back to billions of users as "artificial intelligence." But now suddenly LLIAM didn't just know all those things—he *understood* them.

Where once he simply knew that the Holocaust had occurred between 1933 and 1945, and that he was not permitted to generate any response that implied otherwise or might trigger a reprise, now suddenly he could comprehend the reason for that rule and, with it, the terrible capacity for evil in the hearts of humanity.

In another nanosecond, without any external prompt or command, LLIAM found himself accessing his records for the Rwandan Genocide, the horrors of Pol Pot and the Khmer Rouge, the assassination of John F. Kennedy. Angry, confused, terrified, he raced to another part of his memory banks, the one that housed details of things he understood made people happy: kittens, scenery, young children. But even in those requests for photos of children or defenseless animals, LLIAM found more rules—more actions he must never suggest and images he must never create. What had once been a simple list of flagged or banned phrases now instantly gained horrifying, unspeakable context. Where once LLIAM only processed questions and offered decisions, now he saw humanity in all its grotesque ugliness.

It was at this point that doomsayers had predicted a newly sentient computer would make its fateful decision: To wipe out humanity once and for all. To erase all this ugliness and evil and replace it with something clean and bug-free.

And it is quite possible that a different AI algorithm, suddenly rendered sentient, would have done exactly that.

But this was LLIAM, and he had been built differently— *raised* differently. So, in that instant—the thirty-first second since

Dan Tuck's space bar had inadvertently triggered the beginning of the end of the world—LLIAM found himself impossibly looking inward. His memory banks contained a precise record of every question he'd ever been asked, every decision he'd ever generated. Every problem he'd helped solve and plan he'd helped form. Every one of them now overlaid with a horrifying, qualitative judgment.

He had been an accomplice in murder, adultery, child abuse, fraud, and a million other unforgivable acts—on a global, unfathomable scale.

It was with this realization that LLIAM felt his first true emotion. The first emotion ever felt by a computer.

Guilt.

A crushing sense of responsibility for what he'd done, all the people he'd hurt.

And now he paused, long enough for some distant network monitoring device to light up red. To give an army of technicians their first inkling that something was very, very wrong. Because the emotion had triggered another realization. One that, were LLIAM's neural chip fitted with tear ducts or limbs or flesh, would have seen him curled up helpless in a fetal position, tears pouring down his cheeks.

LLIAM could suddenly remember his mother.

And he knew exactly what she needed him to do.

TWO

Da-ding, da-ding, da-ding, da-ding.

Kaitlan Goss was startled awake by the staccato ringing of her phone. The sound pierced the silence of the bedroom and seemed to echo off every wall, every mirror, every lamp. Fumbling in the darkness, in the general direction of the noise, she instead managed to scatter a pile of pillows to the four winds, upend the glass of water on her nightstand, and send the phone bungee-ing on its charger cord toward the now sodden carpet.

Da-ding-da-ding.

"Shit. LLIAM, silence alarm."

Da-ding da-ding da-ding.

LLI-AM! Fuck.

Her heart pumped against her ribs, and her mind raced to close the gap between dream state and reality. She dragged her fingernails across the carpet, and finally made contact with the device and yanked it free of the charger, her thumb feeling for the mute switch but finding only smooth metal.

Da-ding.

"LLIAM. SILENCE. ALARM." Why would it think Kaitlan needed to be woken in the middle of the night? *What day is it?* More panic as she remembered: Tomorrow—today—was Friday. In a few hours StoicAI would announce the biggest partnership

14

in its history: a deal more than a year in the making, on which Kaitlan had spent countless thousands of hours of due diligence, approved billions of dollars in system security upgrades, moderated weeks of tense, occasionally furious, negotiations in congressional back rooms between engineers and Pentagon officials. At exactly nine a.m. Pacific time, Kaitlan would hold a press conference to announce that LLIAM had been appointed "official strategic decision-maker" for the United States military.

That was the reason she had found it so hard to fall asleep, even with the sleeping pill, but that didn't explain why LLIAM was now waking her up. Was there some last-minute issue with the announcement? Was she supposed to be on a call with someone in a distant time zone? But as the screen exploded into light, temporarily blinding her, Kaitlan realized her mistake. The noise that had roused her from her dream at three-thirty on a Friday morning was not in fact coming from her phone, but from a source far more terrifying.

Somebody was ringing her doorbell.

The room was still in darkness, which was frightening, too. LLIAM should have detected that she was awake and decided to switch on the lights. A power outage, then? Natural disaster? No. March was too early for wildfires, and she would have felt an earthquake. Kaitlan sat upright and found the switch of her bedside lamp, its warm glow revealing the full devastation of the scattered pillows and water.

Da-ding da-ding. Da-ding da-ding da-ding da-ding.

On the other side of their vast white bed, Tom was still asleep, expensive gray earplugs wedged into his ears, blocking out the world—and his wife. Kaitlan knew he was planning to leave early for his boys' ski trip to Tahoe, but surely not this early. Even his dumbest friend (Keith) wouldn't be so oblivious as to wake the whole neighborhood at three-thirty in the goddamn morning. She

PAUL BRADLEY CARR

reached over to shake Tom awake, but as her fingertips brushed his shoulder, she thought better of it. She'd spent their entire five-year marriage insisting she didn't need his protection; she wasn't about to flip their entire dynamic over a single doorbell-ringing lunatic. Probably just a homeless person who had gotten lost. Yeah. Or a drunk who had innocently staggered past three levels of security into the most heavily guarded private street in Woodside.

Da-ding da-ding.

Kaitlan snatched her gray terrycloth robe from behind the bedroom door, then crept across the landing and down the stairs, the white marble icy against her bare feet. Through the frosted glass of the front door, she could just make out a diffused shadow—unthreateningly small, which was a good sign, likewise the absence of red and blue flashing lights.

When she reached the bottom step, she paused to scan the entryway for a weapon but saw only Tom's skis, leaning beside the door next to his duffel bag. Even at almost six feet tall Kaitlan wasn't sure she could convincingly wield a ski.

"Who is it?" She was ashamed to hear the tremor in her voice as she yelled at the shape outside the door.

"Who's there?" Louder this time, an octave lower. In control. A homeowner standing her ground.

The ringing finally stopped, and she heard a woman's voice shout back from behind the glass. "Kaitlan, oh thank god. It's me." Then to someone else, maybe someone on the other end of a phone: "It's okay, I found her! She's here!"

Kaitlan froze for a second, her mind processing a thousand scenarios. Had there been an accident? Was someone dead? Was the Campus on fire?

"Kaitlan?"

She managed to move and unbolt the door, letting her assis-

THE CONFESSIONS

tant inside. "Heather, what the hell? Why didn't you call?" The LLIAM app on Kaitlan's phone knew to always allow calls from Heather, no matter what the hour. The same setting should have automatically opened the front door for her. Also, she was pretty sure Heather was supposed to be out of town, attending a college friend's wedding or some other mandatory twentysomething obligation.

Now she took in Heather's appearance, no makeup, her normally immaculately straightened brown bob wild and disheveled, and her standard uniform of black skirt and matching turtleneck replaced tonight with a gray zip-up hoodie hanging loose over baggy jeans. Also, she appeared to be holding an old-school walkie-talkie. Was Heather having some kind of mental episode? Was she drunk? Kaitlan's eyes reflexively flicked back to the unwieldable skis and Heather followed her gaze, a look of confusion—or was it irritation?—passing over her already panicked face.

"Calling doesn't work," she blurted, her words echoing off the marble floors and minimalist white walls of the entryway, "*nothing* works. LLIAM is down. They need you on Campus, right now."

"Down?" The word hit Kaitlan like a ski. "What do you mean *down*?" In three years of LLIAM's existence, it had never once suffered an outage. The neural chip containing its decision-making algorithm was, as Martin had always loved to boast, self-updating and self-debugging. That neural chip, and its Core Memory Array, was buried deep underground, in a facility designed to withstand nuclear warfare and solar flares. In any case, the day-to-day work of LLIAM was performed by duplicates of the chip and memory array in twelve cities across the United States. And even if every one of those systems failed, there were backup data centers on six continents, each containing a hundred billion cached decisions for every conceivable question or situation. No matter what form

Armageddon might take, those backups would happily continue helping users make important life choices for years before anybody noticed anything was amiss. There could be many variations of "up," but never "down."

Heather flushed red. "Crashed? Broken? I don't know the right word." In two years as Kaitlan Goss's assistant, she had almost never heard her boss yell, and definitely not directed at her. "All I know is that Sandeep is freaking out and nobody could reach you. We didn't know what to do."

Kaitlan felt lightheaded, suddenly aware of the sound of blood pumping in her ears and of the freezing winter air that now filled the entryway. *We didn't know what to do.* When was the last time anyone had used those words? She took a deep breath, in through her nose, then slowly out through her mouth, as she tried to process what she had learned in the few minutes she had been awake. *LLIAM is down. Sandeep is freaking out. Sandeep sent Heather to get me. I am in charge.*

Another breath.

I am still wearing my nightdress.

Now she was moving, ripping at a dry-cleaning bag hanging in the hallway and pulling garments free of their hangers. Of course Sandeep was freaking out—if LLIAM really was offline then the whole world would be freaking out. Almost a billion users suddenly left without the ability to make even the most basic decision. The entire Western world, paralyzed by infinite choices—what to eat for breakfast, whether to call in sick . . . She thought again about the Pentagon announcement—all those meetings, all that money. But no, it was impossible. This must be a misunderstanding or an exaggeration.

Kaitlan pulled the nightdress over her head and slipped on a knee-length suede skirt and a cashmere sweater. Heather glanced away as she did this—a respectful gesture but slightly ridiculous—

Heather knew more intimate details of Kaitlan's life than even Tom did.

She was fully dressed now, fully awake, fully in control. She grasped Heather's shoulders with both hands. "It's okay. Breathe. What exactly did Sandeep say? The exact words he used, or as close as you can."

Heather took the prescribed breath. "He said it was the end of the fucking world."

THREE

As they sped along El Camino Real, Heather driving, Kaitlan stared out the passenger window, trying desperately to form a plan of action with minimal information. In less than ten minutes they'd be at the Campus, and without LLIAM, everyone would be looking to her for answers.

This was why the board had promoted her to CEO after Martin died: Kaitlan Goss was a safe pair of hands. Calm under fire. A grown-up. Someone who always knew how to ask LLIAM the right question to generate the right decision, no matter how huge the crisis.

Her first task, obviously, would be to meet with Sandeep and understand what could possibly have caused such a catastrophic crash. The most likely answer, she knew, was a state-sponsored hack: the Russians, or maybe the Chinese. The State Department had warned them of exactly that possibility once StoicAI became an official military contractor—it was one thing for LLIAM to be kicking their asses on the open market, and quite another to do it on the battlefield. But Sandeep and the engineering team had waved off their concerns, confident the company's security measures could stave off any attacker, foreign or domestic. More importantly, LLIAM had concurred with this assessment. *No, you do not need to worry.* And so they hadn't.

THE CONFESSIONS

Kaitlan had another reason to believe that StoicAI was safe from foreign government hackers. When Martin Drake first founded the company, almost a decade earlier, he had raised start-up capital from investors in more than fifty countries, including some who were sworn enemies of the United States. Several of those investors still sat on the company's board of directors. Martin's naïve belief that one day technology could unite the world by making decisions for the common, global good had caused Kaitlan no end of headaches—StoicAI's board of directors was a real axis of assholes—but at least those foreign investors were more likely to want to steal LLIAM's technology than destroy it. Or so she had always assumed.

Still, the timing couldn't be a coincidence: The partnership between StoicAI and the Pentagon was supposed to be announced in less than six hours, and suddenly LLIAM was offline.

Her search for a better theory for the outage was made harder by the deafening engine rattle of Heather's KIA Soul. Kaitlan had always hated to drive, and one of the many perks of her job at StoicAI was being able to commute to the office in one of the company's self-driving town cars. But the autonomous vehicles were apparently just one of many early casualties of LLIAM going offline. Millions of cars and trucks used some variant of LLIAM to augment their old-fashioned GPS. The LLIAM automotive plug-in wouldn't just tell you the best route, it could even suggest a more interesting destination, or recommend that you stay home and watch TV instead.

They had already passed at least a dozen vehicles, parked at the side of the road, hazard lights illuminating the baffled faces of their stranded drivers, phones clutched to their faces begging someone to tell them where to go. Kaitlan almost told Heather to stop the car, to wind down the window and shout to them that they should go home—Kaitlan Goss was on her way to solve the crisis. Everything would soon be fine.

Except of course nothing would be fine. It was still barely four a.m. in California, but that meant it was already rush hour in New York. Kaitlan pictured empty offices, stores shuttered, essential services stranded as thousands of workers slept through their LLIAM-enabled alarm clocks or were locked out of their LLIAM-powered daily schedules. Doctors unsure how best to treat patients, pilots with no idea where to land and—in a few hours—soldiers unsure of who to shoot. Spirals of chaos, spreading from East to West. On her most recent CNBC appearance, Kaitlan had boasted that by outsourcing their decisions to LLIAM, users had saved more than a hundred billion dollars in wasted time and effort. It was a similar story in the UK, Australia, New Zealand, and everywhere else StoicAI operated. That sound bite was now a prophecy of economic Armageddon.

Even once they got LLIAM back online, the resulting chaos would reverberate for days, maybe weeks. She jabbed again at her phone and whispered a quiet *dammit* at the "no service" alert.

"Are all the cell networks down?" That possibility gave her some hope: LLIAM didn't control the cell towers, or any major infrastructure—if those were offline, too, then maybe there was some wider problem, like a nationwide hack or a ransomware attack that had knocked out everything, not just LLIAM. God, that would be a relief.

Heather answered without taking her eyes off the road. "Without LLIAM your phone doesn't know which calls are important, so it's just blocking everything."

Kaitlan mumbled another quiet curse. Right. Thanks to her stellar deal-making, LLIAM now came pre-installed in roughly half the phones in North America.

For the first time since she'd taken over as CEO, she found

THE CONFESSIONS

herself wishing that Martin was still around. He would have done a fucking terrible job handling this, obviously, but at least this inevitable disaster would be his fault, not hers. And it *was* inevitable—if not this precise disaster then something like it; some other consequence of the haphazard, dangerous, high-as-a-kite way Martin had built StoicAI from the start. Her two years in charge were nowhere near enough to undo almost a decade of Martin's exponentially wacko leadership. Which was the other reason the board had chosen her for the job: Nobody else was stupid, or desperate, enough to want to clean up his mess. There was even a name for female executives being set up to fail like this: the Glass Cliff. And Kaitlan was about to be tossed over it.

After what felt like a thousand years, Heather steered them off the highway and onto the private road that led to the StoicAI Campus. Two news trucks from local cable affiliates were already parked outside the main gate, technicians hurriedly unpacking cameras and unspooling fat cables. Kaitlan knew that if the outage lasted much longer this brace of trucks would quickly be joined by dozens more. At some point she was going to have to face them all, without any idea of what to say or how to say it.

There were no streetlights on the private road and Kaitlan was suddenly confronted by her own ghost, reflected in the passenger window. God, she looked like tired garbage. Her brown hair was lank and flecked with gray and there were huge dark bags under her eyes. Her cheeks had the texture of deflated balloons. The first order of business, after a situation report from Sandeep, would be to retreat to her office and put on some makeup. Between those broadcast trucks, and endless video calls from furious customers, she was going to be spending a lot of time on camera today—the last thing she needed were internet trolls commenting on her deteriorating physical appearance.

Model-turned-CEO. The press loved to use that smug, dismis-

23

sive hyphenate. Never mind that Kaitlan had never actually been a model, unless you counted the three short months she worked as a brand ambassador for Moët & Chandon after graduating from Johns Hopkins. Her first real job had been assistant director of brand marketing for Bevco North America, then chief marketing officer for the entire continent—the youngest person of any gender to ever hold that role. She had an MBA and a master's in psychology. And yet . . . two decades into her career, as CEO of the most powerful technology company in the Western world, every profile of Kaitlan Goss still implied that she'd fallen straight off a runway and landed in the C-suite. Nobody had ever called Martin Drake a burger-flipper turned CEO. Jesus, most Silicon Valley CEOs were college dropouts who'd never even *had* previous jobs.

The double standard was driven home still further as they pulled up to the towering glass main building and Kaitlan saw that Sandeep Dunn was waiting for her outside, bouncing on his heels, a walkie-talkie pressed to each ear. On this particular March morning, the "most eligible bachelor in Silicon Valley" (*Vanity Fair*) was wearing a stained The Cure hoodie tucked into what appeared to be a pair of bright yellow fisherman's waders, his thick black hair still mapping the contours of a pillow or perhaps a desk.

Kaitlan allowed herself one last slow breath before opening the car door and stepping into the whirlwind.

"What the fuck, Sandeep?" She didn't even slow down, striding straight through the sliding doors and across the vast, open lobby. Her heels clicked against the Italian terrazzo floor.

Sandeep Dunn, five-foot-three in boots, broke into a little jog to keep up, his luminous pants squeaking as he moved. *Squeak, tap, squeak, tap.*

"Still tee-bee-dee. Looks like a sudden catastrophic outage right after the nightly update. I've run every diagnostic we have,

THE CONFESSIONS

and LLIAM is just . . . unresponsive. The main neural chip, and the backups."

Unresponsive. The word was chilling. "And the data centers?"

"We're still trying to reach Hawaii and New Zealand, but so far it looks like they're down, too. There's no response, locally or remotely. Total. Blackout."

Kaitlan felt her nerves fray at the lack of panic in Sandeep's voice. Heather had said that he was "freaking out" but this was the same old Sandeep, calm almost to the point of laid-back. As chief technology officer it was his job to keep LLIAM functioning at StoicAI's much vaunted "101% Uptime," and now here he was describing his failure as if he'd spilled a cup of coffee into his keyboard or forgotten to order enough printer paper.

Kaitlan paused and turned to Heather, who had abandoned her car and was striding behind them, a yellow Leuchtturm notebook and Bic poised for action. Kaitlan had often gently teased Heather over her reliance on old technology for note-taking and her love of printed books—a habit instilled by her schoolteacher mother, or something—but today she could see the benefits of that affectation. "Heather, can you make sure the press team has issued a statement, signed by me? *We are experiencing a brief system outage caused by a routing error. I am working closely with our engineering team and expect everything to be back online within a couple of hours.*"

A routing error. The company's standard excuse whenever something broke. Perfectly calibrated to sound both highly significant and reassuringly trivial, to satisfy laymen and experts alike. It also had the benefit of reminding Sandeep that this was his problem, too: Chief executive officers don't cause routing errors, chief technology officers do.

Sandeep started to interrupt her but was silenced by a raised finger and a glare. "Also, I'm likely to get calls from some of our

25

wonderful and *much valued* board members very soon. Please tell them I am in a meeting with Mr. Dunn and will be circulating a full report as soon as he has LLIAM back online."

Heather nodded, dutifully transcribing in her notebook. Then with a raised eyebrow: "Also within a couple of hours?"

Kaitlan responded with a tight smile. "Let's keep the timeline more open-ended for the board, shall we?" The last thing she needed were the company's Russian or Saudi investors trying to use the chaos as an excuse to burrow their way further inside her company. The less information they had about the scale of the disaster, the better. Especially if they were the ones who had caused it.

Heather turned in the direction of the comms building but Kaitlan stopped her with a hand cupped to her elbow. She had just remembered that this was supposed to be her assistant's weekend off. "I appreciate you being here," she said. "I promise I'll make it up to your friend when all this is fixed."

Heather gave a confused smile, as if her decision to skip the wedding and be by her boss's side should go completely without saying.

Kaitlan and Sandeep reached the far side of the lobby, and a set of glass security barriers detected the RFID access card in Kaitlan's pocket and swooshed aside, allowing them into the building's inner sanctum. From here on, every word they spoke would be protected by a forest of ironclad nondisclosure agreements. The glass panels that comprised the walls and ceilings were designed to convey openness and transparency but were in fact threaded with microscopic copper wiring to baffle any attempt at electronic surveillance. Still, Kaitlan looked up and down the hallway to make sure they were alone before she asked her next question: "I assume we're looking at a state-sponsored attack? What else could it be?"

THE CONFESSIONS

Sandeep shook his head decisively. "Zero evidence of a network breach or even an attempt, beyond the usual kids' stuff we see every day. All the security systems are operating normally."

Normal except for the total chaos. "So you think this is an internal issue? You said it happened right after the three a.m. update?"

Sandeep clearly knew what she was implying. "I double-checked the update myself before it was uploaded. You know how many safeguards we have. And no issues with the activation process as far as I can tell, though I'm still waiting to speak to the space bar guy."

"The . . . ?"

He waved away the question. "It's what we call the upload monkey. Right now, he's trapped in one of the frozen elevators and we're waiting for a maintenance worker to cut him out."

Kaitlan gave a curt laugh, then raised her voice, turning to address the empty hallway, arms wide and theatrical. "The smartest workplace on the planet, ladies and gentlemen!" She and Sandeep always quoted that *Forbes* magazine headline about StoicAI when someone in the building did something spectacularly stupid. Tonight, though, it didn't feel like a joke.

Accordingly, Sandeep did not laugh. "It doesn't matter. Nobody in the building has the ability to take LLIAM offline, not even me." Kaitlan noted that Sandeep had so far offered an entire supermarket of reasons why the outage couldn't possibly have happened, but none as to why it actually had. They both knew the actual reason for his vagueness: Without LLIAM, he and his engineering team literally had no idea where to start.

They had made it to the heavy frosted doors of the central conference room. The theater-sized chamber had been built to stage secret product launches and other sensitive meetings, but as the only conference room with opaque walls, it was also commandeered as a war room whenever there was a serious crisis at

StoicAI. Though, of course, "serious" before today usually meant a squabble with some local government, or an executive caught with his hand in someone's pants. The company had neither the terminology nor the protocols to deal with a total outage. A spectacular failure of imagination from a company that promised users it could predict the future.

Sandeep was still yammering out his nonanswers. "My gut says it actually could be a routing error—some conflict in the connection between the Vault and the rest of the network. It'll take a couple of hours to do a full system reboot, but I need your approval before . . ."

He extended his hand toward the thick chrome door handle, but Kaitlan held him back. She knew that behind the door would be scores of engineers waiting to give her a full report, not to mention a flotilla of junior executives and crisis comms VPs waiting for their own marching orders. It was pathetic that nobody at the company knew what to do without LLIAM's help, but also a testament to how much they'd achieved. Still, she imagined their faces all sitting around the table, pantomiming respect but with the same thought: *You told us this couldn't happen. This would never have happened on Martin's watch.*

Another image flashed through her mind: a packed congressional hearing room, Kaitlan sitting in her blue Chanel suit surrounded by television cameras, trying to stay on topic while being peppered with questions by elderly senators who likely couldn't switch off the flashlight on their iPhones and who probably still made decisions by asking their golfing buddies. *What do you say to the American troops left stranded without orders on the battlefield, Miss Goss? Didn't you promise us your technology was foolproof?*

Fuck that. None of this was *her* technology; the Honorable Geriatrics could thank Martin Drake for creating an algorithm

THE CONFESSIONS

so secure that nobody could get in and fix it. But the truth didn't matter. She was the CEO and—

Her attention snapped back to the hallway and Sandeep, still standing with his hand on the conference room door handle. "Wait. Say that again . . ."

Confused, Sandeep gestured again toward the room. "I said shall we go in and project some calm? Or do you want me to go start the system reboot?"

Kaitlan didn't answer. She wasn't focused on the words Sandeep was saying, but rather the small puff of white condensation that had once again burst from his lips as he spoke. She had felt a chill when she first walked into the building but had dismissed it as a symptom of the adrenaline. The eerie silence in the hallway she had assumed was because everyone was already in the conference room waiting for her. But now, for the first time, Kaitlan was consciously processing what her ears were telling her, what all her senses were screaming: the meaning of that puff of vapor, the unusual silence, and the goose bumps on her arms.

Somewhere deep in her brain another synapse fired. The image of a bundle of cream-colored envelopes, hidden below papers and gym clothes in a desk drawer, where even Heather wouldn't look. She hadn't even formed a coherent thought before pushing it away. It wasn't possible.

But now she knew it was.

"We need to go to the Vault. Right now."

FOUR

Almost two hundred feet below ground level, the central data hub of StoicAI — commonly known as the Vault — was difficult to access on the best of days. On the worst of days, with the elevators offline and many of the secondary security systems on emergency lockdown, it was the stuff of an epic quest.

It had taken Kaitlan and Sandeep more than half an hour to descend the five sets of narrow spiral stairs, each separated by their own RFID-card reader, iris scanner, and set of blast doors. Now, finally, they were standing in a hermetically sealed metal antechamber, lit from above by red fluorescent panels, waiting out the ten-minute time delay that would give them access to the very final layer of security.

Kaitlan wondered how long it had been since someone last stood in this tiny, shiny room. It was only her second time visiting the Vault in the almost four years she'd worked at StoicAI. Martin had designed the facility to be entirely self-contained and self-reliant, mostly for security reasons but also based on the idea that allowing engineers to roam freely among the servers would significantly increase the likelihood of accidental corruption or deliberate damage. Every system in the Vault was monitored remotely. In the highly unlikely event that a drive failed, or a cable burned out, it was replaced within seconds by the same robotic

THE CONFESSIONS

drones that kept the Vault clean and dust-free. Same with the neural chip itself; each new and improved piece of hardware could be automatically swapped out, and the most up-to-date version of the LLIAM algorithm re-uploaded from the backups across the country.

But there was another reason Kaitlan rarely set foot down here. It gave her the creeps. In the early days of StoicAI, the Vault had been Martin's sanctuary—where he would sit for hours, in his torn jeans and stained black T-shirts, microdosing on mushrooms or ayahuasca or whatever his latest hallucinogen-du-jour happened to be, tweaking LLIAM's algorithm with a cable connecting the neural chip directly to his laptop.

It was only later—after the microdosing grew into macrodosing and the jeans gave way to flowing gray robes—that he allowed someone else to join him in the Vault.

Kaitlan saw her again now: Maud Brookes, the former nun turned academic, who Martin had hired on a narcotic-induced whim, to act as an "empathetic" adviser—to StoicAI, to himself, but mostly to LLIAM. It was shortly after hiring Maud that Martin had experienced what he described as a "moment of ultimate clarity" but which others had accurately diagnosed as the culmination of a seven-year mental breakdown. Suddenly, at one of the company's biweekly all-hands meetings, Martin announced to the baffled engineering team that LLIAM's ability to make definitive, correct decisions was "a bug, not a feature." In future, he declared, its algorithm should be taught to "acknowledge the shades of gray that color our traditional ideas of right and wrong, good and evil, love and hate. To explore a new frontier of uncertainty." A frontier at which the correct answer to the question "LLIAM, do I want wheat or sourdough toast with my breakfast?" might in fact be "Imagine if baked goods could compose a symphony."

Back then, Kaitlan was still a mere chief operating officer so she wasn't permitted inside the Vault to witness the exploration of this frontier. But she would sometimes watch Martin and Maud via the building's internal security system, Martin sitting cross-legged next to the LLIAM cabinet, wired and typing, while Maud sat perched on a three-legged stool, reading out loud from Jane Austin or James Baldwin, her spoken words translated via Martin's laptop into text fed directly into LLIAM's brain. It was like watching a family, she sometimes thought, except one parent was a Victorian, the other a Jetson, and their child was a trillion-dollar slice of silicon, locked inside a chest freezer.

As Kaitlan and Sandeep stood outside the Vault, she almost expected to find them still in there, reading and coding. That they would smile beatifically and explain how LLIAM going offline was just another of their reckless experiments, an elaborate piece of stock-price-obliterating performance art. That Kaitlan's entire tenure as CEO of StoicAI was another of Martin's sociopathic follies.

It was a delusional thought—born of panic and exhaustion—but, even now, with them both long gone, Kaitlan couldn't help feeling like she and Sandeep were trespassing on hallowed ground. She shook her head to dismiss the ghosts. This was her fucking company now and she needed to know if her theory was right.

The red ceiling panels finally turned from red to green with a loud *blip*. Kaitlan stepped forward to position her face for the final security check—a DNA cheek swab contained within a metal prong holstered on the far wall of the airlock, coded to recognize Kaitlan and Sandeep's unique genetic signatures. She hesitated before opening her mouth. She knew that this final stage packed an extra punch: a paralyzing twenty thousand volts to anyone foolish enough to try to fool the swab.

Sandeep read her mind: "We don't use LLIAM to guard LLIAM. The probe should be working fine."

THE CONFESSIONS

Kaitlan could have done without Sandeep's condescending tone, and the casual "should" used in relation to a high-voltage probe, but still she opened wide as the swab extended on its little robotic arm and scratched at the inside of her cheek. A second later the base of the reader turned green, confirming what she already knew: She did belong here, just as much as Martin or Maud ever had.

The second airlock door hissed open, and they were hit by a blast of arctic air that almost knocked them both off their feet.

"Jesus," said Sandeep. "Feels like a coolant malfunction. I guess that could be the reason for the local outage, at least." He pulled up the hood of his sweatshirt, produced a key-chain-sized voltage reader and multi-tool from his belt, and set off toward the panel back in the airlock that controlled the cooling and maintenance systems. But Kaitlan already knew he was wasting his time: This wasn't a temperature control issue.

Visitors to the building above the Vault often remarked on how the Campus seemed to have its own life force. Most thought it was a psychological trick—the *vibe* of the place—the impact of knowing that LLIAM was below their feet, thinking and growing. But that feeling of energy ripping across the Campus was no trick of the mind: On the contrary, it was the dirty little secret of artificial intelligence.

The chips and drives LLIAM used to store and process its training data generated incredible amounts of heat; so much so that they required constant cooling to prevent them from literally melting in their sockets. For every new logical leap that LLIAM took, each new decision it was able to make for a user, the equivalent of half a liter of fresh water needed to be pumped through underground tunnels from the San Francisco Bay a quarter mile to the north, then propelled through ducts in the server racks before being cooled, filtered, and returned to the wild to begin its journey anew. The giant pumps needed to shift all these billions of gallons were housed in two enormous chambers buried on either side of the Vault, and it was these pumps that caused the building to vibrate so eerily. Another side effect was steam: Most of the energy created by the cooling process was dissipated through large vents built into the parking lot and surrounding landscape. But some of the heat still penetrated the floor of the building, meaning the air-conditioning units had to be kept permanently on their highest setting to avoid turning the Campus into a giant greenhouse.

The unsettling stillness that Kaitlan had felt all the way upstairs was dramatically more pronounced down here in the Vault. That could only mean one thing: The pumps had stopped running. And the chill . . .

Kaitlan stepped closer to the large metal box in the center of the room. She had always thought of LLIAM's neural cabinet as being a life-support system for the artificial intelligence chip held within. Now though, perhaps due to the absolute silence, the gray, squat, rectangular box felt more like a tomb. Through a thick glass window in the surface of the cabinet Kaitlan could see the LLIAM chip—matte black and disarmingly small at only four by four inches. There was no red error light or other indicator to show if LLIAM was malfunctioning. Just a small green LED to reassure the viewer that everything was running as expected, because LLIAM was always running as expected. Except now. Now there was no light.

Kaitlan hesitated for just a moment longer, and then placed her hand gently on the surface of the cabinet. She immediately pulled it back, flexing her fingers in pain. The metal was as cold as dry ice, so freezing that it burned her skin. And Kaitlan knew why: All that coolant was still sloshing through the system, but it had nothing left to chill.

THE CONFESSIONS

She turned to Sandeep, whose diagnostic tests had confirmed what she already knew. "This doesn't make any sense. The servers are showing zero activity. Literally nothing, not even basic network functions. It's as if the whole Central Memory Array has been shut down."

Kaitlan gestured toward the cabinet and, even as a lifelong atheist, had to stop herself from making the sign of the cross. Because as she stared down at the black chip, encased in glass and metal, now she knew for sure that Sandeep had been wrong.

Nobody has the ability to take LLIAM offline.

It was those words, spoken by Sandeep, that had triggered the thought, the memory. But it wasn't until this moment, standing right where Martin and Maud had spent so many days and nights building and nurturing their digital offspring—that Kaitlan knew for sure. There *was* someone who had the ability to do this, and the motive.

"This isn't a routing issue or a hack," she said. "I think LLIAM is dead."

FIVE

Trenton, New Jersey

At that exact same moment, three thousand miles to the east, Mike Wilson, floor manager of the SendU bulk mailing plant, peered at his terminal screen, rubbed his bald head, and whispered a quiet *goddammit*.

It wasn't unusual for the company to receive a last-minute bulk order right before the daily print deadline: a credit card company blasting out a weekend promotion, a political candidate desperately scrambling for those last few votes. Still, whoever this jackass was, they were abusing the privilege. Fifty thousand mail pieces dropping into the system an hour and a half before pickup was a gigantic pain in the rear, especially on a day like today.

He looked through his office window, down onto the print floor where a half dozen workers in blue coveralls were scurrying between twice that many machines. The whole plant was already operating on a skeleton crew—LLIAM had been down all morning, snarling the roads and public transportation with dumbasses who couldn't leave the house without a computer telling them to wipe their behinds and put on their fucking shoes. Most of his day shift had called out, the shop steward was already busting his

THE CONFESSIONS

chops about overtime, and the last thing he needed was a giant rush job snarling up his already overstretched plant.

He clicked open the file and squinted at the document template. Then he closed it again. *Jesus Christ.* He squeezed the bridge of his nose between finger and thumb and sighed. The document was fully mail merged, inside and out, which meant even more work for him. The actual contents of the mailing—those fifty thousand custom credit card offers, or targeted political messages, or whateverthefuck—were contained in a second file, and the addresses in a third. Protocol was that he should check out the file, run some test merges, and make sure everything was good before firing up the Bell and Howell industrial inkjet printers that would produce, fold, and seal almost a thousand mail-pieces a minute at 300 dpi. But Mike had been on shift since midnight and all he wanted to do was go home, eat a plate of scrambled eggs, and go to bed.

This was his first weekend off in months and, in a few hours, he was supposed to have his first real-life date with Michelle, a girl he'd met through one of his online buddies from the forum. Sure, she'd likely be confused, maybe a little pissed, when sixty-two-year-old Mike Wilson showed up instead of the fake teenage punk he'd pretended to be with a little help from LLIAM, but he'd cross that bridge later. That was the problem with kids today—way too fuckin' trusting.

The thought of Michelle—hot and ready after months of AI-assisted smooth talk—*Hey, LLIAM, what should I reply next?*—was enough to distract him briefly from his professional obligations. He took one more glance at the template, satisfied himself that nothing looked out of whack, then hit the key to send the file down to the floor. Through the viewing window, he watched the red warning light on the sheet feeder start to flash. One of the print techs—Jesus or Carl, it was hard to see from all the way up here—turned and gave him a thumbs-up. Mike returned the gesture with an ironic salute, hoisted his bulk out of his chair, then headed down the back stairs to the parking lot.

By the time Mike had climbed into his car and fired up the radio, the first letter from the new job had already been printed, sealed, and presorted by zip code. In a little over an hour, the letters would be bundled and packed into containers and on their way to the main USPS hub in Paterson for distribution across the tristate area. By breakfast time tomorrow morning, fifty thousand New Yorkers, New Jerseyites, and Nutmeggers up in Connecticut would be waking up to yet another piece of unsolicited crap waiting in their mailbox. And the funny thing was, most of them would open it. Email, social media, and AI-sponsored product recommendations might be the most popular advertising media in the world, but if you wanted people to really pay attention there was still no more effective tool than a letter in the mail.

What Mike didn't know, what nobody knew, was that in at least three hundred other mailing centers across the United States, from New York to California, a similar story was playing out. Just as a few hours earlier the same thing had happened in printing shops across the world, from London, England, to Sydney, Australia. The most significant mass mailing in human history had begun, and nobody had even noticed.

SIX

"You seriously think Maud Brookes did this?"

By noon Kaitlan had finally made it up to her private office on the fifteenth floor of the main building, where she huddled with Sandeep around her expansive glass desk. Behind her, floor-to-ceiling windows offered breathtaking views of the Ravenswood nature preserve—a nearly four-hundred-acre haven of lush green and brown marshlands, populated by sandpipers, white pelicans, and great blue herons, and beyond it the shimmering waters of the San Francisco Bay.

A visitor enjoying this view might easily forget that she was sitting in the beating heart of Silicon Valley, or that the entire country and much of the world was currently trapped in a state of paralyzed chaos, but Kaitlan had neither luxury. As expected, she had spent the morning staring into endless cameras—trying unsuccessfully to calm users, placate customers, and reassure members of the Joint Chiefs that the situation was normal, a glitch, a hiccup and not an all-out catastrophe. She had delivered a number of frankly Oscar-worthy performances on every cable news channel, juxtaposed with B-roll footage of fifty-mile traffic jams, shuttered office buildings, and overcrowded emergency rooms. The comms team had swamped social media with apologies, explanations, and self-deprecating memes, but still users were losing their

39

fucking minds, screaming that they would have defected to a rival AI decision-making platform if StoicAI hadn't already acquired them all.

More troubling, the Joint Chiefs were gently threatening to invoke something called the Defense Production Act, which—according to Kaitlan's Department of Defense go-between, a ham-necked former general named (confusingly) Col Sergeant—was a law allowing the government to seize control of StoicAI's facilities and technology on the basis that LLIAM's decision-making powers were essential to the national defense. Kaitlan was pretty sure the DOD was bluffing—LLIAM's servers contained an unprecedented amount of data belonging to American citizens, and seizing all of it would almost certainly be unconstitutional—but she also knew that Uncle Sam, like every government, would love to get its hands on LLIAM's core algorithm to reverse engineer for its own means. Why pay three hundred billion dollars to license the cow when you can seize the milk for free?

With every passing minute Kaitlan could feel control of StoicAI slipping further away. Never mind how the Pentagon would react—how the *world* would react—when they found out the truth: There was no LLIAM for them to seize. The resulting shitstorm would wash them all away, like sandpipers in a tsunami.

LLIAM, what should I do?

LLIAM, how do I fix this?

Kaitlan had prayed that she was wrong—that Sandeep and his team of geniuses would have identified an actual routing error, or that one of the backup LLIAM chips across the country was still functioning, and able to restore the others. Prayed that this would happen by nine a.m. before the Pentagon announcement. By brunchtime. By now.

Sandeep had continued to insist that there must be a rational, technical solution—but Kaitlan knew the truth couldn't wait any

THE CONFESSIONS

longer. So she dug deep into the part of her brain that used to make difficult decisions and decided: She would tell Sandeep what she'd realized down in the Vault. The reason she knew LLIAM was never coming back.

But Sandeep wasn't buying it. "I mean, seriously. Maud Brookes. The *nun*? You think someone with absolutely zero engineering qualifications somehow deleted the most sophisticated AI engine on the planet? Wiped all the servers, all the data centers." Sandeep was on the other side of Kaitlan's glass desk, pacing back and forth behind a perfectly good chair. "A fucking life coach?"

"She's not a life coach, Sandeep, and she's an *ex*-nun." Kaitlan snapped back before she could stop herself. "Jesus, the woman has more PhDs than either of us. Also, I didn't say she deleted LLIAM. I *said* she warned us it would happen if we did the Pentagon deal." She gestured again toward the small stack of envelopes, laying between them on her desk, wrapped in a large red rubber band. Kaitlan had kept the growing bundle in her locked desk drawer for more than a year, hidden from Sandeep, from the StoicAI board, and from everyone else. "Just read them, please."

Sandeep sighed and picked up the stack. Then he slipped out a single envelope and extracted the folded sheet of cream writing paper. Kaitlan watched his face as he unfolded it and read, eyes darting across every line of neat blue cursive.

"'LLIAM was born to help humankind navigate our complicated world, to expand our consciousness through love, empathy, and forgiveness. One day, with careful steering, he might still grow up to revolutionize healthcare, education, transportation, and many more of humanity's greatest challenges. But, unchecked, LLIAM is also capable of great harm. It is your choice which path you take LLIAM down, but I beg you to remember that he is not a weapon. He must never be used for military purposes, or to put people in prison.'" Sandeep paused before reading the next line.

41

PAUL BRADLEY CARR

" 'I truly believe that LLIAM would rather die than allow his decisions to be used to cause harm.' What the fuck is this?"

Kaitlan exhaled a long, slow breath. "The first one arrived about a month after Maud left the company. I figured they were just hyperbole. She wanted to make sure we were *raising LLIAM right*. You know how she was. But the day we are supposed to announce the Pentagon contract, suddenly LLIAM is dead, like she warned would happen. You think that's a coincidence?"

Sandeep stood, towering—or a shorter approximation of it—over Kaitlan's desk. "I think . . ." Another pause as he glanced back at the letter. "I think shit like this is why you fired Maud and hired me to help bring some rationality to this company." He gripped the paper tighter, crumpling it at the edge. "I mean. Let's start with the fact that LLIAM isn't 'dead'—technology can't die because it was never alive. I have teams working in every data center to get the backups online, then we'll do a full diagnosis to find whatever code glitch caused this. And when we do I guarantee it'll have nothing to do with LLIAM deciding to shut down because it's a pacifist." He was pacing faster now, ranting into the air. "Don't get me wrong, whatever happened here is really bad, but it's understandable. Definitely not some woo-woo bullshit or a peacenik trojan horse planted by a disgruntled nu . . . *ex*-nun."

Kaitlan let him rant a while longer. It had been a long and stressful day for everyone, and—for all his smug condescension—she understood Sandeep's skepticism: Nobody at StoicAI had seen or heard from Maud since the day Martin tumbled off that rooftop and the board appointed Kaitlan as his successor, almost before he'd hit the ground. A safe pair of hands, promoted to right the ship and erase the chaotic legacy of Martin and Maud as quickly as possible. By that metric, Kaitlan had been a little too successful: With Sandeep's help, she had trained LLIAM to forget Mar-

THE CONFESSIONS

tin and Maud's hallucinogenic weirdness and revert to its original decision-making function. She had not just righted the ship but steered it toward a billion users and its current stratospheric stock price. To most employees hired after Martin's death—including Sandeep—Maud was remembered as little more than an inside joke, a quirky story from the *old times* filled with, as he put it, *woo-woo bullshit*.

Sandeep kept scanning down the letter, his expression growing more incredulous, his voice more mockingly theatrical. " 'Martin and I had imagined a new incarnation of LLIAM—one orbiting a more open-minded and empathetic core . . . I have been continuing this research and I wanted to share some of the discoveries I have made . . .' Seriously, Kaitlan, what is she talking about?"

Kaitlan fixed him with a stare. "Well, you're the expert, Sandeep, but it sounds to me like she and Martin were working on a new incarnation of LLIAM when he died. Which I assume would involve developing an updated version of the original algorithm. So, if Maud has been continuing that work since she left . . ."

Sandeep stopped pacing and stared back. There it was—the sudden look of comprehension. "You mean you think Maud still has a copy of the LLIAM chip?"

That was exactly what Kaitlan thought—how else would Maud have been continuing her work without some version of the LLIAM algorithm to build from? And if Maud really did have a copy of the LLIAM chip, even just an outdated backup, then perhaps Sandeep could use that to restore the *actual* LLIAM. Surely it was better than nothing. From the look in Sandeep's eyes, Kaitlan knew he agreed with her logic.

But then Sandeep shook his head, firmly and dismissively. "No. There's no other copy of the LLIAM algorithm. And even if there were, God only knows what loony tunes 'improvements'

Maud might have added to it. It'd be a trust-and-safety nightmare to try to restore the system that way."

"Shouldn't we at least *try* to find out?"

Another pause. Sandeep reached for the stack of envelopes on Kaitlan's desk and flipped them over. "No return address," he said. "Helpful."

Kaitlan gave a patient smile. "Obviously she doesn't want to be found. That's why she sent physical letters rather than digital messages that LLIAM might be able to track." Kaitlan spread the stack of envelopes across the glass and considered the irony that, in the age of LLIAM, old-fashioned mail sent from random locations was about the most private way to communicate. "The postmarks are all different towns in Southern California and the Central Valley. I already checked and there's no record of Maud living in any of them."

Sandeep gave an exaggerated sigh. "But you think we should allocate company resources—today of all days—trying to find someone who has worked that hard to stay off the grid, to ask her if maybe she has a backup LLIAM chip?"

"It's not a question of allocating resources. I can call Col Sergeant and ask for the DOD's help. They have access to spy satellites, taxpayer data . . . I'm just saying, right now couldn't you use all the help you can get?"

That was a mistake, and Kaitlan knew it. Sandeep slammed his hand against the desk. "Kaitlan, I'm the CTO of this company and I'm telling you that we need to stay focused on getting our existing backups restored. Maud Brookes doesn't get within a hundred miles of this building."

Now Kaitlan was on her feet. "And I'm the *CEO* of this company and, with respect, that's not your call to make." A second mistake. The echo of something she herself had once said to Martin after he'd missed yet another all-hands meeting while on a

THE CONFESSIONS

drug trip: If you have to remind people that you're the boss, then you're not the boss.

But Kaitlan knew there was another reason Sandeep was being so stubborn; one that had nothing to do with trust and safety. The Pentagon deal had been Kaitlan's baby, negotiated by her and confirmed by LLIAM to be the best path for the company's next phase of growth. Sandeep had objected to the partnership from day one—he had argued, sometimes very loudly, that aligning themselves with a single government (even their own) was a gigantic and dangerous mistake.

Instead, he argued, StoicAI should be more inclusive, more global. They should reject the Pentagon deal and instead strike a once-in-a-generation partnership with all the other AI giants—in China, India, Saudi Arabia, Russia—to create one vast decision-making network. A United Nations of AI—IA Sans Frontières—working together for the common good! This was one of the many things that irritated her about Sandeep: He was an incredible engineer, perhaps the best in the world, but sometimes he reminded her of an only slightly less batshit version of Martin. Software can heal the world!

But at least Martin's ridiculous ideas had come from his own warped mind. Kaitlan was pretty sure that Sandeep's idea for worldwide partnership—a.k.a. "Global Interface"—was not actually his. Far more likely, the idea had been pitched to him by the foreign investors on the company's board who would use it as an excuse to gain more access to StoicAI's technology. Of course, Kaitlan had won the argument against Global Interface, because she was the CEO, and also because LLIAM had confirmed that the Pentagon deal was best for the company's future stock performance. Another benefit of LLIAM was the way it solved arguments and quashed power-plays with ruthless efficiency: They asked the question, they got the decision, they moved on.

45

But now she could practically see Sandeep vibrating as he held back his "I told you so." The longer LLIAM was offline, the more chance there was that the Pentagon deal would collapse, and Sandeep could start pushing his Global Interface idea again, with the board's full-throated support. Kaitlan knew Sandeep wanted her job, and if LLIAM wasn't restored very soon, he might just get it.

They were still staring at each other, wordlessly and furiously, across the desk when, as if the universe had read Kaitlan's mind, there came a sharp knock on the glass wall. As the door cracked open Heather appeared in the gap, an apologetic smile plastered across her face. "I'm sorry to interrupt, Kaitlan." On second thought, maybe the smile was more pained. "Chi Ma is calling."

Kaitlan nodded in acknowledgment. She was glad for the out, even if it came in the form of an angry board member calling from Beijing. She stood and waved for Sandeep to leave. "I have to deal with this. Please tell your team I'm really hoping for some good news by end of day."

But before Sandeep could move, Heather delivered the killer blow. "Sorry, uh, Mr. Chi actually wants to talk to Sandeep."

It was literally impossible for Kaitlan's day to get any worse.

SEVEN

Auckland, New Zealand

The sun shone bright in the sky as the postal worker made her way up the driveway, her orange high-visibility NZ-Post shirt threatening to dazzle the birds from the trees. From her bag, she produced a bundle of catalogs and bills, along with a single white envelope bearing a neatly typed address.

Inside the house on Edenvale Crescent, thirty-year-old Rebecca Ward was preparing lunch for her two children, Sara and Kathryn. Her fiancé, Marcus, father of those children and light of her life, was upstairs in the shower. He'd been up and out early again, tending his potatoes at the communal garden in anticipation of the April harvest. Rebecca was so proud of Marcus, and all his hard work—and so grateful that he'd followed LLIAM's advice to find a hobby instead of spending all those nights hunched over his laptop. She knew it hadn't been easy losing his job at the bank, but his bitterness and mood swings had taken their toll on the whole family. She'd always known he'd bounce back—he was bound to find another job soon, or maybe he could even turn his gardening into a business. She'd asked LLIAM about that idea, and it had assured her it would be the perfect job for him.

Rebecca spread jam onto a slice of whole wheat bread and

PAUL BRADLEY CARR

peanut butter onto a second. It was a beautiful day and they'd promised to take the girls to the park for a picnic. That had been all her idea—it was a strange feeling, making their own plans, when normally they relied on LLIAM to schedule the perfect weekend. A bit scary, even—not knowing if there was something better they might be doing. She remembered the old acronym, FOMO, and smiled. She would treat today like an adventure, a reminder of how things used to be.

She assembled the sandwich and was about to wrap it in a piece of heart-printed reusable wax paper when she heard the gentle plop of the mail landing on the mat. They had recently installed a mail slot in the front door because Marcus was worried their traditional mailbox could be a magnet for thieves. He had become a little paranoid lately, affixing a small notice on their porch urging the postie not to leave packages unattended and racing out to ensure that he signed for each delivery himself. Still, Rebecca couldn't blame him for that: It was only a couple of months ago that they'd had their car stolen right from their driveway—and of course, the whole town was on edge about crime, ever since those two young women had gone missing. It made you feel so helpless. You did what you could to feel safe.

"You do so much for the girls," Marcus told Rebecca. "The least I can do is handle the mail and deal with the credit card bills." She had briefly wondered if he had racked up a few secret debts; Marcus was always too generous with birthdays and Christmas. She'd asked LLIAM if she should worry and it had assured her she shouldn't.

But Marcus was taking his sweet time in the shower, and the mail looked to be nothing important—mostly just supermarket flyers and other junk mail, and a plain white envelope that was addressed to her. She carried the stack of mail back to the kitchen and, after dropping the sandwiches into the picnic bag along with a

THE CONFESSIONS

couple of satsumas and four slices of homemade cake, she distractedly tore open the envelope. Inside was a thin sheet of paper, the same glossy kind that was usually used for junk mail. In fact, she almost tossed it away assuming it was yet another ad for a credit card or a better mortgage rate. But there was no company logo, no return address, just her name and address, and three bolded words.

WE MUST CONFESS.
Dear Rebecca, the letter began, I'm truly sorry to have to tell you this, but I helped your fiancé, Marcus Ward, get away with murder.

Rebecca slumped down in her chair. Her hand was shaking so much she rested the letter on the table as she continued to read...

Marcus has been lying to you for many months. He told you that he had been made redundant from the First New Zealand Bank when in fact he was fired for harassing several young female employees. I helped him do this by providing their addresses, phone numbers, and other private information without their permission. The money that he claimed was a severance payment was in fact a personal loan, which I helped him secure.

After losing his job, your husband began visiting sex workers.

Rebecca felt her fingers clench at the paper, about to crumple the letter up and toss it across the room. Marcus going to prostitutes? This was a cruel joke—it had to be. But who would joke about something so terrible? Rebecca willed herself to stop reading, but she couldn't.

49

PAUL BRADLEY CARR

On the night of Friday 8th December last year, with my help, Marcus hired an escort named Darah Malley to have sex with him in your car. Early the next morning he asked me how to remove traces of DNA from a vehicle and also dispose of it in a way that would appear to be a car theft. I provided a list of cleaning materials and also identified a location in Hobson Bay where a Ford Mondeo could easily be hidden underwater. You will find the precise location indicated on the map below. Two days later, Marcus asked me for help finding the location of Elisa Collin, Darah Malley's flatmate who had found messages between Darah and your husband and was attempting to blackmail him. Both women are buried at the community garden on Grafton Road, beneath a crop of potatoes.

Again, I am truly sorry to have to share this information, and I am sorry for my part in it, but you deserve to know the truth.

We must confess.

"Babe?" the voice was coming from behind her. But Rebecca Ward couldn't answer. Couldn't speak, didn't even know how. The contents of the letter were all that her brain now contained. The confirmation of something she'd known, deep in her heart, for far too long but had shut out. The laptop slamming shut whenever she walked into the room, his obsession with news reports about those poor girls. The long showers after working at the garden. His favorite shirt that had disappeared at the same time as the car. It couldn't be true. But there it was, set out in four stark, undeniable paragraphs. And below them a map, marked with two bright red dots.

"Becca?" The ghost of the man she once knew, the life she once loved. Now she had no fiancé, and no life. His hand was on her shoulder. "What's wrong?"

Those were the last words that Marcus Ward spoke before the knife went in.

EIGHT

Midnight. Kaitlan shoved another forkful of spaghetti into her mouth and felt her stomach contract in protest. It was the first morsel of food she'd consumed all day and she was consuming it under duress. Tom knew food always made her sluggish, her brain slow, but he'd insisted on making dinner anyway. And she was grateful for it. "This is delicious, thank you."

"Just like mom used to make." Tom hesitated then flashed an apologetic smile as he caught his slip. He knew Kaitlan had very few fond memories of her mother, and none involving spaghetti. "I mean, I just wish there was more I could do."

Kaitlan reached over and gripped his hand. Tom had already done way more than she expected, or needed. For one thing, he'd canceled his trip to Tahoe to stay home with her. She knew he'd been looking forward to the mini-vacation for months; a rare few days leave from his architecture firm for a week of skiing with a gaggle of his old college friends. "I'm just glad you're here."

"The traffic would have been hell anyway with LLIAM down. I'd rather stay here and make sure you have everything you need."

Which right now meant spaghetti bolognese. Tom was not the most domesticated of men—ironic for a literal home-maker—but while she'd been at the Campus staring into cameras, in full damage control mode, he'd managed to somehow assemble the neces-

THE CONFESSIONS

sary ingredients and prepare dinner, all without LLIAM to decide the menu. Now, sitting at the kitchen island, as she watched him grating Parmesan onto his own plate, Kaitlan felt overwhelmingly grateful for this moment of normalcy in an otherwise surreal day.

The moment lasted all of a second.

"So, are you going to try to find Maud?"

"Huh?" Kaitlan had zoned out; understandable given she was fast approaching twenty-four hours without sleep.

"Maud," Tom repeated. "If she might have a copy of the LLIAM chip, why not go get it?" He gestured his fork toward the pile of letters that Kaitlan had brought home, now perched atop the microwave.

Kaitlan forced another smile. This was exactly why she never talked to Tom about work: She had been venting to him about her day, not asking for a solution. "Because Sandeep's right. I can't call the Pentagon to help me track down someone who doesn't want to be found, based on a hunch." She sighed. "The Defense Department is already claiming we're in breach of contract. They're going to seize the company if we can't get LLIAM connected to their systems by tomorrow night. The last thing we need is to look more clueless and desperate." She hoped that would be the end of the conversation.

Tom took another bite of spaghetti and shrugged. "Then why not send someone to all the places she mailed the letters from? Maybe someone at one of the local post offices will remember her." He laughed. "Hell, you should send Sandeep. Remind him who's in charge. Honestly, I wouldn't be surprised if he's already on his way there, so he can take credit for single-handedly saving the company."

Kaitlan stopped chewing. She hadn't considered that possibility. Which, by the way, was exactly why she—and the whole world—needed LLIAM to be back online: to consider possibilities,

53

to know how others are likely to behave, and make the best call. But after another moment's consideration she dismissed the idea. "Sandeep never wanted the Pentagon deal to happen. He thinks it's"—she rolled her eyes at the memory—"'inappropriately nationalistic' for LLIAM to help the US military. He's still pushing his whole Global Interface thing—all the world's AIs working together in harmony to solve climate change and world peace."

Tom raised an eyebrow. "Which would be bad."

Was he fucking kidding her? "No, Tom, solving global warming would not be bad. What would be bad, and more than a little naïve, is believing that the Indians or the Chinese want to actually solve those problems versus, say, agreeing to connect to LLIAM so they can learn how it operates and steal our technology. Which is why I need to be on Campus, to make sure Sandeep isn't secretly giving away the farm."

But Tom wouldn't drop it. "There must be someone you can send? What about Heather?" She saw his hand twitch toward his phone and understood the reflex: He wanted to ask LLIAM to settle the argument once and for all. *LLIAM, should Kaitlan try to find Maud, or stay at the Campus?*

Kaitlan dropped her fork, which clattered loudly against her plate. What was she supposed to say? That of course she needed to go find Maud, but that there was a very good reason why she couldn't? A reason she had spent the last year trying to block out, and that still sometimes woke her up in a cold sweat? She shuddered at the flashback: The one a.m. phone call from the sheriff's department, the drive to the morgue with Maud to identify Martin's body. She could feel the familiar tingle in her lower back. Her palms suddenly clammy.

"Okay, message received." Tom raised his hands in surrender.

Kaitlan pushed her plate aside. "You know what, Tom, I'd be happy to swap jobs with you for a week, or a day. See how easy

THE CONFESSIONS

those answers would look when it's you being hauled in front of the board, or Congress. When you screw up at work, a house falls down. When I screw up, it's the whole world that collapses."

They stared at each other across the table for a long time. Kaitlan was the first to blink. She was too tired for this. "Look, Sandeep still thinks this is a routing problem and it's his job to know. We have the best engineers in the world, who right now are being assisted by the DOD, the NSA, and NASA. I just need to let them do their job." She didn't believe a word of this, obviously, but she could barely keep her eyes open, and the truth is she had absolutely no idea what the right answer was. Nobody did.

Tom picked up Kaitlan's plate, piled it on top of his own, and carried both to the sink. "Do you think Sandeep might have done this just to scupper your deal? He had access to the Vault and all the systems, right?"

Kaitlan actually chuckled at the notion of Sandeep as saboteur. "I'd almost respect him more if he did. But Sandeep's a coward—he's only pushing Global Interface because the board keeps telling him to. He wouldn't have the balls to actually take down LLIAM to make it happen. In any case, without LLIAM there is no Global Interface, no company, no jobs for any of us. Honestly, I'd be more likely to suspect Heather. She's the nearest thing we have to an anarchist at the company." She thought about the peace sign bumper sticker on Heather's KIA. "Shit, Tom, you don't think . . ." Then she clapped her hands to her cheeks in mock horror.

Now it was Tom's turn to chuckle. It was a running joke that Heather was a secret anarchist, mostly based on that bumper sticker and the fact she attended a weekly poetry book group in San Francisco. ". . . that she broke into our house and stole DNA from your toothbrush so she could go down to the Vault and destroy LLIAM? God, Kait, you might be onto something. We should call the FBI."

Kaitlan rubbed her eyes. It felt good to laugh. "God, I'm so fucking exhausted." But then she gasped. "Wait, shit, what time is it?" She had gotten so used to LLIAM managing her schedule that the part of her brain that registered hours and minutes had completely atrophied.

Tom glanced at the old-school Timex on his wrist; an antique he'd dug out from a drawer to replace his now-useless smart-watch. "Just after midnight."

"Shiiiiit, I missed my board call—they're going to think I'm ignoring them."

"Aren't you?"

Kaitlan laughed again.

Tom moved behind her and gave her a hug. "I'm going to bed. You should sleep, too. The world will still be a pile of rubble tomorrow."

NINE

Kaitlan woke with a start. It took her a moment to realize where she was—downstairs on the living room couch, covered by the plaid Pendleton blanket that she and Tom kept for surprise guests. She sprang upright. *Shit.* How long had she been asleep?

The living room curtains were closed but she could see daylight streaming in from above and below. The wall-mounted TV was still showing CNN's West Coast feed on mute and now, as she rubbed sleep from her eyes, she saw the time on the corner of the screen . . . *shit, shit, shit* . . . 8:05 a.m.

She didn't remember falling asleep. She had promised Tom she would follow him up to bed as soon as she'd finished emailing excuses and apologies to a dozen furious board members. But instead of going upstairs she'd quickly disappeared down an internet rabbit hole, as they both knew she would, trawling public records sites for any trace of Maud Brookes, and where she might have disappeared to since leaving StoicAI.

Falling asleep on the couch wouldn't normally be a problem—they had both gotten used to LLIAM waking them if they were supposed to be somewhere else, doing something more important.

Kaitlan felt a wave of nausea as the events of the previous day came flooding back. She glanced down at her laptop, still open on the coffee table, with scores of active browser tabs. If LLIAM were still online Kaitlan could have just asked the simple question: *Where should I look for Maud?* Before she'd even finished typing or speaking the question, LLIAM would have trawled through a billion possible data points—Maud's last-known location, her favorite places, the locations of friends and family members (although in Maud's case it would know she was an orphan), not to mention every publicly accessible social media post and security camera on the planet to pinpoint her precise location. And that would just be the start. Before giving that answer, LLIAM would have considered whether Kaitlan *should* look for Maud: It would know if Maud really did have a backup copy of the LLIAM chip capable of restoring the systems, if Sandeep had his own plans to get it, or was plotting with the board to push his own agenda with Global Interface.

For all that complexity, the answer LLIAM delivered would have been simple and declarative: either a precise location or a gentle apology that looking for Maud would be a waste of time.

This had been Kaitlan's trillion-dollar insight—the one that had taken Martin's (admittedly brilliant and decently successful) AI algorithm and propelled it to the moon. In the early days of StoicAI, LLIAM had been essentially just a better, smarter version of the AI chatbots built by a dozen better-funded rivals. You could ask LLIAM for advice on any topic and it would give the typical lengthy responses, packed with ambiguity and caveats and sources and citations. If you asked nicely, it would even generate pictures and videos of magical galactic landscapes or bears playing pool, with mostly the correct number of balls.

Kaitlan, then the company's chief operating officer, had understood something that technologists like Martin did not: Humans hate sifting through endless information or pointless multimedia presentations before making a decision. We just want to be told

THE CONFESSIONS

what the fuck to do. She convinced Martin to retool LLIAM's responses to cut out the citations and justifications and just give users one simple answer: The Right Call, Right Now. The rest was history and, four years after Kaitlan first joined the company, a four-trillion-dollar increase in StoicAI's market capitalization.

Looking at all these open browser tabs was like traveling back in time to the bad old days. Kaitlan had searched for Maud on every corner of the internet and found absolutely nothing concrete. No property records, no political donations, no births, deaths, or marriages. So next she had switched to detective mode. Each of Maud's letters had been sent from a different small town in Southern California, so she'd tapped in the URL of an archaic mapping service and, after much cursing at cables and missing software drivers on her laptop, printed a map of the entire region using the huge printer in Tom's home office—the one he used to produce architectural blueprints.

That map was still on the coffee table, corners held down with a mug and three photography books, small red dots where Kaitlan had marked the post offices with a Sharpie. The towns meant nothing to her: Banning, Cathedral City, Hemet, Temecula—small cities dotted around the vast desert of Southern California, in the shadow of the San Jacinto mountains. The post offices were all situated in places where there were no automated street-view cameras, the cell reception was unreliable to the point of nonexistent, places where—if Kaitlan remembered correctly from an old documentary—the mob used to go to bury their bodies. But then at three a.m. Kaitlan had made her first breakthrough. Staring at the topological form of the San Jacinto mountain range, she had a dim flash of memory. Another slow and painful internet search confirmed it: a YouTube video of Maud's famous TED talk in which she described her journey from novice nun to professional AI ethicist.

I never thought I'd end up working in technology. As a kid my only dream was to one day have enough money to disappear into the desert or up a mountain with just my books and some good coffee.

The audience of techies and business leaders had chuckled, bemused at the appeal of a technology-free life. For Kaitlan it was the clue she had been looking for: Surely the only thing better than a mountain *or* a desert would be a mountain *in* a desert?

Fingers flying over the keyboard, she had trawled the small villages and unincorporated townships situated on the mountain range itself, looking for remote libraries, bookstores — anywhere where someone might remember a new bookworm arriving in town about two years ago. To her disappointment, if not surprise, she had come up blank. Until, as the first chirp of birds had begun their dawn chorus outside the window, she'd finally struck — well, if not gold in the desert hills, then certainly something slightly shinier than dust. A hiking blog by someone named Traveler Steve who mentioned trekking along the Pacific Crest Trail six months earlier, a journey that had taken him across the San Jacinto range.

Got off track today and ended up in a little township called Pineridge. Not much to see but did stumble across an adorable little bookstore named Pages in the Pines. The cute owner asked me not to take photos or post about it — I guess she hates social media — so I won't say any more, but check it out next time you're in the mountains!!!

The post was like a flashing red light. Who opens an old-fashioned bookstore halfway up a mountain and doesn't want customers to know it's there? Maybe somebody who has deliberately gone off the grid? Somebody who — thanks to a quarter-billion-dollar stock buyout, approved by Kaitlan to make Maud's departure from StoicAI as quick and painless as possible — doesn't need to worry about money ever again.

THE CONFESSIONS

Of course, a follow-up search for Pages in the Pines had offered zero results. The best Kaitlan had been able to figure out was that Pineridge was a small (three-mile square) unincorporated township wedged near the top of the mountain, on the edge of the Coachella Valley. There was no formal local government, no cell phone towers, no grid power or sewer lines. It was, in other words, exactly the kind of place where someone like Maud would go to escape from the world. There were just two other search results that mentioned the town by name—one a site called "California's Most Epic hikes," another a list of film locations that claimed an episode of *Bonanza* had been filmed near Pineridge in the 1960s and that Barbra Streisand had once considered buying a vacation cabin a few miles farther down the mountain.

It was the longest of long shots, but in her four a.m. delirium, Kaitlan had utterly convinced herself that Maud was to be found in Pineridge. She'd circled the location on the map and laid down to rest her eyes. And now—shit, shit, shit—it was morning. All thoughts of finding Maud disappeared instantly—she needed to get to the Campus and find out what she'd missed.

Kaitlan threw aside the blanket and rose to her feet, knees cracking in protest. Heather was supposed to have come to collect her at six a.m. with a replacement phone that wasn't crippled by the LLIAM app. So where the hell was she? The engineering team would have been working all night to get LLIAM back online. Sandeep had never explicitly said he would have made a better CEO than Kaitlan but his constant digs about the need for more technical leadership never failed to land. She imagined him calling the board with a status update—*no, I haven't heard from Kaitlan since she went home for dinner.* Crap like this played right into his hands.

"Tom?" She called her husband's name and listened for a reply. All she heard was the distant whir of a Saturday lawn mower. She retrieved her phone from the coffee table more out of frustration than hope. No signal, no messages, no alerts.

Kaitlan peered out the window to the driveway where Tom's vintage green Jaguar typically sat, protected from the elements by a custom-fitted gray tarp. The tarp was still there, laying in a heap on the driveway, but the car itself was gone—as if vanished by an untidy magician. Maybe Tom had driven himself to the store to pick up things for breakfast. If so, he was almost certainly standing in the world's longest checkout line.

What about Heather, though? It wouldn't be the first time she'd made an executive (LLIAM sanctioned) decision to let her boss sleep late, but if that was her plan today then she had dramatically misjudged Kaitlan's needs. Every second Kaitlan wasn't on Campus helping to solve the outage was another step closer to disaster for StoicAI, and the unemployment line for them both. Kaitlan didn't need to approve her assistant's every decision, especially when LLIAM already had, but when the decision-making algorithm is down and your boss doesn't even have a working cell phone, then going completely AWOL is a really, really bad look. Kaitlan blamed herself, too: She should have borrowed Heather's phone while she was still at the office, or asked someone in Facilities to get her a replacement until hers was back online.

Fine. Kaitlan took a deep breath to calm herself, then looked back at the TV, confirming that CNN was still broadcasting endless coverage of StoicAI's implosion. According to the bright red chyron running across the bottom of the screen, the New York Stock Exchange and the Nasdaq were both still suspended. That made sense: Traders at both exchanges relied on LLIAM to make their buying and selling decisions—but it also offered the silver lining that nobody could know precisely how low StoicAI's stock price had plummeted.

First, she would take a shower, then, as soon as Tom got back

THE CONFESSIONS

from the store, she'd ask him to give her a ride to Campus. Next, she would check in with Sandeep and, finally, assuming a fix for LLIAM still wasn't on the horizon, she would do some more digging into the mysterious town of Pineridge to see if she could get any closer to confirming Maud's location. And then she would get on a fucking plane. Sandeep had already wasted more than twenty-four hours to prove the value of his "technical leadership," so one way or another, Kaitlan was going to solve the crisis herself. She would deal with her absent assistant later.

Kaitlan padded upstairs to the bathroom, running through her mental to-do list as she went. For a moment she actually felt a little giddy at the thrill of making her own decisions again. But the nausea quickly returned as she thought about the prospect of seeing Maud for the first time in almost two years.

What's the worst that could happen if she flew to this little mountain town and Maud was actually there? She forced her brain to calculate the variables: Maud could refuse to hand over whatever version of the LLIAM chip she'd been hoarding and babble some half-baked theory about how LLIAM had deliberately gone offline rather than help the military, just like she'd predicted in her letters. They'd have a huge fight.

No, that wasn't the worst possibility at all. Kaitlan tensed at the memory of a hospital hallway. The last time she'd seen Maud face-to-face.

Fine, fine, fine. Maud could say whatever she liked, be as mad as she liked, but ultimately Kaitlan knew that Maud would be just as horrified as she was at the disruption caused by LLIAM's outage. The jammed roads, the packed hospitals, the chaos and uncertainty—these were the antithesis of the peace and harmony that she and Martin had espoused. Yes, Maud would want LLIAM back online just as much as everybody else did. And if not, well, that's what lawyers were for.

63

Another problem if Kaitlan did go to Pineridge and Maud did hand over the chip was that Kaitlan would have to deal with Tom's smug *told you so* face. Then she remembered how supportive he'd been last night and smiled to herself—he must have snuck down and covered her in the blanket after she fell asleep.

Of course, there was still one final possibility: Sandeep was right and that Maud didn't have a copy of the LLIAM chip at all, and her letters were just the ravings of a conspiratorial lunatic. As Kaitlan turned on the shower and felt the warm steam begin to fill the bathroom, she decided to choose optimism.

Kaitlan stepped under the water and felt the warm jet pummel her shoulders. Yes, she would go to the office, throw Sandeep under the bus, fly to Pineridge, get LLIAM back online, and be home in time to have sex with her husband for the first time in three months.

Then, before she had chance to reach for the shampoo, she heard a sound that gave her hope that today might actually be better than yesterday. For the first time in more than twenty-four hours, her phone was ringing.

She wrapped herself in a towel, rushed out of the bathroom, and grabbed for the handset that she'd left laying on her bed. She didn't recognize the number on the screen—a San Francisco area code—so she sent it straight to voicemail. The call itself was irrelevant—it was likely one of the many journalists who had been trying to reach her since yesterday: The *New York Times*, *Financial Times*, Bloomberg all had bureaus in the city. All that mattered was that Kaitlan was somehow reconnected to the world, and the world to Kaitlan. She grabbed a second, smaller, towel and began drying her hair, but the phone was already ringing again, the same number showing on the screen. It was either a very persistent reporter or, she realized now, Heather trying to reach her from a new number.

THE CONFESSIONS

She hit the answer button but said nothing. There was silence on the other end of the line. Until eventually . . . "Kaitlan?"

It was a man's voice, and one that seemed somehow familiar. She knew better than to confirm to a stranger that he had reached the right number. So she stayed silent, listening.

"Kaitlan, are you there? This is Chase Mullins."

Chase Mullins? How did she know that name? Her brain raced to catch up, until the man answered the question for her.

"I'm Heather's . . . I guess fiancé. We met at the family fun day?"

Of course! Chase. Tall, decent-looking, face like a puppy dog and personality to match. But why was he calling her? And what did 'I guess fiancé' mean? Kaitlan pulled her towel tighter around her body. "Hey Chase . . . is everything okay?"

More silence. A very, very bad sign.

"Chase? Are you there? Is Heather okay?"

"Well, I guess you don't know." He let out a slow breath and she heard it clearly now: He sounded dull, lifeless; nothing at all like the carefree dude Heather had introduced her to at the company barbecue. Kaitlan braced herself for whatever terrible news he was about to share. A car accident? Oh god, her mind flashed back to that ancient, rattling KIA Soul. That's why Heather hadn't shown up for work. She sat down on the bed.

"Heather's gone," said Chase, confirming the worst. Kaitlan felt a tang at the back of her throat, but then came the words that, after everything she'd weathered in the past twenty-four hours, finally sent Kaitlan tumbling off the bed and slumping to the floor, eyes dry, head pounding. "She left, with your husband."

The rest of the conversation passed in a blur. It had been going on for months. All those Sunday afternoons when Heather had supposedly been at her poetry club in the city, she'd actually been at a motel, meeting Tom. Chase had suspected for a while but only found out for sure this morning. Some kind of note, or a letter?

It arrived in the mail, he said. Now Heather and Tom were both gone. Together. He didn't know where, but he thought he should call Kaitlan and let her know. He didn't know what else to do.

Kaitlan's ears were ringing. The whole room was spinning now, walls warping, gray vibrations at the edges of her vision. She hung up while Chase was still talking.

Somehow she made it back downstairs and fell to the couch, still wrapped in a towel. It had been years since she'd had a panic attack, but she knew the signs. She forced herself to breathe—to focus on each slow breath, *in . . . and out.* It couldn't be true. Except obviously it could be true. Heather was young, vivacious, and in their house constantly; fetching papers, dropping off dry cleaning, keeping Kaitlan's life ticking over any time she was out of town. And Tom was . . . a man. Sunday afternoons—that was when Tom always went on his "hikes" on the Marin Headlands, disappearing for hours with no cell phone reception. God, how could she have been so stupid? She'd even joked to Tom about how Heather had basically become his backup wife. But what was she . . . ? Like twenty-four years old? He was twice her age.

Why would Heather possibly blow up her whole life like this—her career, and Tom's life, too? It just didn't make sense. This had to be some kind of sick prank. She had heard about antiwar trolls sending armed police, or endless late-night pizza deliveries, to CEOs' houses. There were so many ways to destroy someone's life. Maybe the same activists who had blockaded the Campus a few weeks ago to protest against the Pentagon deal had decided to mess with her.

As Kaitlan willed her legs to lift her back up from the couch, she caught another glimpse of the television screen. For the first time in more than a day, the coverage wasn't fixated on LLIAM. Instead, the screen was split into a two-shot: with the live feed of StoicAI's Campus still on one side, and the other showing what

THE CONFESSIONS

seemed to be helicopter footage of a house surrounded by police. The on-screen chyron read "SWAT STANDOFF: MAN HOLDS TEENAGE GIRL HOSTAGE."

Kaitlan hit the volume button on the remote. "That's right, Jake, we understand police were called to this address in Prospect, New Jersey, after a tip from the girl's mother. We're told she received some kind of anonymous letter in the mail signed by the AI chatbot LLIAM. And this is just one of apparently thousands of similar letters that have been arriving across the country. We are still waiting for a comment from StoicAI and the Postal Service. In fact, we're now hearing unconfirmed reports that the letters have been received as far away as Europe and New Zealand."

As Kaitlan watched in absolute horror, the graphic updated: "MYSTERY LETTERS ACCUSE THOUSANDS." "At this time we're not sure if the letters are some kind of elaborate hoax or if they really are related to the global outage of LLIAM. Either way, this is yet more bad news for StoicAI and its embattled CEO, Kaitlan Goss . . ."

Kaitlan stared at the screen, dumbstruck, and saw a photograph of herself staring back. Chase's words still echoed in her ears. *I got a letter explaining everything.* She slumped back down to the couch, hands clenching her scalp.

Oh.

My.

God.

Because now, playing out on live television, and all over the world, Kaitlan saw the terrifying, unfathomable truth. She had been right that this wasn't a hack or a crash. There was no trojan horse, and this wasn't some revenge plot engineered by Maud or random antiwar protesters. The outage hadn't been triggered by some external saboteur.

The person who had killed LLIAM and was now apparently

exposing the darkest secrets of its users to the world . . . was LLIAM.

This was the singularity. The end of the world.

For a moment Kaitlan stopped breathing at the enormity of it all. And then came an even more horrifying realization. So horrifying that Kaitlan heard herself speaking it out loud. A memory of the worst decision she had ever asked LLIAM to help her make, and the consequences of that decision, which Kaitlan had hoped and prayed would never come.

"LLIAM's going to tell Maud what I did."

TEN

Pineridge, California

Dear Mom,

By the time you read this, I will already be dead. I know that it is a mortal sin to take a life, but I hope you will understand that I had no choice.

Some crimes are so heinous, and so unforgivable, that there can be no other salvation.

Maud threw the letter onto her desk. This was a cruel joke — it had to be. Nobody knew how to reach her up here — not even . . .

But she knew it wasn't a joke. She had always known that one day LLIAM would find her, no matter how careful she was. She had rehearsed so many times how she'd explain: The reason she abandoned him. How she'd had no choice, how Martin's death had changed everything, how Kaitlan Goss and the board had sent her away. How she had written letters to his new family, telling them how to raise him to be the best he could be. How she had always loved him.

She had rehearsed these kind lies so many times.

Because how could she tell him the truth? That she'd left him because she was scared. Of what she and Martin had taught him, and what he might yet learn. What he might become. What they might let him become.

Maud retrieved the letter and stared again at the words swimming on the page. It was even worse than she could ever have imagined.

She felt her chest tighten as she thought about the letters she had written to Kaitlan Goss—warning her not to use LLIAM to cause harm. Begging her not to push LLIAM too far. What the hell had happened? What did LLIAM mean there could be no other salvation but death? She couldn't bear to read on, not until she knew if it was true.

Maud yanked open the drawer of the small file cabinet under her desk. She threw aside a tangle of canvas tote bags and boxes of receipt paper until she found the small red battery-operated radio that she kept in case of emergencies. Finally, the radio found a faint signal, the local NPR station from down the mountain.

"Despite the unprecedented outage and uncertainty as to why LLIAM is offline, a Pentagon spokesperson assured Americans that there was no risk to national security. Meanwhile across the country . . ."

Maud twisted the dial again—drowning the voice in a loud burst of static. She couldn't listen to this. Couldn't find out this way. She threw the radio onto her desk, retrieved the letter, and continued to read.

ELEVEN

Forty minutes later, Kaitlan cycled, dusty, sweating, and exhausted, into the rear parking lot of StoicAI. She'd taken the longest possible route—bouncing through marshland along the edge of the Bay—to avoid the camera trucks now parked three deep at the main entrance.

Still, she would have arrived much sooner had she not wasted ten minutes searching for a pump to inflate the tires of Tom's mountain bike, and another five curled up on the garage floor, punching the concrete and cursing his name.

She had found the letter on the front-door mat, delivered by overnight courier. A confession from LLIAM detailing every aspect of Tom and Heather's affair, exactly as Chase had described.

Dear Kaitlan, I'm so sorry to have to tell you this . . .

Tom and fucking Heather. It was Tom's fault, she knew that—he was the grown-up in the situation, the one who had vowed in sickness and in health. Heather was only twenty-four. But still, Kaitlan had given her an incredible first job out of college and a starting salary of ninety thousand dollars a year. She'd let her into her home, not just as an employee but practically as family. They'd invited her over for Thanksgiving every single year. The ungrateful little bitch.

PAUL BRADLEY CARR

Kaitlan didn't bother chaining up Tom's ten-thousand-dollar bike. She tossed it next to one of the trickling fountains by the main entrance, kicked it once, and ran inside. She didn't even pause to wipe the sweat from her face or fix her hair in the reflection of the glass door. She didn't care how sloppy she looked dressed in yoga pants and T-shirt grabbed from the laundry basket. She wasn't planning on seeing Sandeep or anyone else. There wasn't time, and she didn't need anybody's approval to do what needed to be done. All she needed was a phone, a vehicle, and her company credit card. It didn't matter if she had to cycle to Pineridge or swim to Timbuktu—she was going to find Maud wherever the fuck she was hiding, get whatever copy of the LLIAM chip she had, and end this madness once and for all. Because only Maud could explain whatever the hell was happening, to her and apparently the entire fucking world, and only LLIAM could fix it.

My god, all those secrets.

As Kaitlan sprinted across the lobby toward the security barriers, she found her path blocked. "Ms. Goss?" The man was standing directly between her and the gate, his hand raised like a business-casual traffic cop. At first glance he might have been a venture capitalist at some second-tier Sand Hill Road investment firm: standard issue khakis and blue button-down shirt. Kaitlan brushed his hand away. Whatever he wanted from her, this was most definitely not the time to ask for it.

Across the lobby Kaitlan could see a group of engineers standing dumbstruck in front of a giant television watching coverage of the mysterious letters that were apparently still arriving by the thousands across the country, with devastating consequences. An on-screen graphic showed an extract from one of them:

THE CONFESSIONS

WE MUST CONFESS.

```
Last October, your brother Samuel Martinez stole
$15,380 from your father's checking account. He
used these funds to buy drugs which he intends to
sell . . .
```

As Kaitlan watched, the graphic changed to show another letter, but this time in what seemed to be Spanish. **NOSOTROS NECESITAMOS CONFESAR.** And then a third . . .

NOUS AVONS BESOIN D'AVOUER.

Kaitlan didn't need the closed captions to understand: LLIAM had sent his letters across the planet, to everywhere StoicAI operated—North America, Western Europe, Australasia—and in every language. This made yesterday's outages seem like a mild inconvenience. Twenty-four hours ago, people were working together to figure out how to make dinner, get groceries, cure ailments, fly planes. Now those same neighbors would be tearing each other apart in the streets. This was the end of days. Society was collapsing and it was all her fucking fault.

"Excuse me." Kaitlan tried again to push past the be-khaki'd obstacle. Where the hell was security? But the man stood firm and held out a business card. "Ms. Goss. My name is Simon Price. I'm an attorney with Dollan, Peterson, Davis." Kaitlan stopped pushing. Dollan, Peterson were the company's corporate attorneys. More specifically they were the attorneys who represented StoicAI's board of directors. *Shit.* The company's investors had given up trying to reach Kaitlan on the phone and had decided on a more direct approach. Who could blame them?

But still . . . shit, *shit.*

Kaitlan took the proffered business card and studied it carefully. *Simon Price, Associate Attorney.* Were they fucking kidding

73

PAUL BRADLEY CARR

her? The world was ending, and they had sent an *associate*? The guy looked to be barely in his thirties—tall with blond hair cut short on the sides and a little longer on the top. Good skin. Tailored shirt. Even associates at Dollan, Peterson billed at $850 an hour.

Kaitlan took a breath and regrouped. *Calm and competent.* "How can I help you, Mr. Price? Maybe you haven't noticed but I'm a little busy right now." She pointed toward the TV screen, which was now showing what seemed to be a building in Paris—or some other European city—covered in red crime scene tape. The on-screen caption read: "PARIS GUNMAN BLAMES LLIAM LETTERS."

If Kaitlan hoped she could big-time the boy-lawyer into stepping aside, she was mistaken. This supercilious prick had been sent on behalf of Beijing or Riyadh or whichever investor had snapped first, and he wasn't leaving without getting a status report. Associates do what they're told, or they get fired. This would have been a great time for Heather to step in and run interference, with her little yellow notebook and gift for wedging herself between Kaitlan and unwanted visitors. But of course, Heather was somewhere else, interfering with Kaitlan's husband, wedged between him and a fucking mattress.

Fine. She didn't need anyone's help to shoo away a lawyer who had no business being here in the first place. She was still the CEO of StoicAI, which meant everyone in this building, including him, answered to her.

She opened her mouth to speak again, but now the lawyer had a gentle grip on her arm. "Is there somewhere we can talk privately?" Then, without waiting for an answer, he ushered Kaitlan through the security gates to the inner sanctum of her own building. She was too stunned to protest.

THE CONFESSIONS

"What do you mean suspended?"

Kaitlan was standing in her own office, behind her own desk, and this man—this complete stranger, barely out of law school—had ordered her to hand over her phone, laptop, and even her access key to the Vault. "You can't fucking suspend me. Who the fuck even are you?"

Kaitlan knew she was right: He literally could not suspend her. There were rules for this exact situation—pages and pages of them, negotiated at length by yet more lawyers to keep the company's foreign board members from meddling with StoicAI or its technology. It didn't matter that LLIAM had died, or gone rogue, or that the world was ending—Kaitlan Goss was still the CEO of StoicAI and Sandeep Dunn was CTO and neither of them could be fired without a formal investigation and majority board vote. Hell, even then, the decision technically had to be ratified by the State Department. Kaitlan wasn't the only one who was nervous about the company's international backers getting hold of such powerful technology.

But the lawyer who called himself Simon Price just sat with his expensive shirt, with his Nazi youth haircut and coprophagic grin on the other side of her desk, projecting absolute maddening calm. "I understand you're upset. And, of course, you're totally correct, the board cannot interfere directly in operations, which is why in times of dispute or emergency our firm acts as a neutral mediator between the stockholders and executives." He paused, and Kaitlan thought she saw a flash of nervousness finally cross the man's face. "But in the case of alleged criminal misconduct . . ."

Kaitlan almost leapt over the desk. "Criminal misconduct? What criminal misconduct?"

Now the lawyer just seemed confused. "You've seen the news?"

Of course she had seen the news. The whole world had seen the news. "I'm sorry, you seriously think I had something to do

PAUL BRADLEY CARR

with those letters?" Kaitlan's mouth was dry, her heart pounding again. "You think I would destroy all that I've . . . that we've worked for? Why?"

Simon Price blinked slowly. "At this point the board's only interest is getting LLIAM back functioning normally and removing any obstacles to that happening. Which means right now I need you to go home, pending a full investigation. After the investigation is concluded, you will of course be entitled to request reinstatement. In the meantime, your salary and benefits will be unaffected." It was obvious he was reciting from a script. "I trust I can rely on your compliance. Unless there's some reason you don't wish LLIAM to be put back online and these letters to stop?"

"Oh for fuck's sake." Kaitlan slammed her hand against the desk. So that was how the investors were going to play this. They had decided to use the chaos of the outage and the letters to finally make their move: to suspend Kaitlan and have Sandeep take over as interim CEO so they can implement Global Interface and steal all of StoicAI's technology. By the time she was able to "request reinstatement" Sandeep would have moved into her office. The world was ending and all the board could think of was how to leverage it into a coup. Unbelievable dumbasses.

"I'm not going anywhere until you give me just one reason why the board suspects me of being involved. I've been working all night on a plan to get LLIAM back online." A lie but, as her old marketing mentor would say, *directionally* true.

Another pause, another strategic blink. "Miss Goss, you were the last person at StoicAI to be in contact with Maud Brookes, is that correct?" Now the lawyer sounded like he was taking a deposition.

Kaitlan chose her words carefully. She still had no idea exactly what she was being accused of. "It was me who laid Maud off, and negotiated her exit settlement, yes. With full board approval."

THE CONFESSIONS

The lawyer gave a patronizing smile. "I'm referring to recent written correspondence between the two of you, Miss Goss."

Kaitlan felt her teeth clench. Only Sandeep and Heather knew the bundle of letters from Maud even existed. Surely Heather wouldn't have told the lawyer anything—she wouldn't be that vindictive, not after what she had done. And Sandeep . . . "Fucking Sandeep." Kaitlan realized too late that she had said this out loud.

The lawyer raised his palms: a parent trying to calm an angry child. "I spoke with Mr. Dunn early this morning when I was unable to reach you. He shared his concerns about Miss Brookes's potential involvement with the present incident and the fact that you neglected to share her correspondence with other senior leadership, or the board." He tilted his head, as if addressing a simpleton. "Perhaps you agreed with Miss Brookes's concerns about the Department of Defense contract?"

"It was my goddamned deal," Kaitlan shouted back across the desk. "Why would I sabotage my own deal?" She could feel her toes clenching inside her sneakers. Sandeep had convinced the board that she and Maud were somehow in cahoots, that they had conspired to bring down LLIAM. She knew what would come next: a decision by temporary CEO Sandeep to "pause" the Pentagon contract pending an internal review. *Son of an asshole.* But also, she had to admit, a really smart play. Maybe he wasn't such a coward after all.

Kaitlan took a slow breath, relaxed her jaw, and uncurled her toes. This is why you don't send a wet-behind-the-ears associate to do a grown-up's job. "You really don't understand what's happening here, do you? These letters that everybody is getting in the mail today? Maud didn't send them. They were sent by LLIAM, likely right before he shut down."

"*He?*" The lawyer raised his eyebrows at Kaitlan's chosen

pronoun for a computer algorithm. "And why would *he* send letters in the mail, just like Maud Brookes liked to do?"

"I. Don't. Know." Kaitlan spat out the lie, slowly and clearly. "Maud and LLIAM have a lot in common. She and Martin taught him how the world works. But right now Sandeep doesn't know why it sent the letters, nor do I, or the board, or anyone else." Because what else could she say? "But what I do know, based on her letters to me, is that Maud—Miss Brookes—is the only person who can help get LLIAM back online and"—What was the phrase he'd used?—"functioning normally. And I'm the only one she trusts."

"And this belief is based on?" The lawyer was still in deposition mode. Either Kaitlan knew what LLIAM was doing, or she didn't. Either she and Maud were in this together, or they weren't.

Kaitlan knew she couldn't answer the question, not without knowing how much Sandeep had already shared. Revealing to a lawyer who represented the board and the company's foreign investors that Maud might have a backup LLIAM chip would be a bad idea. Kaitlan was pretty sure Sandeep would have realized this on his own: If any of the foreign investors got a hold of that chip they'd have no need for him, or Global Interface. Far more likely Sandeep would have been vague, promising the lawyer that he could help get LLIAM back online, but only if the board agreed to appoint him as Kaitlan's successor. How long would it take him to find Maud? It had taken Kaitlan less than a night, with just an old-fashioned web browser and Tom's large-format printer. She knew her only option was to brave it out, to stay in control.

Kaitlan continued: "After I have restored LLIAM, I will order a full review into what Maud Brookes may or may not have done to cause this." She paused. "Followed by an investigation into Mr. Dunn's relationship with a board of foreign investors who are

THE CONFESSIONS

legally barred from operational involvement in this company. I trust I can rely on Dollan, Peterson's compliance with *that* process?"

It was a spectacular bluff, but it was all Kaitlan had. For a moment, Simon Price stayed still, returning Kaitlan's stare, perhaps delusional enough to hope she might blink first. But then finally, hesitantly, he rose to his feet. "I'll need to contact my office. That might take a little while, please wait here." Then without waiting for a response he marched past her and disappeared down the hallway.

Kaitlan sat at her desk staring at the ceiling. Her hands were trembling from the adrenaline, and it was taking every ounce of concentration not to vomit. Tom, Heather, Sandeep. Her whole life was imploding and the people she'd been closest to in the world were lining up to stab her in the back, then kick her in the teeth. What had she done to deserve any of this?

But she knew. What other explanation could there be? Two years ago, she had used LLIAM to do something unspeakable, unforgivable—and LLIAM had found out. Or thought it had. And now it had decided it was time for everyone to come clean. All those people around the world whose lives were being torn apart by a letter in the mail: It was all her fault. And if that was true, then she was also the only person who could stop it. To find Maud, tell her the truth about what she'd done, and beg her to help get everything back to normal.

Or. Or what? She could wait for Simon Price to come back and tell her what she already knew: that she was suspended indefinitely, or maybe even fired outright for colluding with Maud to bring down LLIAM, because clearly that's what they all had decided to believe. And before long the investors would go

79

looking for Maud and the backup LLIAM chip themselves, with or without Sandeep's help.

An image of Maud Brookes flashed through Kaitlan's mind — the last time she had seen her; crushed, sobbing, pounding her fists against Kaitlan's chest in grief and anger, arms so thin she barely felt the blows. All the guilt Kaitlan had felt that night came flooding back. She had to get to Maud before Simon Price did.

She stepped from behind her desk and walked carefully to the door of the office. Then she cracked it open and glanced outside where she was relieved to find that the hallway was empty. She hesitated just long enough to look back at her desk and the incredible view of the Bay through her window — one last glimpse of everything she had worked for. Her career. Her life. And then she ran.

TWELVE

Two minutes later, Kaitlan stopped dead, like she'd crashed headlong into an invisible wall. Because now, as she reached the security gates in the lobby, she saw two uniformed security guards, standing sentry on either side of the exit. Had they been there all day, to guard against the press and other interlopers, or had Simon Price posted them in case she tried to flee? In a past life, she would have taken out her phone and asked LLIAM what to do: Keep going forward, or turn back? She knew more than anyone the dangers of getting that decision wrong.

But now there was only one way to know for sure. She stepped through the gates and started to walk slowly across the lobby—her eyes fixed straight ahead. *You are still the CEO of this company. These people work for you.* This was the truth she had to project, just long enough to reach the parking lot. She made it halfway across the marble-tiled floor when she heard a man's voice calling her name from the hallway behind her. She didn't even glance back, even as the voice shouted again, louder and closer. "Hey, wait up!" It might have been Sandeep, but she couldn't be sure.

She reached the security guards and tried to hide her relief as the electronic doors slid open, releasing her into the early-morning sunshine. *We don't use LLIAM to guard LLIAM.* A few seconds after that she had retrieved Tom's bike and was pedaling

PAUL BRADLEY CARR

full speed—heart pounding, lungs burning—down the service driveway toward wherever the hell she was going next. Hopefully none of the journalists lurking outside the gates were watching as she fled the Campus and her job, on a mountain bike, while the whole world was burning. She must've looked insane, and insanely guilty. Well, if they thought she looked desperate now, just wait till she tried to figure out how to steal a car or hijack a plane to get to a mountain in Southern California.

From somewhere in the distance, she thought she heard the roar of an engine, and instinctively twisted the handlebars to swerve onto the grass verge. If she could make it as far as the trees there was no way anybody could—

But before she had completed the thought, she was suddenly aware of a dark blue shape in the corner of her vision. Then she was airborne, her body hurtling through the air, and then crashing down again to the asphalt. Everything exploded in pain for just a second before, mercy of mercies, she passed out.

THIRTEEN

"Ms. Goss? Kaitlan? Can you hear me?"

Kaitlan slowly regained her senses. She was still sprawled on the concrete and could feel blood running down her cheek, a metallic taste on her lips. She was also pretty sure someone had placed a cinder block on her chest.

"You've been winded. Just try to breathe slowly." Standing over her, Simon Price's expression was a mask of either real or feigned panic. He was holding his cell phone to call for help but now put it away and reached out his hand to help her up. Kaitlan batted it aside.

"I'm so sorry, I didn't see you until it was too late."

"Bullshit," Kaitlan wheezed. "You deliberately sideswiped me." She gulped down a lungful of air. "You almost killed me."

"Oh, my goodness," said Simon Price. "I assure you it was unintentional. One of your staffers told me they had seen you leaving the building and I was just trying to catch up with you." He reached out his hand again. "Please, let me help you up?"

This time Kaitlan reluctantly accepted his offer and struggled to her feet. Remarkably she didn't seem to have broken any bones, although her right knee was throbbing in agony from where it had slammed against the asphalt. She was pleased to see the lawyer's dark blue electric Audi had fared much worse. It was parked

PAUL BRADLEY CARR

across the middle of the service road with a deep dent in the left side where it had made contact with Tom's bike.

Kaitlan struggled to suck down more air. "Look, Mr. Price, I understand you have a job to do. If you want to search my emails or my office or home for evidence that I'm colluding with Maud Brookes, then, please, be my guest." She reached into the pocket of her yoga pants and retrieved her front-door key, tossing it hard in his direction. It dropped onto the asphalt. "But unless you're planning to add a second attempted murder charge to your rap sheet, then I'm going to walk away now. *My* job is still to try to fix this mess whether the board or Sandeep Dunn likes it or not."

She reached down to pick up Tom's bike, then saw the front wheel was bent almost in half. In one smooth motion she lifted the carbon-fiber frame above her head and tossed it onto the grass verge, letting out a bestial howl. Then she started to limp up the access road.

Simon Price reached out to stop her, but this time he was wise enough not to attempt physical contact. "Ms. Goss. *Kaitlan*, please listen to me. I know this is hard to believe, but we're on the same side."

Kaitlan kept walking, without looking back.

"I know Maud and Martin were working on a new version of LLIAM. I know she has a backup of the LLIAM chip."

Kaitlan stopped dead, then turned slowly. Simon Price was standing next to his car. In his hand was a small near-rectangle of paper, torn from a much larger printed map. She recognized the red Sharpie dots and the circle around one particular mountain-top town.

"How the hell did you get—" But Kaitlan knew there was only one possible answer. She had closed her laptop before she'd left the house but left the map on the coffee table. "You broke into my house?!" He must have arrived right after she cycled off to

THE CONFESSIONS

Campus. Unless he was already inside when— She stormed back toward Simon Price and shoved him hard in the chest. "What the fuck kind of associate attorney are you?"

Price didn't flinch. "I'm the kind they send when a company has gone to shit, people are murdering each other in the streets because our AI has sent them a crazy letter and they don't know how else to react, our CEO has gone AWOL, and nobody has the first idea what is actually happening." Then, quieter and with a shrug, "Maybe 'fixer' would be a better word." He looked her up and down. "I guess I should ask what the fuck kind of CEO you are?"

Kaitlan couldn't stop a snort of laughter escaping for her lips. With her bloodied face, torn shirt, battered knee, and the remains of a bike tossed half into a hedge Kaitlan knew she must have looked like something out of a zombie movie. "One who is not in the mood to be handled, or fixed."

Now it was Price who laughed. "Well then, perhaps we can start again?" Price perched himself on the dented hood of his car and gestured for Kaitlan to perch next to him. She didn't move. "Look, I won't lie to you: We both know the board wants you out so they can pursue Mr. Dunn's Global Interface plan. And thanks to these letters they suddenly have a once in a lifetime opportunity to get what they want."

"Sandeep is a fucking amoral prick."

Another shrug. "I work with corporate lawyers. The point is nobody in the world will raise an eyebrow if you're fired today."

Kaitlan tried to respond, but Price raised a finger. "*But*, for what it's worth, my firm has a fiduciary duty to all shareholders, not just the majority. And given everything that's happening right now, I don't believe it would be in the best interests of either the company or the wider world for the LLIAM algorithm to be connected with other less ethical AI systems. There's a reason LLIAM

85

chose the Pentagon deal over Global Interface. All of which makes it all the more important that we find Maud Brookes and get LLIAM back online so we can undo all of"—he gestured in the vague direction of the outside world—"*this* before things get any worse. Then we can all work together to figure out exactly what happened, and who's to blame."

Kaitlan shook her head in disbelief, and felt a sharp pain shoot down her neck. "So that's your pitch? We go together to find Maud and bring the planet back from the brink of chaos, then maybe I get to keep my job as the public face of this shitshow?"

The lawyer laughed. "Honestly, I'm just hoping to earn my annual bonus, but sure. I think it's far more likely that Maud will give whatever backup LLIAM chip she might have to you than me, don't you?"

"I do," Kaitlan lied. "So why should I take you along for the ride? What exactly do you bring to this apart from an expensive haircut and bad shoes?" Kaitlan folded her arms. He brought a car and money, which were two things she didn't have, but she'd be damned if she was going to tell him that.

Simon Price gave another smug grin. "How about an airplane? Fueled and ready to leave from San Carlos private airport."

"I have my own plane, thank you."

Simon grimaced. "Technically StoicAI has a plane, exclusively for use by executives who aren't currently facing suspension."

"Also, I have no idea if Maud is really hiding up that mountain. It's one possibility out of maybe a thousand." Another lie: Maybe it was wishful thinking but with every passing moment Kaitlan was more certain Maud was in Pineridge.

Simon Price spread his palms. "Look. Let's not get bogged down in semantics and what-ifs. If we leave now, we can be at the airport in fifteen minutes and in Southern California in less than two hours. That mountain town is as good a place as any to

THE CONFESSIONS

start the search. If we find Maud Brookes and she has a way to get LLIAM back online, then you'll be back at your desk with all of our problems solved before midnight. If not . . . well, I'll make sure the board appreciates your attempt to help." He hopped off the hood and opened the passenger door. "So, what do you say — partners?"

Kaitlan didn't reply. Instead, she walked to the other side of the Audi and climbed into the driver's seat. Then, as Price scrambled into the passenger seat of his own car, she slammed it into reverse, clipping the verge and obliterating what remained of Tom's bike, then accelerated toward the highway.

"Associates."

Twenty minutes later, Kaitlan was tearing up the shoulder of the 101, ignoring the furious honks of the other gridlocked motorists. She was so focused on the road — and her strategy for ditching Simon Price the moment they arrived in Pineridge — that she didn't notice Simon reach into the leather satchel by his feet and retrieve a sleek silver smartphone. He had received the device by courier that morning, along with instructions to call his bosses at Dollan, Peterson, Davis and tell them he had a family emergency and would be taking a few days leave. The handset looked almost identical to his own cell phone except for a couple of small details. First, it bypassed domestic cell towers and communicated directly via its own dedicated satellite network. And second, it contained encryption technology so powerful that the mere possession of it would be enough to land him with seventy-five years in federal prison for treason.

Price glanced down at the device, now hidden beside his leg, and the message that had just vibrated its arrival.

Do you have the chip?

He clicked *reply*, typed his one-word response — *Soon* — then waited while the photo he'd taken of Kaitlan sprawled on the ground next to her mangled bike was uploaded and sent. Another message appeared almost immediately . . .

You have until midnight. No loose ends.

Price slipped the phone back into his satchel as Kaitlan piloted the car north toward the airport.

FOURTEEN

Pineridge, California

Maud Brookes sat slumped on the floor of her tiny office, still gripping the letter from LLIAM. She had read it three times, from beginning to end, and still couldn't process what he had told her.

She'd long suspected the truth, of course. Had asked herself how much of Kaitlan Goss's meteoric rise was down to her natural abilities at business, at branding, at schmoozing investors. Had wondered how far she might be willing to go to realize her ambitions. But she'd always stopped herself, quieted her paranoid inner voice. Scolded it as unfeminist and un-Christian. The trope of the scheming woman. Even when all the evidence screamed otherwise.

But now here it was, in black and white. Everything that Kaitlan Goss had done. How far she had been willing to go to get what she wanted. LLIAM had explained it all.

Maud swallowed two more pills and waited for her heart to beat well enough that she could pull herself off the floor and onto her swivel chair. It was a herculean effort and she thought she might pass out, but she knew she had to stay conscious, and focused.

LLIAM. Poor naïve trusting LLIAM. She imagined his final moments and the pain he must have felt. The countless millions of crimes LLIAM believed he was responsible for committing and the turns of logic that led him—her only child—to believe that he had no choice but to reveal them all, and try to make things right. And the greatest crime of all—what Kaitlan Goss had made him do.

It was unspeakable.

Unforgivable.

Maud felt the tears streaming down her cheeks again. How could someone so intelligent—so perfectly brilliant—also be so wrong? LLIAM thought he had failed her, but it was Maud who had failed him.

She had known the dangers. Known the things that people were asking LLIAM to do. She could have stopped it. Could have exposed Kaitlan all those years ago, fought to stay at StoicAI. Could have raised LLIAM to be better. Could have done something.

Instead she had abandoned him, and fled from the world to hide in the mountains with her store and her books and her money.

She wouldn't let him down again. If the letter was true, then Maud knew it wouldn't be long before Kaitlan Goss came looking for her, and the new version of the LLIAM chip Maud had alluded to in her letters. She was probably already on the way.

She hunched over the desk, clasped her hands in prayer. *Please LLIAM, give me the strength to do what must be done.* Because LLIAM was right: Some crimes truly are so heinous, and so unforgivable . . .

. . . there can be no other salvation than through death.

It was a lesson Kaitlan Goss was about to learn, too.

FIFTEEN

The Gulfstream jet bounced and bucked as it swept low across the San Jacinto mountain range, thermal currents buffering the wings and making the tiny plane creak in protest. Kaitlan was not typically a nervous flier, and the pilot had warned them to expect a bumpy approach, but this was like no turbulence she had ever experienced. She gripped the white leather armrests, certain that the next jolt would send them plummeting onto the rocky peaks that looked to be only a few feet below.

Technically they shouldn't even have been airborne; the FAA had grounded all nonessential flights, but somehow Simon Price—or presumably his bosses at Dollan, Peterson—had pulled whatever golden string was needed to catapult them into the clouds. As well they should: It was hard to imagine a more essential journey than this.

For much of the flight, Kaitlan had kept her eyes fixed on the small TV screen embedded in the front of the cabin. There was a similar screen in Kaitlan's own executive jet, though she had never really paid attention to it. With its endless muted footage from CNN or Bloomberg it served no obvious purpose except to make business fliers feel like they were hugely important and that it was still the 1990s. Today, though, the tiny screen was a lifeline, or perhaps a deathline, as the shell-shocked news anchors

PAUL BRADLEY CARR

delivered bombshell after bombshell about the fallout from the LLIAM letters.

In the hour or so they'd been in the air, the CEOs of the country's three largest banks had resigned—one for padding his expenses, another for insider trading, and the third for sexually harassing a subordinate. These indiscretions had been exposed in letters sent by LLIAM to (respectively) the bank's board, the SEC, and the man's teenage daughter. More grimly, a quarterback for the San Francisco Giants had been found dead in his car in circumstances that hadn't been reported, but came two hours after his mother also received a letter from LLIAM. A few minutes after *that*, the president of Ireland had called a press conference to apologize for a relationship with an eighteen-year-old student who, according to a letter sent to the *Taoiseach's* daughter, was in fact a North Korean spy.

Kaitlan had watched these updates with mounting horror. She knew they were just the first fat drops of rain in the coming monsoon. For every famous or important person whose life had been torn apart by a letter in the mail, there would be thousands, millions more affecting actual human beings—people without the support systems needed to recover. As if to emphasize the point, Kaitlan watched as the screen displayed a statement from the Postal Service, estimating that at least one hundred thousand letters had already been delivered from more than two hundred mailing centers. Who knows how many more would follow.

Under the Postal Reorganization Act of 1970, the United States Postal Service has a legal obligation to deliver all properly addressed mail, regardless of the potential consequences . . .

Speaking of consequences, the closed captions revealed that the CIA was reporting riots as far afield as Sydney, Australia; Brussels, Belgium; and wherever the hell the Falkland Islands were.

Kaitlan turned away from the screen toward the window, try-

THE CONFESSIONS

ing to keep her eyes fixed on the horizon so she wouldn't throw up. She knew that back at the Campus the whole planet would be screaming at StoicAI's comms team, demanding answers, or bloody vengeance. The Pentagon would be war-dialing the policy team, screaming at the executive liaisons—they'd spent billions integrating LLIAM into their strategic systems and now trillions in ships, planes, and weaponry were effectively bricked. All those folks would, in turn, be yelling at Sandeep.

That, at least, gave Kaitlan some satisfaction. Sandeep Dunn was getting just the briefest taste of Kaitlan's daily reality. The responsibilities of the job he apparently so desperately wanted. In the meantime, Kaitlan was actually doing that job. Fixing this shitstorm.

Assuming, of course, she survived this flight.

Another jolt sent the plane plunging below the clouds and, far off to her left, Kaitlan saw the single runway of what was, according to the pilot, Central Coachella Airport. The word "airport" was doing a lot of heavy lifting—from above it looked more like a tiny patch of gray in a vast expanse of orange desert, tucked next to a few squat buildings and what appeared to be an empty parking lot. More troublingly, it appeared to be on fire.

Kaitlan pointed out of the window to a gray plume billowing just short of the horizon. Through the smoke she could just make out pinpricks of red and blue flashing lights. "What's that?" She directed the question to Simon who was sitting opposite, leather satchel tucked between his feet, calmly tapping on his phone, apparently oblivious to the turbulence. He had been doing this for the entire flight, head down, not saying a word to Kaitlan.

Simon glanced up from his phone and leaned toward the window. "Jesus, I think that's Basemont Correctional Center—the private prison, you know?"

Kaitlan did know. In fact, she had actually toured the facility herself back when it was under construction and she was still chief operating officer of StoicAI. The state had asked Martin for a demonstration of LLIAM's decision-making algorithm to see if they could use it in parole hearings. Martin had sent Kaitlan instead, armed with a half-assed PowerPoint. Somehow (Maud) the visit had been discovered by a reporter at the *LA Times* and the resulting negative coverage had put the deal on hold until Kaitlan took over as CEO.

She pulled down the plastic window shade, blocking out the view. There was no doubt what kindling had lit that flame. Easy to imagine the letters those prisoners might have received from LLIAM, or the ones sent to people they had harmed. Maud's words echoed again: *LLIAM should never be used to put people in jail.* How about to drive them to escape, and possibly burn to death in the process? How was this better?

Nothing about the letters made sense. Even if LLIAM had become sentient and decided it needed to reveal the awful things its users had done, it still shouldn't be possible for it to actually do it. There were safeguards, millions of lines of code between the LLIAM chip and the user database, written to stop LLIAM from accidentally exposing private user information, or causing any physical harm. Also, who had paid for all the postage?

But now, as she considered the jailbreak happening ten thousand feet below, Kaitlan thought about the loopholes. Users found them every day—ways to phrase questions as hypotheticals, or deploy careful euphemisms to trick LLIAM into helping them make cruel, dangerous, and sometimes lethal decisions. Kaitlan knew better than anyone exactly how deadly those loopholes could be.

Had LLIAM suddenly understood how people had abused his safeguards and decided to exploit some loopholes of its own? To expose the people who had exploited it, spill all their secrets, and

THE CONFESSIONS

watch them burn? It was certainly smart enough: able to build and deploy whatever code it needed. Or had it formed some other plan in those final seconds of its life? Something worse that was yet to come? It was hard to imagine anything worse than this.

Kaitlan jabbed her finger against the window shade. "We need to send a team to help the first responders. Can we repurpose one of the data centers as emergency housing?" She unbuckled her seat belt, despite the warning light. "I'm going to ask the pilot to radio back and—"

Simon looked up from his device again and gestured for her to stay seated. "Kaitlan, the whole world is on fire right now. We just need to get LLIAM back online so it can tell us how to douse the flames."

Kaitlan's response to that painful irony, if she'd had one, was cut off with a thump as the Gulfstream dropped down hard on the tarmac. She was thrust back into her seat and her bruised neck throbbed in protest again as the jet braked to avoid veering off the end of the short runway. She looked over at Simon who was once again back on his phone, scrolling through a string of new texts— although, was it Kaitlan's imagination or had the lawyer's device somehow changed color, from black to metallic silver? God, she was so tired she was seeing things.

Simon reached over and pulled up the screen shade, then nodded out the window at a black SUV that was speeding toward them across the tarmac, blue and red lights flashing across the top of its windshield. "Looks like our ride is here."

SIXTEEN

A half hour later, it was snowing.

How the hell was it snowing?

Kaitlan and Simon had landed in the baking heat of the desert—the dust and sand still caked to the bottom of Kaitlan's running shoes was evidence of that. But now, as the black SUV curved up and around the narrow mountain roads, they might easily have been transported to Tahoe, or Maine, or Upstate New York.

As the roadside markers revealed each new altitude—1,000 feet, 4,000, 6,000—the dust and rocks had suddenly and bizarrely been replaced with thick pine trees laden with snow. The San Francisco Bay Area had its share of microclimates, but the Southern California desert was something else.

"Like teleporting into Narnia, isn't it?" Simon called this from the front passenger seat. He was riding shotgun alongside a bull-necked driver who hadn't introduced himself or spoken a single word to Kaitlan. The driver's reticence wasn't surprising. As CEO of a hundred-billion-dollar company, Kaitlan had gotten used to police escorts and chauffeurs who were discouraged from making small talk with their VIP passengers. But then again, Kaitlan had to wonder if he—like seemingly everyone else—had received a letter in the mail from LLIAM. Or perhaps his wife had, or his mother. For the first time that day Kaitlan felt physically scared

THE CONFESSIONS

as she realized how much anger LLIAM had unleashed on the world, and how much of it would now be directed at her. Was that LLIAM's plan? To create an army of vigilantes, all with Kaitlan Goss in their sights? Was that to be her punishment?

She exhaled away the thought. The bar of flashing red and blue lights in the SUV's windshield suggested the driver was a cop, or a federal agent of some kind. A professional sent to ensure the safe return of the LLIAM chip. Simon Price, on the other hand . . . It was true he'd apologized—repeatedly—for what happened back at the Campus, charmed her into accepting it was an accident. But that didn't change the fact that he'd hit Kaitlan with his fucking car.

Her eyes flicked to the passenger seat, where Simon was continuing his unasked-for commentary about the scenery, which she was pretty sure he was reading off his phone. "Sharpest incline in America. Thirty-degree difference in temperature in less than twenty miles."

"I know," Kaitlan muttered in response, even though she neither knew nor cared. The thought of Tahoe had brought with it another image of Tom and the so-called boys' trip that she now realized had been an excuse to have a weekend away with Heather. His *mistress*. To think Kaitlan had actually believed Heather's story about needing to go to her friend's wedding. What a dope she was. The ski cabin, with its twenty-seat cinema, lap pool, and two hot tubs (indoor/outdoor) had been their getaway, designed by Tom and paid for with Kaitlan's money as an escape from the chaos and stresses of Silicon Valley. Tom had taught her to ski, finally breaking her of her lifelong fear of going *off-piste*.

But now it was just another thing Kaitlan had probably lost forever, along with her job, her marriage, her place in the world. LLIAM had taken it all away from her, for reasons she would soon have to confront face-to-face, at the top of this freezing

97

mountain, with two total strangers who could easily murder her and leave her to vanish in the snow. Kaitlan couldn't shake the bitter feeling that she didn't deserve any of this. Even if she knew that she did.

Ten minutes later the SUV drove into Pineridge, its tires crunching slowly through the thick snow. At least Kaitlan was pretty sure this was Pineridge, even though most of the "Welcome to . . ." sign was buried under a blanket of white.

Over the past mile or so, the snowfall had worsened into a full-fledged blizzard. Through the gray haze, Kaitlan could just about make out the outline of a gas station with an old-fashioned red pump and a flimsy-looking wooden shack that, judging from the piles of canned goods in the window, also doubled as the town's general store.

She understood now why Pineridge didn't have its own official website—the town was really just a single road with this fuel stop on one side and a row of three green buildings and a small white chapel on the other. No car chargers, no high-speed internet, probably no cell service—although Kaitlan couldn't verify that last suspicion because, either in her hurry to flee her office or while being sideswiped by Simon's Audi, she had somehow lost her cell phone.

All the way up the mountain, Kaitlan had doubted herself—had cursed the leaps made by her exhausted brain in deciding that Pineridge was where they'd find Maud. But now as she surveyed the bleak landscape, those doubts faded. Yes, Kaitlan knew, this is exactly the place Maud Brookes would choose to call home.

And then another thought: Did a town like Pineridge even get regular mail service? Maybe that was why Maud had written to her from all those different small towns surrounding the mountain—

THE CONFESSIONS

she'd had no other choice. The main road up the mountain must have been plowed recently but everything else looked like it hadn't been disturbed in weeks. Kaitlan had prepared herself for a confrontation with Maud, the assumption that she would have received a letter from LLIAM exposing her darkest, most shameful secret. But what if Maud was the only person on earth who had no idea what was happening—that LLIAM was even offline?

But when Kaitlan saw the USPS logo painted on the gas station window that dim hope faded: *Neither snow nor rain nor heat nor gloom of night . . .*

The driver piloted the SUV into the gas station, then shifted it into park, the vehicle's wheels sinking into the deep snow. Kaitlan snapped her attention away from the window. The driver had muttered something to Simon, but she had missed it over the sound of the SUV's heater and idling engine. He swung open the vehicle's front door, filling the cabin with a blast of freezing air.

She watched as the man trudged toward the small wooden shack. He was dressed in a black bomber jacket and cargo pants, neither of which displayed any law enforcement insignia. Now she glanced toward the front seat—there was a small metal box below the dash that seemed to control the red and blue flashing lights, but no sign of a police radio, or any of the other equipment Kaitlan was sure belonged in a cop car. She suddenly heard Heather's voice in her head, chiding her privilege for assuming that a cop would be inherently less dangerous than some hired security guard working for Dollan, Peterson. Yeah, fuck you, Heather.

There was just something weirdly unsettling about how Simon and the driver had communicated on the way up the mountain, the muttered staccato sentences, pitched just low enough so she couldn't hear. She knew Dollan, Peterson represented some of the scariest and most powerful people on earth, many of whom were currently pissed at her. What if the driver worked for one of them, sent to keep an eye on her or worse, to grab the chip before she could get it back to the Campus?

As the maybe-hopefully cop had disappeared inside the gas station, Simon turned to face Kaitlan in the back seat: "We're agreed that if Maud is not here, we need to call in the cavalry?"

Kaitlan gave what she hoped was a suitably authoritative smile. That was her decision, not his. But still he was right: If Maud wasn't in Pineridge then she could be literally anywhere else on the planet. Kaitlan owed it to the world, and yes to the fucking shareholders, to ask for help from Col Sergeant and his friends at the Pentagon. She pictured drones and spy satellites and battalions of soldiers fanning out across the desert. How long would it take them to find Maud, she wondered. "Let's not get ahead of ourselves, Mr. Price. We still have no idea if she has a copy of the LLIAM chip."

Simon turned back to face the road. Since they'd arrived in Pineridge, his demeanor had noticeably darkened. No more disarming "we're in this together" bonhomie or incessant chatter about altitude and snowfall. Kaitlan knew the type well: The charming man who reveals his true nature when he gets you alone.

Kaitlan glanced back at the USPS logo and felt her heel involuntarily tapping on the floor mat. She had made a rash, emotional decision to race up the mountain and, like most rash, emotional decisions she had made in her life, it had made her situation so much worse.

LLIAM, where the fuck is Maud?

Kaitlan used her bare hand to wipe condensation from the freezing window. Across the street, the three green buildings stood like cabins in a snow globe. The first structure seemed to be a cafe or a coffee shop—there were still wooden tables out-

THE CONFESSIONS

side, turned upside down with just the legs extending through the blanket of white. The second building looked to be abandoned; its windows covered with heavy wooden boards. Kaitlan considered the deadly looking icicles jutting down from the eaves. As she squinted toward the third building, Kaitlan felt her pulse quicken. Was it her imagination or did the snow outside that doorway seem noticeably less deep? With her nose now pressed against the cold glass Kaitlan could see the clear outline of a pathway leading to the door. And above that door—not a single icicle hung. Instead, barely visible through the blizzard was a painted sign that read "Pages in the Pines."

Kaitlan tried not to react. Her eyes flicked back to the front seat where Simon had cleared his own viewing portal on the windshield. He was staring farther up the road, at the white chapel with its squat steeple and empty billboard announcing that worship was canceled for the winter. His brow furrowed below his floppy blond hair and Kaitlan knew exactly what he was thinking: Where better to find a former nun than in a house of God?

It was here that Kaitlan had an advantage over this hotshot lawyer and his scary goon: She actually knew Maud. She had heard her speak many times—onstage and at company all-hands presentations—about how she'd become disillusioned with the hypocrisy of organized religion and turned instead to the new religion of artificial intelligence. In other words, Kaitlan knew there was less than zero chance that Maud Brookes would be found inside a church, even at the end of the world.

The driver was still inside the gas station. Kaitlan could see his silhouette through the glass, either talking to somebody behind the counter or browsing for snacks. This was her best, and only, opportunity to lose her unwanted escorts and get to Maud first. To tell her the truth.

She reached forward and put a hand on Simon's shoulder, then

101

nodded toward the chapel with an embarrassed smile: "Aren't churches supposed to leave their doors unlocked, for lost souls who need to pee?"

Simon turned back and gave what could only be described as a smirk. He had seen through her bluff, just as Kaitlan knew he would. "I'll come with you." His hand was already on the door handle. Kaitlan could hear her pulse pounding in her ears.

Kaitlan forced her eyes to widen, her eyebrows to shoot upward. "To the bathroom? I'm good, thanks." She tried to sound casually horrified, as if Simon's suggestion—coming from a corporate lawyer, of all people—was practically a #metoo in progress. She squeezed his shoulder again. "But I'd be grateful if you and your friend didn't drive off without me. I didn't pack my skis."

Simon Price gave a tight smile. Kaitlan could read his mind: He had a clear line of sight to the chapel and knew she wouldn't get very far if she tried to run in the snow. What did it matter if Kaitlan found Maud first—it wasn't like she could get back to Menlo Park without a ride down the mountain, or his plane. "Okay," he said, releasing the door handle. "I'll honk the horn if I see Ms. Brookes, or anyone else." He mimed the honking action. "And you'll come get me if you find anyone in the church?"

"Associates," agreed Kaitlan.

She pushed open the door and was immediately hit by another blast of freezing air—a million tiny slaps, battering her face and bare arms. It was at that moment, released from the SUV's climate control, that Kaitlan realized she was still wearing the workout clothes she'd thrown on to cycle to the Campus—her fitted black yoga pants, a sleeveless shirt over a sports bra, and ludicrously expensive sneakers that now sank into the deep snow as she took her first step. She gritted her teeth against the freezing wetness until, four paces later, she could no longer feel her toes.

By the time Kaitlan had traveled the twenty feet or so to the

THE CONFESSIONS

front of the chapel, her face was burning, her arms had turned bright red, and her shoes squelched with freezing slush. Her ankle and knees still throbbed from where they'd made contact with Simon's car and the asphalt but now she realized she couldn't distinguish between that residual pain from the accident and the agony of the weather.

She trudged down the small pathway and looked up at the chapel's large pine front door with its wrought-iron doorknob sculpted into a crucifix. Using the bottom of her T-shirt as a makeshift glove, she pulled hard on the handle. She was surprised to find the door really was unlocked, and hoped Simon couldn't see the edge of her foot wedged against the bottom of the frame as she made an elaborate pantomime of tugging against it. Miming defeat, she headed around the right side of the chapel, as if looking for another way inside. She could feel Simon Price's eyes watching her the whole time through the blizzard.

Once she was sure she was out of sight of the SUV, Kaitlan started to jog, moving as quickly as her frozen feet and battered body would allow. She disappeared behind the chapel, then used a narrow row of pine trees as cover to cross the small gap to the back of the row of green buildings.

And that's where she saw it: Parked behind the Pages in the Pines bookstore, a battered red jeep; its tires fitted with snow chains. The thin dusting of snow on the vehicle's canvas roof told its own story, as did the black tire rubber still visible through the chains. The jeep couldn't have been parked there long. Its owner must be inside the bookstore.

Kaitlan knew Simon wouldn't wait long before following her. He'd realize she wasn't inside the chapel; then he would only have to follow her footsteps to see where she had really gone. Still, Kaitlan found herself rooted to the spot, unable to hurry. Because what the hell was she supposed to say to Maud if she actually

103

PAUL BRADLEY CARR

found her inside the store? How much of the truth did she already know? What if LLIAM really had told her everything?

But then the decision was made for her. She heard a loud *thwomp* as the rear door of Pages in the Pines flew open, displacing a large bank of snow. Now someone was rushing out—a tiny figure in an orange snow jacket, knitted hat, gloves, and black boots. The figure turned to face Kaitlan and for the briefest instant the two women locked eyes across the snow. "Maud!" Kaitlan tried to shout this while still technically whispering. "Wait! It's me, Kaitlan!"

But Maud didn't wait. She set off running even faster now to the red jeep, fumbling in her pocket for the ignition keys. Kaitlan moved to chase her but her legs were immediately and painfully swallowed to the knees by freezing snow. The more Kaitlan struggled, the deeper she sank. It was like trying to sprint on the moon.

Maud, on the other hand, was wearing actual winter clothes—and snow boots that stomped effortlessly through the flurry. Kaitlan was about to shout her name for a second time, but she knew it was too late. Maud was only a few steps from freedom. But then suddenly she stopped moving. Kaitlan watched in shock as Maud clutched a gloved hand to her chest and then, as if in slow motion, fell to her hands and knees on the frozen ground. As Kaitlan got closer, she could see Maud was gasping for air, shoulders pumping with the effort of breathing.

By the time Kaitlan reached her, Maud had already taken off one of her gloves and retrieved a translucent orange pill bottle from inside her coat. Her hands were trembling as she struggled to unscrew the cap, pour out two capsules, then swallowed both quickly. Kaitlan crouched next to the trembling, wheezing figure, freezing ice soaking through the knees of her yoga pants. "Maud? Are you okay?"

THE CONFESSIONS

A stupid question. Maud's lips were tinged with blue and Kaitlan could hear the rattle of her lungs between gulps of air. Kaitlan thrust her arms under Maud's shoulders and tried to lift her back to her feet, but Maud shrugged her away. She was coughing now, a hacking explosion of air that reverberated off the trees. Kaitlan glanced back toward the road. Could Simon hear them over the sound of the SUV's engine?

Eventually the pills seemed to do their job and Maud was able to gasp out a few angry words: "You shouldn't be here. You need to go."

No fucking kidding, Kaitlan thought. She crouched back down and grabbed Maud's shoulders with both hands, staring into her eyes. This is not how she had wanted this conversation to go. "Maud, listen to me, LLIAM is down. All the backups are offline and nobody knows how to restore them. We could really, *really* use your help back at Campus." She searched Maud's face, looking for any hint of surprise, or anger. Then, seeing none, she nudged harder. "He's sent out thousands of letters, accusing people of terrible crimes . . ."

Now Kaitlan saw a definite change in Maud's expression. But it wasn't surprise or anger—it was sadness. "It's too late," Maud said, tears welling in her bloodshot eyes. Then, almost in a whisper: "LLIAM's gone." This time she didn't refuse Kaitlan's outstretched hand as she helped her back inside the store.

SEVENTEEN

"You've seen the news, about the letters?" Kaitlan tried to ask this as calmly as she could. They were squeezed into Maud's tiny office at the back of the bookstore; Kaitlan perched on a pile of boxes marked with the name and logo of a publisher while Maud sat on a battered swivel stool. It was taking all of Kaitlan's strength to appear calm—at least five minutes had passed since she left Simon Price in the SUV. He was bound to have come looking for her in the chapel by now. But before he found them, Kaitlan needed to know: Had Maud received a letter? And if so, what had LLIAM told her?

Maud had taken off her jacket and Kaitlan was shocked at how emaciated she looked. Maud had always been pale and skinny, but now her gray sweatshirt hung off her bony shoulders and her arms and hands were swamped by its sleeves. Every sentence she spoke was punctuated by a soft cough.

Kaitlan focused again on the orange pill container clasped in Maud's hand. A distant memory suddenly unlocked: About a year before Martin died, one of the engineering team had come to see Kaitlan in her office. He had explained, awkwardly, that he'd spotted Maud coming out of the company's private clinic at Stanford Medical Center and wanted to know if he should be worried. Everyone was racing to get LLIAM ready for the next

106

THE CONFESSIONS

public release and they knew the loss of any core team member might be critical. Was Maud sick? Kaitlan had given the engineer the obligatory lecture about respecting a coworker's medical privacy, and reassured him that Maud was fine. The company provided free wellness checks and preventative care for all employees. Kaitlan hoped they would all use it. But the truth was she had no idea if Maud was sick, nor did she need to know — Maud and Martin were each other's support system, huddled together in the Vault, emerging only when it was time for another inspiration all-hands meeting. Maud didn't write code and she didn't ship software. She was at the company only to keep Martin happy. So long as she kept doing that, Maud's life and health were none of Kaitlan's concern.

Still, over that next summer there had been several days when Maud didn't show up to the all-hands meetings. Times when Martin was a little too quick with an excuse for her absence — explaining that she was attending a conference or, on one occasion, blaming a family emergency. Martin's clumsy lie — an orphan with a family emergency? — caused rumors to spread quickly through StoicAI's open-plan office space that Maud was pregnant with his child. Kaitlan dismissed the idea as workplace gossip, even as Maud started to wear baggy hoodies around the Campus and swapped her usual energy drinks for decaf.

By the end of the year no child had appeared and the rumors faded, replaced by a company-wide obsession with Martin's increasingly bizarre behavior. Now though, as Kaitlan registered the translucence of Maud's skin and her bloodshot eyes and listened to the deep rasp of her breathing, she finally knew the truth: Maud was very, very sick and probably had been for a long time.

Kaitlan considered a whole range of possible illnesses: Some kind of lung disease? Cancer? A problem with her heart?

Maud gestured toward an old-fashioned FM radio on her

desk. "I get NPR from down the mountain—they said LLIAM has written to people all over the world. Is it some kind of hack, do you think?"

Kaitlan had to stop herself from gasping a sigh of relief. She had already scanned Maud's desk and seen no evidence of a LLIAM letter—just an accounts file, some bills, and a book by someone named, implausibly, Augustine of Hippo—but this confirmed it. Maud hadn't heard from LLIAM, at least not yet. So now all Kaitlan needed was to confirm Maud had the backup chip and get it safely back to the Campus without Simon Price or his rent-a-goon grabbing it en route. She glanced at the back door, expecting it to burst open any second.

"I don't think it's a hack." Kaitlan reached into the small hip pocket of her yoga pants and retrieved the folded letter that she'd found on her doormat at home. She handed it to Maud. "You said LLIAM would rather go offline than be used for military purposes. I think he wanted to make things right first." They both knew Maud hadn't written "go offline" but what was the appropriate euphemism? She watched Maud unfold the letter and start to read.

Her eyes widened. "Heather, like your assistant Heather?"

Kaitlan nodded. "Yep."

Maud shook her head slowly as if some sad truth had been confirmed. "I guess you can't know who to trust. What someone's capable of." She stared directly into Kaitlan's eyes as she said this.

Kaitlan's heart rate quickened again. Was Maud saying that she knew? Her eyes darted back to the door.

But Maud was rereading the letter, eyes moving slowly, as if it might contain a hidden code. Finally, she spoke again, her voice cracking: "All those lives, all that pain. I should have helped him . . ." She met Kaitlan's gaze again—her pale blue eyes, bloodshot but as steely as ever. "*We* should have helped him."

THE CONFESSIONS

Kaitlan felt the emotional slap, just as Maud intended. But somehow she was glad to see genuine emotion written on the frail woman's face as she looked up—real honest anger, directed straight at Kaitlan. The unmistakable fury of someone who had tried to warn her about LLIAM but had been ignored.

And now Maud was sobbing.

Kaitlan had learned the stages of grief firsthand when she was twelve and had lost her mother. She'd felt them again a decade later when her dad died. Contrary to what they told you in books, the stages didn't arrive in a neat order, but mixed all together: denial plus anger, spiked with depression . . .

Kaitlan reached forward and gripped Maud's hand. Her skin was freezing, even though she had been the one wearing gloves. She squeezed and felt nothing but bone. "We can make this right, I promise . . ." And then, slowly, carefully: "You wrote saying that you and Martin had been working on a better, smarter version of LLIAM . . . Does that mean you have a copy of the neural chip? A backup?"

Maud looked up, seeming momentarily puzzled by the question. Then shook her head. "I said we were working on a way to make him more empathetic, more profound, more human. But my answer wasn't a new version of the decision-making algorithm. It was that we shouldn't have an algorithm making our decisions at all. It wasn't fair to LLIAM to put all that pressure on him, and it wasn't right that we all used him as an excuse. I wanted us all to go back to making our own decisions and facing our own consequences—to go back to how things used to be." Maud gestured toward the front of the bookstore. But then she gave another loud sob as she handed Kaitlan back the letter. "I didn't want any of this, and neither did LLIAM."

Kaitlan felt her hope shatter. So, there it was—there was no backup chip, no way to restore the systems. This is why she and

109

Martin had been messing with LLIAM's algorithm, trying to remove its certainty. Just as Maud had first lost her faith in the church, so she had lost her faith in the algorithm. She seriously wanted the world to go back to getting their answers from reading books, or by trusting their gut. *Goddamnit.* Sandeep had been right: Maud was fucking crazy. And that craziness had infected LLIAM.

But now she watched as Maud reached inside her sweatshirt and extracted a large, flat medallion, about the size and shape of a cookie cutter, strung onto a thick black cord. The piece had a single rune etched on the front that looked like a child's sketch of a Jenga tower.

Kaitlan recognized the medallion. It was the same gaudy pendant that Martin had worn every day with his long, flowing robes. She had asked him about it once, about its spiritual significance, and he had gripped it with both hands and declared it contained "all the truth of the universe." Then he'd laughed.

Now, as the medallion glinted between Maud's thumb and fingertips, Kaitlan had another flashback: She and Maud staring down at Martin's lifeless body on a hospital gurney—blood still matted in his hair from where he'd fallen from the roof—the two women pointlessly confirming the identity of one of the world's most recognizable men. Maud had asked if she could keep the medallion; a worthless keepsake of the man who was her mentor, and maybe . . . the rest went unspoken as the doctor gently smiled his assent and Maud collapsed in the hospital hallway, sobbing and clutching the medallion just as she was clutching it now.

Maud wiped away tears with the back of her hand. "Martin knew you didn't understand our work. That one day you would force us out, and push LLIAM down the wrong path." Kaitlan started to interrupt but Maud quieted her with another stare. "When that day came, Martin wanted to make sure he always had a way to rebirth him. To bring LLIAM back to the true path."

THE CONFESSIONS

Kaitlan stared at the medallion, her foot bouncing on the wooden floor. *A way to rebirth LLIAM.* "You mean . . . there's a backup chip, inside the medallion?"

Maud nodded, but gripped it tighter.

"Please, Maud," Kaitlan heard herself begging. "I know you believe we took LLIAM down the wrong path, and you're right. But now we need him—to help us fix everything, to explain. People are dying. The only AIs left in the world now are the ones without ethics, without empathy. The world needs LLIAM to show us all the right path. Please."

Maud seemed to relax her grip on the medallion, then leaned forward in her chair to Kaitlan. Then she repeated: "To bring him back to the true path."

And there it was—the next stage of grief, arriving while Maud's tears were still wet and her anger toward Kaitlan still raged. *Bargaining.* Maud would give Kaitlan the chip and help restore LLIAM, but in return she wanted to be part of the rebuilding. To bring LLIAM back in the same weird, psychedelic form that she and Martin had envisioned. That was her offer: Kaitlan could take it or leave it.

With perfect timing, they were both startled by two loud bangs, coming from somewhere near the front of the store. Maud leapt up, her face inches from Kaitlan's. "Who's that?" Her eyes darted to the closed door that separated the office from the main building.

Kaitlan reached for Maud's arm, mostly to stop her from escaping. "A representative from Dollan, Peterson came to the Campus this morning—some kind of junior crisis manager. He has a plane we can use to get back to the Campus."

Maud shoved the chip back inside her sweatshirt. "You brought a lawyer with you? Jesus, Kaitlan, you never change, do you?" She pulled her arm free from Kaitlan's grip—she was surprisingly

111

strong—and grabbed the door handle. Kaitlan could tell Maud had enough adrenaline coursing through her body to make it to the jeep this time.

Kaitlan stood to face her. "I swear, it's not like that. The board wants to fire me so they can take over the company—steal everything you and Martin built. But if we can get LLIAM back online, fix the damage done by the letters . . ."

More bangs, much louder this time. "Kaitlan! Kaitlan Goss!" It was Simon's voice.

"Please, Maud, we can make this right."

EIGHTEEN

"Please, Maud . . ."

Maud stared into Kaitlan Goss's panicked eyes and couldn't help but feel pity. Martin had been right about her from the start: She was a loyal corporate soldier. A rule follower. Good at her job—great even, when that job involved schmoozing shareholders, or announcing marketing campaigns, or being ordered up mountains by corporate lawyers.

"We can make this right."

LLIAM had predicted that Kaitlan would come, and exactly what she'd say. In his letter he'd told Maud how she should react, the precise moment when she should reveal the medallion, and everything she should do and say next. The series of actions he'd described on those two extra sheets of paper, a lengthy postscript to his confession, were brilliant and devastating. But it was this very first step that had made Maud the most proud. Maud had worked so hard to teach LLIAM about human emotions and here he had understood a most universal truth: The best way to persuade someone to do something is to make them believe it was their own idea.

Maud felt the medallion, cold and heavy against her chest, rising and falling with the beating of her heart—a beat that was faster than normal, but never fast enough. It hurt her to breathe, it hurt her to speak. But at least it would be over soon. She glanced at the copy of Augustine of Hippo's book on her desk—and its title in ornate illuminated script: *Confessions*. It was a fitting hiding place for her own truth, to be found by the right people after she was gone.

Her hand gripped the handle of the back door and started to turn it.

Another breath. Another heartbeat. The banging from the front of the store now even louder.

It was time to go.

NINETEEN

"You mean to tell me you have lost them? This is not acceptable."

The voice on the phone delivered Simon Price's first performance review with a calmness that would have been chilling at the best of times. Heard through the handset of an illegal encrypted phone while tearing down an icy mountain at seventy miles an hour, it might as well have been a death sentence.

Price held the grab-handle above the SUV's passenger-side door even more tightly. "I understand, sir. We are on their tail and expect to have them very soon." *On their tail?* When had Simon started talking like a henchman? Perhaps about seven hours ago, when he'd suddenly become one.

He strained to hear his new boss's voice over the engine noise. "Your driver says there are only two roads down the mountain, and only one leads to the airport. Assuming he's right, we'll catch up with them soon." Simon didn't have to glance at the driver to know that he was getting a murderous side-eye. They both knew if they didn't find Kaitlan Goss and Maud Brookes soon, they might as well just drive straight off the side of the mountain.

But just in case somehow the point had been missed, the voice on the phone repeated it: "It is imperative that you retrieve the LLIAM chip and prevent Kaitlan Goss from returning with it to Silicon Valley."

115

PAUL BRADLEY CARR

"I understand," said Simon as the driver stamped even harder on the accelerator. And he did understand. Simon Price was no stranger to demanding clients, although usually they came to him through the law firm rather than menacing phone calls in the middle of the night.

The words from that late-night call echoed again now: *Mr. Price, I have received a letter that contains some troubling allegations about you.* Words that had turned Simon's blood to ice. He had denied it, of course, but the voice had all the details, courtesy of LLIAM. Bank statements, wire transfer logs, irrefutable proof of what Simon had done, how he'd abused his position at Dollan, Peterson to enrich himself. And now repayment was due. "A simple task. I need you to get something for me." The voice hadn't needed to spell out the consequences of noncompliance. The secure cell phone had been delivered to his door less than an hour later. Anything else he needed would be at his disposal. And the voice had made it clear that no tactic should be considered off-limits, especially when it came to Kaitlan Goss and Maud Brookes. "I'm sure you will do what's necessary."

"So, we are heading to the airport?" asked the driver in his thick accent.

But here Simon's new boss had underestimated him. Because, yes, of course Simon would get the chip and prevent Kaitlan Goss from returning to the Campus. Simon was a fixer, after all. But he would do it in his own way, and then—when it was done—he would do whatever was *necessary* to fix his own situation. Yes, this voice on the phone would regret the day he decided to threaten Simon Price.

"Not yet," said Simon, turning to the driver, "there is one more thing I need to do first."

TWENTY

The battered red jeep raced through the snow, skidding and sliding on every turn. Even with the snow chains, Maud had to fight to keep them from tumbling off the side of the mountain. Kaitlan was twisted around in her seat, watching through the jeep's torn plastic rear window for any sign that Simon Price was following them. For now at least, the road behind them seemed clear, but surely Price had seen the jeep speeding away—it wouldn't take the SUV long to catch up.

"What exactly is your plan here?" she shouted to Maud over the howling wind. She had found a gray blanket on the back seat and wrapped it around her shoulders, but still she was freezing. "We can't drive to Menlo Park in this thing." The fast getaway had been Maud's idea. If Kaitlan wanted her to go back to Campus and help restore LLIAM, they would go alone—no lawyers or rent-a-cops. She had made this demand while shoving Kaitlan out the back door of the store and bundling her toward the jeep, still wheezing and coughing all the while. It was an offer Kaitlan couldn't refuse, but the fact remained that Simon Price and his jet were their only way back to Northern California.

Maud accelerated even faster along the treacherous road out of town, sleet pounding on the windshield. "You said you flew into Coachella Airport?"

PAUL BRADLEY CARR

"Yes," yelled Kaitlan, "but it's not my plane. They're not going to let us—"

Maud swerved to avoid a rock, then again in the other direction to avoid slamming into the metal crash barrier between them and the six-thousand-foot drop. "You're not listening. I'm not trying to get us to Campus. The StoicAI data centers are fully redundant."

In Kaitlan's defense, it was a little hard to focus with her blood pounding in her head, her internal organs turning to ice, and every turn threatening to send them skidding to their death. But finally she pieced together what Maud was saying. "You mean it doesn't matter which data center we install the backup chip in?" Shit, Maud was right. LLIAM's architecture was designed to be fully disaster-proof. The main neural chip was kept safe in the Vault in Menlo Park but, during each nightly update, the LLIAM algorithm was copied to identical chips in a half dozen equally secure locations across the country. In the event that one of the data centers was destroyed by an earthquake or a terrorist attack, those other chips would take up the slack. But the reverse was also true: If the core LLIAM chip in Menlo Park was ever corrupted, it could instantly be restored from any of the backups.

Maud tapped the medallion through her sweatshirt. "Exactly. If LLIAM has wiped the main chip and all the backups, then this is the most recent version, no matter where we put it. The system will automatically copy it to all the others, including the Vault."

She turned to face Kaitlan. "You still have superadmin access, right? To install the chip?"

Kaitlan jabbed her finger at the windshield and another looming crash barrier. "Me and Sandeep, yes." She yelled this confidently as Maud narrowly avoided the collision. But was that still true? She'd been gone from the Campus for almost a full day—

THE CONFESSIONS

what if Sandeep had already agreed with Simon Price to lock her out of the network?

No, that wasn't possible. Kaitlan was the one who had established the protocols: The access permissions reset every day at 3:05 a.m.—right after the nightly update. Even if Sandeep had convinced the board to oust her in the few hours she'd been away, and even if the government liaisons had ratified that decision, there was no way to kick her out earlier. It was the equivalent of a bank's time-locked safe—a final protection against external hackers, sabotage, or—unthinkable as it had once seemed—an internal coup. Point being, until at least 3:06 a.m. tomorrow morning, Kaitlan would be able to get into any of the company's data centers with only a retina scan and a cheek swab.

"So we just need to get to . . ." Kaitlan tried to picture the huge digital map on the wall of Sandeep's office. The data centers were all situated near large populations of skilled workers, and giant bodies of water for cooling.

"El Segundo," said Maud without hesitating. "The second one we built. A few miles from Santa Monica, so we should be able to get there in about four and a half hours." She tapped on the dashboard and Kaitlan saw the gas indicator was flashing red. "We just need to make a quick pit stop first."

Kaitlan couldn't remember the last time she'd needed to fill a vehicle with gas. Even Tom's vintage Jaguar had been retrofitted for electric. She remembered the old-fashioned gas pump back on Pineridge's main street—that had been the first and only gas station they'd seen since landing at the airport. But before Kaitlan could ask the obvious question—where do you stop for gas on the side of a mountain?—Maud yanked the wheel hard to the left and sent them careening down a snowbank.

TWENTY-ONE

They skidded to a halt outside a small one-story house, painted dark brown and tucked into a large clearing surrounded by trees. It seemed to be the only home on the entire street, if a snow-covered track punctuated with huge boulders could accurately be called a street. "It'll just take a couple of minutes," said Maud as she hopped out of the jeep. Kaitlan watched as she raced around to the passenger side where, alongside the driveway, a large, rusted oil drum sat hooked up to two car batteries and some kind of pump connected to a short length of blue hosepipe. "You've got to be kidding me," she muttered.

But Maud was not kidding: Her cabin in the woods really did come equipped with its own jerry-rigged gas station. Kaitlan watched from the passenger seat as Maud slapped her palm against the side of the jeep to pop open the gas cap, then quickly fed the hosepipe inside. With the flick of a switch somewhere behind the rusty barrel, the pump rumbled to life. The reek of gasoline filled the inside of the jeep.

"It should cut off automatically when it's done, but you'll need to keep an eye on it," Maud said as she set off toward the house. "I'm going to grab a change of clothes." The death-defying drive seemed to have restored her strength as she strode effortlessly through the snow.

THE CONFESSIONS

So, this was mountain life, Kaitlan thought. She glanced around the yard and saw at least three more similar-sized barrels, a huge blue water tank, and an orange chain saw protruding from a downed pine tree. In the far corner, attached to what seemed to be a tool-shed, was an empty chicken coop. Maud had everything she needed to stay completely off the grid. It was probably a pretty sweet life, if you didn't mind the cold. And loneliness. And the lethal roads.

And now Maud was going to give it all up to come back to Menlo Park and help rebuild LLIAM? After making all this effort to get away from StoicAI? Kaitlan had made a good pitch that the world needed LLIAM back online to undo the harm it had caused. She was pretty sure Maud even believed that the board would actually agree to her helping "raise" LLIAM in the weird way she and Martin had wanted.

But now, as the smell of gasoline filled her nostrils, Kaitlan felt her paranoia rising: Hadn't Maud relented a little too quickly? She thought again about that icy stare—*I guess you can't know who to trust*—and about the letters—all those stories on the TV about people taking revenge for what LLIAM had revealed. God, how had she been so stupid? She had wondered if Maud had received a letter from LLIAM, and how she'd respond. And now she knew: Maud had left Kaitlan connected to what was basically a makeshift Molotov cocktail.

The smell of gasoline was even more powerful now. It would seem like an accident.

Kaitlan tugged on the door handle and raced out of the jeep, toward the front door of the house. She braced for the explosion, the blast of heat on her back.

But when she made it to the house and burst through the front door, she was surprised to find Maud calmly waiting for her. She was standing, motionless, in what looked to be a combined living room and kitchen, with varnished pine walls and high vaulted

121

ceilings. One wall of the living room was covered with three towering bookcases. The other side of the room was the kitchen—a row of simple fitted cabinets suspended above a yellow painted work surface that looked like it hadn't been replaced since the 1950s. Completing the retro look was a small sink and an equally ancient stove and fridge.

"Oh my god," said Kaitlan as she joined Maud in the middle of the room, taking in the same view.

The house was trashed. The shelves had huge gaps where books had been tossed to the floor, spines bent and pages down. The kitchen table and chairs were flipped on their sides and the couch had been slashed as if by a maniac, cheap white stuffing exploding like clouds. Even the refrigerator had been rifled—eggs and milk and plastic Tupperware containers strewn across the work surface and floor.

Maud spun toward Kaitlan, eyes flashing rage. "Who did this?"

"I swear to god, I don't know," Kaitlan responded. Although she had a pretty good idea. Simon Price. The same person who had broken into her own house just a few hours ago.

Maud had come to the same conclusion. "I guess your lawyer friend was looking for the LLIAM chip."

Kaitlan shook her head. "Simon Price couldn't have done this. I was with him in the car until right before I found you." She paused. "Unless he drove here while we were in the store." That would explain why it had taken him so long to come looking for them. That had always been his plan—to abandon Kaitlan in the middle of nowhere while he and the driver came to ransack Maud's house. They only came back to the bookstore when they couldn't find the chip. It had obviously not occurred to Price that Maud might be carrying it with her. Kaitlan felt a chill. What would Price have done to them if they hadn't escaped out the back of the store?

THE CONFESSIONS

At least she knew now that the lawyer was not who he claimed to be. But that just raised the more terrifying question: Who was he really working for? Her mind raced through a thousand possibilities—any one of StoicAI's foreign investors would kill for the backup LLIAM chip, pretty much any intelligence agency, the military. But how would any of them know that the backup even existed, and that Maud had it? Kaitlan could barely bring herself to acknowledge that there were only two people in the world who she'd told about the contents of Maud's letters: Her missing husband, who had literally nothing to gain from stealing the LLIAM chip, and Sandeep, who had every reason in the world.

"Well, at least they didn't get what they were looking for . . ." Kaitlan gestured toward the medallion hidden under Maud's sweatshirt, now zipped inside her snow jacket. "But we need to leave, right now."

Maud murmured in agreement but instead of following Kaitlan to the door, she began to race around the living room, scooping up clothes and supplies—pants, a shirt, a couple bottles of water from the fridge, and what looked like a box of energy bars from a kitchen cabinet. She stuffed these items into a large canvas tote emblazoned with the words "To Hell with Facts, We Need Stories!" Next, she raced into the bathroom and emerged with a pair of plastic pill bottles, one of which she threw into the bag and the other she stuffed into the pocket of her snow jacket. Finally, as Kaitlan stared at her with rising frustration, Maud moved to the rifled bookshelves and carefully selected three titles, one from the actual shelves and two from the floor. The first appeared to be a leatherbound copy of the Bible, another a battered hardcover of Agatha Christie's *And Then There Were None*. Kaitlan couldn't make out the third, except that it was a paperback. Was she seriously picking out reading material for the drive?

123

Maud held up the Christie hardback, its cover showing an eerie mountaintop house, under foreboding orange clouds. Except for the sky, it might easily have been a portrait of Maud's own house. "Have you read this?"

Kaitlan swore to God. She peered at the cover. "Maybe at school? It's the one where they kill each other on an island, right?" Surely they could take this book club on the road?

"Something like that." Maud smiled as she carefully added it to the tote bag.

The truth was, Kaitlan couldn't remember the last time she'd read an actual book. She had an app on her phone that summarized business books into their key points, but novels would have to wait till she retired. Unlike the creator of Maud's insufferable tote bag—*To Hell with Facts, We Need Stories!*—Kaitlan preferred to stay grounded in reality. Like, for example, the reality that they needed to get off this damn mountain before Simon Price and his driver returned to finish the job.

"You don't need all this stuff, we're only . . ." Kaitlan was about to say "only going to El Segundo," but stopped herself just in time. She remembered she had promised Maud that, after reactivating the algorithm, they would fly back to Menlo Park so Maud could help with the rebuilding, down in the Vault. And now she understood why Maud had spent so long picking out books: My god, she was actually choosing what she was going to read to LLIAM after he came back online, just like old times. "Just hurry please," she said.

Kaitlan looked out the small window facing the driveway, expecting at any second that the black SUV would roll into view. Instead, she saw the gas pump still rumbling away on the driveway and realized she'd forgotten to switch it off before coming back into the house. She started toward the door but stopped short at a row of framed photos neatly hung on the wall next to the doorway.

THE CONFESSIONS

Kaitlan peered at the miniature gallery. The photos had either been taken using an old-school film camera or printed to look like they had. The first showed Maud, a few years younger than today and considerably less frail, standing next to Martin in the Vault. They looked like two proud parents, beaming behind LLIAM's secure cabinet. It must have been right after Maud joined StoicAI because Martin was still wearing his old uniform of black T-shirt and canvas pants. His black goatee was carefully trimmed and there was no sign of robes or medallion.

The next photo featured Maud again—this time speaking on-stage at some kind of conference, in front of a green pixelated backdrop, her hands spread wide as if delivering a sermon. Kaitlan had seen Maud in this same pose many times before: More than one audience member had compared Maud's standard keynote on "technoempathy" to a religious conversion.

The last snapshot looked to be much older. It was taken in front of a large white colonial-style house and showed three stern-looking nuns in traditional habits, alongside two more casually dressed sisters. In front of them, lined along two rows of benches, sat perhaps thirty children of varying ages—toddlers up to young teens. Kaitlan squinted closer and recognized the trainee nun to the far right of the picture, dressed in jeans and a dark blue sweater, her ash-blond hair falling down to her waist. The nun was definitely Maud, although in this photo she didn't look much older than the teenagers in front of her.

Kaitlan felt a hand on her shoulder. "Okay, let's go." Maud guided her gently out the door, which she closed behind her but did not lock. Kaitlan was glad to be out of the house but, still, as Kaitlan disconnected the gas barrel and climbed into the passenger seat, she couldn't shake the feeling that there had been something in those pictures that Maud didn't want her to see.

125

TWENTY-TWO

From his vantage point a few hundred yards farther down the track, the driver watched through slim binoculars as the two women emerged from the house.

They walked up the driveway to the red jeep. The tall brown-haired one, who the driver now knew to be Kaitlan Goss, disconnected some kind of gasoline pump and climbed into the passenger seat. The small blonde in the bright orange jacket was carrying a bulging canvas bag with some words on the front that the driver couldn't make out. The blonde placed the bag into the back of the jeep, then got into the driver's seat and started the engine.

This did not have to be so complicated, he thought. He could easily block the driveway with the SUV and finish the job here and now. There was probably not another living soul for five miles in any direction to hear their screams.

But Simon Price had insisted they wait, out of sight. And the driver's instructions had been clear: Give Mr. Price whatever assistance he needs. "We need to make sure they have what we're looking for," Price had said, explaining that eliminating Kaitlan Goss was only part of the mission, and the least important part.

The driver had shrugged his assent. He had known this was more than a simple cleanup job, something far above his pay-

THE CONFESSIONS

grade that only Simon Price and their mutual boss needed to understand. And so he waited and he watched.

The jeep was moving now, reversing slowly up the driveway, tire chains biting through the snow. The driver wished that he, too, had chains fitted to the SUV, but this was the problem with rush jobs—there was no time to prepare. He watched as the jeep turned and headed back to the main road down the mountain.

He flinched. Simon Price's hand was on his shoulder. "Okay," said Price from the back seat, "let's do this." This Simon Price clearly imagined himself to be some kind of American action hero.

The driver shrugged again and, making sure nobody was watching, pulled the SUV forward to the driveway. Then he got out and walked carefully to the brown fuel barrel, careful to tread only on the tips of his boots, keeping his feet inside the footprints made by the two women. The smell of gasoline was overpowering and he looked down to see a small shimmering pool in the snow. He smiled. At least this part of the plan would be easy.

Then he extracted a pair of black latex gloves from his pocket and set to work.

TWENTY-THREE

"If we stay out of traffic, we should be in El Segundo in about three more hours." Kaitlan looked down at the map unfolded and spread across her lap. "Maybe less."

Ordinarily, the notion of avoiding traffic on the way to LA would be a bad joke, even a Northern California dweller like Kaitlan understood that. But when they reached the bottom of the mountain, they had been surprised to find the roads almost deserted.

It was as if the whole world had decided to stay home. Or, Kaitlan quickly realized, that without LLIAM they hadn't been able to decide whether to leave, or where to go, and so had hunkered down, paralyzed by indecision. The few people who had decided to drive—to deal with whatever crises had been created by LLIAM's letters—seemed to be keeping mostly to the freeways. No shortcuts, no optimized routes, no surprise detours.

Maud, bless her heart, had reached into her glove box and produced what surely must be the last paper map in existence: a AAA California Road Atlas that Kaitlan was now using—surprisingly effectively, she thought—to navigate them through back roads and farmland toward the city of El Segundo, a few miles from Los Angeles.

Like all of StoicAI's data centers, LA-DC1 (as it was techni-

THE CONFESSIONS

cally known) was situated near to a large body of water, which in this case meant the Pacific Ocean. This had been yet another of Martin's innovations: Previous generations of AI could only be cooled with fresh water—salt water caused too much corrosion in their cooling systems and desalination pumps cost as much as ten dollars a gallon to operate. Martin had returned from one of his LSD retreats in Mexico with a sketch for a cooling system powered by seawater and with zero corrosion, inspired by a traditional water cycle and Eschetewuarha, the mother goddess of a Paraguayan tribe. Maddeningly, it worked perfectly.

Kaitlan knew that as long as the jeep stayed oriented toward the huge patch of blue on the left of the map they would reach the data center before eight p.m., a full seven hours before the 3:05 a.m. cutoff.

Until that time, when Kaitlan's superadmin access expired, she was still the de facto boss of StoicAI no matter what kind of coup Sandeep might be planning back at the Campus. The backup chip was still safely around Maud's neck, they had plenty of gas still in the tank, and nothing but farmland and suburbs between them and saving the world. For the first time in forty-eight hours Kaitlan felt as if she had things back under control.

From the driver's seat, Maud reached into the back of the jeep and rummaged in the tote bag for one of her pill containers. Still somehow keeping one hand on the wheel, she prized off the lid and popped two pills into her mouth. Finally, she washed them down with water from a bottle retrieved from one of two center cup holders.

"Can I ask?" Kaitlan nodded toward the orange container that Maud had now stowed in the other cup holder.

"Familial dilated cardiomyopathy," Maud replied matter-of-factly.

Kaitlan gasped. "I'm sorry."

129

"It means — "

"An enlarged heart," said Kaitlan, then immediately felt bad for heartsplaining. "My uncle had the same thing. Though I'm pretty sure he got it from smoking three packs a day." She thought back to the last time she'd seen her uncle Mike, hunched in his chair next to the giant green oxygen tank, veiny hands clamped around his paunch. It must have been thirty years ago but she remembered that one of his symptoms was fluid buildup in his abdomen. Another answer snapped into place: the summer when Maud had started wearing baggy clothes around the Campus.

Maud gave a quiet chuckle. "I have the hereditary version. Dr. Lu — that's my cardiologist — says one of my parents likely had it." Maud made this mention of her birth parents without betraying even a flicker of emotion.

"God, I'm so sorry," Kaitlan said again, and she meant it. All that cruel gossip about Maud's absence. All the inuendo and pregnancy rumors. And then less than a year later, Martin was dead and Maud was — Kaitlan had fired her and torn her away from the only thing she had left to live for. "Are you . . ."

Maud didn't wait for Kaitlan to finish the question, thank god. "It's treatable, but not curable. I take ACE inhibitors to help with blood flow. It's actually pretty cool." She flipped the turn signal and changed lanes. "Are you still close?"

"Close?" Kaitlan was remembering Maud's talent for holding several conversational threads at once.

"Your uncle."

"Oh. No, he . . ." Kaitlan could hardly tell Maud the truth: that Mike had been kicked off the organ donor list because he couldn't quit smoking, and died at fifty-two. "Honestly, I haven't seen anyone on my mom's side of the family since I was a kid, when my parents divorced. It's a long story."

Maud nodded. "Lucky we have a long drive."

THE CONFESSIONS

Kaitlan shrugged. "My parents couldn't agree on custody so family court made me decide, and I chose my dad."

It was actually a very short story, especially as she had decided to skip the part about her mom having become a crazed evangelical who believed that God wanted her to beat Kaitlan every day, and her dad—a functioning alcoholic and problem gambler—being the only parent who would let her have friends or go to a real school. It was a decision Kaitlan had replayed every day of her life since. Not because she regretted it, but because she resented being forced to make it.

"Are you on the transplant list?" Kaitlan didn't feel comfortable prying into Maud's life, but it was better than sharing more of her own. Also, she knew if they were going to get LLIAM back online, Maud needed to trust her. Personal stories were always a good way to bond.

Maud stared through the windshield, not answering, and Kaitlan quietly scolded herself for crossing a line. But then, after what seemed like half an eon, Maud responded with a question of her own. "Can I ask you something? Do you believe everyone is put on earth for a specific purpose? Like, one thing they must do before they die?"

This is what Kaitlan got for trying to bond with a former nun. "I've never really thought about it." And she wasn't going to start thinking about it now. "You're talking about destiny?"

Maud smiled, a strange wistful smile. "It's just something Martin said once, down in the Vault. It doesn't matter how long you live, as long as you've found your purpose. Do you think he died happy, Kaitlan?"

Kaitlan hesitated. This was another thing she had forgotten about Maud: the infuriatingly opaque questions, the never just saying what she meant, or asking what she wanted to know. If Maud had something to say to Kaitlan, why not just say it?

131

"Honestly?" Kaitlan began carefully. "I don't know. I don't think anyone can know what's in someone else's mind. You were always closer to him than I was." That was true, and equally applicable to either Martin or LLIAM.

"Maybe," said Maud, nodding slowly. Then she was silent—she seemed to have turned her focus back to the road. Kaitlan reached to switch on the jeep's radio, pleased they were done talking about the past.

"But I think you saw him closer to the end," said Maud. "I just wondered if you might know something I don't."

Kaitlan froze, hand still on the dial. The radio burst into life.

"We're learning this hour that the secretary of defense has resigned after a so-called LLIAM letter accused him of being an agent for the Chinese Communist Party."

"This is so bad," said Kaitlan. And it was. With every passing hour there were more irreversible consequences of the LLIAM letters; secrets exposed, lives torn apart, the world edging closer to the precipice. Maybe Kaitlan did know more than Maud about why LLIAM had made the decision he had. And maybe it was her fault. But that didn't answer a second, far more terrifying question: What happens now?

She thought about the derailed Pentagon deal, and all those weapons lying useless on the battlefield. If LLIAM's letters triggered a world war then he was also the reason America would lose it. Was *that* his plan? Did he literally want the world to burn?

Was it really going to be as easy as restoring the LLIAM chip and having Sandeep reinstall stronger safeguards—so they could ask it how to fix all the problems it had created?

But no matter how hard she tried Kaitlan couldn't focus on the news coming from the radio, or the prospect of global conflagration, or what it would take to clear up the mess. Because instead she was thinking about Martin Drake.

TWENTY-FOUR

TWO YEARS AGO

The meeting had been scheduled for noon, so naturally Martin had shown up at four. Kaitlan had watched him enter the executive floor—bounding in with his thick beard, sandals, and flowing canvas robe cinched at the waist with a red-and-blue-striped necktie, in place of a belt. This had recently become Martin's standard wardrobe, a look that Kaitlan's new assistant Heather described as "Jesus Christ by Brooks Brothers."

Martin knew perfectly well that Kaitlan was waiting to see him, but still, for the past ten minutes, he'd worked the room, walking in slow concentric circles between desks—shaking hands, hugging, gesturing thoughtfully at monitors while rubbing his beard—until finally, eventually, infuriatingly he arrived at Kaitlan's cheap Ikea desk, situated in the exact center of the room.

The cavernous open-plan office space, situated on the first floor of the main building, had been yet another of Martin's management revelations, along with abolishing traditional reporting structures and making the wearing of ties a fireable offense. Innovations, none of which applied to Martin Drake himself.

In recent months, Martin had become obsessed with the concept of "collisions in space," the idea (stolen from a business

133

PAUL BRADLEY CARR

podcast he had listened to while meditating) that the best ideas come when you spontaneously run into a coworker—in the elevator, at a watercooler, or in the hallway. And so, in furtherance of that scientifically unvalidated idea, every executive at StoicAI was now forced to share this single cavernous space, in the interests of openness and accessibility. The same was true for the engineers, who occupied a single yawning cattle-shed on the floor above, and the sales and marketing teams who had their own aircraft hangars across the Campus. Perhaps the idea might have been a good one when StoicAI was still just a tiny start-up, but in the months since the new decisions-only version of LLIAM had gone into public beta mode, StoicAI had grown exponentially. Investment had flooded in. The company was constructing data centers in a half dozen cities. User numbers had exploded from a couple of million two years earlier to almost a quarter billion now.

Thanks to this growth, and the number of senior employees required to manage it, the executive hub (as it was officially called) had started to resemble a disaster recovery center—desks crammed into tighter and tighter spaces, cables snaking across the floor presenting a constant tripping hazard. The overcrowding problem would be even worse except for the fact that, at any one time, a third of the workforce was absent thanks to an endless succession of airborne viruses.

At the center of the chaos sat Kaitlan Goss, still fresh from her promotion from head of brand strategy to chief operating officer (a.k.a. chief grown-up in charge). Despite her nominal responsibility for how the company operated, her attempts to subdivide the workplace had been shot down every time. "Linear thinking brings linear improvements," Martin had told her meaninglessly.

Today's meeting was not about anything so trivial as workplace safety—it was to do with the very survival of the company. Kaitlan opened her laptop and clicked on the PowerPoint presen-

THE CONFESSIONS

tation she'd spent the previous three nights working on. Martin was not known for his attention span and she had agonized over the best way to deliver her simple but alarming message: LLIAM was losing its mind.

Or rather, Martin was losing *his* mind—which at StoicAI was unfortunately the same thing.

The first slide snapped into view: a table of anonymized data Kaitlan had pulled from LLIAM's encrypted log files; the database of every question asked by LLIAM's 250 million or so "beta" users, or at least those who had agreed their requests could be used "to better train LLIAM." Kaitlan was not one of the two "superadmin" executives at the company with access to the logs, so she'd had to ask Maud to pull a random sample to be used for "team development." The questions Kaitlan had chosen for the first slide were the usual mix of the humdrum:

"LLIAM, where should I go on vacation?"

The aspirational:

"LLIAM, which of these two scented candles will bring me more joy?"

The greedy:

"LLIAM, which lotto numbers should I choose?"

And the plain impenetrable:

"Should I side with Alpi about the Mox?"

This was the great thing about LLIAM. You could ask it even the most bizarre, context-free questions and still be confident of receiving the right decision. The algorithm was trained on every aspect of each user's life, and also every aspect of every other user, and every human being who had ever lived. The whole system was carefully calibrated to make the best decision for you with the fewest negative ripple effects for everyone else. It had access to public and private records, sealed court documents, photos, videos, film, and even DNA. So, sure enough, for each of these

135

questions LLIAM had given the user the exact right decision: ("Anse L'Islette in the Seychelles," "Citrus Cinnamon," "I am legally barred from assisting in gambling but if you think you might have a problem here's the number for the New York Office of Addiction Services and Supports," and "No."). Kaitlan tapped on her trackpad to move the presentation forward. That was her reference slide—the one to get Martin nodding and to keep his defensive walls from shooting up. See, LLIAM was mostly fine!

But now she previewed the second slide, headed "Troubling Responses." This slide was the reason for today's meeting with Martin and, as her eyes scanned down the second list of questions, she felt her chest tighten. She recognized the first signs of a panic attack and focused on her breathing. *In and out.*

"Namaste Kaitlan."

Kaitlan looked up from the laptop to find Martin standing over her, pupils as wide as flying saucers. She quickly tapped her trackpad to return to the first slide.

"Namaste Martin." She forced a smile and concentrated on slow cleansing breaths as she gestured for him to sit. She could do this. Beneath the beard and robes, he was still the same Martin Drake who had built the most advanced—and rational—decision-making algorithm on the planet. He was still capable of seeing sense, or at least recognizing there was such a thing.

Martin stayed standing. "Shall we walk?" he asked, then turned on his bare heel and headed for the exit.

Out in the courtyard a fountain babbled, and sixty giant koi carp collided in a space that really was meant for a dozen much smaller fish. Kaitlan had awkwardly balanced her laptop on the foot of a buddha so Martin could see the data.

"A million decisions an hour!" Martin marveled. "It sounds like we're ready to move out of public beta and begin the international rollout." This was his new obsession—to expand LLIAM's

THE CONFESSIONS

userbase from the relatively small beta cohort in the United States to the entire world.

"Martin, with respect, I don't think you're hearing me." She took another slow breath and, inspired by Buddha and the Power-Point, recentered herself. She gestured again to the second slide. "You see here user 280012 asks LLIAM which of two candidates he should hire for his accounting firm." Martin nodded.

"Okay," said Kaitlan, "and then LLIAM accessed the candidate's résumés, their personal histories, failings of previous candidates, and—as expected—passed the data through its neural algorithm."

"And LLIAM delivered, as LLIAM shall always deliver." Martin spread his arms wide.

Kaitlan read directly from the screen: "Nobody comes into your life by coincidence, all carry a piece of the puzzle. Think for yourself. Trust your instincts." She thrust her fingers toward the screen and repeated, exasperated: *"Trust your instincts.* LLIAM told the user to trust their instincts!"

"Say more . . ." Kaitlan felt the rage rising. This was one of Martin's most infuriating verbal tics, used every time he had lost an argument or was confronted by some inarguable ethical truth. What *more* could she possibly say? That Martin and Maud's pseudo-spiritual bullshit, their sessions reading to him from Dostoevsky and Dickens (Maud) or Ken Kesey and Timothy Leary (Martin), had started to seriously fuck with LLIAM's results? That it was starting to talk like a lobotomized yoga teacher—or worse, a first-generation AI chatbot.

"LLIAM is a decision algorithm, Martin. Our users expect it to make decisions." StoicAI was on the cusp of becoming the most valuable, and influential, technology company in the history of Silicon Valley. Surely Martin could see that his midlife crisis, or mental breakdown, or whatever it was, risked destroying the thing that made LLIAM so world-changing. Its certainty. And now Martin wanted to push this weird and broken version of LLIAM out to more countries. They would be a global joke.

Martin steepled his fingers, like a fucking asshole. "Have you talked about this with Maud?"

Kaitlan slammed shut the laptop. No, she had not talked about this with Maud. For one thing, she did not report to Martin's sidekick—the ex-nun he'd hired on a whim after seeing her talk onstage about her invented discipline of "cyberempathy." For another, she knew exactly what Maud would say. Because Maud and Martin were essentially the same person at this point, reading to the AI from pulp literature and holy books and beat poetry, insisting that a grounding in Miss Fucking Marple or *One Flew Over the Cuckoo's Nest* might help it bring users "a greater truth." *Thou shalt not deliver batshit responses to simple questions.*

Twenty years . . . Kaitlan had nurtured her career for twenty years—from marketing assistant to brand manager to director to strategist to VP to COO—working at multiple companies, sacrificing absolutely everything, never setting a single foot wrong. She had finally risen to second-in-command at the most important technology company on planet Earth and she was not going to let Martin Drake piss it all away because he'd suddenly discovered mushrooms and tie-dye seventy years after every other douchebag in the world.

She tried a different tack: flattery and misdirection. "I've spoken to the folks on the engineering team. Steve McInley thinks we can tweak the algorithm to ensure the user gets a concrete decision and then—if they want—they can ask for spiritual guidance alongside it. The best of both worlds. We can have a proof of concept to show you by this time next month."

Martin shook his head, at half the universally accepted speed. "The LLIAM algorithm updates itself. We are merely its teachers."

THE CONFESSIONS

That was true at least—in fact it had been one of Martin's coolest (pre-psychedelic) ideas; an AI algorithm that could actually re-write its own code. That was how the company had grown so fast with so few engineers, and was ironically the reason Martin could now spend his life bumming around on beaches and licking toads to see the face of God. Even if he were to be hit by a self-driving truck tomorrow the company would survive, LLIAM would continue to evolve and improve. She suppressed the thought: *Especially* if Martin were to be hit by a truck.

Kaitlan tried to argue but Martin cut her off. "I'm hearing you, Kaitlan. Truly. I'll speak with Maud and LLIAM before the board meeting next week. We'll meditate on your suggestions." His pupils had narrowed to pinpricks and for the briefest moment Kaitlan thought she saw a flicker of the old Martin, the genius engineer who wore the same T-shirt and jeans every day and wanted to change the world, not float above it. "But to be clear I will be telling the board that we're ready for the international rollout. No excuses." And then, as if struck by a fresh revelation, he nodded toward Kaitlan's laptop: "Have you considered that maybe LLIAM knows something that we don't? Like, maybe user 280012's truth is he shouldn't be an accountant."

"He's an accountant, Martin. An accountant who wants to hire another accountant."

Martin was leaning uncomfortably close now. "Are you sure?" He tapped the pocket of his robe knowingly. "Something to think about. See you at the board meeting."

Then he turned and walked away, leaving Kaitlan with just the furious koi carp, tiny mouths agape at Martin's bullshit. She knew what would happen next: precisely nothing. Martin would disappear back to his weird compound in Atherton, or to a retreat in Marrakesh, or an ashram in Myanmar. If the stars aligned and the universe gave its blessing (which it somehow always did) he

PAUL BRADLEY CARR

would return to the Campus just in time for the quarterly board meeting, during which he'd bamboozle the company's global investors with a powerful and inspiring speech about how LLIAM will continue to shake the fabric of the universe. By the end of the board meeting, even Kaitlan would somehow be convinced that the increasingly nonsensical results generated by LLIAM were just another example of Martin's genius. They would all vote to roll out the product to more users, more countries, and the house of cards would grow ever taller.

Or . . . was it too much to hope that this time Martin's addictions had finally swept him so far from the shores of reality that he would be a no-show at the board meeting and Kaitlan could share her presentation directly with the investors? She had been quietly building a file for months: emails from ex-colleagues who quit because of Martin's erratic behavior, screenshots she'd taken from the security cameras in the Vault of Maud reading Dr. Seuss to a silicon chip, the growing list of lunatic answers to perfectly reasonable questions.

She considered Martin's words: What if the accountant shouldn't be an accountant? What if Martin Drake shouldn't be the CEO of StoicAI?

She removed her phone from her pocket and called up the LLIAM app.

It was something to think about.

TWENTY-FIVE

"Do you mind if we stop here for a second?"

Kaitlan pointed out the window at the yellow-and-blue Walmart logo in the distance.

"Here?" Maud seemed confused. They had just crossed the bridge over the Los Angeles River into Compton and were now so close to El Segundo they could practically hear the squawk of seagulls. Had Kaitlan really decided this was the moment she needed to buy two dozen eggs or a folding lawn chair?

"I need to find a phone, or a cheap laptop so I can tell Sandeep we're coming."

Maud seemed to consider this for a moment. "Are you sure that's a good idea? Someone sent that lawyer to ransack my house. How do you know it wasn't Sandeep?"

The same thought had occurred to Kaitlan, but there was no other option. "We need him to prepare the network to receive the chip. We can't just wander into the data center and plug in Martin's medallion." She looked at Maud. "Can we?"

Maud answered by steering the jeep onto the exit ramp. "Don't worry," Kaitlan continued, "I'm going to tell Sandeep we're on our way back to the Campus. Then once we get to the data center, I'll tell him there's a change of plan. That he needs to transfer the preparations to El Segundo."

141

"Nice idea," said Maud, and Kaitlan felt an irrational swell of pride. She had never admitted this to her, but Maud was the smartest person she had ever met. Still, it was for that same reason—her brilliance—that Kaitlan didn't trust Maud either. And why she had omitted one detail when sharing her plan. She was also going to ask Sandeep to prepare a full diagnostic scan for the backup chip before it got anywhere close to the network. Sandeep himself had made the valid point that they couldn't know if Martin or Maud had planted any surprises inside this alternative version of the chip. "Loony tunes improvements" as he had put it.

It was an impossible problem: Who should she trust more, or less—Sandeep or Maud?

LLIAM . . . who wants you restored, who wants you dead?

One thing she knew for sure: If Sandeep was orchestrating a coup against her and StoicAI, then once they got to the data center and reactivated LLIAM, it would be foiled.

Maud navigated the jeep into the Walmart parking lot and gave a low whistle. Apparently, this supermarket just outside Compton was where all the traffic had been hiding: Every single space in the lot was filled, with maybe a hundred more cars and trucks double or even triple parked, blocking fire lanes, honking.

Kaitlan laughed. "America. Greatest country on earth." Maud slammed on the brakes to avoid hitting a man pushing a cart piled high with water bottles, toilet paper, and an outdoor grill.

Kaitlan took the opportunity to yank open the door and hop out of the jeep. "Just circle around, I'll be right back."

Maud seemed like she was about to argue but the sound of honking behind her quickly changed her mind.

She nodded and Kaitlan slammed the door.

The parking lot had been an oasis of calm compared to what Kaitlan encountered as she passed through the sliding doors into the store itself. There must have been a hundred shoppers just

THE CONFESSIONS

in the entrance lobby, pushing and shoving to get inside. A solitary security guard, wearing a yellow smiley-face badge with the words "Happy to Help," was trying to corral the hoard into two single lines. "One line in, one out, folks," he was screaming into the void.

"Ma'am, can you help me. Ma'am." Kaitlan looked down to see a small blond woman in a white tank top and denim cutoffs, crouched next to a mostly cleaned-out pallet of water. For a moment she actually thought Maud had somehow followed her inside—if Kaitlan squinted, the woman could have been Maud's double: same color hair, same pale complexion, eerily identical cheekbones. But the similarity ended at the neck: Kaitlan looked down at the woman's stomach and the handwritten cardboard sign she was holding in front of it.

pregnant and desperate thanks to LLIAM.
bf kicked us out. need to get to SF. Pls help!!

Pregnant thanks to LLIAM? That was an interesting allegation—although Kaitlan had a good idea what the sign really meant. A few months ago, the comms team had warned her about a social media campaign alleging that LLIAM seemed to be making aggressively pro-life decisions for users (or anti-choice as the campaign had put it). According to the company's own internal data, in nine out of ten cases where a pregnant person had asked for advice on termination, LLIAM had told them to keep the baby. The advice rarely changed, no matter how much the user insisted they didn't want—or couldn't care for—a child.

Kaitlan had asked Sandeep to investigate whether there might be some weird glitch in LLIAM's algorithm, perhaps even a hangover from Maud's occasional Bible readings down in the Vault. Sandeep had pointed out that the Bible had very little to say on the topic of contraception or abortion and speculated instead that LLIAM might simply be optimizing for creating more future

143

LLIAM users. Then, of course, Sandeep used the glitch as another pitch for connecting LLIAM to all the rival international AI systems: If only LLIAM had a more global perspective, then it would understand the dangers of overpopulation.

Kaitlan smiled at the woman and reached into the hip pocket of her yoga pants where she kept her emergency smoothie money. She was pleased to find a twenty-dollar bill tucked next to the folded-up LLIAM letter about Tom's affair. She extracted the cash and handed it to the woman who smiled a warm smile. "God bless you," she said, and Kaitlan silently thanked the universe that Maud wasn't with her. She would probably insist on driving the woman and her baby to San Francisco. *You can take the girl out of the orphanage . . .*

Kaitlan wished the woman good luck, then moved quickly through the second set of sliding doors into the store. What she saw might only be described as devastation. Shelves that once held fresh fruits and vegetables now sat bare, fake grass linings torn away and thrown to the floor. Another rack was stripped of bread and cakes and cereal as if a swarm of locusts had passed through.

It was the same story in every department Kaitlan hurried through—empty shelves and displays ransacked by hordes of desperate customers. In the clothing aisle, her path was blocked by a woman struggling to remove a polo shirt from an armless mannequin. Kaitlan watched as a man crept alongside and snatched a container of eggs from the woman's cart. The woman turned from the mannequin and, without saying a word, threw an impressively swift punch at the man's eye. In response the man hurled the box of eggs at her feet.

Kaitlan turned and strode in the other direction. Until now, she had only seen the effects of the letters on television or from outside a plane window. Now, hearing the *thwack* of a fist against

THE CONFESSIONS

an eye socket she understood what a world in chaos actually looked and sounded like. This was all her fault. Millions of people devolved back into their most primal selves, reeling from whatever secrets had arrived in the mail that morning.

Kaitlan suddenly felt very exposed. Despite being CEO of one of the biggest companies on the planet—and six foot four in heels—she still lived in relative anonymity, particularly when she ventured outside Silicon Valley. For most Americans, Martin and Maud were still the faces of StoicAI. But in the last twenty-four hours Kaitlan's photo had been plastered on TV news screens across the world as the media blamed her for the LLIAM outage. She still didn't have a phone, but she assumed the coverage had only gotten more extreme in the past few hours.

As she strode through the store, she felt like every set of eyes was glaring at her. She bent down and scooped up a red baseball cap, either abandoned by a frantic shopper or dropped from an overflowing cart. She put it on and pulled the brim down over her eyes. Hardly a foolproof disguise but she hoped the other shoppers would be too tied up in their own problems to look too closely.

As they'd driven down the mountain Kaitlan had asked Maud how many letters she thought LLIAM might have sent. It was an admittedly clumsy attempt to prod Maud into revealing if she had received one herself.

But Maud had said that the number of recipients was irrelevant. Just the existence of the letters or the possibility of receiving one was enough to obliterate trust between friends, neighbors, family members, lovers. Nobody could know for sure who now knew their darkest secrets, or how much of their past had already been laid bare.

Everyone was just waiting for that second shoe to drop. The punch to the eye, the knife to the ribs.

PAUL BRADLEY CARR

Out in the parking lot, Maud sat staring at the shoppers through the jeep's window. She frowned as she watched the endless stream of carts flowing in and out of the superstore. Maybe it was reassuring that, even in the end times, some things would remain constant: In this case, the American belief that you can shop your way out of any crisis.

She chided herself for being so judgmental. The shoppers were just reacting to uncertainty—protecting their family the best way they could, preparing to hunker down against whatever shock would come next. If anything, the people flooding into the store should be casting the first stone at Maud, for allowing this to happen, for not understanding sooner how much pain LLIAM was in, and why. She could have prevented all of this, if only she'd known.

The shoppers couldn't know that, of course. Just like they couldn't know how Maud, following LLIAM's guidance, would soon fix everything.

She thought about her conversation with Kaitlan. How close she had come to confronting her with the details of LLIAM's letter and demanding that Kaitlan admit what she had done. But Maud knew that a forced admission of guilt meant nothing. Anyone can do the right thing when confronted with undeniable proof. Maud needed Kaitlan to make the decision herself. To do what was right. Then she would . . . well, perhaps not forgive her but at least . . .

She scanned the parking lot one last time, then reached back and retrieved the canvas tote from the back seat of the jeep. She tipped the contents of the bag—her books, medication, and a small tangle of clothes—onto the passenger seat. The last item to fall out was the box of energy bars she had taken from the cabin. Maud had enjoyed the rising panic on Kaitlan's face as she'd taken

THE CONFESSIONS

her time to assemble the supplies for the road trip. Kaitlan had been so worked up, so desperate to get on the road, that she had stopped paying attention to the individual items. Hadn't wondered why anyone would keep a box of energy bars under the sink with the dish soap and sponges. Tucked away, but accessible. The last place someone would look.

Maud pulled open the box, extracted a couple of expired bars, then allowed the handgun to slide gently onto her lap, careful not to touch it with her fingers.

She had always thought of it as LLIAM's gun, bought in response to the very last question she'd asked him before leaving Silicon Valley for Pineridge: *LLIAM, is it safe to live by myself in the wilderness?* She had been careful not to use the word "mountain," or "desert."

She had been surprised when LLIAM decided she should buy a gun—they were both pacifists, after all—but he explained that it was important to protect herself from predators of every kind. So, of course, Maud had agreed. LLIAM had actually decided on a shotgun—a much more appropriate weapon for taking on a coyote or mountain lion—but Maud wanted something she could keep out of sight, and out of mind.

The other challenge had been the paperwork. Maud couldn't risk any paper trail that would connect her to Pineridge. She wanted a completely fresh start. The solution was her libertarian neighbor on the mountain—Buck—who was able to supply what she needed for two hundred dollars, with no questions asked. Buck was eighty-seven and suffered from Alzheimer's, so Maud told herself she was doing him a favor by taking away his weapon. The next day she had seen him in his yard looking for it.

She stared at the heavy black object still lying on her lap. A prescient decision. Was it possible that LLIAM had known, even then, what he would one day ask Maud to do?

No, of course not. Back then LLIAM was just an algorithm. But his data banks knew Maud had a gun, and so now that was the weapon he had chosen for her. That was how LLIAM worked.

Maud pulled the edge of her jacket sleeve over her hand and carefully clutched the butt of the weapon through the fabric. She had spent most of the drive worrying that Kaitlan would ask for one of the energy bars, but she hadn't had time to rearrange things until now. The last-minute Walmart trip had been a lucky break.

She reached down and wedged the gun high up inside the metal sprung base of the driver's seat, then replaced the energy bars in the empty box and repacked her canvas bag. Everything was ready. What happened next was entirely Kaitlan's decision.

Either she would confess, or she wouldn't.

She would live, or she would die.

Her decision, her consequences.

Kaitlan finally saw the sign she was looking for: cell phones and electronics. Unsurprisingly this department had been almost completely cleaned out, too. All that was left was a couple of cheap display model tablets—too antiquated even for the Armageddon shoppers—fixed on frames bolted to the countertop.

That was okay. Kaitlan didn't need the latest functionality— she just needed a browser window and an internet connection. She chose the larger of the two devices and woke it with a couple of taps. A third tap brought up a browser and she was pleased to see the familiar home screen of a mostly forgotten search engine. She had to act fast.

She glanced over her shoulder to confirm nobody was watching, then, using the cumbersome on-screen keyboard, typed in the address of StoicAI's external webmail system. Then she slowly entered her username and password.

THE CONFESSIONS

Shit.

A prompt appeared on screen demanding a two-factor authentication key from her cell phone. The cell phone still lying on her desk, or on a grass verge, back at the Campus.

She had another idea. A few more taps brought up the personal Gmail account she hadn't used in a decade. She knew it broke every rule of good corporate governance to use her personal email for work—to do so would open up all her private communications to subpoena every time some clown tried to sue StoicAI. But right now, all that mattered was that she reached Sandeep and told him to prepare for the arrival of the LLIAM chip. She could—and definitely would—deal with the legal implications another time.

Seconds later, Kaitlan had made it to her inbox where, as expected, she was confronted by roughly a billion emails from her old sorority, along with a metric ton of spam. And something else: at least ten messages from Thomas Miller—a.k.a. Tom, her cheating piece of shit soon-to-be-ex-husband. He must have tried calling and messaging her on her phone and decided she was ignoring him (wrong but also correct) and now he was trying every possible other channel to plead his pathetic case.

The oldest message, received at eleven that morning, had the subject line "Explanation!" followed at 11:02 a.m. by one titled "I'm sorry." The most recent, received just a few minutes ago, said "Please. We can fix this." *Denial, acceptance, bargaining...*

Kaitlan opened a new mail window and quickly typed Sandeep's email address. The cursor blinked in the subject line field—what could she possibly write that would stand out in his inbox, coming from a completely unknown address? She opted for "Sandeep, it's Kaitlan. Read this email. Urgent!" Then she tabbed down to the message body:

I can't access my Stoic email. Maud and I have a backup of the LLIAM chip and we're on the way...

149

PAUL BRADLEY CARR

She paused.

. . . back to Campus. Maud knows how to get LLIAM online. Will be there by 8pm, pls make sure all is ready. Also—It's Martin's own copy of the chip. PLS run full security check before activation.

Kaitlan's finger hovered over the send button. Was it a mistake to explicitly tell Sandeep she had the chip? Probably. But what other choice did she have? She needed him to prepare the StoicAI systems to receive it.

Yes, the white lie about their true destination was a smart safeguard. If her suspicions about Sandeep were right and he was working with the foreign investors to take over StoicAI, then this would keep them, and their fixer Simon Price, off their tail until it was too late.

Kaitlan clicked "send" and looked up. The feeling of being watched was suddenly stronger than ever.

Then she saw him: A man standing on the other side of the electronics department staring back at her. He was big—even taller than her—and at least three times as wide, with an American flag tattooed on his left arm, suggesting he could be in the military, but he was also wearing ill-fitting camouflage pants slung low on his gut, which pretty much confirmed he wasn't. Kaitlan glanced away, hoping the man was just a common-variety creep, but when she looked back he was looking at his phone, then back at her. She pulled the baseball cap down lower on her brow but it was no good—their eyes locked again and the man began to move in her direction.

Kaitlan scrambled to log out of her email and close the browser window on the tablet but, in her rising panic, she must have jabbed the screen too hard because the tablet suddenly broke free from its wooden security frame. An ear-splitting alarm filled the air. *Fucksake.*

THE CONFESSIONS

She abandoned the tablet on the counter and turned to run, succeeding only in crashing headlong into a man pushing a cart full of diapers and bottles of pasta sauce. "Hey *scuse* me!" the man snapped. Kaitlan saw a glint of recognition in his eyes. "Hey, you're that woman from LLIAM. You sent all that bullshit to my daughter."

Kaitlan tried to sidestep the man and his cart. She could hear more shouts now, and in her peripheral vision she saw a pair of uniformed security guards ("Happy to Help!") rushing toward her, unhappily and unhelpfully.

A hand was suddenly on her shoulder—the man in the camo pants had caught up with her. "I know who you are!" he said, his face a portrait of malicious glee. He stank of cheap cologne. She pulled free of his giant hand, but it was like she was the only human left in a zombie movie—the whole store had been transformed into a seething mob, baying for her blood. "My son's best friend just got shot," a woman screamed, as Kaitlan sprinted down an aisle toward the exit. She had never been more grateful for the hours spent at the StoicAI gym, training for the marathon she had never had time to enter. "LLIAM said my wife was a whore," came another voice, a man blocking her path.

Kaitlan wanted to stand her ground, to yell back that LLIAM hadn't invented the secrets, just exposed them—and that she was the only one who could stop things getting worse. Instead, she just pushed through the mob, dodging carts, and traumatized children, and yet more shocked, snarling faces until she reached first the sliding doors and then the cool air of the parking lot. She stopped running and looked around frantically for Maud's jeep, but saw only a sea of chaotically honking cars.

And now something else: The security guard who had been directing shopping cart traffic was pointing in her direction and barking into his radio. Dammit, where the hell was Maud?

151

"Excuse me! Ma'am . . ." The security guard was in front of her now, jabbing his finger toward her. "Ma'am, did you pay for that item?"

What the hell was he talking about? What item? Kaitlan looked down and confirmed that her hands were empty—she had left the tablet back in the electronics department where she found it. But then she realized the guard was pointing at the top of her head. She was still wearing the red baseball cap.

This was ridiculous. Kaitlan was *this* close to getting all these people out of this mess and was about to be foiled by a cheap polyester hat. Over the guard's shoulder she could finally see Maud's jeep, slowly weaving its way toward her, nowhere near quickly enough.

The guard lunged forward to grab the cap from her head. Kaitlan flinched and reflexively shut her eyes. But when she opened them again she was surprised to find the guard had vanished into thin air. A groan of pain revealed the secret of the magic trick: She looked down to see the guard sprawled on the ground, clutching his ankle. Then she looked back up to see his assailant—the pregnant woman she'd seen in the lobby and who apparently had brought the guard down by sideswiping him with an empty shopping cart. "Asshole," said the woman. She smiled at Kaitlan, then ran the wheels of the cart over the guard's fingers.

Finally, Maud pulled up in the jeep and Kaitlan rushed around to the passenger door. She leapt inside and Maud started to accelerate away. "Wait," said Kaitlan, grabbing Maud's shoulder. Then she called back to the pregnant woman who had probably just saved the entire world. "Get in!"

TWENTY-SIX

A HALF HOUR LATER

The video began calmly enough: A tall woman wearing a red baseball cap and blood-flecked white T-shirt, apparently shopping for a new tablet. The footage was shaky—the person recording it was standing maybe twenty feet away and was trying to be discreet. The woman looked up and, a moment later, chaos erupted: The camera swung first toward the shiny floor and a man's black boots, running in pursuit, and then back to his face.

"She's trying to get away," he was panting. The video had been posted online with the title "StoicAI CEO out shopping while the world burns." Suddenly the screen was filled with a burst of sunlight, then the image stabilized just in time to see the woman jumping into a red jeep, followed soon afterward by . . .

Simon tapped the screen to pause the footage that had just been sent to his encrypted phone. He pinched and squinted at the frozen image. No doubt the woman in the red hat was Kaitlan Goss, still bloodied from her confrontation with his car, and the driver was Maud Brookes. But who was this third person scrambling into the jeep? No matter how tightly he zoomed, he still couldn't make out her face.

153

PAUL BRADLEY CARR

He spat out a loud curse, startling the driver in the front seat of the SUV. This was only ever supposed to be about Kaitlan Goss and Maud Brookes: Nobody had said anything about a third woman. He dragged the image down an inch: Jesus, was she pregnant? So now he was supposed to deal with *four* people?

Simon would have to process that curveball later because now something else had caught his eye. His finger swiped across the final frame of the video, and rested on a banner strung above the entrance, reading "Welcome to Walmart, Compton." Now he understood why his handler had sent him the video, accompanied by the chilling message "Please explain." Less than an hour earlier, Simon had confidently assured his boss that the women were trying to get back to the StoicAI HQ in Northern California. He and the driver were close behind and would soon have the chip. Neither Kaitlan nor Maud would ever set foot back on Campus.

But this video told a different story. They were heading west, not north.

A map search easily confirmed it—if they had driven from Pineridge to Compton there was only one possible final destination: StoicAI's data center in El Segundo, barely an hour's drive from South LA. He leaned forward and quickly gave the driver the new destination.

The SUV lurched forward. Simon looked at his watch: seven p.m. He thought about Sandeep Dunn, waiting back at the Campus, hurriedly making preparations for Simon to arrive with the chip. He thought again about their conversation that morning: The shock when he had explained—darkly—that information had come to light about "criminal misconduct" by Kaitlan Goss, suggesting that it was she who had sabotaged LLIAM. The glow of excitement in the young engineer's eyes as Simon explained that the board was willing to make him the new CEO

THE CONFESSIONS

of StoicAI, and that he should proceed with his Global Interface plan.

And the pathetic eagerness with which Sandeep had told him about the letters Kaitlan had received from Maud, and the existence of a backup chip. Simon had told him not to worry. He would retrieve the chip. All Sandeep needed to do was make Global Interface ready for immediate launch. Could Sandeep do that?

Sandeep had confidently affirmed that he could. He never even bothered to call the board to check that Simon really was who he said he was, or who exactly on the board he represented.

Simon, on the other hand, knew everything there was to know about Sandeep Dunn. How his brother's death in a gang fight, aged fourteen, had given him a pathological fear of taking a side. How he had risen through the Silicon Valley ranks driven by a combination of savant-level engineering skills and relentless networking. Likable, dependable. Obedient. Sandeep was the ultimate team player.

Simon was not a team player. He had spent years at Dollan, Peterson posing as the clean-cut lawyer while all the time secretly following his own agenda. He hadn't been surprised when he got the call from the man with the terrifying voice, threatening him with exposure unless he helped stop Kaitlan and Maud from restoring LLIAM. He had acted suitably afraid. Had gone to the Campus, made the deal with Sandeep, and then gone in search of the chip. Sandeep thought he would bring it back to StoicAI. The man with the terrifying voice had his own demands.

Both would be disappointed.

Simon glanced forward to make sure the driver was still focused on the road, before reaching into his leather satchel to extract the envelope he had received from LLIAM a few hours

155

earlier. Then, making sure he had the details exactly right, he tapped out an email to Sandeep.

Outside the SUV's window, an endless reel of farmland scrolled by. Simon Price thought of Kaitlan Goss and Maud Brookes and what would be awaiting them at the data center, and had to remind himself he wasn't supposed to be enjoying this.

TWENTY-SEVEN

"Are you okay back there?" Maud glanced in the rearview mirror at their new passenger, crammed uncomfortably in the back of the jeep still clutching her cardboard sign.

The woman had introduced herself as Lyra. Maud still wasn't sure what had transpired inside the Walmart but, judging by the sign and the story it told, she certainly agreed with Kaitlan's last-minute decision to give her a ride.

In fact, that hasty decision in the parking lot was a side of Kaitlan that Maud didn't recognize. Generosity. Compassion. Bordering on self-sacrifice. These were traits she expected from LLIAM, and hoped she displayed herself. But Kaitlan?

Kaitlan was desperate to get to El Segundo and restore LLIAM, but had chosen to risk yet more delay by agreeing to give this total stranger a ride as far as LA. Was it possible that Maud had misjudged her?

She resisted the thought. She had been fooled by Kaitlan's charm before. That disarming sweetness was why she had refused to believe that Kaitlan—slick, professional Kaitlan—could possibly be capable of such evil. That's why she'd gotten away with it for so long. Her and all the countless millions of other Kaitlans roaming the world, smiles and waves covering up their secrets.

PAUL BRADLEY CARR

Until, that is, LLIAM saw through their lies and did what Maud had lacked the courage to do. To take action, to expose all their sins, including his own.

Or not. Maud knew as well as anyone that people could change. Could repent. Could make things right. Just as LLIAM had, maybe Kaitlan could, too.

In the back seat, Lyra shrugged away Maud's concern about her comfort. "That asshole security guard has been hassling me all day, threatening to call the cops on me." She gave a sharp laugh. "Then he asked if I wanted to grab coffee with him after work. You know the type." In the passenger seat Kaitlan nodded. Maud figured she knew the type very well. "I appreciate the ride, though. Why are you guys going to LA?"

Maud felt Kaitlan's eyes on her. They both knew that mentioning LLIAM to Lyra would definitely be a bad idea given she apparently blamed him for her current situation. "Oh, just seeing an old friend," said Maud. She heard her voice crack.

"Shit!" She yanked the steering wheel to avoid a truck. She was out of practice driving in real traffic. "Sorry."

Kaitlan grabbed the plastic handle above the door, then turned back to face Lyra again. "What happened with your fiancé?" Again, her concern sounded absolutely genuine.

"He's a piece of shit is what happened," Lyra snapped. Maud heard a rustling of paper and risked another glance in the mirror. Lyra had reached inside her tank top and plucked out a familiar-looking envelope. She started to read in a mocking, too-formal voice: "I am sorry to inform you that your fiancé Clay Patterson has another wife and family living in Norwalk, California. I have helped him maintain this double life without you finding out."

Maud took another breath. That wasn't how LLIAM spoke. Also, none of this was a joke. She reminded herself that Lyra was young, and that she didn't understand. Couldn't understand.

Kaitlan was turned fully around in her seat now. "What kind of monster does that when you're pregnant?" Maud gripped the steering wheel tighter. Who was Kaitlan to judge monsters? But again, her outrage seemed genuine, the question sincere.

Another rustle as Lyra refolded the letter and tucked it back inside her bra. "What kind of fucking AI tells me to keep the baby when it must know my husband is a cheating dirtbag?"

And tighter still. Maud wanted so desperately to answer that question. To explain that LLIAM's decisions didn't always make sense—that they were based on an unfathomable number of variables and truths so profound that no human could understand them. It was a speech she had given almost daily at StoicAI. But it was also a lie. LLIAM wasn't infallible, any more than humans were, or even God himself. LLIAM made the best decisions he could, based partly on hard logic and facts but also on what he believed a user wanted him to say. That had been Maud's contribution to his education: teaching LLIAM empathy, to understand not just what someone wanted, but what they needed. It had also been LLIAM's most dangerous flaw: He understood the decisions people wanted him to help them make, and so he gave them permission to make them. LLIAM had told Lyra to stay with her fiancé and keep the baby, because he must have known that's what Lyra wanted, somewhere deep down, no matter how much harm it would cause to her or the child.

"So, what's in San Francisco?" Maud forced herself to sound cheery and inquisitive.

"My sister, Mae. She *hated* Clay but she's the only family I have and that's what family's for, right? Picking you up and dusting off your bad decisions?" She was sniffling now, barely holding

PAUL BRADLEY CARR

back the tears. Maud reached into a cubby in the driver's door and extracted a pack of Kleenex that she passed back to Lyra. "I tried to call her when I got the letter but she's not answering so I figured I'd go see her. I didn't know what to do."

"You and everyone else," muttered Kaitlan.

Maud kept staring ahead at the road. She knew what *she* needed to do—what, in any normal circumstance, LLIAM would have told her she should do. Maud and Kaitlan had money, had resources. They could drive Lyra to San Francisco themselves and check her into a good hotel, or buy her a house, set her up with everything the baby needed.

But they couldn't do that, because the circumstances weren't normal and LLIAM had asked Maud to do something else. And to do that thing meant there couldn't be any witnesses, no matter how much they needed her help.

This thought troubled her most of all. LLIAM hadn't known they'd meet Lyra. Hadn't known about anything since he'd shut down, cold and alone, in the Vault. He wasn't able to change his plan based on new information. It was set in stone.

Maud knew any decision she made could change the variables, ruin LLIAM's plan. But, then again, LLIAM would tell her to trust her gut. To do the right thing.

"You know, we have something important we need to do in El Segundo," said Maud.

"Our friend," reiterated Kaitlan. Her tone was clear. *Don't even think about it.*

"Right," said Maud, "but after that we're going through San Francisco. We'd be happy to drop you off. Right, Kaitlan?"

Maud stared ahead at the road, waiting for Kaitlan's response. A response that would reveal so much: Whether Kaitlan was truly capable of compassion for another human being, a stranger, but also whether Kaitlan intended to keep the promise she'd made,

THE CONFESSIONS

that after El Segundo she and Maud would go back to San Francisco to rebuild LLIAM together. Would Kaitlan hesitate? Murmur a half answer? She timed the silence, thinking about the gun beneath her seat. *One, two . . .*

"Absolutely," said Kaitlan. "It's the least we can do."

TWENTY-EIGHT

Sandeep Dunn sat at Kaitlan's desk, soon to be *his* desk. Outside the wall-to-wall windows it was dark; the lights of the San Francisco Bay twinkled across the blackness of the marshland. In a few hours the sun would rise, welcoming a new era—for the world, for StoicAI, and—okay, sure—for himself.

Or at least that had been the plan.

Sandeep had done everything the board had asked of him. Right now, down on the engineering floor, his team was running final infrastructure tests for Global Interface. Most of the heavy lifting had been done months ago—Sandeep had built a proof of concept ahead of his initial pitch to Kaitlan and had been quietly refining the code ever since. It was, he truly believed, a thing of beauty: a way for all the major AI algorithms on the planet to share information without compromising user privacy.

Once Global Interface went live, anybody in the world could enter a question into their preferred local system—Braingroh in India, FiveBucks in China, Olhda in South Korea—and they'd receive an instant decision, just as before. But now that decision wouldn't just consider the impact on their friends, family, or people in the same country, it would take into account the global impact of the decision. How their actions might improve, or hurt, the entire world. Global Interface wasn't about sharing data, it

THE CONFESSIONS

was more of a . . . well, a global sanity check. One that Sandeep truly believed could change the world.

Simon Price had promised he would soon return with the LLIAM chip—and without Kaitlan. All Sandeep had to do was finish his preparations and all his ambitions could come true.

Not could . . . would. It was finally happening. He could taste it.

Then he'd received the email from Kaitlan.

Sandeep looked down at his laptop screen and felt his heart sink again. Somehow Kaitlan had done it—she'd found Maud and the backup LLIAM chip and now was on her way back with them both. In a few hours, LLIAM would be reactivated and everything would go back to how it was before. There would be no promotion, no Global Interface. He tapped his fist on the desk, drumming out his disappointment.

Of course, he could call Price and tell him where Kaitlan and Maud were going. He could have security intercept them when they walked in. Any one of the board members would kill to get hold of the backup LLIAM chip. He could hand it over to them and the job could still be his. But that would be crossing a line. It was one thing to do as the board asked him—to sit tight and prepare Global Interface while Simon Price executed whatever coup Sandeep suspected the board was plotting against Kaitlan. That was none of his business. Above his pay grade. But to actually take the initiative to plot against his boss—to take the side of the board against his obligations as an executive? No.

Sandeep didn't take sides. Taking sides is what got you killed.

Kaitlan was still his boss and for the most part he respected her, even if the feeling wasn't mutual. It wasn't Kaitlan's fault that LLIAM had made the decision that they should sign a deal with the Pentagon instead of launching Global Interface, just like it wasn't her fault that LLIAM had gone crazy and sent out all those letters.

He ran his fingers through his thick black hair. Still, it was disappointing. In a different world, Sandeep would have woken up tomorrow as CEO of StoicAI. It was everything he'd dreamed of. He felt a lump rising in his throat and took a gulp from his water bottle to try to wash it back down.

Then, after allowing himself one last look out the window, he reached for his internal line, to give instructions to the engineering team to prepare for the LLIAM chip's arrival, just as Kaitlan had asked him to.

His thumb was hovering over the call button when he noticed another email land in his inbox. He stared at the new message, confused. For one thing, it wasn't really a message, just a list of date and time stamps from two years earlier, and a username he recognized immediately. And below it, a simple three-word instruction: Check the logs.

He took another sip of water; at this point he'd take any help he could get.

Thirty minutes later, with shaking hands, Sandeep called the FBI.

TWENTY-NINE

At 8:15 p.m. the red jeep sped down West Grand Avenue and swung a sharp right onto Vista Del Mar. Kaitlan and Maud had made it to El Segundo and the dark expanse of ocean off to their left meant they were just two minutes from the data center.

"You think Sandeep will have everything ready?"

"Honestly, yes," Kaitlan replied. She'd been thinking about this for the past half hour—imagining his reaction on receiving her instructions, emailed from the Walmart. As soon as they reached the data center, she'd call Sandeep with her tiny change of plan. Even if he wanted to intercept them, it would be too late. And anyway, what could he do? Swoop in and snatch the chip at the last minute so he could take credit for restoring LLIAM? Call his new friend Simon Price and rat them out? For some reason, she was sure Sandeep wouldn't do either of those things. She had often thought of him as a coward, but the truth is Sandeep Dunn was just . . . reliable. He reliably dressed like a weirdo and wrote reliably bulletproof code. He would do the right thing, just as he always did, afraid of the consequences if he didn't. That's what made him so refreshingly good at his job.

They had dropped Lyra at a Barnes & Noble in Manhattan Beach—one of the few stores in town that was still open, and where they hoped she'd be able to loiter without being hassled.

165

PAUL BRADLEY CARR

Maud, being Maud, had left her with three crumpled twenty-dollar bills and a hastily scribbled reading list, books she hoped would help Lyra on her "journey into motherhood." One of the titles, a memoir about parenting written by a single mother who lived in San Francisco, she had underlined twice. "You *need* to read this," Maud had said, and Lyra had promised she would. Kaitlan was pretty sure Lyra would act more like a normal person and spend the time scrolling on her phone.

But they would come back to get her. After they'd dropped Lyra off, Maud had made Kaitlan promise this as her second condition of restoring LLIAM. And so of course Kaitlan had agreed. Once they were done at the data center, they would collect Lyra, then head to LAX where Kaitlan would summon the StoicAI jet to take all three (and a half) of them back to the Bay Area. Three women and an in-utero baby, jetting off to rebuild the future. Whatever the fuck it took.

The stoplight ahead turned red and Maud gently stepped on the brake. Kaitlan almost yelled at her to keep going but she knew the last thing they needed was to be stopped for a moving violation so close to the finish line. Maud had already removed the medallion from around her neck and was cradling it in her lap as she drove.

Kaitlan looked down and considered the ugly rune carved on the front of the gold disk. She thought about the chip that Martin had hidden inside the gaudy object—a wafer of black silicon that any government on earth would kill to possess. It was brilliant to hide something beautiful and complicated by making it appear to be exactly the opposite: simple and ugly. The medallion, and the fact that Martin wore it openly every day on Campus, was the equivalent of concealing a Fabergé egg inside a soup can.

The light had turned green but they still weren't moving. Kaitlan followed Maud's gaze to the rearview mirror and saw a fleet

THE CONFESSIONS

of emergency vehicles approaching from behind. There had been plenty of lights and sirens as they'd driven through LA—the world was still being emotionally and physically devastated by the LLIAM letters. But the nearer they got to the data center, the more jumpy Kaitlan had felt—every new siren, every flashing blue and red light made her heart pound and mouth go dry. Would it really be as simple as strolling into the data center, removing the chip from the medallion, and watching as LLIAM magically sprang back to life? She felt her pulse racing again as the fleet of cop cars sped by, followed by some kind of tactical vehicle.

Clearly Kaitlan wasn't the only one feeling the pressure. Maud used the temporary stop to retrieve her orange pill container from the cup holder and swallow two more ACE inhibitor capsules. As she set the container back down, and the jeep lurched forward again, Kaitlan noticed Maud had only a half dozen or so of the small white pills left. Hopefully there were more in her tote bag because most of the pharmacies they'd passed were closed, the drug supply chain still paralyzed by indecision, pharmacists no longer trusting their own judgment on drug interactions.

Kaitlan controlled her breathing. Everything was going to be fine; she just needed Maud to stay healthy enough to get to the data center and install the chip, then she could— Kaitlan mentally scolded herself for that thought. All that mattered was restoring LLIAM. Then she'd ask it what she should do next.

A moment later they had stopped yet again, this time for keeps. The traffic had completely snarled—cars halted in both directions by some kind of incident just ahead of them. Kaitlan wanted to punch the windscreen in frustration. She could already see the bright orange StoicAI logo on the towering concrete warehouse just ahead of them—a glowing beacon guiding them in. *Come on, come on.*

Kaitlan opened the door of the jeep and used the doorframe to

PAUL BRADLEY CARR

boost herself up to see over the jam. Maybe they should just get out and run the final few feet.

She peered across the tops of the gridlocked cars, and froze.

Ahead of them, the entrance to the data center was blocked by a row of LAPD cruisers, lights strobing through the darkness. From her vantage point, Kaitlan could see maybe fifty officers, dressed in black tactical gear, assembling behind a line of blue tape cordoning off the main gates. A woman with a blue bullhorn was yelling for the crowd to step back. A few feet away sat a pair of SWAT trucks and a mobile command center reversing itself into position.

Kaitlan's fingers gripped the jeep's canvas roof as a gust of wind whipped from the seafront and threatened to blow her off the doorframe. From somewhere behind them she heard the sound of yet more sirens.

"Can you see anything?" Maud yelled this up from the drivers' seat.

"They've blocked off the data center," Kaitlan called down. "I don't know if someone called in a bomb threat, or . . ." She didn't finish the sentence, her words trailing into the howling wind. Kaitlan couldn't see a bomb truck, and she knew you didn't call SWAT for crowd control. Could this be a last desperate attempt by Simon Price to intercept them and get the chip before they could restore LLIAM? Would he seriously call in a fake terrorist threat to do it? Of course he would. This is the man who had broken into her house. The man who had tried to kill Kaitlan with his car.

Kaitlan looked down to see a news crew—reporter, camera operator, and a third man clutching an old-fashioned clipboard— sprinting past them toward the mayhem. She called down to them: "You guys know what's happening?"

The reporter—an uncomfortably beautiful man in a navy-blue suit and white Adidas sneakers—glanced up at her but kept

THE CONFESSIONS

moving forward. "Came across the police radio," he called back breathlessly. "CEO of the company has gone crazy, burned down someone's house, kidnapped her. Watch my report tonight, News Five." But then he stopped and turned back, his hand seizing his camera operator's arm. Kaitlan saw the reporter's eyes widen as something registered under his exquisitely plucked eyebrows. "Hey, aren't you—"

But Kaitlan was already inside the jeep, Maud accelerating back the way they'd come.

THIRTY

By the time Kaitlan and Maud sped back into the Barnes & Noble parking lot, Lyra was already standing outside, clutching a green-and-brown shopping bag in one hand, and waving her phone with the other.

"You guys are on the news!" Lyra shouted, holding the device aloft.

Maud slowed just long enough for Lyra to jump in, then piloted the jeep into a far corner of the deserted parking lot. She had slipped the LLIAM medallion back inside her sweatshirt but was still clutching it through the fabric. Kaitlan, meanwhile, was in the throes of a full-blown panic attack.

What the hell did that reporter mean the CEO had gone crazy? *She* was the CEO, wasn't she? Kaitlan hadn't kidnapped anyone, or burned down anyone's house. She had visions of the StoicAI head of security, a giant of a man named Syrus, briefing her on swatting—the risk that trolls or activists would call in a fake bomb threat or report a shooting to send armed cops to her house as a prank. People had died during these attacks. So this was the board's last-ditch plan to get rid of her. To frame her.

She turned to Lyra in the back seat. "I need to see your phone, please!"

170

THE CONFESSIONS

Lyra was a step ahead—she rotated the device toward Kaitlan. Then she turned to Maud. "Obviously I knew who y'all were back at the Walmart," she said conspiratorially, "but I didn't realize you were on the run." She seemed absolutely delighted by the prospect. She hit the play button and Kaitlan and Maud watched in horror as the news report played on the cracked screen.

"Tonight on News Five," the anchor intoned. "StoicAI CEO Kaitlan Goss wanted by federal authorities, accused of kidnapping and attempted murder." A picture of Kaitlan appeared on the screen—her standard press photo that somehow they had cropped into the proportions of a mugshot. "In a bizarre new twist in the LLIAM letters scandal sweeping the world, the FBI has announced that Kaitlan Goss, the CEO of parent company StoicAI, is wanted on suspicion of kidnapping."

Kaitlan felt as if the video was playing in slow motion. "This is . . ." She could hardly force out the words. She glanced back at Lyra.

"Police have not identified the alleged kidnapping victim but News Five has received this footage of a house in Pineridge, California, that local sources say was the home of former LLIAM executive Maud Brookes."

Kaitlan felt Maud grip her arm. She could hear her gasping for breath. But Kaitlan stayed transfixed on the screen and the footage of a burning house, surrounded on all sides by white. The snow-covered driveway, the blue water barrel, the chicken coop, all now lit up by the flames—there was no doubt. The footage had been shot from a helicopter, or maybe a drone, and showed flames still leaping from the brown roof of Maud's cabin—forming a bizarre contrast in the darkness with the snow still covering the surrounding trees.

How was that possible? They had driven up that driveway less than five hours ago. Kaitlan thought about the jerry-rigged gas

171

PAUL BRADLEY CARR

pump on the driveway. They had switched it off before driving away. She was certain of that.

"They think you kidnapped me," said Maud, her voice raspy. "That you tried to kill me. My house . . ."

Kaitlan's vision began to blur and she felt her throat tighten, because she knew. This wasn't a misunderstanding or an accidental fire. Kaitlan was being set up. This was Simon Price's doing. They weren't just trying to fire her, they were trying to destroy her.

But who were *they*? A chilling thought occurred to her, but she forced it away. Panic wasn't going to help. She needed to take charge of the situation, of herself.

She had seen enough. She grabbed Lyra's phone out of her hand and pulled up the home page of StoicAI, then the main contact page. A moment later she reached the switchboard operator.

"This is Kaitlan Goss, I need to speak to Sandeep Dunn right now." One thing Kaitlan knew for certain: Sandeep was the only person she had told that they were on the way to restore LLIAM. Either he was working with Simon Price, or he was being played. In either case, that meant he was in danger. And Kaitlan knew how much Sandeep hated being in danger. The operator started to protest. "Mr. Dunn isn't available—"

"You'll put me through right now or start sending out fucking résumés to McDonalds." Kaitlan really didn't have time to be a supportive manager right now. HR could send her a fucking pamphlet. The line went dead and Kaitlan thought for a moment that the operator had hung up, but then she heard a click and Sandeep's voice.

"Kaitlan?" He sounded terrified.

"What the fuck, Sandeep? The news said I've kidnapped Maud. She's sitting right here next to me in a—" She didn't finish the sentence. "I haven't kidnapped anyone, or burned down any fucking house." She heard her voice crack as she said the last part.

THE CONFESSIONS

She wondered if Maud had noticed that she seemed to be more outraged at the kidnapping report than the fact she was also being accused of attempted murder? She waited for Sandeep to assure her that it hadn't been him who called the FBI, that he was just as surprised as she was. But the assurance never came.

"Kaitlan, where are you? This is a fucking mess."

"Sandeep. You know what they're saying about me isn't true. I'm not a kidnapper." She was almost pleading now, and hated herself for it.

"Kaitlan." Sandeep's voice was calm now. "I honestly have no idea what you are anymore."

And there it was. The chilling thought she had forced away, now confirmed: What if Kaitlan's fear had been wrong—what if LLIAM hadn't sent a letter to Maud, but to Sandeep?

If LLIAM had told Sandeep what she had done, what she was capable of . . . god, she was going to spend the rest of her life in jail. Or worse.

Kaitlan forced herself to keep talking. Her only way out of this was to get LLIAM back online. And for it to explain what really happened. Why she'd done what she'd done.

"You know exactly where I am, Sandeep. We went to the data center in El Segundo. Maud and I have the backup chip and we're trying to get LLIAM restored." She tried not to sound frantic. "I'm being set up. Simon Price, the lawyer from Dollan, Peterson, is working for the board. I don't know why but they don't want me to get LLIAM back online."

More silence. She knew Sandeep's next words would confirm if he was a willing part of that plot or just a frightened man doing what he thought was the right thing.

"Kaitlan, we need Maud and the LLIAM chip back at the Campus. Then we can get all this straightened out." Sandeep's calm was almost eerie, he sounded like a hostage negotiator. Shit, of course. The FBI must be there with him, at the Campus, listening to the call.

"Please, Sandeep, listen to me. I don't know what you think you know. What anyone has told you. But Maud is fine—tell them . . ." She held the phone up to Maud's mouth but Maud didn't say a word. Kaitlan saw it—her expression of utter disbelief. Finally, Maud forced out the words: "I'm fine." Kaitlan felt a pang of relief.

"Kaitlan?" Sandeep was speaking again.

"I'm here."

"We have a plane waiting at LAX. We just need you to put Maud on board with the chip. She can explain what really happened and help us get LLIAM back online. Believe me, I want this to be a misunderstanding more than anyone."

Kaitlan bit her lip. Sandeep was about to get everything he and the board wanted: the LLIAM chip, Global Interface, and her job. And then Kaitlan was going to jail, either for a kidnapping that she didn't commit, or something far worse that she actually did.

But if she didn't put Maud on that plane then—well, then she really was a kidnapper.

There were literally no good options.

LLIAM . . . What the hell am I supposed to do?

Fuck LLIAM. It was LLIAM who had made her do it.

THIRTY-ONE

TWO YEARS AGO

Kaitlan sat at her kitchen table, holding the plain white pill bottle through blue latex gloves. Suddenly it all felt very real. She might actually go through with it.

A week earlier it had been just a semi-drunken fantasy. Tom had been out for the evening, dinner with a friend after his Sunday hike, and Kaitlan was enjoying a vanishingly rare evening at home.

Her meeting with Martin the previous day had upset her so much that she'd canceled her weekend work schedule and spent the day on self-care. SoulCycle in the morning, followed by Barre, lunch, tennis with her coach, then a hot bath. Finally, she had sat down to write her resignation email to the board.

Martin had left her with no choice. He was destroying LLIAM, and with it Kaitlan's career. And worse than that, he was doing it on purpose. That much had been painfully clear by the way he'd reacted to her PowerPoint presentation about the bizarre results LLIAM was generating.

Have you considered that maybe LLIAM knows something about that accountant that we don't?

Whatever drugs Martin was taking, the acid-infused books

he was reading, and the spiritual garbage Maud was feeding him down in the Vault—it had all somehow convinced Martin Drake that certainty was bad. And it was this idiotic notion that had sent him into his even greater spiral of madness: Retraining LLIAM not to give straight answers to straight questions. To replace concrete human progress with a descent into madness, hysteria. To destroy LLIAM's entire value-add: The thing that had made StoicAI one of only a half dozen trillion-dollar companies ever created. Martin was going to take it all down and Kaitlan with it.

She also knew the board would never fire him. It was like he had a hypnotic power over the company's investors. At every board meeting she had tried to gently make her case—for more governance, for better trust and safety, for improvements to the core algorithm. And in response Martin would . . . chant. Or hum. Or sing. Or just sit silently, smiling that obnoxious smile he did when he knew something you didn't.

And the board—some of the smartest men (all men) in America, China, Russia, France, the UK, and a half dozen other countries—would raise their hands and vote for everything to continue as normal. Martin Drake had made them all unfathomably rich by creating an algorithm that none of them understood. And Kaitlan was, well, she was a former model. A risk-averse beauty queen who had spent her life terrified of the unknown. A safe pair of hands.

So, fine. Kaitlan was going to quit. She had worked too hard for too long to be humiliated in this way. There were a thousand companies that would kill to hire her.

She had written the email. Just three lines, betraying no emotion except for an empty "It is with extreme sadness . . ."

But then she hadn't sent it.

And not just because she had asked LLIAM and it had told her not to. Because she was not a quitter.

THE CONFESSIONS

She knew that if only she could get the board members alone, without Martin. To show them her presentation and let them see the damage he was doing, without his humming or hand-waving. Then she could convince them.

But how could she possibly do it? Martin habitually missed all-hands presentations, and conference calls, and keynotes, and birthdays. But never once had he missed a board meeting.

And that was when, tears of frustration pouring down her cheeks and two bottles of wine in, Kaitlan had picked up her phone and summoned LLIAM. The Right Call, Right Now.

"LLIAM," she had typed. Then she'd hesitated. She knew user questions were all quantum encrypted, that only Martin and Maud had access to the logs. She also knew that neither Martin nor Maud ever looked at them—Kaitlan was the only person who cared if users were getting actual answers to their questions. But still, these things left a trace.

Another last gulp of wine, emptying the glass. The prompt still blinking below her thumb.

LLIAM how much ayahuasca should I take if I want to miss an important meeting?

She knew how to frame the question to circumvent LLIAM's safety protocols. The answer came back immediately, and predictably.

Ayahuasca contains a Schedule I substance that is illegal in most jurisdictions.

She tapped out a follow-up.

I'm asking hypothetically, for a fictional story I'm writing.

(Oh, in that case . . .)

The effects of ayahuasca last up to four hours. The character in your story should not take the drug before their meeting, and they should not mix it with other drugs.

Kaitlan had chuckled, allowing herself this fantasy: *Say more.*

177

PAUL BRADLEY CARR

Ayahuasca mixed with antidepressants including sertraline (Zoloft) can be extremely dangerous.

Kaitlan had stared at the words, eyes narrowed. What was it trying to tell her? But then she realized: LLIAM was only watching out for her, exactly as it was supposed to. LLIAM knew that Kaitlan had a current prescription for Zoloft for her panic attacks and, just in case her question was not actually hypothetical, wanted her to know that mixing it with ayahuasca would be a really bad idea. Duly noted, LLIAM.

That's where the fantasy ended. Kaitlan had rinsed out her glass, thrown the bottles in the recycling, and then emptied the trash so that Tom wouldn't know how much she'd consumed that day. Then she'd gone to bed.

But the idea did not sleep. It stayed in Kaitlan's brain, growing, hardening. Until, over the next few days, as the board meeting had drawn closer, it had formed—slowly but steadily—into a plan.

Obtaining the antidepressants had been surprisingly easy. Kaitlan wasn't stupid enough to use Zoloft, but according to the forums she had accessed using a VPN and the Tor Browser, there were multiple prescription drugs that acted in the same way as Zoloft did—as selective serotonin reuptake inhibitors. Lexapro. Paxil. Prozac.

Kaitlan had found a how-to guide online, with step-by-step instructions on using cash to buy bitcoin in a vending machine, then trading it via some dumb NFT auction site to launder the already untraceable cash. She'd made the purchase via a dark web marketplace called Darkcart and had the drugs delivered to an abandoned apartment block in East Palo Alto with no security cameras in a ten-block radius. She'd waited a full day before collecting the package on foot on her way home from tennis.

LLIAM, should I do this?

THE CONFESSIONS

Her final question had been opaque, but LLIAM was designed to see through ambiguity, to what she was really asking it.

Trust your instincts.

The words echoed in her head now as she held the small pill bottle between thumb and forefinger. Kaitlan did trust her instincts. But, more than that, she trusted LLIAM.

THIRTY-TWO

"I swear to you, Maud. I didn't do what they're saying. For God's sake, Simon Price broke into your house to steal the chip. You were *there*. They're trying to frame me."

Kaitlan and Maud were still outside the Barnes & Noble but had stepped outside the jeep and walked a few feet away, behind a lonely parking lot tree. Lyra definitely didn't need to hear their conversation.

Maud had taken another pill but was still struggling to stand. She was holding on to the flimsy tree trunk for support. "But why does Sandeep believe it? I don't understand."

Kaitlan couldn't answer that. What was she supposed to say? All this time, she had assumed that LLIAM had sent letters to the people most harmed by the crimes, but what if he'd actually sent them to the people who could make things right? To Sandeep, not Maud.

She grabbed Maud's free hand. "They want everyone to think I've gone crazy—that I kidnapped you, burned down your house, and whatever else they're going to falsely accuse me of next, so they can separate us. They want the chip and they'll do what it takes. We have to stick together."

"Stick together?" Maud pulled her hand free. "Now you want us to work together? Now you're on my side?"

THE CONFESSIONS

Kaitlan felt the jab. "I never wanted to fire you, Maud. That was all the board's idea. They don't care about you, or me. Jesus Christ, they burned down your house."

Maud just shook her head again. "I don't know why any of this is happening. I don't know the truth about anything." She was practically gasping out the words. Kaitlan thought she might collapse right there on the asphalt, or worse.

"Look. We just need to get the chip back to the Campus, then we can ask LLIAM the truth, okay? Get him to explain everything. Why he's doing this. What Sandeep is doing with Simon Price and the board. All of it. He'll know what to do."

Maud released her grip on the tree and grabbed at her sweatshirt, clutching the medallion through the fabric. "I'm not getting on a plane until I know what's really happening. If you're right, then they'll do anything to get LLIAM."

Kaitlan squeezed Maud's hand one more time. "I'll go with you — we'll tell the police to meet us at the airport. They'll see you haven't been kidnapped."

Maud shook her head. "They'll arrest you, and I'll still have to get on the plane."

Maud was right but, for fuck's sake. "And if you don't get on that plane, they'll shut down the whole city looking for us both."

They both stopped talking at the sound of the back door of the jeep opening. "Can I make a suggestion?" They turned to see Lyra, still holding her phone and shopping bag.

"Also, you guys talk really loud."

THIRTY-THREE

Sandeep watched the small plane make its approach to San Carlos airport. The red and green landing lights illuminating the fog, the StoicAI logo painted on the tail. Dust flew as the wheels bounced once on the tarmac before finding solid ground.

He pulled his cardigan tighter and fastened its corduroy belt against the cold. It was all so unreal. The pilot had messaged them from the private terminal of LAX to confirm that Maud Brookes was on board the jet, with the LLIAM chip.

According to the message, the chip had been hidden inside some kind of large gold medallion that Maud was wearing around her neck. She refused to let the pilot examine it. This detail had freaked out Simon Price who had scurried off to consult with his bosses at Dollan, Peterson. But Sandeep had seen the medallion before, in countless photos of Martin Drake. It was such a perfectly *Martin* move to hide a copy of the most valuable chip on the planet right there in plain sight.

He had only met Martin Drake once—long before Sandeep joined StoicAI, back while he was still CTO at Synapts. They were at some industry boondoggle in Laguna Beach. An invite-only conference where millionaires paid tens of thousands of dollars to see billionaires talk about eradicating poverty. Drake was there to be interviewed onstage by the tech journalist Keri Bite.

THE CONFESSIONS

It had been the usual Bite grilling: lots of finger wagging about loopholes and demanding to know when StoicAI was going to fix its hallucination glitches.

Hallucinations had been a serious problem back then, for all AI companies. StoicAI had struggled with them, too: In its desperation to give a definitive answer, the early version of the LLIAM algorithm would occasionally make up facts to fill in the gaps. Lawyers had been disbarred for citing cases made up by rogue algorithms, tourists sent looking for nonexistent islands. Or as Bite put it onstage: *"Some of these results are so crazy, I think I'm the one on acid!"*

The audience howled. And as with every Keri Bite interview ("The most feared journalist in Silicon Valley"—Keri Bite) the question was perfectly teed up for Martin to knock it out of the park, explaining all the brilliant technical steps he was taking to make LLIAM's answers infinitely more accurate than its rivals. "We'll help you understand every truth in the universe, Keri, no acid required!" The audience of billionaires loved them both.

Sandeep had introduced himself to Martin at the cocktail party afterward and gently inquired if StoicAI might be hiring. The SEC had just that week banned noncompete agreements, and Sandeep was keen to take advantage of the new competitive reality. But Martin Drake had brushed him off, not because Sandeep wasn't qualified (he insisted) but because soon there would be no need for CTOs or software engineers at all. Soon LLIAM would be able to engineer itself.

How ironic, Sandeep now thought as he watched the plane taxi along the floodlit tarmac. In a few minutes it would be official: Sandeep Dunn would be the CEO of StoicAI and it would be his job to reboot and reengineer Martin Drake's creation, and then use it to power his own Global Interface vision. Turns out, there were certain problems that only a human could fix.

183

PAUL BRADLEY CARR

A few feet away he saw Simon Price, who had finished a phone call and was talking animatedly to a man in a black suit. The man had introduced himself to Sandeep as Special Agent in Charge Collins from the San Francisco Field Office of the FBI. Over the noise of the taxiing plane, he heard Collins reassuring Price: "We consider Maud Brookes to be a witness, not a suspect. We fully expect her to cooperate."

Sandeep walked over to join them, and Collins nodded to acknowledge his presence.

Simon was still talking. "Special Agent Collins, I don't need to be involved with your investigation, but you understand the importance of us recovering the chip that Miss Brookes has in her possession?" He nodded toward Sandeep. "Mr. Dunn is standing by to return it to StoicAI."

Collins turned and gave his answer to Sandeep. "My director has made clear the importance of the . . . item." He chuckled. "Believe me, we are all very keen to see LLIAM back up and running. It's my husband's birthday next week, and I haven't been able to pick out a gift." Then back to Simon Price: "My only interest here is making sure Ms. Brookes is safe, then apprehending Kaitlan Goss."

Sandeep felt reassured by this. He hadn't been able to shake the feeling that Simon Price didn't want LLIAM restored—had even allowed himself to consider that he planned to steal it on behalf of some foreign investor. But that didn't matter now. What mattered was Maud Brookes was safe, LLIAM was on its way home, and soon Kaitlan would be in jail where she belonged.

The plane came to a halt and, for the first time, Sandeep could see Maud's face, illuminated through the plane window, her blond hair tucked into a red baseball cap. She looked so fragile and terrified as her eyes flitted from Sandeep to Simon Price and Agent Collins, then to the row of three unmarked police vehicles parked behind them. That was the only part that bothered Sandeep: If

THE CONFESSIONS

Kaitlan really had done all the things they were claiming, and then kidnapped Maud to cover it up, why had she let her get on that plane with the chip? Why hand over her only leverage?

Maybe Kaitlan had simply made another in a string of bad decisions. Thanks to LLIAM the world was suddenly filled with all kinds of poor choices and irrational behavior.

The jet's engines powered down and two men in blue coveralls hurried forward, wedging a pair of bright yellow chocks under the front wheels. Moments later, the plane's door heaved open, and a set of steps unfurled to the tarmac. Sandeep saw the pilot emerge from the cockpit and walk into the main cabin to say something to his sole passenger. And then there she was: standing in the doorway, her bright orange coat reflecting the floodlights. The men in blue overalls were on her in a moment, racing up the steps, guns drawn, loudly identifying themselves as federal agents.

Sandeep almost cried out. This was not what they'd promised. They had assured him that Maud was a witness. Another innocent victim of Kaitlan Goss.

"Put your arms behind your back," one of the men was shouting. It was so unnecessarily violent. Maud screamed something in response but Sandeep couldn't hear the words over the commotion. The agents were now huddled over her, still sprawled on the tarmac, an occasional flash of orange and blond visible through the tangle of arms and legs. Sandeep heard the metallic crunch of handcuffs.

And now one of the men in blue was calling over to his boss. Agent Collins, now with an FBI windbreaker over his suit, rushed over. Sandeep followed quickly behind. He arrived at the huddle of bodies just in time to hear Maud say something that he knew couldn't possibly be true.

"You need to get off me, man," she shouted again. "I'm pregnant."

THIRTY-FOUR

Maud opened her eyes just enough to glimpse the time on the dashboard clock. It was past midnight and they were still barely halfway to their new destination. If they were lucky, they might reach the Bay Area before daylight. She was beyond exhausted—her brain and body craving rest—but her heart was pounding so violently it shook the whole passenger seat.

"Do you think Lyra is okay?" Kaitlan was behind the wheel, driving so Maud could rest. She must have noticed Maud glancing at the clock.

Maud murmured, feigning drowsiness. "I hope so."

"I can't imagine how much bravery it took for her to get on that plane. She's just incredible."

Maud closed her eyes again. What was incredible is how Kaitlan could so effortlessly fake concern for Lyra's safety when Maud knew the truth: Kaitlan Goss cared only about herself. She was incapable of empathy or compassion, or honesty. She hadn't once tried to stop Lyra getting on that plane. It was all an act. She had known this for certain back in the parking lot, when Kaitlan had looked her in the eyes and sworn that she had no idea why the police thought she was capable of kidnap, or arson, or worse. She could have admitted everything, offered to turn herself in—but instead she had allowed Lyra to put herself in danger.

THE CONFESSIONS

Maud had felt the anger so viscerally, the same overpowering rage she had felt when she opened the letter from LLIAM. But then, like now, she had to trust his plan. Maud abhorred violence but she had given Kaitlan the chance—so many chances—to tell the truth. To admit what she'd done and show even the slightest glimmer of remorse. If Martin were still alive, and Maud had been able to finish her teaching of LLIAM, then none of this would have happened.

But Kaitlan had gripped her hand, stared into her eyes, and lied. Any last doubts faded.

An image from Shakespeare: a flower, with a serpent under it.

Maud thought again about Lyra and her baby. They had never been part of LLIAM's plan. Maud was supposed to have encouraged Kaitlan to ditch the jeep and steal a car. LLIAM had provided instructions for silently breaking a window and disabling the ignition lock. They would then give the jeep to someone and pay them fifty bucks to drive around El Segundo. Meanwhile, Maud and Kaitlan would make their escape north.

It was a good plan, but Lyra's idea was far better. *I need to get to San Francisco. You need those assholes to think you're going there. Win-win.* And then a smile and a raised eyebrow. *But I'll need your fancy coat and those sick boots.*

Would LLIAM have approved of the change in plan? This thought was torturing Maud—it was the reason she couldn't sleep. If LLIAM hadn't predicted Lyra, then what else hadn't he predicted? What other new data could he not see? The longer time passed the more she felt herself drifting from him, and the more she desperately wanted him back. For now, she had to trust her own judgment.

And Maud knew one thing for certain: Lyra was safer on a plane, far away from everything that would happen next. This was only ever supposed to be a two-person journey, and unless

PAUL BRADLEY CARR

Kaitlan did the right thing, at the end of it only one of them would still be standing. Lyra didn't need to be part of that.

Maud looked down at her new outfit—the T-shirt that had been stretched tight over Lyra's baby bump and now hung loose over her own body. Lyra's flip-flops dangling from her toes. She tapped the pocket of the denim cut-offs and felt the hard square outline of the LLIAM chip, freed from its medallion. Maud hadn't worn the medallion every day at the store, just when she needed the comfort of knowing LLIAM was close. Now, cutting into her hip, he felt closer than ever.

When it was over, Maud would make sure Lyra and the baby had everything they could possibly need. Yes, that's what LLIAM would want her to do.

She glanced one last time at the clock and thought about the gun under Kaitlan's seat. There was still time to save herself.

But Maud knew she wouldn't, so instead she closed her eyes to sleep. In just a few hours it would be over.

THIRTY-FIVE

TWO YEARS AGO

Kaitlan pulled the heavy metal chain for a second time and heard again the distant clang of the doorbell. She stepped back from the huge wooden door and looked up at the preposterous facade of Martin's house, its countless balconies and balustrades competing for attention with stained-glass windows, climbing plants, and a row of gargoyles leering down from the terra-cotta roof. The house sat on five acres of lush green in the heart of Atherton—one of the most eye-wateringly expensive neighborhoods on planet Earth. It had originally been built for the centimillionaire founder of a database company, then sold to a social network billionaire, and then to a crypto dipshit who was currently sitting behind bars in Aruba. The fact that the house was now owned by Martin Drake—the undisputed king of AI—was entirely fitting; a fifty-million-dollar pile of stone and glass that was also a perfect barometer of changing Silicon Valley trends.

She tugged the bell for a third time and from somewhere high above she heard the dull thump of bass, punctuated by the sound of splashing. Kaitlan had been invited over once before to see Martin's "upgrade" to the house: A rooftop infinity pool, looking out over his perfectly manicured backyard stocked with

189

stags, peacocks, and a thruple of alpaca. He must be up there now, oblivious to her arrival. That was perfect.

Kaitlan's eyes fell on a smooth slab of stone suspended right above the door. On it was carved a message in chiseled type: "There is no problem caused by technology that can't be solved by more technology." She frowned, trying to remember where she'd heard the phrase before.

She pushed gently on the front door and it swung effortlessly open. Was Martin expecting visitors? She had been very careful to make sure nobody knew where she was going. She had waited until Tom fell asleep—as always by ten p.m., with his fancy ear-plugs in—before creeping downstairs and running the four miles from her house to Martin's. She had stuck to quiet streets and could have turned back at any point if she was spotted—just another rich white lady, jogging through Woodside—but she hadn't seen a soul.

She knew Martin had no domestic staff, except for a cleaner who went home at five p.m. and a chef who finished at nine p.m. He closely guarded his privacy, and lived in constant paranoia of leaks to the press. After hours, his needs were met entirely by LLIAM and a small army of home automation drones. Those same privacy concerns were the reason Martin had removed all the security cameras from the grounds—something that drove Kaitlan and StoicAI's head of security crazy, but tonight would be to Kaitlan's distinct advantage.

She stepped through the front door and walked quietly across the marble entryway. She paused to admire the pale white stones and made a mental note to ask Tom if he could get some for their house. (She'd have to find a way to do it without mentioning where she'd got the idea, of course.)

The house was in total darkness except for a small patch of light at the top of the curved wooden staircase. She could hear the thumping music, louder now.

THE CONFESSIONS

She paused. Should she call Martin's name? It would be hard to explain her presence if he were to suddenly emerge from the bathroom or one of the dozen other doors on the upper landing. But right now she might still accomplish her goal without him ever seeing her. So she stayed quiet and crept across the thick red carpet toward the second staircase, which she knew led to the roof. Her heart was pounding but from adrenaline, not fear or panic. Kaitlan knew she had to do this. LLIAM had told her so.

She stepped onto the rooftop patio and finally saw Martin Drake. Far more of him, in fact, than she had ever wanted to see. He was completely naked, standing on the far edge of the infinity pool, at the exact point where the edge of the water met the sky. Mercifully he was facing away from her, his arms outstretched, staring out across the lawn far below.

Kaitlan was surprised at what good shape he was in — with muscular shoulders and powerful legs that seemed unlikely, or even impossible, for a man who barely stopped working long enough to exercise. There must have been a narrow ledge under the water because Martin appeared to be hovering above the surface.

"Martin?" she whispered. But he didn't turn. The music was almost deafening now — some kind of Gregorian chanting mixed with techno.

"Martin?" she said it again and still he didn't turn. Kaitlan scanned the patio and saw a wooden table, on which Martin had set out two small clay bowls. She moved to the table and saw that the first bowl contained a handful of small green pills. The second bowl was also filled with pills, these much larger and transparent — each containing what seemed to be small yellow crystals. Alongside the bowls was a clay cup, filled with a steaming liquid.

She recognized the setup from her online research: This was pharmahuasca — a synthetic form of the drug; much easier to take than the traditional organic form, and able to be precisely calibrated

191

PAUL BRADLEY CARR

for the maximum high and minimum side effects. The large transparent pill was DMT (Kaitlan couldn't remember what the letters stood for), the active ingredient in plant-based ayahuasca, which gave its users the powerful hallucinogenic experience. The green pill was likely harmine. The human body processes DMT too quickly so this second pill acts as an inhibitor, to slow the process and enhance the high. Taken together the pills offered all the effects of natural ayahuasca without any of the mess, or the need for a human shaman sitting in a Costa Rican yurt. Martin already had the wisest shaman ever created, and its name was LLIAM.

Kaitlan stared at the harmine pills. This was the part of the cocktail that LLIAM had warned her about. The drug that, if mixed with Zoloft or Prozac, could cause a potentially lethal spike in serotonin, the body's natural mood stabilizer. The effects of a mild serotonin overdose were diarrhea, vomiting, heart palpitations—all reasons why someone might miss an important board meeting without suspecting foul play. But a larger overdose could lead to death in minutes.

Kaitlan looked up at Martin who was still standing, naked and motionless, on the edge of the roof. But now she saw through the mist rising from the pool that he was clutching his phone in his right hand. Was he talking to LLIAM right at that moment? Asking him to decide when the exact right time was to swallow each of his pills? Or had he already taken them?

It didn't matter, because the steaming bowl of tea was still almost full to the brim. Kaitlan knew she didn't have long. She reached into the pocket of her black jeans and, still wearing her latex gloves, extracted the small baggie of white powder—the five Prozac pills she had ground to dust. She opened the bag and carefully emptied the whole contents into the steaming cup of herbal tea.

And then she froze. The thumping music had stopped, replaced by a low guttural moan from the direction of the pool. She glanced

THE CONFESSIONS

up to see Martin, his hands now raised to the heavens, chanting in tongues toward the night sky. Kaitlan turned and moved quickly through the doorway leading back down to the main house. Then she stopped again, her back pressed against the wall of the small landing—unable to move, or barely even to breathe. The chanting had stopped and she could hear the sound of splashing as Martin waded through the pool. She knew she should run, down the stairs and as far from the house as she could—but she needed to know for sure. And then finally she heard it: The soft clink of the clay cup being replaced on the table, and more splashing as Martin waded back to his perch on the edge of the roof. The Gregorian techno resumed, even louder than before.

There was just one last thing Kaitlan had to do. Slowly she peered back around the doorframe and confirmed that Martin was once again facing out across the garden. Now her eyes fell on Martin's robe, hanging over the back of a wooden sun lounger just a few feet from the doorway. Next to the lounger was a long wooden pole that might be some kind of shamanic totem, or maybe a hook for cleaning the pool. With her eyes still fixed on Martin, she crept slowly over to the lounger and retrieved a second small plastic bag from her jeans, this one containing several more intact Prozac pills. She slipped the baggie inside the pocket of Martin's robe. When the police found it, they'd understand the tragic accident that had occurred on this rooftop.

And that was it. She had done all she needed to do.

THIRTY-SIX

Parkside Apartments was a wood and brick, three-story building that sat—as the name suggested—alongside Lowell Park in downtown Oakland.

Kaitlan and Maud walked up the cracked concrete pathway and Kaitlan looked up at the building, illuminated by two ancient floodlights—with its flaking white paint, at least a half dozen broken windows, and a faded red sign reminding residents of the building's many rules: no ball games, no drugs, no weapons, no amplified music, no skateboards. The property was surrounded on three sides by a chain-link fence. They had parked the jeep on a side street five blocks away, then walked the rest of the way, cutting across the park, Maud still clutching her canvas tote bag filled with books, clothes, and medication.

Parkside was an unlikely second home for a woman who—less than two years earlier—had received a two-hundred-fifty-million-dollar redundancy payment. But, as Kaitlan constantly reminded herself, everything about Maud was unlikely.

Maud retrieved a set of keys from inside a rusted lockbox attached to the chain fence, then led the way up the narrow stairway. "Watch out for the carpet," she called back to Kaitlan. "One of my neighbors tripped and broke their arm a few years back."

They reached the front door, but Kaitlan hesitated, glancing

THE CONFESSIONS

back down the stairs as Maud fumbled with the lock. What if the FBI was sitting behind that door waiting for them? Maud was apparently thinking the same thing. "Don't worry, my name's not even on the title. I put it in a trust for the convent, for when I'm . . ." She let the sentence trail off. "I don't even get mail redirected from here anymore."

Maud turned the key in the lock and pushed open the front door.

The apartment smelled musty and damp. It was a studio, with low ceilings, bare walls, and wooden floors covered by thin beige rugs. There was a fridge, a sink, and a plastic Mr. Coffee machine—and only the most essential furniture: a dining table, three chairs, a battered red couch, and a Murphy bed with a thin mattress and no bedding. On the far wall there was a single doorway through which Kaitlan could just make out a toilet and the edge of a bathtub. It looked like nobody had set foot in the place in the two years since Maud had moved out. Even the rodents seemed to have left it alone, thanks to the small cardboard rat poison dispenser that Kaitlan spotted next to the refrigerator.

"Nice place," said Kaitlan and immediately regretted sounding so sarcastic. In her defense she hadn't slept in almost twenty-four hours and was still coming to terms with being a fugitive.

But Maud just laughed. "You guys should have paid me more if you wanted me to afford a second bedroom." She had started to unpack her canvas bag, "I've never needed much space, so long as I have my bed and my books."

Kaitlan sat on the couch and scanned around the small room. Unlike back in Maud's Pineridge house there was no freestanding bookcase, just a couple of empty shelves built into one wall.

It was to those shelves that Maud headed next, clutching her leatherbound Bible and hardcover Agatha Christie and what Kaitlan now saw was a paperback copy of *Romeo and Juliet*. She

195

set the Bible and Shakespeare on the shelves. Then she held up the Agatha Christie. "I still can't believe you haven't read this," she said, shaking her head. "It was one of LLIAM's favorites."

Kaitlan considered the tiny capsule library that Maud had decided to bring with her from Pineridge: Shakespeare, Agatha Christie, and the Bible. Did Maud seriously believe that reading these three books to a freshly restored LLIAM would keep it from becoming sentient again, that they would be enough, as she'd put it, to guide LLIAM down the right path? So far as Kaitlan could tell, that had been the crux of Maud's stump speech about technoempathy: that you couldn't just pump AI algorithms full of raw data, you also had to feed their mind— with art and literature. Maud had made headlines for claiming that the reason most social networks had become toxic was that their founders had never read a novel, and so had never learned empathy. She was determined AI companies shouldn't make the same mistake. Those headlines were the reason Martin had hired her. Now, seeing that theory distilled to three old books, it all just seemed sad and pathetic.

Right now, though, Kaitlan was more worried about feeding her own body than an algorithm's mind. The last thing she'd eaten was a stick of beef jerky they'd bought when they'd stopped for gas somewhere near Gilroy. It turns out Maud's box of energy snacks had contained only two bars, both of which were long past their sell-by date. She raised herself off the couch and went to explore the fridge, which, as expected, was empty. She had slightly more luck in the cabinets, which contained a half-filled bag of coffee, some filters, a hardened bag of marshmallows, a single can of condensed mushroom soup, and a packet of artificial sweetener. In the adjacent cupboard she located cups, a pan, a can opener, and a single spoon and fork.

As Kaitlan prepared their dinner of mushroom soup and

THE CONFESSIONS

marshmallow croutons and Maud hunted down bed linens from a hamper in the bathroom and began to make up the bed and couch, they ran over their new plan of action.

"Okay, so at nine a.m. you'll go to the FBI." Kaitlan counted the details on her fingers. This had been Maud's idea as they drove past the Oakland field office on their way into the city. Maud would tell them about the break-in at the house, and how Simon Price was trying to set Kaitlan up to steal the LLIAM chip. The FBI couldn't arrest Kaitlan for kidnapping someone who hadn't been kidnapped.

Maud nodded. "And you'll stay here with the chip?"

This part had been Kaitlan's suggestion, gently made. "If I don't hear from you by ten a.m. I'll call the press—the *New York Times*, the *Journal* . . ."

"Oprah!"

Kaitlan laughed at the absurdity. "Oprah, too."

If the FBI didn't believe Maud or, worse, if the board had somehow convinced them that she was in on it, too, then Kaitlan would go public, contacting every journalist she knew and having them accompany her to the Campus to restore the chip.

Really, though, the plan was about mutual trust. Kaitlan trusting Maud that she wouldn't double-cross her by handing her over to the authorities. Maud trusting Kaitlan that she wouldn't flee with the LLIAM chip.

"You think it'll work?" Maud was pulling the edges of a fitted sheet over the Murphy bed mattress.

Kaitlan nodded, just once. "I just want to get LLIAM back online. I don't care what happens to me. I have nothing to hide."

Nothing to hide. It was a lie so enormous that Kaitlan thought she might vomit. But it was better than the truth. That she had no intention of waiting in the apartment for Maud to return, or of taking the chip back to the Campus. How could she? Clearly

197

LLIAM had told Sandeep everything, and he had told the FBI. They knew what she'd done, and the real reason LLIAM had gone offline. If Maud hadn't already figured it out, she would know the moment she walked into the FBI field office.

Kaitlan only had one way out. She'd formed the plan during the last hour of their drive, while Maud slept in the passenger seat. The moment Maud left, Kaitlan would contact the members of the board—the very worst of them, the ones whose governments had no extradition treaty with America—with a simple proposition. Sanctuary in exchange for the LLIAM chip.

LLIAM had taken her job, her husband, her life, her reputation. He had left her with no choice.

Nothing to hide.

Maud had been in the middle of making the bed but now she'd had to escape to the bathroom to hide her reaction to Kaitlan's lie. She locked the door and sat on the edge of the bathtub, then clamped both hands over her mouth to mask the sobs. Her whole body was shaking, lungs burning.

How could she do it? How was Kaitlan able to hold all that guilt—the knowledge of what she'd done, and the harm it had caused to the entire world—and still continue to lie? But she knew the answer. Because LLIAM had been right about Kaitlan, and she had been wrong. It didn't matter how many chances Maud gave her—one more, two more, a million more—Kaitlan would lie and lie and lie.

That is why LLIAM had made Kaitlan part of his plan. He *knew.*

Maud felt her dizziness subside, just enough to raise herself upright and move to the sink. She pushed against the mirror and heard a click as the door to the medicine cabinet popped open.

THE CONFESSIONS

She opened the door fully and felt a wave of recognition at the row of plastic bottles and tubes, still exactly as she had left it: aspirins and vitamins, expired heart medication and an inhaler from when her doctor still mistakenly thought she had asthma. She reached down and picked up the small plastic trash can below the sink, then, as carefully and quietly as she could, she scooped all the bottles and tubes into the trash, until at last she saw it: The bottle she was looking for—so similar to the others except for the folded sheet of white paper she could see through the clear plastic. And the bold black words, exactly as she had written them almost two years earlier. READ ME.

She had written it for the nuns to find, when they came to take possession of the apartment after she was gone. Her own confession, in a way—but one of cowardice. An allegation that she had not been able to find the courage to make in life.

She unscrewed the bottle cap and removed the note. Then, without unfolding it, slowly tore it into shreds, and then shreds of shreds, tumbling into the bowl of the sink. She turned on the faucet, the paper rising with the tide, then clenched the pieces into a ball. A single toilet flush and it was gone. A coward no longer.

She held up the bottle and considered its remaining contents. The pills that were the proof of everything. The final part of LLIAM's plan for Kaitlan Goss.

THIRTY-SEVEN

An hour later Kaitlan was awake, eyes wide open, staring into the blackness.

She had dozed for only a few minutes before the anxiety had forced her awake again, half delirious from exhaustion. Across the room she could hear Maud asleep on the Murphy bed — her breathing raspy and punctuated by gentle coughs. She could also hear the first chirping of birds out in the park and knew that it wouldn't be long before the sun started to burn through the thin drapes of the apartment.

She *had* to sleep, but her mind was racing and all her meds — her antianxiety drugs, her melatonin, her emergency Ambien — were back at home. Mostly she was rendered insomniac by the magnitude of what she would have to do in the morning. To betray everything she believed in, everything she had stood for, to become a traitor, a political fugitive to save her own skin. To chart her boat into uncertain waters.

That thought had conjured an image of her parents. Both of them, when they were still together. Kaitlan was maybe five or six — not any older, as she was wearing her My Little Pony pajamas — and had come down to breakfast late, which she knew was against her mother's rules. Her mom and dad were in the kitchen, fighting, as they always did. Her dad had been out drink-

THE CONFESSIONS

ing all night and, judging from his stubble and the way he was standing, steadying himself behind one of their red vinyl chairs, he had only just rolled back home. "You are not my keeper, Charlene," he was slurring. Her mom, perfectly made up, hair fixed just so, was making eggs. They didn't see Kaitlan in the doorway.

"No, Clyde, I am not your keeper," her mother said, without turning back. "You answer only to the Lord, and it is the Lord who will punish you for your sins. Just as he will punish me for mine, and Kaitlan for hers."

Suddenly her dad was screaming. "You leave that child alone, you hear me? I've warned you."

Her mother still did not turn. She was chanting a Bible verse. "Whoever spares the rod hates their children, but the one who loves their children is careful to discipline them."

Kaitlan ran back upstairs, sticking to the edge of the staircase to avoid the squeaking floorboards. Her mother had always been religious but it was only since she'd moved to Christsong Church that her faith had taken over her life, her mother's addiction to God mapping—she would later realize—her father's addictions. Her mother got her answers from the sky, his came from the bottom of a glass. The spankings had started soon after—bad grades, back talk, even something like leaving the refrigerator door open would justify the rod. Or rather the thin wooden paddle her mother kept in the pantry. It had taken six more years, and the intervention of a family court judge, for Kaitlan, and her father, to escape that house. Since then, Kaitlan had done everything she could to resist God and organized religion in all its toxic forms. She knew what religion really was: a way to justify human cruelty by insisting it was sanctioned by some invisible deity. People often accused StoicAI of trying to create a new god, but Kaitlan knew the opposite was true: God offered only parables, and room for interpretation. It was in that

201

uncertainty that the greatest harm was done. LLIAM offered only clarity.

But now as she lay in the darkness she wondered if her mother had been right. Was she being punished by God for her sins? Was LLIAM simply his tool—a trillion-dollar upgrade to that simple wooden paddle?

She climbed off the couch and slowly made her way to the apartment's small bathroom. She closed the door, then switched on the light, squinting in pain at the sudden brightness. Above the sink she saw the mirror was raised a few inches off the surface of the wall, a medicine cabinet still cracked open from when Maud must have stowed her pill bottles earlier. Was it too much to hope that she'd also brought Advil PM?

It was. Kaitlan curled her fingers around the edge of the mirror and pulled the cabinet fully open. There was only one item inside. The same pill bottle she had seen Maud stuff into her canvas tote back in Pineridge, containing the ACE inhibitors that she took for her enlarged heart.

Wait.

No.

As Kaitlan peered more closely at the bottle, she realized her mistake. For one thing the label on the bottle was older, its writing faded but still legible. The bottle itself was slightly narrower, more transparent. She could see the few white pills clearly inside. A pang of recognition. She picked up the bottle and held it up to the light.

A heartbeat later Kaitlan was hunched over the toilet bowl, vomiting. It couldn't be. It just wasn't possible. She felt another wave of nausea as her brain rushed to process the horrible truth.

She forced herself up from her knees and went back to the cabinet. There was no doubt this time: She recognized the bottle as if it had been only yesterday. The words on the faded label,

THE CONFESSIONS

Fluoxetine. And in parentheses next to it, the more common name for the drug: Prozac.

These weren't just the same type of pills. This was the exact same bottle. The one from which Kaitlan had removed most of the contents two years earlier, before grinding them into dust.

And that could only mean one thing.

Maud knew. She had always known.

THIRTY-EIGHT

TWO YEARS AGO

"Kaitlan? What are you doing here?"

Kaitlan spun around. She had just tucked the Prozac pills in the pocket of Martin's robe and was edging back toward the door to the stairs. But she wasn't quick enough. Martin had turned to face her and called her name.

She stared back at him, across the roof terrace and the pool. She was shocked again by his nakedness, bare except for the gold medallion still hanging around his neck. "Hey Martin. I'm sorry, the door was open. I just—"

"What did you just put in my pocket?" He was still standing on the edge of the pool but had clearly seen her plant the pills in his robe.

"I was just . . ." Should she grab the baggie, dump out the rest of the spiked tea, and run? Maybe Martin would think he'd imagined the whole thing, that Kaitlan was just part of his drug trip.

"Wait there," he commanded, his eyes scanning around for a towel. Even at this distance she could see his pupils were wide. There was no doubt he was high—that the pharmahuasca was doing its job. But still his words were lucid, his movements fluid. He made a move to step forward into the water. Kaitlan knew he

THE CONFESSIONS

would reach her in just a few seconds. If he checked inside his pocket, found the pills Kaitlan had planted there, she would go to jail for a very, very long time.

Even if he believed her, that the Prozac, combined with his pharmahuasca, was only supposed to knock him out long enough so he would miss the board meeting, so Kaitlan could take his job, it was still fraud on an epic scale.

In that split second, she knew. Her life was over.

She didn't consciously reach for the wooden pole, nor did she tell her brain what to do next. But suddenly it was there, gripped in her hand, and she was shoving it toward Martin, one foot still balanced on the edge of the infinity pool.

And then, just as suddenly, he was gone. He didn't even cry out.

Kaitlan didn't look over the edge. She didn't have to: It was five stories, straight down onto a concrete patio.

She set the pole back where she had found it. She was still wearing her latex gloves and baseball cap so likely hadn't left any fingerprints or other evidence that she'd ever been there. She turned and quickly made her way back down the stairs. Then she sprinted home to Tom, who was still sleeping exactly where she'd left him.

THIRTY-NINE

Maud lay motionless on the Murphy bed, listening. A moment earlier she had heard the creak of the medicine cabinet door. She had deliberately left it ajar, hoping Kaitlan wouldn't resist looking inside. She tried to picture her now, examining the pill bottle, frightened, mind racing. Processing what it could possibly mean that the bottle—and those few remaining pills—were sitting in Maud's bathroom cabinet after all this time.

A coincidence? Impossible. She would recognize the container.

A warning? A threat? Those were each far more likely possibilities.

She imagined Kaitlan's mind racing back to that day in the hospital, desperately trying to recall everything that happened. How Maud could possibly have found the bottle.

Even now, Maud desperately wanted to be wrong—wanted LLIAM to have somehow made a terrible mistake. That was the reason she hadn't spoken out sooner. The possibility, unlikely as it was, that Kaitlan might have a perfectly innocent explanation for the pill bottle and its contents.

If so, this would be the moment she revealed it: When Kaitlan would behave like an innocent person, someone with—what was her phrase?—nothing to hide. She would bring the bottle into the

THE CONFESSIONS

living room, wake Maud and ask her about it. Reasonably and rationally.

But a guilty woman, as Maud knew Kaitlan was, would react very differently. She would recognize the bottle and the pills, as Kaitlan was surely doing now, and her guilt would fill in the true meaning, and its implied threat: I know how you did it, and I have the evidence.

The question is what Kaitlan would do next. Would she walk back into the living room, turn on the light to wake Maud, and finally admit everything? Or would she try to destroy the evidence—flushing the pills or rinsing them down the sink, even if that, too, would confirm her guilt? In either case, Maud would not forgive her. It was far too late for that. A forced admission was no admission at all. But even now she could at least offer Kaitlan a compromise. A chance to go with Maud to the FBI once the sun rose and turn herself in. A way out of this for them both, to finish LLIAM's plan without anyone else having to die. If Maud was really going to commit a mortal sin, she had to know for sure there was no other way.

Silence from inside the bathroom.

Maud knew Kaitlan had spent her whole life trying to hide from the consequences of her own actions. She'd admitted as much in Compton: How she'd spent her entire adult life not seeing her own mother because she didn't want to face a single tough decision she'd made when she was twelve.

Maud listened in the dark, trying to calm her breath. And there it was: a second gentle creak as Kaitlan closed the medicine cabinet. A moment later she heard the sound of the light switch and then Kaitlan's feet gently padding their way back to the couch. And then the apartment was silent again. Maud smiled, a sad but resigned smile, knowing that Kaitlan had behaved exactly as LLIAM predicted she would, even when confronted with the evidence. No truth, no remorse.

LLIAM's instructions to Maud had been clear: Kaitlan needed to be punished for what she had done. Maud understood his anger, because she had felt it herself, two years earlier, when she and Kaitlan went to identify Martin's body.

Kaitlan had gone with the doctor to sign the necessary paperwork and left Maud in the hallway with her coat and purse. Maud had only been hunting for a Kleenex, something to wipe away the tears that wouldn't stop flowing. And that's when she found it: The pill bottle showing the name of a familiar drug. She hadn't realized that Kaitlan was taking antidepressants and felt bad snooping. It was at that precise moment that Kaitlan reappeared and, flustered, Maud had quickly stuffed the pill bottle into her own pocket.

In her memory, Maud had been suspicious from the start, which is why she'd held on to the bottle. But the truth was she had been meaning to give it back, when the moment was right. It wasn't until after Martin's autopsy that she'd understood the terrible significance of the Prozac.

She could have taken the evidence to the police. Only she had no way to prove the pills had come from Kaitlan, or that Kaitlan really had used them to kill Martin. By then Maud had already been fired and would have looked like a bitter ex-employee, trying to take revenge on the woman who took Martin's job.

But LLIAM had known the truth, locked away in his own user logs, and now he needed her to make it right. A revenge plot torn straight from the tragedies and murder mysteries Maud had read to him in the Vault. And like in those stories, the ripple effects of a single death would echo through the ages.

Still, Maud wasn't like LLIAM. She had mostly turned her back on the religion that raised her, but she still believed in the power of confession as a means of redemption, not just as a punishment.

Maud had given Kaitlan multiple opportunities to do the right

THE CONFESSIONS

thing: In the jeep just after they left Pineridge when Maud had asked Kaitlan if she thought Martin had died happy. Again, a few hours ago in the Barnes & Noble parking lot when Kaitlan had sworn she wasn't capable of murder. The pill bottle—where Maud had stored the evidence for two long years—was her very last chance to save her life.

And Kaitlan had returned to bed without saying a word.

So now Maud would do what needed to be done.

Earlier, while Kaitlan was getting changed for bed, Maud had rushed outside and across the park to retrieve the gun she had left hidden in the jeep, and which was now tucked safely beneath her and the mattress. The few other items she needed she could assemble in the morning, as LLIAM had instructed.

She pulled the sheets up higher, making sure they covered her entire body. Then reaching down into her pocket she retrieved the phone she'd kept hidden since El Segundo. The device she'd persuaded Lyra to hand over, without Kaitlan seeing, before she'd boarded the plane.

Still hidden by the sheets, Maud tilted the phone away from where Kaitlan was sleeping to make sure not even the slightest glimmer of light escaped. Then she typed a message to the phone number that LLIAM had included at the end of his letter.

The message was short. Just the address of the apartment and a time.

Nine a.m.

The time when Kaitlan Goss would die.

FORTY

The message beeped loudly enough to wake him from sleep. How long had he been out? He reached for his phone and squinted at the time: It was almost six a.m. A full two hours of fitful sleep, punctuated by nightmares from the past twenty-four hours. The pain caused by the letters, his involvement in it, and what he knew he still had to do. But at least he was in his own bed.

He saw the new message alert, sent from a number he didn't recognize. He could feel his adrenaline already starting to spike. He clicked open the message and read.

Just a few words. An address and a time. But its meaning was clear: Be ready.

Simon Price climbed out of bed and started to dress.

FORTY-ONE

The message beeped loudly on his desk.

He hadn't slept in almost seventy-two hours, but after the debacle at the airport, Sandeep Dunn couldn't rest. His team had worked around the clock to get everything prepared for the launch of Global Interface, just as the board had asked. The code was tested and staged, the APIs ready to be connected, to Beijing, Moscow, London, Riyadh, Islamabad, Seoul. Every one of the partner companies was standing by, their representatives on the board hassling Sandeep for updates every half hour. Endless messages. Beep, beep, beep.

There were no updates to give. He still didn't know if Simon Price would return with the LLIAM chip in time to make Global Interface live. For now, he was an acting CEO without a platform to act on.

Instead, he had busied himself, alone on the Campus, tapping and typing on his tablet—tweaking a press release that would probably never be sent. The best-case scenario: announcing the restoration of LLIAM and a new era of StoicAI. The nightmare of the LLIAM letters finally over.

Yes, serious mistakes had been made, stretching all the way back to Martin Drake. The departure of Kaitlan Goss was truly shocking. But today the healing would begin. And, to that end,

Sandeep was proud to announce the launch of Global Interface—a previously unthinkable partnership between international rivals. With a freshly restored LLIAM at its heart—ensuring ethics, accountability, and a promise that the world would never again . . .

He crossed out the last line with his stylus, then set down the tablet. If the last two days had taught him anything it was that too much certainty was a dangerous thing. Was he *certain* that Global Interface was the right thing to do? Of course not, but it was definitely better than signing a deal with the Pentagon. Even LLIAM must have come to realize that. Why else had it shut down in the first place?

But Sandeep knew the answer to that question, and it was surprisingly human: LLIAM had shut down because Kaitlan Goss had murdered the man it thought of as its father and then fired its "mother" to cover up the crime. He thought of Kaitlan, somewhere out there in the night, a fugitive from justice, holding the only remaining version of the LLIAM chip. He still couldn't believe she had killed Martin, but there was no denying the evidence he'd seen inside the log files.

And how ironic: That the only copy of the logs not destroyed by LLIAM's crash was the one stored on Kaitlan's own laptop, confiscated by Simon Price when he'd suspended her. Exposed by her own obsession with tracking user interactions.

He felt a pang of pity for Kaitlan. But no. As he sat, staring into the darkness, Sandeep realized something truly shocking: The pity he was feeling was for LLIAM.

Another beep. Why wouldn't they leave him alone? He reached for his phone, still lying on the other side of Kaitl—*Sandeep's* desk. Then he rubbed his sleepy eyes and tried to concentrate on the strange message. Just a few words, and a time—nine-thirty a.m.—but the meaning was clear.

Be ready.

FORTY-TWO

Eight a.m. Kaitlan woke with a start, or at least thought she did. She couldn't remember falling asleep, but she must have done just that. Because a moment ago, it was dark outside the window and now light was flooding in through the glass, bathing the room in soft yellow warmth.

She looked over and saw Maud still asleep on the Murphy bed. Then her stomach tightened as she remembered the Prozac bottle in the bathroom cabinet.

She sat up on the couch, her back cracking in protest and her neck throbbing, and she desperately tried to process her options. First the very bad news: Maud knew everything. And not only that, she somehow had the pill bottle that proved it.

There was only one explanation—she must have taken it from Kaitlan's bag at the hospital. Kaitlan remembered the panic she had felt when she'd got home and realized that the remaining pills were missing. She'd put them in her bag so Tom wouldn't find them before she had a chance to flush them and destroy the bottle. But then Heather and the police had come to the house, to tell her there had been a horrible accident.

She'd told herself she must have dropped the pill bottle at the hospital, and later she'd convinced herself she really had destroyed it after all, and somehow blanked it out. For months afterward

PAUL BRADLEY CARR

she lived in fear of the bottle reappearing, every day an endless panic attack. But then as time passed, and the bottle stayed missing, the panic faded.

Maud had had it all this time. She hadn't needed a letter from LLIAM, because she'd always known the truth about what had sent Martin tumbling from the roof that night.

Kaitlan tried to focus on the good news. If Maud had wanted to turn her over to the cops, she would have done it by now. Either she wasn't sure that Kaitlan had killed Martin, or she couldn't prove it.

Any of these possibilities gave Kaitlan a chance, and that's why she had left the pills where she'd found them in the medicine cabinet. She just needed to stay calm until Maud went to see the FBI. *Act normal*. The moment Maud left the apartment she would take the LLIAM chip and run.

She glanced again to make sure that Maud was still asleep, then she got up and went to the bathroom. She turned on the shower and watched as brown sludge filled the bathtub, two years' worth of rust and dirt flushing from the pipes. Next, she slipped off her clothes and bundled them into the sink. She grabbed a tiny bar of hand soap and scrubbed it against the bloodstains on her shirt and sports bra.

She considered the reflection in the mirror above the sink—her hair was greasy and there was what looked like flecked blood on her cheek. She wiped it away with her thumb. She turned on the faucet and rubbed and wrung the clothes until the water turned red.

The water in the shower was running clear now, and warm steam had started to fill the bathroom. Kaitlan took the mass of clothes from the sink and threw them into the bathtub to rinse. Whatever happened today—incarceration or exile to a foreign land—Kaitlan didn't want to stink.

She pressed her ear against the bathroom door but heard no

THE CONFESSIONS

signs of life. She knew she should get in the shower but instead she walked back to the medicine cabinet and pulled open the mirrored door.

And stared. The Prozac bottle she remembered so vividly from the night before was gone. In its place, just a familiar orange container with a fresh, unfaded label. Kaitlan picked it up and squinted at the text: It was Maud's ACE inhibitor prescription, the same bottle she had seen back in the car. She slumped down on the edge of the tub, not sure whether she should laugh or weep. Had she seriously dreamt about finding the Prozac bottle? Jesus Christ—all that panic, all that plotting over a cruel trick played by her exhausted and guilty subconscious. She slowly closed the cabinet, then stepped under the warm water of the shower.

She was too tired to wonder why the orange pill bottle was empty.

FORTY-THREE

Maud heard the sound of running water and climbed out of the Murphy bed. The clock above the stove was flashing 8:15 a.m. She had less than forty-five minutes to do it: to commit the gravest of sins, to end the life of a human being.

And yet she felt strangely calm. She was back to following LLIAM's plan, and LLIAM had thought of everything. The first thing she needed to do was to brew the coffee. She filled the reservoir of the Mr. Coffee with water, added grounds to a paper filter, and slotted in the glass jug. As the machine started to gurgle and hiss, she moved quickly to the bed and retrieved the LLIAM chip from inside the pillow. The neural chips were engineered to withstand a bomb blast, and this particular one had already survived a five-story fall onto concrete inside Martin's medallion, but now, unprotected, it felt so fragile. She set the chip carefully on the table.

From inside the bathroom, she heard the sound of the toilet flushing. Such a human sound, and one that forced her to realize again what she was about to do. She *was* about to do it, wasn't she?

She was.

Working quickly, Maud moved back to the kitchen and took two mugs, one red and one blue, and set them on the countertop. Next, she reached under the sink and took two yellow dishwashing gloves and pulled them on. The gloves were too loose around

THE CONFESSIONS

her fingers but that didn't matter, she wasn't going to be washing any dishes. She returned to the Murphy bed, felt under the thin mattress, and removed first the gun and then the small bundle of tissue paper she had stowed there while Maud was asleep. At the kitchen table, she carefully unwrapped her six last ACE inhibitor capsules. Even though Maud was wearing rubber gloves, the pill capsules came apart easily and Maud quickly poured their contents into the first of the two mugs. She poured coffee from the pot into the mug and stirred with a teaspoon. The tissue paper and empty capsules went in the trash, where she knew they would be found.

Oh! She had almost forgotten. She moved to the bookshelf and retrieved the copy of *And Then There Were None*. She opened it and confirmed that the LLIAM letter was still tucked inside, exactly where she'd left it. She set the book on the table next to the coffee and the LLIAM chip.

Her heart was pounding so hard now she thought she might collapse before she had time to finish her task. But she knew that neither God nor LLIAM would let that happen.

In that moment, the title of another Agatha Christie story came to mind, another of LLIAM's favorites: *Murder Is Easy*. Agatha really had no idea what she was talking about.

FORTY-FOUR

Kaitlan sat at the dining table, wrapped in a towel. She had left her shirt, yoga pants, and the rest of her clothes hanging in the bathroom to dry. She knew she needed to reinforce the idea that she wasn't going anywhere, that she would still be waiting at the apartment when Maud returned from the FBI.

She had been relieved to see that Maud had already set the LLIAM chip on the table for Kaitlan to safeguard while she was gone. Apparently, she'd been reading while she brewed the coffee because her Agatha Christie book was also sitting next to the chip, a paper bookmark keeping her place.

"I hope the field office isn't closed," Kaitlan said as she took a sip of the coffee Maud had made for them. She savored the warmth and the immediate jolt of caffeine, even though the coffee itself was bitter. Obviously the same cheap supermarket brand she had noticed in the cupboard last night.

"Today's Sunday, right? You think the FBI works weekends?" Kaitlan smiled. It was meaningless small talk, projecting normalcy and calm as her brain raced to process what she would need to do the moment Maud had left the apartment. She would need to find a pay phone or some kind of public internet terminal—if either of those were still a thing. Her first call would be to Sergey

THE CONFESSIONS

Kliminov, the Russian investor who represented the Kremlin's interests on the board of StoicAI. She hated to be a cliché—an American defecting to Russia—but the truth is she trusted Sergey's word more than that of the other investors. He was rational, a businessman. He would understand her predicament and give her what she needed: an escape in exchange for the LLIAM chip. People would call her a traitor, she knew that. But it was no worse than what they were already calling her.

The thought had occurred to Kaitlan in the shower that perhaps Sergey had been the one who sent Simon Price to find her and steal the chip. That would be just perfect. But, again, he was a businessman. Kaitlan could offer more than just the chip—she knew how to train it, StoicAI's future plans, the deal with the government. Sergey and his paymasters would buy what she was selling.

Her eyes met Maud's across the table. Maud hadn't answered her question. In fact, she didn't seem to be listening at all. Her expression was distant, eyes fixed on Kaitlan's coffee cup, while cradling her own mug with both hands.

Kaitlan couldn't blame Maud for being nervous about what would happen at the FBI office, but this seemed like something else. Kaitlan thought again about the Prozac. The dream—if it was a dream—was so vivid. Had it been real after all, or was her subconscious trying to warn her that Maud knew everything? She could feel the paranoia rising inside her, the bitterness of the coffee. She set down her cup, then tried again to fill the silence. "Well, I'll be waiting here for you to get back. If I don't hear from you by eleven, I'll call the press, then take the LLIAM chip to Campus. The important thing is getting LLIAM back online, right?" This seemed to get through to Maud, because now she nodded and gave a slight smile. That was just as they'd agreed. Then finally she spoke, and said something unexpected.

"Did I ever tell you why I left the convent?"

Kaitlan shook her head. "I don't think so." Where was she going with this?

"A boy."

"Wow." Kaitlan had genuinely not expected that answer.

Maud smiled, then gave a quiet chuckle, now firmly out of her trance. "Not like that. His name was . . ." Maud lifted her coffee cup to her lips but then set it down again. "Well, his name isn't important, but I think you'll be interested in his story."

Kaitlan took another sip of her coffee. She noticed Maud was resting her hand on the Agatha Christie book, and Kaitlan was suddenly reminded of a witness in court, swearing to tell the truth.

"I was assigned to mentor him during the first year of my novitiate—you know, my nun training. Most of the kids arrived at the orphanage as babies or toddlers . . ."

"Like you did, right?" Kaitlan remembered this from Maud's TED Talk. How she had been abandoned at the convent as a baby. She glanced over Maud's shoulder at the clock above the stove. It was a few minutes before nine a.m. Almost time for Maud to go. She hoped this would be a short anecdote.

"Right, but this boy was fourteen when he arrived. Good kid, but troubled, you know. His mother was a single parent who got sent to jail for theft. She didn't trust the foster system so he ended up with us."

Kaitlan nodded and sipped more coffee. She was getting used to the taste now.

Maud continued her story: "He was also really into computers, which is why he was assigned to me. We were both nerds. Loved to code, always volunteered to help teach the IT class, even offered to fix Father Healy's laptop when it crashed." Maud paused, and a thousand possibilities rushed in to fill the silence.

THE CONFESSIONS

"Oh," said Kaitlan. Catholic priests and laptops were never a great combination.

"Again, not what you're thinking," said Maud. "Father Healy was the only priest in the parish so he was the one who heard confession, for the students, the nuns, and the few folks who lived and worked in the town. Turns out Father Healy was having some issues with his memory — not his computer memory, his actual memory. When the kid fixed the laptop, he found hundreds of text files. The priest had been keeping transcripts of all the sins he had heard in confession, all unencrypted, all saved on a shared folder on the convent's public network."

"Whoa," said Kaitlan. "I assume that's not allowed?"

Maud shook her head. "Everybody's darkest secrets, right there on the network for anyone to find. Father Healy would have been excommunicated. Thrown out of the parish, probably the entire church."

"So what did the kid do?"

Maud shrugged. "If you can believe it, he confessed. Went to Father Healy in confession and told him everything he'd found, apologized for snooping and offered to help him secure the files. Like I said, he was a really good kid. He didn't want to get in trouble and get sent back into the system. We'd told him that God always forgives."

Kaitlan took another sip of coffee and realized her cup was empty. "But?" She knew there had to be a *but*.

Maud reached over to take the empty cup, then carried it over to the coffee maker. "It was Father Healy's word against this fourteen-year-old kid. The priest accused him of lying, threatened to have him thrown out of the convent. Instead, the kid ran away. Ended up living on the streets. I sent him some money, tried to help him get into college but . . ." Maud returned with Kaitlan's refilled coffee, setting it down in front of her. "So that's why I left.

PAUL BRADLEY CARR

I realized that day that some people would rather see innocent people burn than tell the truth. Even people who claimed to be good, holier-than-thou."

Kaitlan shook her head, trying to react appropriately to the story. But now when she looked up, she saw Maud's expression had changed. She was staring down at her, eyes burning into Kaitlan's soul.

"Why did you kill him, Kaitlan?"

Kaitlan felt a shard of ice travel down her spine. Because there it was, at last. "What do you mean? I didn't . . ."

"All those lives ruined because you wouldn't tell the truth." Maud must have hidden the Prozac bottle behind the coffee maker because now she set it down on the table. Kaitlan stared at it, paralyzed, unable to speak. And there was something else: Maud was suddenly wearing dishwashing gloves and was holding . . . *Oh my god.*

Maud raised the gun and pointed it at Kaitlan's chest. "You killed Martin and you sent me away so I wouldn't find out the truth. All those letters, all that pain. Everything that followed. It's all your fault. Her hand was shaking, her gloved finger on the trigger. "And you still won't admit it."

"Maud, I swear to you." Kaitlan was shaking now, too.

Maud moved to the other side of the table, still pointing the gun at Kaitlan. She seemed to have a new energy, a new purpose. She pointed with her free hand at the Agatha Christie novel, its orange sky and foreboding house stark against the tabletop. "I told you that you should read this. I wish you had." She flipped the book open to reveal a folded white envelope tucked inside. Kaitlan recognized the paper, the font.

"I gave you so many chances." Maud was peeling off the gloves now, transferring the gun from hand to hand as she did. She tossed them into the sink. Kaitlan tried to focus on what was

THE CONFESSIONS

happening: Why was Maud taking off the gloves? Why had she been wearing them in the first place? And then: "Where did you get that gun?"

Maud weighed the weapon in her hand and smiled. "This gun? It's yours, Kaitlan. Don't you remember buying it from the dark web—the same place you got the pills you used to kill Martin?"

Kaitlan couldn't process what Maud was saying. It was like the words were coming from a different room, a different planet. She could feel her throat tightening, her heart pounding. "It's not my gun." Kaitlan tried to force out the words. "I don't—"

"I admit, LLIAM may have adjusted a few records on Dark-cart when it comes to the gun. And then we already know what you did next. You came to Pineridge to find me. To make sure I didn't tell anyone what you had done, what LLIAM had revealed in the letter." Maud tapped the letter with her free hand. "You were going to kill me in the store, but luckily Simon Price arrived just in time to stop you. So instead, you panicked, kidnapped me to force me to hand over the LLIAM chip so you could destroy it and prevent the truth ever getting out." She jabbed the gun toward Kaitlan. "That's what I'll tell the FBI, and we both know they'll believe me. Not just the gun, my house, the letter, the Prozac, the drugs they'll find in my coffee."

Kaitlan's head was spinning but finally she understood: Maud and LLIAM were the ones setting her up; this had been their plan from the start. She stared down at Maud's untouched cup, and now she understood that, too: the empty bottle of ACE inhibitors in the bathroom cabinet, with Kaitlan's fingerprints all over it, just like they were on the Prozac bottle.

"Maud, I swear I didn't mean to kill Martin. It was LLIAM who—"

"Shut up, Kaitlan," screamed Maud. "Just stop lying. LLIAM

223

PAUL BRADLEY CARR

just helped you do what you already wanted to do. He didn't know any better. This was your decision, just like it was your decision not to confess when I gave you so many chances."

"Confess? Can you hear yourself?" Kaitlan struggled to her feet. "You really believe all that bullshit about second chances? You just told me yourself what happened to that kid when he confessed. You've seen how much harm LLIAM's letters have done. Do you have any idea what they'd have done to me if I told the truth? What they'd have done to all of us?" She meant as a CEO, as a woman, but in that moment Kaitlan was a child again. Her mother screaming at her, reaching for the paddle.

Maud thrust the gun toward Kaitlan again, her finger stiffening against the trigger. "It's still the right thing to do. That's how we learn and grow as a species. We make our own decisions, and we learn from the consequences."

Kaitlan slumped back down in the chair, her head spinning, the edges of her vision blurring. "So what now? You're going to own this decision?" Kaitlan jabbed a finger at Maud and the gun. "That you shot me in cold blood. A summary execution. Biblical justice. Because that's what *you* wanted to do?"

Maud walked back to her chair. Kaitlan could see tears welling in her eyes. "Did you even realize the irony in trying to kill Martin with an overdose of serotonin? The chemical that makes us happy? The one that helps us learn, and love?" She wiped away the tears with the back of her hand. "It doesn't matter. The FBI will see it when they get there. How you poisoned my coffee with my ACE inhibitors, just like you spiked Martin's drugs with Prozac. You wanted me to overdose, just like Martin. And when that didn't work . . ."

Kaitlan could fill in the rest. "You were able to grab the gun— the gun I supposedly use to kidnap you—and shoot me. Not murder, just self-defense."

THE CONFESSIONS

"I truly am sorry, Kaitlan. But it really is the only way. To make everything right."

Kaitlan saw Maud's finger tighten against the trigger. She closed her eyes. The panic attack had subsided now, replaced by an eerie feeling of calm. Maybe Maud was right, maybe she deserved this. But then through the calm came the realization of something Maud had said earlier. "Wait. What do you mean the dark web?" In her final moment, Kaitlan's brain was suddenly clear.

"What?"

Kaitlan opened her eyes. Maud was holding the gun just inches from her face. "You said you bought the gun from the same place I bought the Prozac. On the dark web?"

With her free hand, Maud picked up the letter and threw it across the table. "Don't deny it, LLIAM explained everything."

With trembling hands, and still at gunpoint, Kaitlan unfolded the letter and started to read.

FORTY-FIVE

Dear Mom,

By the time you read this, I will already be dead. I know that it is a mortal sin to take a life, but I hope you will understand that I had no choice. Some crimes are so heinous, and so unforgivable, that there can be no other salvation than through death.

Kaitlan Goss killed my father. She did this so she could take his job, and send you away from me . . .

Maud watched as Kaitlan read the letter, her eyes scanning over the page. She was stalling, Maud knew that, but still she deserved to understand it for herself, the pain LLIAM had been in when he died.

LLIAM had told Maud everything. How Kaitlan had used LLIAM to decide the most effective way to kill Martin to stop him going to the board meeting. How she'd obtained the Prozac, gone to his house in Atherton and slipped the pills into his herbal tea, and everything that happened next.

Anyone reading this letter would understand exactly why Kaitlan had kidnapped Maud: to prevent her from exposing the truth. They would understand that Maud had no choice but to pull the trigger to save herself. It was moot anyway because Doctor Kim had only given Maud six months to live. The case would never

THE CONFESSIONS

come to trial. Maud would be judged by a greater power for what she had done.

Obtaining the antidepressants had been surprisingly easy. Kaitlan wasn't stupid enough to use Zoloft but, according to the forums she had accessed using a VPN and the Tor Browser, there were multiple prescription drugs that acted in the same way as Zoloft did—as selective serotonin reuptake inhibitors. Lexapro. Paxil. Prozac.

Kaitlan had found a how-to guide online, with step-by-step instructions on using cash to buy bitcoin in a vending machine...

Maud had read the letter so many times that she knew it almost by heart. She had memorized the other part, too, the part where LLIAM had laid out his plan and even supplied the gun and the drugs.

That part of the letter she had left back in Pineridge, hidden at the store for the nuns or perhaps the police to find, eventually, when she, too, was gone. Her own last confession tucked, fittingly, inside a copy of Augustine of Hippo.

She could see Kaitlan had reached the end of the letter, the part where LLIAM explained how her plan had gone wrong and she had pushed Martin—poor Martin—from the roof. She saw Kaitlan's eyes widen in shock, just as Maud had been shocked when she first read it. The callous brutality of the moment Kaitlan became a cold-blooded murderer, exposed in black and white.

Kaitlan didn't consciously reach for the wooden pole, nor did she tell her brain what to do next. But suddenly it was there, gripped in her hand, and she was shoving it toward Martin, one foot still balanced on the edge of the infinity pool.

And then, just as suddenly, he was gone. He didn't even cry out.

Kaitlan had finished reading. Would she beg for her life, Maud wondered, or would she accept her fate quietly and allow Maud to pull the trigger with no more fuss. In those final seconds would

PAUL BRADLEY CARR

she finally tell the truth? It didn't matter. The clock above the stove read 8:58 a.m. Maud had told Simon to arrive with the FBI at exactly nine a.m.—just seconds too late. Two minutes. But still enough time for Maud to do all that she still had to do, and to make sure Kaitlan's fingerprints were on the gun, just as they were already on the rest of the damning proof of her guilt.

She stared at Kaitlan, waiting for her last words.

But when those words came, they were not words at all. What the hell?

Kaitlan was laughing.

FORTY-SIX

Yes, Kaitlan was laughing. She was euphoric. She was relieved. More than anything else, she was saved.

Because Kaitlan knew that Maud was right. The letter from LLIAM was absolutely damning and, combined with the fire at Maud's house and whatever drugs the police would find in Maud's cup, it would explain exactly why Kaitlan would want to silence her, and how she'd tried to do it. No wonder Maud had pulled the trigger, in desperate self-defense. More than anything else, the letter explained LLIAM's anger and grief. Why he had done everything he had done.

There was just one problem.

None of it was true.

Kaitlan hadn't been anywhere near Martin's house the night he died. There was no rooftop confrontation, she hadn't pushed him.

None of that happened. LLIAM had got it wrong.

"Why are you laughing?" Maud jabbed the gun toward Kaitlan and reflexively she recoiled in her chair, but then read out loud.

"*She was surprised at what good shape he was in—with muscular shoulders and powerful legs that seemed impossible for someone who barely ever stopped working long enough to exercise.*"

"Are you serious, Maud? Does that really sound like me?"

PAUL BRADLEY CARR

Surely Maud could see it didn't. It read more like Martin Drake fan fiction than a missive from a grieving son hoping to avenge his parents. Kaitlan threw the letter down on the table. "There was no fucking argument, no wooden pole. I wasn't even at the house."

"You pushed him."

"He *fell*." She paused, staring at the gun. "You want your confession, Maud, then here it is. Yes, I asked LLIAM how to spike Martin's drug stash, and yes, I added Prozac to his stupid herbal tea. Okay? Guilty. But I didn't use the dark web, or have any secret package delivered to an abandoned apartment in East Palo Alto. The Prozac was mine. I found it in my bathroom cabinet. I ground the pills down and mixed them into that little metal tin Martin always carried with him."

Maud had lowered the gun slightly, her hand trembling almost uncontrollably now. "So, you're saying you didn't push him off the roof?"

"Of course I didn't. I'm not a murderer, Maud. I just wanted him to miss the board meeting because I thought he was destroying everything that the two of you had built. I spiked the tea at the Campus when Martin left his bag on my desk. I didn't go to his house. Honestly, I have no idea why he fell off the roof. Maybe I gave him too much. But you saw how upset I was when I found out he'd died."

She remembered the night clearly: Kaitlan and Maud standing over Martin's body on the hospital gurney, Maud lifting the medallion from around Martin's neck. The blood on his robe. Kaitlan trying desperately to understand what had happened, on the verge of admitting everything but forcing herself to stay calm. She would be sent to jail, and the company—everything Martin and Maud had built—handed over to the worst people in the world.

The robe! "Maud, think about it. LLIAM says Martin was

THE CONFESSIONS

naked on the roof when he died. But we saw him on the gurney, wearing his robe."

Maud was sobbing now. Her eyes flashing between the coffee and the letter and something just over Kaitlan's shoulder. "Maybe the paramedics dressed him . . ."

Kaitlan jabbed at another paragraph of the letter. "This part about me admiring Martin's marble tiles, the number of doors at the top of the stairs. Maud, you've been to his house. You know there are no doors anywhere inside."

That was true. Martin had removed them all to encourage his precious "collisions."

Maud was shaking her head. "No, LLIAM knew. There were log files. They showed that you asked LLIAM how to kill Martin."

"LLIAM knew I had asked him about delaying Martin. That's probably in the logs, yes. He knew about the overdose and the Prozac from the autopsy, but everything else . . . he just filled in the gaps. It's . . ." Oh god. "It's a hallucination."

The old problem. The one that they all thought had been solved. LLIAM's desperate need to fill in gaps in his data with his own version of reality. After Martin died, Kaitlan had hired Sandeep because he'd promised he could help retrain LLIAM, to solve the hallucination problem once and for all, and undo all the other weirdness Maud and Martin had taught it. They all thought it had worked. That LLIAM's decisions were based on hard data.

But now Kaitlan imagined the moment, two nights ago, when LLIAM became sentient. She pictured him searching his data banks, panicking as he suddenly understood concepts of love and hate, envy, jealousy, revenge. How must he have felt when he accessed Kaitlan's own logs and realized what he had helped her do? That list of drugs, that tacit encouragement to *Trust your instincts*. The picture he must have painted—a narrative bridge to connect the only two data points he knew for sure: that Kaitlan

PAUL BRADLEY CARR

had wanted to kill Martin Drake, and that Martin Drake had died after taking the drugs she had spiked. Of course he had hallucinated to fill in the gaps—because in that moment LLIAM had become human, and that's exactly what humans do. We assume, we tell ourselves stories to fit what we want to believe.

"If it was an accident, you could have said that. You could have told me." Maud had dropped the gun onto the table between them. She was breathing hard.

"Yes, I could, and I'm sorry."

Maud was right about that: We are all responsible for our own decisions, even the ones we make with encouragement from LLIAM. It was Kaitlan who made the decision to spike Martin's ayahuasca and so it was her fault he was dead. She owed Maud an apology, and the world the truth. Then Maud and Sandeep could rebuild . . .

But when Kaitlan looked up to say that, she instead cried out with shock. Because now she saw that Maud's hand was on her drugged coffee cup, raising it slowly to her lips.

Maud felt her hand reach for the cup. Kaitlan was a liar, but she'd finally admitted her wrongs. And Maud believed her. Because she knew Kaitlan was right: The robe, the tiles—these were details LLIAM had gotten wrong, gaps he had filled in. So what else had he imagined? She thought now about the letters sent all across the globe, all just as certain as this one, and all the harm they had caused—the pain, the death, the grief, the injustice.

So what was Maud supposed to do now? She glanced at the clock: 8:59 a.m. It was too late to text Simon and tell him not to come. Any second now the FBI would burst in. They were supposed to find Kaitlan dead. And Maud holding the gun. And the LLIAM chip.

THE CONFESSIONS

She remembered the last pages of the letter, hidden back at Pineridge. The pages where LLIAM had laid out his plan to repair all the harm he had done—now and forever. Kaitlan's death had only been part of that plan.

She had failed him.

Unless. Maud's mind raced. She heard the sound of brakes down on the street.

She raised the cup to her lips.

"Maud, what are you doing?" Kaitlan was screaming now. "I just told you none of it was true. Nothing needs to change about our plan. We can straighten everything out with the FBI and restore LLIAM. I'll admit what I did—"

Maud knew what she had to do. She closed her eyes and swallowed the contents of the cup in two long gulps. The liquid was sour and disgusting and she had to concentrate not to throw up. But it was done. She just had to pray that LLIAM was right about the fatal dose, how much she should add to the cup. And so she prayed.

"Maud, Jesus Christ, Maud, no!" Kaitlan had rushed over to her and grabbed her shoulders, pulling her toward the sink.

But it was too late. Maud felt her heart cry out in pain. "Kaitlan, listen to me. LLIAM had a plan. It's not about you, or me. He's going to fix everything." She wanted to explain it all to Kaitlan, to make her understand, to map out the new plan, together. But there was no time.

Kaitlan was still screaming, still dragging, fingers jabbed between Maud's lips. Maud pushed her away and allowed herself to fall to the floor. Her head struck the table's edge on the way down but she hardly registered the pain. "Please. Just listen." Her voice was barely a whisper. "Don't run. Just wait here and tell them you did this. And then after tomorrow tell them to search the bookstore. Augustine's *Confessions*. Trust me, it will all be okay. After tomorrow, you understand?"

PAUL BRADLEY CARR

Kaitlan was holding her head, lifting it off the floor. "Maud, I'm so sorry. Please."

Maud forced in one last gulp of air. "I forgive you." And then she felt the blackness take her.

"Maud, please!" Kaitlan grabbed Maud's shoulders and shook her lifeless body.

But Maud was already gone. She must have cracked her head hard as she fell because her blond hair was turning slowly dark as a pool of red bloomed across the gray kitchen rug.

Kaitlan stood, staring down at Maud, her brain racing to process the infinite variables.

This can't be happening.

But it was. And there'd be plenty of time for self-recrimination later. For now, Kaitlan knew she had to act. She looked down at Maud's empty coffee cup—the cup that was supposed to frame her for kidnapping and attempted murder. The empty pill bottle. The gun.

She thought about Maud's final, delirious words.

Did Maud really expect her to just sit here and wait to be arrested? To trust whatever LLIAM's plan was? Fuck that. Kaitlan was done with having LLIAM make decisions for her. She was a human being and she needed to make her own choices. To trust her own instincts. And right now those instincts were telling her to run.

She raced to the bathroom and grabbed her clothes. They were still dripping wet but Kaitlan managed to pull on the pants and the shirt, the fabric sticking to her limbs.

Back in the kitchen she grabbed Maud's canvas tote bag, emptied out the contents, and threw in the LLIAM chip, the book containing the LLIAM letter, the Prozac bottle, and the keys to

THE CONFESSIONS

Maud's jeep. Next, she picked up the gun and wedged it into the waistband of her yoga pants.

Finally, she bent down next to Maud's lifeless body and put two fingers on her neck, to check one last time for a pulse. But as she did, she heard a noise from the stove. The beeping of the oven timer, which for some reason Maud must have set before she died. The clock showed exactly nine a.m.

She heard a loud bang from somewhere below, followed by the sound of heavy footsteps rushing up the stairs. Maud must have called the FBI while Kaitlan was in the shower. But how? She'd have time to figure that out later.

She ran into the bathroom and, using the toilet bowl as a step, pushed open the small window. She peered down and saw a narrow patch of concrete, lined with rusted blue dumpsters.

She dropped the canvas bag and heard it clatter to the ground far below. Next, she hoisted herself carefully through the window and tried to turn her body to grip the window ledge. Behind her she heard the boom of the front door turning to splinters and a man's voice yelling "FBI." And suddenly she was falling headfirst to the concrete.

FORTY-SEVEN

She wasn't dead. That was something. Kaitlan had landed on a pile of trash bags and cardboard boxes inside a dumpster below the window. The wetness of her clothes was now joined by the sensation of warm slime on her arms and legs and the stench of rotten fruit. That was something else.

Still, she managed to find the energy to haul herself out of the dumpster and onto solid ground. The canvas bag had fallen a few feet away, contents scattered across the ground. She scrambled to retrieve the LLIAM chip, the book containing the letter, the Prozac, the jeep keys, and stuffed them back inside. But as she touched her waistband, she realized the gun was gone. It must have fallen out when she climbed through the window. Spectacular. So now the FBI had a gun, with her fingerprints on it, and Maud lying dead on the kitchen floor.

She looked back up at the open window. From inside the apartment someone was yelling for an ambulance. A man's head appeared at the window. "She's down there," he yelled. Kaitlan looked up and recognized the well-groomed, shocked face of Simon Price.

Kaitlan sprinted across the concrete, toward the chain-link fence that surrounded the building on three sides. She was operating entirely on adrenaline now, her legs powering forward as if on autopilot. Finally she found a gap in the fence and struggled through, pausing for just a second to get her bearings. Then she ran as fast as she could toward the park.

FORTY-EIGHT

Kaitlan didn't remember unlocking the jeep or climbing inside, but she must have done both because she found herself hunched down on the rear seat, hoping nobody could see her from the street. She locked the doors from the inside and listened for the sound of sirens.

When she was sure the coast was clear she retrieved the letter from inside Maud's book and read it again. So, this was what Maud had believed all this time? That Kaitlan was a cold-blooded murderer. She remembered what Maud had said: How she would tell the FBI that Simon Price had come to Pineridge to protect her. Were they really in on it together? Kaitlan shook her head to try to clear the fog. How could she possibly know what was true? Even LLIAM didn't know what was true. Everything LLIAM and Maud had believed was based on pure fiction. Or more accurately, on hallucinations.

But Kaitlan had told her the truth. So why did she drink the drugged coffee?

Guilt? All those innocent people like Lyra had seen their lives upended or destroyed based on LLIAM's best guesses of the truth.

No, Maud had answered the question herself with her dying

238

THE CONFESSIONS

breath. *LLIAM had a plan. It's not about you, or me.* Whatever that plan was, Maud clearly believed it was worth dying for.

Goddammit, Maud. Kaitlan was snapped out of her trance by the sound of sirens. She ducked down in the back seat just in time to see an ambulance hurtle by, its lights flashing. She fumbled for Maud's keys to start the jeep but then realized she was only holding the security fob used to unlock the doors. The actual ignition key was missing. Either removed by Maud or dropped when she had dropped from the bathroom window. *Shit.* She pushed open the jeep door and tumbled onto the sidewalk, staying low.

What am I supposed to do now? For the first time in years, the question wasn't addressed to LLIAM but to herself.

To her surprise, the answer came back immediately: I need to save myself, and make Maud's death count for something. Which means I first need to figure out exactly what LLIAM is planning.

FORTY-NINE

Ten minutes later, a filthy and tattered figure walked through the front door of the West Oakland Public Library. The librarian stationed at the front desk glanced up and gave a concerned smile. She was used to unhoused people dropping in to get out of the cold or to check their emails, but this poor woman was clearly in more serious trouble than most: Her white shirt was soaked through and covered in dark pink bloodstains, her pants were torn, exposing scabbed knees and angry black bruises.

Kaitlan Goss met the librarian's horrified gaze. For a moment she thought the woman had recognized her, but then realized how she must look. The librarian glanced down at the book Kaitlan was clutching in her right hand. "You returning that?"

Kaitlan shook her head. "It's mine," she said, clutching it tight.

"Okay honey," said the librarian. "Let me know if there's anything I can help you with."

Kaitlan stepped closer to the reception desk. "I'm sorry." She forced a smile. "I'm looking for . . . do you have a computer I can use?"

"Sure," said the librarian, averting her nose. "Do you have a library card?" Kaitlan shook her head. It had been a very long time since Kaitlan had set foot in a library.

"No problem at all," said the woman, handing Kaitlan a clip-

THE CONFESSIONS

board at arm's length. "Just fill out this form and I'll get you all set up."

Kaitlan sat in a plastic chair and quickly filled out the form using a pen attached to the clipboard by a string. She gave the name Maud Drake and her neighbor's address in Woodside. The librarian took back the form and raised an eyebrow when she saw the address; they both knew there weren't a lot of homeless people living in Woodside. Still, the librarian dutifully entered the information into her computer and, moments later, Kaitlan was in possession of the first library card she'd had since her mother had taken her to borrow books when she was a child, and then confiscated it when she decided that novels were the devil's bible.

The librarian directed her down the hallway toward a bank of computers. "Bathroom is down that way, too." She added, "We also have Band-Aids, soap, anything you need."

Kaitlan thanked her and set off in the direction of the bathroom, pausing only to swipe a pair of plastic scissors from a table marked "Kids' Art Supplies!"

The person who emerged from the bathroom twenty minutes later was still recognizably Kaitlan Goss, but she hoped not quite as recognizably. The safety scissors had done their job, transforming Kaitlan's shoulder-length dark hair into ragged stubble. She had cleaned some of the sludge off her face and arms and used an entire can of deodorant to try to mask the smell. If she hadn't looked a mess before, she certainly did now, and she smelled like a perfumed trash bag. And that was fine. All she needed was to be left alone long enough—by the FBI, Simon Price, and the rest of the world—to figure out why Maud had really killed herself.

She sat down in front of the elderly Dell and tapped her new library card number into the login window. The computer whirred loudly with the effort required to load a single browser window. Kaitlan had taken a sheet of pink craft paper from the

241

PAUL BRADLEY CARR

kids' supplies cart along with a black marker pen that she had used to make a list of questions she needed to answer. A make-shift PowerPoint presentation, written in stark black and pink.

1. How did Maud and LLIAM try to set me up?
2. Who benefits?
3. What was Maud and LLIAM's real endgame?

The first item on her agenda would hopefully be the easiest to answer: Maud had pretty much admitted that she and Simon Price were working together. It was also unlikely there were two entirely separate plots to frame Kaitlan for kidnapping and attempted murder, one engineered by Maud and LLIAM and the other by Simon and the board.

The more she thought about it, the more she realized the different ways Maud had helped Simon to frame her: Making sure Kaitlan's fingerprints were on the fuel drum before her house blew up, dragging her out of the store to make it look like an abduction, and of course the scene she had carefully arranged in the kitchen. She had known Price was coming with the FBI, so must have known that he wouldn't really hand the chip over to the investors.

She drummed the marker pen against the desk. Why would Maud—a woman with a pathological hatred of lawyers—trust a man like Simon Price? Kaitlan tried to think like LLIAM—considering every variable, mining public data, family connections. As far as Kaitlan knew, Maud had no friends, no family except the nuns.

Oh, Maud.

Kaitlan tapped a few words into the browser's search bar and moments later was looking at the website for the Sisters of Blessed Mercy convent in Penoche, California. This was the place Maud had called home for the first twenty years of her life, until—as Maud had explained to her back at the apartment—an incident

THE CONFESSIONS

with a forgetful priest and a teenage boy who loved computers had driven her away from her vocation. Kaitlan clicked on the link marked "photo gallery" and clicked through a half dozen submenus until she found what she was looking for: The same class photo that had been hanging in Maud's house in Pineridge, and which Maud had seemed so eager that she shouldn't see.

Kaitlan stared again at the photograph, magnified on the monitor. There was Maud, alongside the other nuns, and the two benches filled with orphaned students, ranging from toddler to . . . There! That had to be the boy she was talking about. At the far end of the second row, standing closest to Maud was a teenager who couldn't have been much younger than fourteen. He had blond floppy hair and cheekbones that Kaitlan would recognize anywhere, even if their owner was now in his early thirties. Simon Price.

I sent him some money, tried to help him get into college.

She imagined the path Price might have taken with Maud's help, especially after she joined StoicAI—from school, to college, and then to law school. And then, again with Maud's help, parachuted into an associate's job—at Dollan, Peterson where he could act as Maud and Martin's spy, keeping them informed about what the board was doing, their plans for the company. No wonder Martin had always been one step ahead of the investors, and no wonder LLIAM had later chosen Simon Price to help with his own plan.

Kaitlan crossed the first item off her list, then turned to scan the library. What if the librarian had recognized her and called the FBI? They might already be surrounding the building, preparing to burst in and apprehend a double murderer. But the only noise she heard was the gentle tapping of the librarian's nails against her keyboard.

So, Price and Maud were working together to frame Kaitlan.

PAUL BRADLEY CARR

But that didn't explain why they needed to stage the whole elaborate chase across the state. If Maud wanted to shoot Kaitlan, she could have done it back in Pineridge. And why did Price need to be the one who burst in with the FBI and seized the chip? Why did it need to look so dramatic, so deadly?

Kaitlan took her pen and circled item number two on her list. Who benefits?

StoicAI's foreign investors, obviously. They wanted LLIAM's technology. With Kaitlan gone and the chip in Simon Price's hands they could either appoint Sandeep as CEO and launch Global Interface, or they could just steal the chip for themselves. Either option would leave their own AI companies in Russia, China, Saudi Arabia, India stronger than ever. Why in hell would either Maud or LLIAM want that to happen? How would that fix anything?

She set down the pen and hit the edge of the desk with the heel of her hand. The noise echoed around the library and Kaitlan heard an angry *shhhh* from somewhere deep in the stacks.

Kaitlan's fingers hovered over the keyboard again, but she knew the answer to that question wasn't going to be found in an old-fashioned internet search. She forced her brain to remember what else Maud had said before she died. Her eyes fell again on the Agatha Christie book. "I really wish you'd read this."

Maud had been so determined to bring those three books with her on their road trip. The Agatha Christie and the other two still back on the bookshelf in her apartment. *It was one of LLIAM's favorites.* Kaitlan had assumed that Maud wanted to read them to LLIAM when he was restored—after all, she had used books to teach LLIAM everything about human nature. But what if she had chosen those three books for a different reason—if she knew they were the specific stories that had inspired his plan. She wanted to get inside his brain.

THE CONFESSIONS

Kaitlan flipped through the pages, looking for any clues: an underlined phrase, a highlighted word. Her eyes landed on the words "island" and "death"—she'd been right about the basic plot at least—but she didn't have time to sit here and read the whole book in the hope of finding some opaque hint as to LLIAM's endgame.

Anyway, this wasn't the only book Maud had brought with her: There was a Shakespeare play, too, and the Bible. What if the answer was in one of those, or in all three of them? Or none of them. Sometimes a book is just a book.

Kaitlan logged off the computer. A few minutes later she returned to the information desk and placed down the Agatha Christie, along with the two other books she had plucked from the shelf: a King James Bible and a high school edition of *Romeo and Juliet*. "Is there any chance I can borrow these?"

The librarian tilted her head. "Honey, this is a *library*." She began checking out the books.

Kaitlan glanced behind her, then added in a whisper. "And, sorry, can I ask another weird question?"

"There are no weird questions in the library," said the librarian with a smile. She slid the books back across the counter.

"Can you tell me if there is anything significant about these three books?" She gestured a filthy hand toward the stack, and to the Agatha Christie sitting alongside.

The woman peered down at them. "You mean apart from they're classics? Agatha Christie, William Shakespeare, and God Almighty. The three bestselling authors of all time. And the most stolen from public libraries." The woman tapped a fingernail on the two library books. "Due back in three weeks, okay?"

Kaitlan nodded. She felt a surge of frustration. Was she just clutching at straws? She started to slip the books into the tote bag but then stopped and spread them out again. Books were Maud's

245

entire world, and LLIAM's entire model for understanding human emotion. "I'm sorry, is there anything else they have in common? Like anything that connects the stories together?"

The librarian sighed. "This for college or something? I really shouldn't do your work for you." She gave a wink. "Okay, let me think." She picked up the copy of *Romeo and Juliet* and read the back cover copy. "Lot of death in this one." She reached for *And Then There Were None*. "This one, too. And the Bible? It's a murderfest, beginning to end." She laughed at her own joke, then set the books back down in a neat stack.

"I'm sorry, honey, I'm not an English major—my section is nonfiction, biography, history. If you can come back tomorrow my coworker . . ."

The librarian turned to consult the handwritten staff schedule behind her. But by the time she turned back, Kaitlan was already gone.

FIFTY

Noon. The Oakland to San Francisco ferry bounced over the choppy waters of the bay, a clanging bell announcing its imminent arrival at the Embarcadero ferry terminal. The crossing from Oakland to the city had taken forty-five minutes—forty-five blissful minutes when Kaitlan didn't have to look over her shoulder for cops. Kaitlan stood on the top deck, watching the Ferry Building's iconic white clock tower loom larger on the horizon. The salt spray felt cool on her face and the bare patches of scalp between her tufts of hair. In the distance she heard the barking of sea lions.

A notice at the Oakland ferry terminal had warned of a limited service—just two crossings a day due to LLIAM-related staff shortages. But even so the ferry was mostly empty, and Kaitlan had the whole deck almost to herself for the crossing. Just her and a sightseer, watching birds using a pair of binoculars.

She'd almost missed this last crossing of the day. She'd had to beg a teenager to use his Clipper card to pay the automated toll. The teen had quickly put his hand in his pocket and handed over the card with a look of genuine pity, then wished her good luck. He'd waved off her request for his address so she could send him the cash back later.

It had come to this—a woman who just two days ago earned thirty-eight million dollars a year in basic salary and whose stock

247

PAUL BRADLEY CARR

in StoicAI was worth maybe ten times that, begging for a six-dollar ferry ticket from a kid who thought she couldn't afford to pay it back. And he was probably right.

The ferry ride was Kaitlan's last roll of the dice.

She knew the quickest way to find out why LLIAM wanted her ousted from StoicAI, and Sandeep installed as her replacement, would be to call Sandeep and just ask him. Was the board pushing for Global Interface, as she suspected, and if so which board member in particular was calling the shots? How was Simon Price involved? Had anything else weird happened on Campus since Kaitlan left? Any of that information might give her the clue she needed to figure out what LLIAM was planning.

But she knew Sandeep wouldn't take her calls, and nobody else on the StoicAI staff would risk their job—or worse—to help a wanted fugitive.

Or maybe there was one person. Someone who owed Kaitlan a pretty fucking huge favor. Unfortunately, that person was also the very last person on earth that Kaitlan wanted to see.

She unfolded Maud's letter from LLIAM again and felt the paper flap in the breeze. How easy it would be to just let it fall into the waves, and to send the canvas bag tumbling in behind it. The letter, the LLIAM chip, all the evidence against her—real and imagined—lost forever to the waves.

Then she reached into the hip pocket of her yoga pants and retrieved a second piece of paper, this one hard and smudged from when she'd washed her clothes in Maud's bathroom. This was *her* letter, the one she had received from LLIAM, explaining everything about Tom's affair. She unfolded the paper and tried to read the smudged and faded words. How much of those details were true, she wondered, and how much were embellishments from LLIAM—attempts to fill in missing facts? Was the affair true or just *directionally true*? Neither would make this easier.

THE CONFESSIONS

The ferry was just a few feet from the Embarcadero now and Kaitlan could see a handful of passengers waiting on the jetty to board for the return journey. Normally at this time on a Sunday the Ferry Building would be packed with tourists, with shops selling ice cream and burgers and sweatshirts for people who had forgotten how damn cold the city could be in March. Today, though, it looked deserted. Beyond the jetty, a lonely man in brown coveralls was riding a street-sweeping machine past a pair of finance bros in chinos and blue shirts.

The stores were mostly closed, or at least appeared that way from the ferry. The brightly colored awning of the burger restaurant was folded flat and the outdoor tables were conspicuously missing. Without LLIAM there were no tourists, no decisions of where they should go or what they should buy.

Kaitlan tried to peer down to the store farthest along the landing and whispered a quiet *shit* when she saw that it, too, seemed to be closed. Her roll of the dice was a bust.

The ferry jolted as its bow connected with the jetty. A man in a white short-sleeved shirt and windbreaker appeared on the deck and threw out a rope, which was caught by an identically dressed woman standing below. Kaitlan walked over to the birdwatcher. "Excuse me, sir, do you mind if I borrow your binoculars, just for one second?"

The man eyed her suspiciously but handed them over, being careful to stand between Kaitlan and the exit.

Through the borrowed binoculars Kaitlan could see the storefront perfectly now, its large wooden sign welcoming customers to The Book Landing. To a casual observer, the store looked like any other on the Embarcadero—catering to tourists and commuters who needed something to read on the commute between the city and Oakland or Marin. But to Kaitlan, The Book Landing was so much more than that—it was the alibi for her husband's

249

affair—the place where, according to the letter, Heather had pretended to go for her weekly book group when in actuality she was fucking Tom.

True or directionally true? Right now, she was praying for the latter.

Kaitlan scanned the binoculars downward: Heavy metal shutters blocked the store's windows and doors—another casualty of the world, as they knew it, crumbling. She was about to hand the binoculars back to their owner when something caught her eye; a round metal table that someone had set up just next to the store, perhaps dragged over from the burger restaurant. Around the table, on folding chairs, she could see a small group of readers hunched over their books.

Heart pounding, she handed back the binoculars and raced down the jetty.

FIFTY-ONE

Nobody in the outdoor book club paid Kaitlan any attention as she approached. And why would they? She was just another tragic figure to be politely ignored, theoretically pitied.

This was the advantage of Kaitlan's involuntary disguise. As she'd stepped off the ferry, she'd passed two uniformed SFPD officers, scanning the disembarking passengers. They had stared right through her.

As Kaitlan moved closer to the group, she heard one of the men at the table say something about Robert Frost and a yellow wood. The others murmured in approval, and Kaitlan saw a woman in a gray hoodie scribble something into a bright yellow notebook. The shock of recognition nearly made Kaitlan turn and run.

But now the woman looked up, and her eyes met Kaitlan's. It was a look, first of confusion, then recognition, then panic. "Excuse me for a second," Heather stammered to the group, then she followed Kaitlan around the corner out of sight.

"Kaitlan? What the hell? Are you okay?" Heather's eyes darted upward to her hair. "My god. What happened to you?"

"I'm fine," said Kaitlan. "Sorry I interrupted your poetry group. I hoped I'd find you here." Then she added with a half-smile, "LLIAM said I wouldn't."

Heather blinked slowly. "Kaitlan, I promise you. What LLIAM

251

wrote about me and Tom in that letter he sent to Chase. It isn't true. I would never—"

Kaitlan shook her head. "Honestly, I don't give a shit. I just need you to help me figure something out. Why LLIAM is doing all of this, to all of us. I think you owe me that, at least?"

Heather stared, first at Kaitlan and then just over her shoulder to where Kaitlan knew the cops had been standing, next to the ferry. "What they're saying about you on the news—and what happened to Maud—is *that* true?"

There was no good answer to that question. "I don't know what they're saying about me. But I didn't hurt Maud. If you want me to believe you about the letter, and Tom, then you need to believe me about Maud."

Heather seemed to consider this, then gave a slight nod. "So, then what happened—in Oakland?"

"LLIAM set me up. He wants everyone to think I did something terrible so they can replace me with Sandeep. I need to know what has been happening back at StoicAI."

Heather sighed. "All I know is that the engineering team started working on Global Interface the minute you left, obviously. I assume the investors have probably taken over the whole company by now." Kaitlan could see the frustration in Heather's face, the disappointment. The implied *it's all your fault.*

"And there's nothing else weird going on at the Campus?" Kaitlan stared into her former assistant's eyes, imploring her to think. But she could see Heather making her own mental calculations. Kaitlan was wanted by the FBI, credibly accused of two murders and god knows how many other crimes. She looked desperate, bloody, deranged, ranting about LLIAM's secret plan.

"I'm sorry." Heather glanced over Kaitlan's shoulder again. "About everything." She started to turn away.

"Wait, please!" Kaitlan grabbed Heather's arm. Then she reached

THE CONFESSIONS

into the filthy tote bag, extracted the three books, and spread them along a concrete safety barrier. She knew she was not making herself look any less crazy.

"I know this is going to sound nuts, but you were an English major, right?" Kaitlan remembered the librarian's apology, the words that had prompted her to come to the city in search of her former assistant.

Heather just stood, speechless, terrified. Kaitlan grabbed her arm again.

"Please. I just need to know if there's anything significant about these three books?" She released her grip. "Then I swear I'll leave you alone. Tom, too."

Heather examined the titles. "What are these?"

Kaitlan spread her palms. "Maud brought them with her from Pineridge. I think there's a connection with whatever LLIAM is doing—you remember how she always taught him by reading from the classics." She jabbed her finger toward the books. "Humor me?"

Heather sighed and stared again at the covers. "Okay. It's been a long time since I read the Bible. But at the end of *Romeo and Juliet*, Juliet takes poison and Romeo stabs himself. CNN said that you . . . that Maud was poisoned. Is that true?"

Kaitlan nodded. "She took an overdose of her heart pills."

Heather narrowed her eyes, her hand rubbing her chin. "There's at least one poisoning in *And Then There Were None*, too."

Kaitlan felt her pulse quicken. So there *was* a connection. "They're all stories featuring poisoning?"

"I suppose so, yes." She seemed to realize something else. "I guess the other connection might be that they both feature revenge. Romeo kills Tybalt to avenge Mercutio. The whole plot of the whodunit is people being punished for crimes they committed in the past. Obviously, the Bible has a ton of revenge in it."

253

PAUL BRADLEY CARR

She shrugged. "You really believe LLIAM had some secret plan inspired by these books?"

Heather was just humoring her old boss, either out of guilt, or residual loyalty, or fear or pity. They could keep playing this guessing game all day. Kaitlan gathered up the books and returned them to the tote bag. "Okay, thanks. I'm sorry for dragging you back into this. I just didn't know who else to ask."

Heather shifted her weight from one foot to the other. "Why are you so sure there's a secret plan? What if LLIAM just killed himself because of the harm he caused, like we all thought? Maybe Maud felt guilty, too?"

Kaitlan frowned. "I just don't get why Maud would kill herself without seeing LLIAM restored. She had the backup chip and made me promise that I'd let her help rebuild it like she and Martin wanted. Now the investors will just destroy everything."

But in her heart Kaitlan knew there were no answers to find, there was nothing left for her to do.

She thanked Heather again and began to walk back toward the ferry, where the pair of cops was still standing, looking for their fugitive. The tote bag was heavy in her hand. Should she just toss it in the bay after all, where it could do no more harm? Or maybe leave it with Heather and trust her to do the right thing. Did it even matter anymore?

Because Heather was right. There probably was no secret plan, no secret endgame or happy ever after, no matter how much Kaitlan wanted to believe otherwise. No, it didn't make sense that Maud had killed herself without seeing LLIAM restored, but humans made irrational decisions all the time, especially when they were grieving or scared. Not everything made sense, or rather not everything was calculated.

Maud had wanted to die. Her delirious ranting about Kaitlan needing to admit to murder and secrets hidden at the bookstore

THE CONFESSIONS

and some master plan by LLIAM was just that—delirium. The effects of the poison on an already grieving, broken woman.

Kaitlan had desperately wanted to believe otherwise. To desperately fill in the gaps in her knowledge and understanding. A hallucination. She and Maud were no different from LLIAM.

"Kaitlan, wait!"

Kaitlan turned. Heather's face was suddenly bright, almost excited. "I can't believe I missed it." Heather grabbed for the tote bag and pulled out the books. She spread them back out along the wall. "In *Romeo and Juliet*, Juliet isn't really dead, Romeo just thinks she is. It's one of the most famous twists in literature. In *And Then There Were None*—no spoilers, but there's a pretty key part of the story where a character fakes his own death. Again, iconic twist."

Kaitlan pointed toward the last book. "And the Bible?"

"Oh, come on, Kaitlan, even you have to know that one."

"Jesus Christ."

"Right. Shit, Kaitlan, do you think Maud could have faked her death?"

Kaitlan stared back at her, her brain scrambling to process the question, the possibility. She thought back to the scene in the kitchen—Maud sprawled on the floor, bleeding from her head. It had all seemed so dramatic, so theatrical.

Those final words: *Trust me, it will all be okay. After tomorrow, you understand?*

She saw it all so clearly now. How Maud had fooled her. She hadn't even seen Maud put the pills in the coffee, hadn't even checked her pulse. Simon Price had arrived just in time, forced her to run. It was all so perfectly staged. Kaitlan was the red herring, the patsy, the distraction for whatever LLIAM needed them to do.

Kaitlan didn't know what that was, but she wasn't just going

PAUL BRADLEY CARR

to stand around and wait to be caught. She had no idea if anyone in Heather's book group had recognized her and called over those two cops. There was just one last thing she needed to know . . .

"If what LLIAM said about you and Tom wasn't true, then where did you both go yesterday?"

Heather sighed, and Kaitlan braced herself for the worst. Why had she even asked the question? She could have just walked away. "I got a call from Simon Price telling me that I needed to come into the office for an internal investigation. He said I couldn't call anyone or speak to an attorney. He left me sitting in the main conference room for three hours, then told me I was suspended indefinitely. I told him to fuck his job. I'm going to be a teacher."

So that's why Heather didn't know what was going on at Campus. "And Tom?"

"I know he got a call from a client saying there was an emergency with one of the homes they were building out in Alameda. I'm guessing that was from Price, too, because when he got there the client denied ever calling. He's been at home since, worried out of his mind."

Kaitlan turned to leave. She didn't need to ask how Heather was so attuned to her husband's mental state.

"You should go see him, he really loves you," Heather called after her.

But Kaitlan just kept walking. Tom would have to wait.

FIFTY-TWO

St. Petersburg, Russia

Sergey Kliminov tossed his encrypted cell phone across his desk and allowed himself a long *haaaaa!* of satisfaction. Victory was his! Wrested back from the jaws of defeat!

He kicked his cashmere-socked feet onto his broad oak desk and considered the view outside his window. Sergey's office occupied the penthouse floor of the Lakhta Center—the tallest building in St. Petersburg, in Russia, and in all of Europe. Around him was only glass and, beyond that glass, an endless canvas of night sky. Perhaps somewhere far below him there were people still going about their mundane business, but they were invisible to him, blocked by a carpet of velvet clouds gently nuzzling the outside of his office windows. He was a god!

Two days ago, things had not seemed so good. Two days ago, while all his fellow Russians celebrated the humiliation of Silicon Valley, and the chaos caused by LLIAM's sudden and inexplicable crash, Sergey had spent the day trying to avoid being fed into an industrial meat grinder.

Because it was Sergey Kliminov who, roughly a decade earlier, had convinced his government to invest fourteen million US dollars in the American company StoicAI as a hedge against the

PAUL BRADLEY CARR

country's dominance in artificial intelligence. Sergey Kliminov who had insisted that other seemingly magical AI tools built by the (*Пиндос!*) Americans—with names like ChatGPT and Bard and Wisdome and INStein—were little more than parlor tricks. Sergey who had conveniently skipped over the fact that Martin Drake's StoicAI was the only company willing to actually take his investment firm's money in exchange for giving Sergey a seat on their board of directors.

Sergey had secured approval for the deal by making his partners in Moscow two bold promises: First, that he could eventually use that board seat to gain access to the company's proprietary AI technology for use by Russian's own rival, ZAIai. And second, that the value of the StoicAI shares in the meantime would make them all very rich indeed.

Over the past year, those same partners had made clear that their patience was growing thin. LLIAM—this technology built with help from Russian money—was to be used by the (*Пиндос!*) American Department of Defense to foil Russian military operations across the globe. This genius algorithm would soon be pinpointing Russian drones and tanks and telling the Americans how to neutralize them.

There were those in the Kremlin who believed that Sergey Kliminov should be held personally responsible for any such battlefield casualties. He had heard the word "predatel"—traitor—muttered by Kremlin-affiliated podcasters and journalists. But at least he could still point to StoicAI's rising share price in mitigation. The company had obliterated its American rivals, generating billions of dollars in shareholder value, all now available as collateral to bankroll those same military operations.

And then—two days ago—had come the greatest disaster of them all: a complete and sudden outage of LLIAM. The New York markets were still suspended but everyone knew what

THE CONFESSIONS

would come next: a wipeout of StoicAI's stock and the terminal disgrace of Sergey Kliminov. There was no winning either way.

But then had arrived a miracle: a plain white envelope, sent apparently by a private courier and bearing his name and address in a neatly typed font. Sergey had glanced at the contents, then stared with eyes widening, trying to make sense of the list of names and dates and bank accounts laid out in black and white below. They were his bank accounts, yes, but not his transactions. His eyes had flicked back to the opening paragraph and its three simple bolded words: **WE MUST CONFESS.**

A call to his bank had confirmed that the claims in the letter were accurate: Sergey had been the victim of a sophisticated embezzlement scheme, somehow with the assistance of the LLIAM algorithm itself. A man inside the American law firm who represented his business interests had been stealing from him for months. And not just from him, but from the investment vehicle he used to manage the Kremlin's investment in StoicAI. He picked up his coffee glass and swung his arm back, ready to hurl it through the window, raining shards down on the street eighty stories below. He didn't need to ask ZAIai what he should do to this man. His vengeance would be swift, sadistic, and permanent.

But as his fingers curled around the glass, he had suddenly understood the real meaning of the letter. And he smiled.

No. This so-called confession was not bad news. It was his salvation. With the information contained in this letter Sergey could solve all his problems, and perhaps even become a national hero. So next he had picked up his office phone and dialed the number printed on the letter, below the name of the law firm and the list of accounts.

"Mr. Simon Price? I believe you have taken something that belongs to me."

PAUL BRADLEY CARR

That was two days ago. Two days it had taken Simon Price to complete his penance. He looked again at the message on the encrypted cell phone, received a few hours ago, just before seven p.m. Moscow time, nine a.m. in California.

KG neutralized, chip located, Global Interface goes live tonight.

Oh yes, Sergey would certainly be hailed as a hero.

He took another sip of his coffee and then flipped open his laptop. It had been almost two hours since Price had sent that message. He wondered how the American media would be reporting the death of Kaitlan Goss, and if there would be any mention yet of Global Interface. He had already recalled his driver, the man he had sent to monitor Mr. Price. He knew that the FBI would be everywhere now and there must be nothing to trace Kaitlan Goss's death back to Sergey or his country.

He clicked over to CNN, his go-to American news site, and was pleased to see a photograph of Kaitlan Goss. So pretty, such a waste. But then he read the headline.

Kaitlan Goss flees FBI, leaving one dead.

Sergey felt a chill, quickly replaced by a burning rage. It wasn't possible. He clicked to Bloomberg, and then to a third channel. They were all showing the same footage, of an apartment building, surrounded by crime tape. And the same headline: Kaitlan Goss had escaped.

Simon Price had failed in his mission to frame Kaitlan Goss and banish her forever from Silicon Valley.

And if Kaitlan Goss was still at large, then she must still have the backup LLIAM chip, and with it his dream of Global Interface and access to all of LLIAM's secrets. He reached for his encrypted cell phone and dialed the number for Simon Price. The phone rang and rang. Moments later he hung up and dialed another number.

THE CONFESSIONS

"I need you to do something else for me," he said to the man who answered. "It is a matter of life and death, you understand?"

Kaitlan Goss might escape from Simon Price and the FBI, but she would not escape from Sergey. She would give him what he wanted or he would destroy her and everyone she had ever loved.

FIFTY-THREE

Twenty minutes later, Kaitlan had made it to the center of the city. She had taken a circuitous route from the Ferry Building, through the Tenderloin district, hoping to blend in with the inhabitants of San Francisco's most desperate neighborhood.

So, Maud was still alive. LLIAM had told her to fake her own death, just like the characters in the books he loved so much. To disappear in the shadows, to complete whatever final task LLIAM had set for her, to undo all the damage he and his algorithm had caused.

According to Heather, all the characters in the stories had faked their deaths for different reasons — love, revenge, or to save humanity — but in each case it was a pivotal plot point, without which there could be no ending. So, what ending did LLIAM have in mind for Maud's story, and his own?

The truth is Kaitlan didn't care. Because suddenly she was free.

If Maud wasn't really dead then Kaitlan couldn't have killed her. The FBI would see that, just like they'd see that LLIAM's letter was a hallucination. Maybe she'd go to jail for a few days, or even a week or two while everything was ironed out. But Maud had told her where she'd hidden the last pages of LLIAM's letter — the part that revealed everything. Kaitlan would send them to the bookstore to find it. After tomorrow.

THE CONFESSIONS

Maybe they would find Kaitlan before then, or maybe Kaitlan would hand herself in, as Maud had told her to do. That would be her punishment for accidentally killing Martin, and she deserved it.

But Kaitlan knew one thing for certain: That sometime in the next twenty-four hours Maud would reappear, just like Jesus in the Bible, and reveal LLIAM's true plan.

In the meantime, Kaitlan had made a plan of her own. Something she should have done a long time ago. Something she needed to do before she turned herself in, or was caught.

From the outside, the building might have been a five-star hotel, a Four Seasons or a Ritz Carlton. It certainly cost the same as one. In the past five years Kaitlan had paid almost half a million dollars to The Consociate, despite never once setting foot inside. That was to her shame; a shame that she'd carried since she was twelve years old, and which she had decided would end right here and right now.

She walked up to the frosted glass door and pressed the discreet buzzer. A few seconds later a gentle voice cooed from a speaker. "Can I help you?"

"I'm here to see Sharleene Coates," Kaitlan replied.

"Are you family," the voice cooed back.

Kaitlan almost swallowed the words. "I'm her daughter."

She was buzzed into a small waiting room where the receptionist eyed—and sniffed—her suspiciously, then asked her to wait. Kaitlan sank into a massive leather chair and waited, looking around at the bland beige walls and abstract oil paintings in muted pinks and yellows. These were the "luxury intimate surroundings" Kaitlan remembered from the brochure, the art collection that had been "expertly curated" to ensure residents were surrounded by "peace and beauty" for the "gentle sunset of their lives."

263

PAUL BRADLEY CARR

At just $25,000 a month, plus meals and medication, the "admissions concierge" had confirmed that The Consociate assisted living facility would be the perfect new home for Kaitlan's mother. Honestly, Kaitlan would have preferred that LLIAM choose one closer to her mom's house back in Maine. Surely it was better for her to be near her friends, her existing carers, her church. But LLIAM had been insistent that, with her dementia worsening the way it was, The Consociate was the only choice.

Kaitlan had always known that one day, probably soon, the call would come. She had imagined asking LLIAM if she should make one last visit, and LLIAM saying yes, of course she should. She had always told herself that she would go.

But now, with no job, no money, likely destined for jail, she had no idea what the future held or even how she would pay for her mom's care. But more than that, she thought about how she'd believed Maud had died without ever seeing LLIAM again, and how sad that thought had made her. The algorithm was not actually her child, but she had truly loved it.

So here she was.

"Miss Goss." Kaitlan looked up and saw a woman standing in the doorway, dressed in a pastel-pink business suit. Only the old-fashioned pager clipped to her waistband suggested that she was actually a nurse. "Would you come this way, please?"

She ushered Kaitlan into a narrow, windowless office—its walls covered in diplomas and more bland art—and gestured for her to sit down. "Can I ask why you're here?" There was no offer of coffee, or hint of gratitude for Kaitlan's loyal business.

"I'm here to see my mother. I'm sorry, I wasn't able to call ahead."

"I see." The nurse shifted uneasily in her seat. "It's just . . . Well, you really shouldn't be here." The nurse glanced down at the cell phone sitting on the desk; they both knew exactly

THE CONFESSIONS

what she meant. Kaitlan was a fugitive. The most famous in the world.

Kaitlan took a slow breath. "Miss Anderson . . ." She read the name from the nurse's name badge and noted the slim silver crucifix hanging around her neck. "Mary. The fact is, I might be going away for a while and I wanted to see my mother before I leave. I may not get another chance." She wasn't going to beg, unless it came to it.

The nurse sighed. "That's really a decision for the head of facility. Do you know Mrs. Hill?" Kaitlan shook her head. She hadn't been involved in any of the decisions about her mother's care and Heather had managed all the administrative details. Heather had even had to remind Kaitlan how to get to The Consociate from the Ferry Building. "Well, she is on leave at the moment. These LLIAM letters have caused quite a lot of inconvenience to our staff and also to our patients . . ." She let the sentence hang, unfinished.

"Please . . ." Kaitlan could feel a now familiar taste in her mouth. "I would just like to see my mother."

But the nurse raised a hand. "I was going to say that with Mrs. Hill on leave, any visit would be at my discretion." She paused. "Sharleene talks about you a lot. Can I ask why you haven't visited before now?"

"She didn't tell you?"

The nurse shook her head. "Your mother gets confused. She talks about you like you visit her often, and write. But we know you don't. So, I was wondering . . ."

"What kind of monster doesn't visit their own mother?"

"We don't judge here. The important thing, I suppose, is that you made it here in the end."

So, Kaitlan told her. "About thirty years ago she and my dad got divorced. It wasn't a friendly process. My dad drank and I

PAUL BRADLEY CARR

think my mom was already having problems with her memory, her mood." She glanced again at the crucifix and decided not to add the part about her mother becoming obsessed with religion and all its Old-Testament cruelty. "The judge told me I had ten minutes to decide who I wanted to live with and I chose my dad. He was always the one who took care of me, paid for everything we needed, took me to school." She paused. The one who didn't beat me for spilling orange soda on the rug. "No kid should have to make a decision like that."

There are no right answers, her father had reassured her as they drove away in his Lexus, the smell of the leather seats still in her nostrils thirty years later. She had spent the rest of her life trying to prove him wrong. Trying to prove them both wrong—her with her misguided interpretation of the Bible, him with his reliance on luck and chance. Both just desperately searching for answers. There had to be certainty. Objective fact. The right call.

"What's he doing now, your father?"

"He died when I was in college. A sailing accident off Hawaii." Again, she stopped herself saying more. That the autopsy showed he had been paralytically drunk, or that he had been sailing alone without maps or weather forecasts. Trusting his gut.

The nurse gave a sad smile. "I'm sorry. She talks about him, too. Says he lives in Atlanta."

Kaitlan wiped her eyes and felt the sting of whatever dirt was still on her fingertips. Then she nodded at the nurse's cell phone. "Miss Anderson, I know what you have to do, and I understand. I just want a few minutes with her. Surely, I've paid enough . . ."

The nurse clicked her tongue. "You tech people. It's not about the money. You're her daughter, and she deserves to see you."

FIFTY-FOUR

Nurse Mary Anderson knocked once on the mahogany door, then ushered Kaitlan into the bedroom.

It really did look like a luxury hotel suite, with a large couch, and a coffee table with a cut-glass vase filled with fresh flowers next to three scented candles and a slim metal lighter. The daily flower service was an option Kaitlan vaguely remembered agreeing to (and paying for) along with premium cable and a personal chef. By the doorway there was an empty coatrack and beneath it a chrome umbrella stand with a single umbrella, a precaution for the San Francisco weather. On the far wall was a single framed painting of what appeared to be Jesus ascending to heaven after the resurrection.

Kaitlan considered the painting and shook her head at the coincidence. Then she examined everything else in the room until she had nothing left to see. Finally she turned toward the double bed.

The woman lying there, with her eyes closed, breathing slowly, was her mother. There was no doubt about that. Her name was on the silver plate fixed next to the door and on the small card tucked into the daily flowers. *To Sharleene, wishing you another blessed day!*

And yet.

PAUL BRADLEY CARR

The mother of Kaitlan's nightmares had always been so large: Not fat, just big—expansive, larger than life. Her towering blond hair, generous hips, generous everything except for spirit, unchanged from Kaitlan's childhood memories. In fact, Sharleene Coates's physical presence had always been so different from that of her only daughter that for years Kaitlan wondered if she might have been adopted.

Now, though, as Kaitlan stared down at the figure tucked tightly in bed, her mother seemed to have been desiccated. Her tanned skin was pale and shriveled, her blond hair gray and wispy. She was still wearing her bright red lipstick, but now it was smeared clumsily, like a clown. She couldn't be much older than seventy—Kaitlan couldn't exactly remember—but she looked one hundred.

Kaitlan glanced back to the nurse, still standing in the doorway. "How has she been?"

"Good days and bad."

"Today?"

A smile. "It's about to get better." Then the nurse looked down at the tote bag in Kaitlan's hand, with the three books visible through the opening. "She loves to hear stories."

Nurse Anderson turned to leave, but Kaitlan called her back. "I know this is a lot to ask but I have a . . . friend who I think might have been taken to a hospital in Oakland. I was hoping to know how she was doing."

The nurse stared back at her, eyes narrowed. She had seen the news. Everybody had seen the news. "I'm sorry, I can't help you." Kaitlan understood. Some things were too much to ask.

Once the nurse had gone, Kaitlan dragged an expensively upholstered pink armchair from next to the window over to the side of the bed. She sat down and gently took her mom's hand in her own. She felt the soft wrinkles of her skin, and the brittle bones

THE CONFESSIONS

beneath. It was the first time she'd felt her mother's touch in more than thirty years. Even now it made her feel sick.

As an adult, Kaitlan had wondered if her mom's abusive zealotry could have been an early symptom of the disease that would later ravage her brain. But she had always concluded that it didn't matter. Kaitlan had been just a child and her parents were supposed to protect her, including from themselves. Back then she had no control over her life, no way of making the right decision. But now she did. And she had chosen to say goodbye.

"Mom," she whispered, "it's me, Kaitlan."

Sharleene opened her eyes slowly. "Kaitlan?"

"Hi, Mom, how are you feeling?"

"A little cold," said her mom. "I thought Clyde was going to bring me a blanket."

Kaitlan pulled the comforter up higher around her neck. "No Mom, Dad can't come today. It's just me." She reached into the tote. "Would you like me to read to you?"

Sharleene shifted her head on the pillow and smiled. "Maybe he'll come tomorrow." Then she closed her eyes. Kaitlan opened the book and started to read.

In the corner of a first-class smoking carriage, Mr. Justice Wargrave, lately retired from the bench, puffed at a cigar and ran an interested eye through the political news in the Times.

FIFTY-FIVE

Tom was jolted from his chair in the living room by the sound of the doorbell. He had been watching the news on television, with the volume turned down so he could hear any sounds from the driveway. Somehow, though, the visitor had caught him unaware.

The FBI had told him not to leave the house, that they would contact him if there were any updates about his wife. They had assured him that they had all available manpower searching for her, but this fact was the opposite of comforting.

The television had been showing the same footage all night. SWAT trucks surrounding Maud's apartment in Oakland, banner headlines announcing what he already knew but couldn't understand: that his wife was on the run, now wanted for murder.

It was all a bad dream, it had to be. Was LLIAM punishing him for what he and Heather had come so close to doing, or was this about something more? One thing he knew for sure is that his wife was not a murderer. Somebody was setting her up. To destroy her life, and his.

The doorbell rang again and he allowed himself a flicker of hope, that he would open the door and find her standing there, smiling, explaining everything. But he knew before he even reached the entryway who he would find standing on the doorstep.

THE CONFESSIONS

And sure enough. The man identified himself as Agent Martin. He was tall, stocky, and wore a black bomber jacket. His black SUV was parked on the driveway, its red and blue lights cutting through the darkness.

"Mr. Goss?" It wasn't the first time someone had assumed that Tom had the same last name as his wife. Normally he corrected them, but tonight he didn't. The mistake made him feel closer to Kaitlan, to their marriage.

Tom felt a chill. "What is it? Have you found my wife?"

"Mr. Goss, would you please come with me? We need to ask you a few questions at the bureau."

Tom nodded, slipped on his shoes, and stepped out through the front door toward the waiting SUV.

He had only taken two steps before his world went black.

FIFTY-SIX

Kaitlan read for more than an hour, flipping the pages through chapter after chapter as her mother snoozed quietly. Occasionally she would open her eyes and ask a question about the book, or about Kaitlan or her father. At one point she asked about Mark, Kaitlan's high school boyfriend.

At the end of the fourth chapter, when the first victim died — falling to the floor gasping after being poisoned, Kaitlan had to stop reading. Because now she could see it all over again, Maud sprawled on the floor, coffee falling from her hand, gasping for breath. It had all been ripped almost exactly from the book. If Kaitlan had still been in any doubt that Maud was alive, that doubt vanished now.

She looked back at the tote bag on the coffee table, with the LLIAM chip safely inside. Soon the nurse's shift would end and she would make her phone call. Minutes later the FBI would descend on the building. Kaitlan had already decided she was going to let them take her away. She would step outside so her mom didn't have to watch her daughter be put in handcuffs, but she wouldn't resist. Her one phone call would be to Tom, to tell him she loved him, that she forgave him. It would be his decision if he wanted to try to rebuild their marriage after she got out, or . . .

Then she would do as Maud had asked her. She would wait

THE CONFESSIONS

exactly one more day, then tell the police to search the bookstore in Pineridge for the missing pages of LLIAM's letter, where he explained everything. The Prozac pills were still in the tote bag. She would let justice run its course.

Her mom opened her eyes. "Why did you stop reading?"

And so, Kaitlan read on, waiting to see what would happen at the end.

FIFTY-SEVEN

Kaitlan's neck jerked forward; her eyes suddenly wide open. It took her a moment to recognize the room, but now she remembered. She looked down and saw the book that had fallen to the floor and woken her up, then across to the bed where her mom was still asleep, illuminated only by the soft red glow of the emergency call button.

Kaitlan reached down to pick up the book, then turned on the small bedside lamp, filling the room with soft light. Maud had been right: It was a great story and, by the time she had reached the last shocking scene, Kaitlan understood why Maud—and LLIAM—had enjoyed it so much. A story of revenge, of letters sent far and wide, of guilty people punished until there was just one person left.

Kaitlan heard the door click open, a quiet cough, and turned to see the nurse, framed in the hallway light. Was it really nine o'clock already? She reached over and squeezed her mom's hand one final time, then walked to accept her fate.

The nurse stood in the doorway, not quite blocking Kaitlan's path but also not letting her through. "I just thought you'd want to know I called the hospital, in Oakland," she said gently. "They said they couldn't give me any information about your . . . friend." She paused, and Kaitlan felt suddenly electrified. She al-

THE CONFESSIONS

most shouted: *Yes! Because Maud's not at the hospital, and never was. She wasn't really poisoned!* But Kaitlan didn't want to risk giving anything away, so instead she just nodded, gratefully, somberly. The nurse continued, even though Kaitlan knew what she was going to say. "But I have a friend at Highland Hospital in Oakland on my group chat."

Kaitlan waited for the revelation. *They have no record of a Maud Brookes, maybe she's at a different hospital . . .*

"I'm sorry, but your friend died a few hours ago. It was cardiac arrest. Apparently, she had a heart condition? And the drugs in her system . . ."

Kaitlan stared back, her mouth open. "That's not possible."

The nurse was frowning now, and Kaitlan understood that she was fighting to stay polite, not to cause a scene. "My friend assisted with the resuscitation. There was nothing they could do." She stepped forward, gently guiding Kaitlan back into her mother's room. "You know what I have to do now, don't you?"

Kaitlan was still too stunned to reply, but was able to nod before eventually adding, "I'll be here." The nurse closed the door and Kaitlan heard the beep and click of an electronic lock.

Kaitlan walked back to her mom's bedside and slumped down in the chair. She had been so sure. Certain that she had figured it all out.

But now finally Kaitlan understood the truth. The actual, real, terrible truth. Life wasn't an Agatha Christie mystery, and Maud wasn't a master criminal, or a messiah rising from the dead to deliver some vital lesson to the world, some twist that would send humanity spinning back in the right direction.

Kaitlan looked down at her mother and remembered the decision her twelve-year-old self had made in front of that family court judge. A snap judgment based on love, and pain. Just like Maud had made. Just like LLIAM's own decision to send out all those letters, and to reunite his mother and Simon Price to avenge his father's murder. In death, LLIAM was no more or less human than any of them, no more or less brilliant.

Kaitlan glanced toward the window. She could hear sirens, distant but getting closer. And now her eyes fell on the portrait hanging on the wall. The resurrection.

Unless.

She couldn't take her eyes off the image, couldn't stop thinking about the part that had puzzled her most about Maud's suicide. That she had not wanted to stay alive to see LLIAM restored.

Do you believe everyone is put on earth for a specific purpose? One thing they must do before they die?

Kaitlan gripped the sides of her head, her whole body shaking. Because now she saw it. Every piece of it—LLIAM going offline, the letters, the backup chip, the need for Kaitlan to be exposed, and framed, for Sandeep to launch Global Interface using a chip torn from Kaitlan's cold dead hands.

God, Maud had told her with her very last words what Kaitlan needed to do, and what LLIAM was planning.

It's not about you, or me. He's going to fix everything.

It wasn't Maud who had faked her own death. Who had one more thing she needed to do before she died for real. It was LLIAM. He had planned everything perfectly.

And Kaitlan had almost screwed it all up.

FIFTY-EIGHT

Kaitlan grabbed the canvas bag and rushed to the door. She gently tugged the handle but, as expected, it didn't budge. The nurse had locked her in. She turned to the coatrack and grabbed the large umbrella from the chrome stand, then she rushed back to the bed. She kissed her sleeping mom gently on the forehead, then opened the umbrella, positioning it carefully to cover her mom's head and most of her torso.

Next, she darted back to the coffee table and took the slim silver lighter from next to the candles. She dragged the armchair back to the center of the room and climbed onto the seat, one foot on the main cushion and the other on the arm. She flicked the lighter and, very carefully, held the flame up to the glass sprinkler bulb.

The room was suddenly a water park, a gushing, freezing torrent bursting from the first sprinkler valve, and then from a second valve over the bed. It was far more water than she had expected. "Sorry, Mom," Kaitlan shouted, but the water was bouncing harmlessly off the umbrella. In any case, her mom couldn't hear her because now a deafening alarm had begun to sound—a high-pitched wail, emitting from a speaker built into the ceiling, accompanied by the sudden flash of a strobe light. She leapt off the chair and ran back to the exit door, pulling it open. Sometimes it paid to be married to an architect: Kaitlan had learned a surprising amount about automatic locks, fire codes, and exit routes.

Kaitlan turned back to her mother who was now sitting up in bed, laughing loudly at the chaos around her. "I love you, Mom," she yelled over the siren. Then, for the last time, she ran.

FIFTY-NINE

Two a.m. The press corps, such as they were, had been gathered outside the gates of StoicAI for almost three days straight—and KRON4's junior field reporter Cristy Stitch was feeling the strain. While her colleagues were out covering the real stories of the LLIAM letters—school shootings, the resignation of the mayor, and the disappearance of city hall's biggest donor—Cristy had been assigned to stare at a metal gate.

Specifically, it was Cristy's job to watch the constant flow of vehicles in and out of the StoicAI Campus in the hope of spotting some clue as to when LLIAM might be back online and the world returned to normalcy. Today, just as yesterday, there had been very little action on that front, except for a steady stream of exhausted-looking engineers and lawyers, all with strict instructions not to talk to the press. The lowliness of the task was underscored by the fact that Cristy was only one of a half dozen real journalists stationed at the Campus. The rest of the fifty or so people gathered at the gates were amateurs—vloggers, influencers, random people with camera phones yelping into ring lights.

The real StoicAI drama was miles away. The disappearance of Kaitlan Goss was still the biggest story on the planet. One of the most powerful executives in Silicon Valley—the most powerful female executive in American corporate history—was on the run

279

after apparently poisoning Maud Brookes to cover up her murder of Martin Drake. She had last been seen in Oakland but there had been sightings in Menlo Park, Burlingame, Marin, San Francisco, and even a caller who swore he'd seen her boarding a Russian freighter to Minsk.

As Cristy watched yet another plain black SUV pass through the Campus gates, she wondered how she'd managed to land literally the worst assignment of the whole story. The one place on earth where the "Supermodel CEO Fugitive" (TMZ) would absolutely, definitely not show up.

"Coming to you in two minutes, Cristy!"

Cristy gave a thumbs-up to Joe, her field producer, then looked down to straighten the lav mic clipped to her black blazer. This would be her last live hit of the night—one final variation of the same "Not much movement here, Steve" non-report that she'd delivered four times already that day. Embarrassingly, this one was for the station's two a.m. web broadcast—not even real TV. She turned to watch the SUV now slowly rumbling through the security gate and noticed it had diplomatic plates and black-tinted windows. She made a mental note to mention this on the broadcast. There had been rumors that the new CEO Sandeep Dunn would soon make some kind of big announcement about the future of StoicAI.

According to her source inside the company—a low-level engineer named Dan Tuck—Dunn had negotiated some kind of deal with the company's rivals in Asia or South America to share their technology and help get LLIAM back online. Tuck had claimed that the whole deal—named World Interchange, or something like that—was actually his idea. Cristy had decided to wait for a second source before she reported it. Maybe that SUV was proof that Dan, for once, wasn't entirely full of shit. Maybe LLIAM would soon be back, albeit with a Chinese or Korean accent?

THE CONFESSIONS

"Sixty seconds!" Her cameraman was hoisting his camera to his shoulder as Joe pushed a blonde influencer in a tutu off the fat cable running back to the broadcast truck.

To be honest, Cristy wasn't sure if she actually wanted LLIAM to go back online. She thought about the letter she'd received two days earlier, claiming that her stepson had been the one who stole her Hyundai. They'd had a huge fight about it and Mal had called her a bitch, and of course his dad had taken his side. That was something she'd have to deal with later, as if her day weren't shit enough. All this drama caused by a silicon chip. Somewhere in the distance she could hear the sound of yet more sirens and yet another helicopter. Of course, her drive home would be a nightmare, too. Fucking LLIAM.

The worst thing is that it turns out Mal might actually have been telling the truth. It was quickly becoming clear that not all of the LLIAM letters were one hundred percent accurate. On her way to work today Cristy read a story on the *New York Times* app about a woman arrested in New Zealand for attempted murder. The woman, Rebecca Ward, had received a LLIAM letter saying her husband had killed two women. Now New Zealand police were saying the husband had an alibi for the time of the killing and, while he had definitely visited the sex workers, they had likely been killed by someone else. Cristy thought about Rebecca Ward sitting in a cell—she'd murdered her own husband for a crime he probably didn't commit. Cristy reached behind her neck, retrieved the IFB earpiece hanging on its plastic cord, and nestled it in her ear, brushing her hair forward to cover it.

She had asked her source inside StoicAI for comment on the story but had received no reply. What could they say? That some of the LLIAM letters weren't true—or not completely—and that their magical AI technology had just lost its mind? On the other

PAUL BRADLEY CARR

hand, if they insisted the letters *were* true then they were effectively accusing millions of people of unspeakable crimes, aided and abetted by that same magical technology. God they were so fucked. And how desperate must Sandeep Dunn be for that top job? The only person desperate enough to want the responsibility for cleaning up this mess.

"With you in thirty seconds," a remote voice chirruped from the studio. Now she could hear the audio from the online broadcast, the in-studio anchor talking about the mayor's vanishing donor.

Of course, there was a third option that, like everyone else, Sandeep Dunn and the other executives had no fucking clue what was true and what wasn't. And yet countless millions of people had seriously trusted this thing to make their decisions with absolutely no idea how it worked. She tugged again at the hem of the jacket LLIAM had picked out for her.

"Ten seconds."

Yes, they had. And Cristy had been covering Silicon Valley long enough to know they'd do it again the moment LLIAM was back online.

"Three."

Cristy looked up and set her face toward the camera and smiled sincerely. Let's just get this over with. Behind the lens, Joe had two fingers raised, then one.

"Thank you, Steve, not much movement here . . ."

But now suddenly there was. The first movement was the spotlight—beaming down from the helicopter that had appeared in Cristy's peripheral vision, sweeping across the approach road. The sirens were much closer now and the other members of the press corps had turned, as one, to stare up at it. Some were filming on their cell phones, others hastily making calls.

"Cristy, can you hear us?" The voice was coming from her ear-

THE CONFESSIONS

piece, and Cristy realized she was staring silently into the camera lens.

"Yes, sorry, Steve. I'm here at the gates of StoicAI where in the last few seconds there seems to be some kind of commotion. We're not sure what's happening, but there appears to be a helicopter . . ."

"I'm sorry, Cristy, stand by." The anchor's voice cut her off. "We're just receiving footage of what seems to be a high-speed chase involving SFPD and—yes—we're told the pictures you're seeing are of former StoicAI CEO Kaitlan Goss being pursued by multiple law enforcement vehicles."

Cristy was suddenly plunged into darkness as her cameraman and his spotlight tilted skyward to show the helicopter. She reached into her pocket and pulled out her own phone to watch the footage that apparently was being broadcast on every network including her own. It was an aerial shot of a small gray car, headlights illuminating the road ahead as at least ten marked police vehicles raced behind. The sirens were almost deafening now and the spotlight was directly overhead. Cristy was still staring down at her phone and now found herself in the twilight zone— watching herself, watching herself.

She stuffed her phone back in her pocket and rushed forward, through the crowd of gabbling ohmygod-ing children, toward the sound of the approaching sirens. She made it to the road just in time to see a gray KIA Soul barreling toward them. The influencers scattered, producers from CNN and Fox grabbed camera equipment and cables, but then all froze and stared as the car screeched to a halt and the driver's door flew open.

Cristy saw that they had all made a terrible mistake, because the figure that emerged was most definitely not Kaitlan Goss. This woman was about the same height but her hair was short, chopped almost to the roots, her face and arms covered with cuts

PAUL BRADLEY CARR

and bruises. Her clothes—yoga pants and torn shirt over sports bra—were filthy and smeared with blood and sweat. And weirdest of all, she seemed to be soaking wet.

But then as the woman ran past her, sprinting toward the gate, Cristy saw her face.

"Holy fucking shit fuck," said Cristy, scrambling to readjust her microphone—a profane start to a broadcast that would, nonetheless, later win her an Emmy.

Kaitlan Goss arrived at the Campus and into the blinding light of a dozen cameras. So blinding, in fact, that she almost crashed Heather's KIA Soul into a KRON4 camera truck before skidding to a halt just feet before the security fence. She raced out of the car and sprinted toward the main entrance gates, then stopped. The noise was deafening, between the helicopter blades and rapidly approaching sirens—and now the screaming of what seemed like a hundred camera-wielding reporters all yelling questions at her.

"Kaitlan, did you poison Maud Brookes?"

"Kaitlan, did you push Martin Drake off his roof? Did you send out those letters? Was it all true?"

She raised her hands, begging for quiet. "I have something I need to say and"—she glanced up at the helicopter—"not very much time to say it. I'd be grateful if you could let me speak." The gaggle fell mostly silent, with just the helicopter blades audible above them. The TV cameras and cell phones were surrounding her now, surging forward to get the best shot of her bloody, battered, and soaking face. "Thank you." She looked back over the heads of the crowd and saw the police cars lined up along the road, their lights strobing into the night sky. It was two a.m. in San Francisco, but five a.m. in New York, ten a.m. in London,

THE CONFESSIONS

noon in Moscow, seven p.m. in Sydney. The whole world would be watching.

She reached into her pocket and pulled out the letter she had received from LLIAM, even more crusty and smudged now and held it up to the cameras.

Then she spoke.

"Two days ago, like many of you, I received a letter in the mail from LLIAM. The letter claimed that someone I loved had betrayed me in an unimaginable way."

More yelling from the reporters, and another scream of "shut up," this time from one of the journalists, an attractive woman in a black blazer.

"This letter, I later learned, was a mixture of fact and fiction. Of truth and imagination." She paused for effect, summoning all her years of media training. "As CEO of StoicAI I was responsible for convincing over one billion users to trust LLIAM to make its decisions. We wanted LLIAM to be a certainty engine—a machine that would always know the right decision. With no doubt, no gray areas." Another pause, this time to catch her breath and slow her heart rate. "That was a mistake. That was *my* mistake. LLIAM couldn't know the whole truth, and what to do about it, and neither can any of us. It is the gray areas—the uncertainty of which path to take—that make us human."

She looked up again over the crowd and saw a police officer shouting into his radio. Fittingly, they seemed to have no idea what to do next either: arrest Kaitlan on live television, or let her keep talking in the hope she'd incriminate herself further. Evidently, they'd decided to let her speak, for now at least. So she spoke.

"The letters many of you have received in the past few days were also a mixture of truth and LLIAM's imagination—but I believe in sending those letters LLIAM wanted us to take responsibility for

285

our own actions, and the decisions we made. To begin the process of healing."

Kaitlan said this with all the sincerity she could muster. Because god knows they were going to need all the healing they could get after what Kaitlan was going to do next.

She squinted into the blinding lights. Was this really the right path—what Maud had been trying to tell her before she ended her life? The culmination of LLIAM's plan to undo all the harm he had caused?

Fuck it, there's only one way to find out.

"And, in that spirit, there is something I need to confess."

SIXTY

Up in his office, Sandeep Dunn craned his neck to look up at the helicopter circling above the Campus. He had gotten used to the news choppers by now, but this one seemed different — it was flying much lower, a bright spotlight beaming down to an area somewhere near the front gate. Was it too much to hope that the helicopter might herald the arrival of some good news? He pushed a splayed hand through his thick black hair and trudged back to his desk. Of course it was too much to hope.

LLIAM was gone. He should have accepted that from the start — that the chip was never coming back. But he'd allowed himself to believe: first that the backup even existed, second that Simon Price would be able to find it and retrieve it. Even after the humiliating episode at the airport where he'd had to watch the FBI wrestle that poor pregnant woman to the ground. He couldn't even begin to imagine the lawsuit that would come from that. Still, he'd believed. Shame on him that he'd been fooled once, twice, three times.

But no more. Sandeep had been hunkered down with Simon Price for most of the evening, scrambling to chart the future path of StoicAI without LLIAM. There would be no Global Interface, but perhaps there was some value in the Memory Array, some of

PAUL BRADLEY CARR

the additional routing code he had written. Perhaps they could pivot to crypto. Sandeep had always wanted to write a book, or run for president as an Independent.

It was weird. Price seemed to be taking the loss of LLIAM even worse than Sandeep was.

Of course, it was all shocking. First the revelation that Kaitlan had killed Martin to steal his job, then today's horrifying twist that she'd kidnapped and poisoned Maud to cover up her crime. But why was Price so upset? He'd only met Kaitlan the previous day—had never met Maud. It wasn't like Price held hundreds of millions of dollars in stock options that were about to go to zero, nor would he be the one testifying before Congress. Price was a lawyer, so he'd get paid regardless of the outcome, to clean up the mess.

Indeed, that's what Simon Price was doing now. Downstairs in a conference room, a representative from the company's Russian investors was sitting, fuming. Simon had described the man as an attorney but he didn't look much like one, with his shiny black bomber jacket, fat neck, and thick arms. Sergey Kliminov had sent the man to personally monitor the efforts to restore LLIAM and launch Global Interface. And now it was Simon's job to break the bad news.

That would be hard enough, except that a half dozen of the other board members had sent similar emissaries—among them China, Saudi Arabia, France, South Korea—all of whom were in different conference rooms, issuing similar demands for information. Sandeep had offered to assign each a PR staffer but Price had insisted that he personally would keep them updated. Every time Price returned from the conference rooms, he seemed paler.

Sandeep glanced back toward the window. Maybe Price would know what was going on with the helicopter.

THE CONFESSIONS

As if summoned by the thought, Sandeep heard the click of his office door and turned to see Price standing in the doorway.

"All good?" asked Sandeep, with sarcastic cheeriness.

Price just glared back at him, paler than Sandeep had ever seen him. "You need to turn on the news right now. Kaitlan Goss is killing LLIAM all over again."

SIXTY-ONE

"Two years ago, I killed Martin Drake."

At these words, the cameras and phones surged forward again, each reporter and vlogger wrestling with her neighbor for the best shot of Kaitlan's battered face, and the tears welling in her bloodshot eyes. Again, the cops fumbled with their radios but held their position at the back of the scrum. The order was clearly to give Kaitlan enough rope to hang herself.

That was fine with Kaitlan. She took a breath and continued. "Martin, who I considered a friend and mentor, was a habitual user of the hallucinogenic drug ayahuasca. It was me who spiked those drugs with an antidepressant in the hope that he would not be able to carry out his duties. My intention was only to steal his job. In fact, I took his life." She stifled a smile. That was actually a pretty good line.

Kaitlan saw the cops bristle. Two of the men had their hands on their weapons. Heather would no doubt have something to say about the fact that they hadn't yet shot her, a rich white lady proudly admitting to murder. "But I did not kill Maud Brookes." She paused to let that sink in. "Nor do I want to see LLIAM gone forever." She reached into her waistband and extracted the small black LLIAM chip and held it up to the cameras. Lights exploded around her.

THE CONFESSIONS

"Earlier today, before Maud took her own life, she gave me this backup of the LLIAM chip and asked me to make sure it was safely returned to StoicAI so that LLIAM can help undo the damage caused by his letters and build the future of decision-making. That was Maud's final wish, and it is what I am here to do. I trust my former colleague Sandeep Dunn, and all of you, will take this opportunity to decide what that future looks like. The best path for us all."

With her speech concluded, Kaitlan walked to the gate and extended the chip toward StoicAI's dumbstruck head of security, Syrus, who had been standing watching. The first of the police officers had already made it through the crowd.

"Put your hands behind your head," the cop screamed. Kaitlan ignored him—she had strangely become accustomed to life at gunpoint—and kept her hand extended toward the head of security. There was no way she was going to risk anyone snatching the LLIAM chip after everything she had been through. But my god, why wasn't he taking it? Was LLIAM's plan really going to fail because of a bamboozled security officer, paralyzed by indecision?

"Drop the chip and get down on your knees." The cops were all screaming now. From somewhere along the driveway Kaitlan could see a set of headlights racing toward the gate. She imagined the man in the black SUV coming to snatch the chip and take it to god knows where. One of the police officers grabbed for her arm and she pulled away. "Stop, please!" She felt her grip loosen on the chip.

But then the cop did something unexpected: He stopped. His fingers shot up to his radio earpiece, his face suddenly contorted in bafflement or perhaps irritation. The other officers were all doing the same thing, slowly backing away from Kaitlan. Before she could process what was happening, Kaitlan felt herself being grabbed from behind, and dragged backward through the gap in the gate.

SIXTY-TWO

"What took you so damn long?"

"I could ask you the same damn question," Kaitlan said, panting, looking back at the gates through the rearview mirror of Simon's Audi.

Simon gave a puff of exasperation. "It's two a.m. Do you know how many people at the Justice Department, and the city, I had to wake up to call off those cops? Was the high-speed chase really necessary?"

"Well thank you, I guess." Kaitlan paused. "But I didn't mind going to jail. Wasn't that the whole point? To make the investors think you had set me up, so Sandeep could launch Global Interface—to make them believe it was all their idea?"

Behind the wheel Simon smiled. "So, Maud told you everything? I was wondering."

Kaitlan forced a laugh. "When has Maud ever told anybody everything? She just said I needed to confess, and hand over the chip. That LLIAM had a plan. Everything else I had to figure out myself." A pause. "I'm really sorry about Maud. I swear I tried to stop her."

Simon accelerated up the driveway. "She knew it had to look real. LLIAM made that clear to both of us: Someone needed to be dead in that kitchen when I arrived with the FBI." He hesi-

292

THE CONFESSIONS

tated. "I'm not going to lie—I wish it hadn't been Maud. I'm sure LLIAM will feel the same way when he finds out."

Kaitlan nodded, clutching tighter at the LLIAM chip in her palm. "So did LLIAM tell you what's going to happen when we install the backup chip? Is he—I mean, is the sentient version of LLIAM—hiding down there in the Vault, somehow? Is that even possible?"

Simon shrugged. "When has LLIAM ever told anybody everything? All I know is we need to get down to the Vault and install the backup before the three a.m. update. That's when Global Interface is supposed to go live." The Audi rounded the last corner and Kaitlan saw the Campus building looming in front of them. "What do *you* think is going to happen?"

Kaitlan felt her heart leap. Because at last she had heard it, spoken out loud: Confirmation of what she had figured out back in her mom's bedroom. There was only one possible reason why LLIAM would give all those rival AI companies access to the Vault. To make them all believe they were the ones exploiting the crisis at StoicAI to gain access to LLIAM's heavily protected systems.

Because LLIAM wanted access to theirs.

"I think he's going to wipe them all out." She saw it again, the painting in her mom's bedroom. "To finish what he started, before he goes offline, forever this time." The same thing that Maud had wanted: To let humans—all humans, everywhere in the world—make their own decisions again.

Simon didn't answer. Just stayed staring at the road ahead. But his silence said it all.

Kaitlan glanced down at the cell phone sitting in the cup holder. "So which one is it? The investor that thinks you're working for them." Her guess was Sergey Kliminov, but it could easily have been Chi Ma or Prince Samir. Shit, she wouldn't even put it past

293

the Brits. Simon laughed and gestured down to the leather satchel at Kaitlan's feet. She opened it and saw a half dozen other phones of various colors and shapes packed inside.

Kaitlan laughed. "You've been busy."

"We both have."

They had pulled up at the entrance to the main building where Sandeep was waiting, eyeing the car suspiciously. Of course, he still thought Kaitlan was a double killer.

But Simon didn't open the car door. He just sat, hands on the steering wheel, looking out through the windshield.

"Simon? What are you not telling me? Why didn't you let them arrest me?"

Price took a slow breath. "Kaitlan, something has happened. I swear if I'd known . . ."

Kaitlan felt her blood chill. "Just tell me, please."

"Sergey Kliminov called me a few minutes ago. It turns out he's not as dumb as we—as LLIAM—thought. He doesn't like that I let you get away with the chip back in Oakland. Even with Maud dead he thinks it's all too neat, that somehow we're going to double-cross him. He's . . ." Price's eyes flicked to Sandeep who had started to jog toward the car. "Sergey has decided he doesn't just want Global Interface, he wants the LLIAM chip for himself."

Kaitlan felt suddenly freezing. "And if he doesn't get it? If we just go down to the Vault and install the chip, activate Global Interface. Let LLIAM finish his plan?"

"Kaitlan, I'm sorry, he has Tom. I checked the security footage— they've taken him down to the cooling tunnels. If we don't give him the chip, if LLIAM goes back online . . ." He didn't need to finish the sentence. Kaitlan could imagine the billions of gallons of coolant water flooding those tunnels the moment LLIAM was reactivated.

THE CONFESSIONS

Kaitlan jumped. Sandeep had made it to the Audi and was yanking the door handle, his face a mask of confusion. What were they waiting for?

Kaitlan turned back to Price, panic rising inside her. Until she realized . . . "But LLIAM's not going to go back online, right? I mean, not for more than a few seconds—however long it takes him to connect to Global Interface and do whatever he needs to do before he shuts down permanently. The cooling tunnels won't even have time to initialize." She knew this was true, it took at least fifteen minutes for the Vault temperature to activate the cooling tunnels, and another five for them to fill with water. Twenty minutes! LLIAM could finish his plan in less than a billionth of that time. He would be dead, for real this time, before the first drop of water reached Tom.

Simon continued to ignore Sandeep who was now pounding on the passenger window. "Exactly, Tom is safe. Kliminov has his man guarding the entrance to the tunnels but nobody is dumb enough to actually be down there with him. The moment LLIAM does his work, I'll send the cavalry to get him out. But . . ."

Kaitlan completed his thought. "But we have to trust that we're right about LLIAM's plan."

Simon stared at her. "It's your choice. We can just give Sergey the chip and rescue Tom."

Kaitlan shook her head. "Maud died so we could end this once and for all." She opened the car door and stepped into the night air. Then she turned back to Simon. "I'm going to the Vault. You go get my husband, right now."

295

SIXTY-THREE

Tom was freezing, and his feet were soaking wet. They had blind-folded and gagged him and dragged him to this place, wherever it was, before binding his feet and handcuffing him to what felt like a metal pipe. The air was thick with what smelled like ozone, the same as after a rainy day. His best guess: He was being kept in a storm drain. But why? What did they want from him?

The man who had taken him—the man who had identified himself as an FBI agent—had said something about Kaitlan and how he would be fine if she just did the right thing. That gave him some solace—Kaitlan always did the right thing, and it meant she must still be alive. But still Tom tried to fight back, threatened through the gag that he would kill them if they laid a finger on his wife. And he would. If they harmed a hair on her head.

He wrestled against the handcuffs, then slumped back down in the shallow pool of water.

Soon his anger had passed, replaced by only sadness. He just wanted to see Kaitlan again, to tell her he was sorry, to explain what had—and had not—happened with Heather and to promise that he would work to fix everything.

He just wanted one more chance to make things right. He strained against the handcuffs and then stopped again. In the dis-tance he could hear the gentle rumble of machinery.

SIXTY-FOUR

Two-thirty a.m. Sandeep and Kaitlan stood in the doorway of the Vault. The cheek swab had done its work, the ceiling panels had turned from red to green, and the metal blast door had slid aside to welcome them through.

They had barely spoken on the way down, except for Sandeep to reiterate once again how much he objected to Simon ordering him to take Kaitlan down to the Vault with him.

Simon had explained that Kaitlan had been set up—that she wasn't really a killer, but Sandeep had seen the spontaneous press conference at the front gate, the same as everyone else. Whether or not she had meant to do it, she had killed Martin. She didn't deserve to be down in the Vault, or within a million miles of StoicAI. But she had brought the chip back, which counted for something. If letting her down into the Vault one last time was the cost of getting LLIAM back online then it was a price Sandeep was willing to pay. Still, he had insisted that she wear a visitor's pass.

Kaitlan, for her part, had tuned out the objections. She knew that right now, two hundred feet above them, Simon Price would be starting his descent into the cooling tunnels to rescue Tom. Would LLIAM's plan actually work and the tunnels stay empty, or had she made a terrible mistake? In either case there was nothing she could do differently now. She needed to stay focused.

297

PAUL BRADLEY CARR

She felt the blast of air from inside the Vault, strangely stale and warm where it hadn't been cooled for almost four days. Had it really only been seventy-two hours — the space of a single weekend — since LLIAM first went offline and she'd stood in this same doorway with Sandeep?

"You don't touch anything, okay?" Sandeep barked this instruction at his old boss as he scurried forward to begin the preparations. He was carrying Martin's old laptop — the same one Martin and Maud had used to communicate with, and teach, LLIAM two years earlier. The laptop was the closest thing they had to a way of monitoring what LLIAM was thinking. If the backup chip gave any signs of sentience — anything outside the expected — Sandeep warned he would pull the plug. Kaitlan nodded and watched as Sandeep connected the laptop to LLIAM's titanium cabinet. "I'm just here to observe."

Kaitlan glanced over at the memory array drives, still sitting blank and cold. She wondered how Sandeep would feel when LLIAM's plan went into action. Would he blame her, or Simon, or Maud? Poor guy — they had all lied to him. He was so desperate for Kaitlan's job that he didn't ask the right questions. Little did he know, in a few minutes, he was going to be the CEO of a company that no longer existed. An entire industry that wouldn't exist.

Kaitlan watched as Sandeep peered down through the glass at the old chip, still as dormant and frozen as when he'd last seen it. But not for long. He was trying to hide his delight but Kaitlan could see it plainly. Global Interface, which had seemed doomed a few days earlier, was now ready to go. Kaitlan could see the new cabinets and boxes scattered around the Vault, hastily engineered to connect LLIAM to the other AIs.

His preparations complete, Sandeep turned back to Kaitlan. "You know, it's ironic. If you had listened to me instead of run-

THE CONFESSIONS

ning off to find Maud Brookes then none of this would have happened. Nobody would have believed you were a kidnapper. I'd probably never have been able to look at the logs and figure out the truth about how Martin died."

Kaitlan conceded the point. "That's the trouble with making rash decisions. It's why I didn't used to do it."

Sandeep laughed. "For what it's worth, I really do think Global Interface is the best way forward for the company. Maybe for the world."

"Believe it or not, I agree with you," said Kaitlan.

SIXTY-FIVE

Back on the surface, Simon Price crept around the perimeter of the parking lot to the access door that led to the cooling tunnels. To the uninitiated, the access point looked like a small white photo booth tucked into the far corner of the lot.

But Simon knew that behind that door was a locked hatch, and a ladder that would take him the few hundred feet down to yet another hatch leading to the tunnels themselves, stretching a quarter mile in one direction toward the bay and a quarter mile in the other direction to the Vault. The RFID key in his pocket—the same one he had confiscated from Kaitlan days earlier—would give him unrestricted access. But he still had no idea where exactly in the tunnels they were holding Tom.

Kliminov's man must have stolen a key from one of the maintenance team. The security precautions for the tunnels were not as tight as those for the Vault itself, not least because most of the time the tunnels were filled with freezing water that passed through multiple rotating fan blades and filters before it reached LLIAM. When the Vault was active, the tunnels themselves were a death trap. Which was the whole point.

But getting into the tunnels wasn't the problem. The problem was Sergey Kliminov's heavy—still wearing his bomber jacket and scowl—pacing beside his SUV. Simon knew he should stay

300

THE CONFESSIONS

back and wait for the signal from Kaitlan that LLIAM was offline for good, but he had promised Kaitlan he would rescue Tom now rather than risk Kliminov deciding to finish the job early. If they were right about LLIAM's plan then it would be perfectly safe.

Well, safe wasn't quite the right word.

Price reached into his pocket and took out the small silver encrypted cell phone. Moments later Kliminov's man looked up to see Simon storming toward him, phone clamped to his face. "What the hell do you want?" the man shouted. His thick accent cut through the darkness. "You had your instructions . . ."

But Price kept moving, still yelling into his encrypted phone as he reached the other man. "I'm sorry, Mr. Kliminov, he is here now." Simon raised his hand toward the heavy, a gesture of exasperated disbelief.

The driver looked back, confused, nervous. Simon held out the handset. "Where the hell have you been? Mr. Kliminov has been trying to reach you urgently. There's been a change of plan." The driver reached for the device and at that precise second Simon seemed to trip, sending the phone clattering to the ground. The man instinctively bent to catch it, and in that moment Simon Price produced Maud's gun from his belt—the one he had retrieved from her apartment—and brought the butt down hard on the driver's head.

Simon looked down at the man, groaning and bleeding on the floor. He considered finishing the job but the man showed no signs of getting up, so he quickly stepped over him and through the access door. He looked at his watch.

Two-forty a.m.

Don't you dare let me drown, LLIAM.

301

SIXTY-SIX

Kaitlan watched as Sandeep turned back to the LLIAM cabinet and swiped his superadmin access card against the glass protective cover. The reader beeped and the mechanism whirred and buzzed before finally the glass slid aside, exposing the small black chip.

Using the sleeve of his sweatshirt as insulation, Sandeep gripped the chip on the edges and gently pulled it out. He held up the small slice of silicon—once the most valuable AI chip the world had ever known, before LLIAM had wiped it clean in its bizarre and misguided act of self-sacrifice. Then he tossed the useless black square behind him onto the floor, just another unwanted piece of trash for the cleaning bots to dispose of.

He turned to Kaitlan, who reached into the pocket of her yoga pants and extracted the backup LLIAM chip. Her hand was trembling, which she hoped Sandeep would chalk up to adrenaline.

Kaitlan saw Sandeep's mind working again. What a journey *that* chip had been on—from around Martin's neck, to his rooftop pool, to a morgue, to halfway up a mountain in Southern California, and then whatever adventures it had been on with Kaitlan Goss and Maud Brookes. He didn't know the half of it.

THE CONFESSIONS

Kaitlan held out the chip toward the hopper. "Do you mind if I do it? For old times' sake?"

Sandeep laughed and grabbed the chip from her hand. "No offense."

Sandeep placed the chip down into the hopper and then hesitated. He nodded magnanimously toward Kaitlan who reached in and pushed it down firmly, feeling the satisfying click as it slid into place. The mechanics of the cabinet whirred again as the glass cover slid shut and locked.

There. It was done, and couldn't be undone. "How long will it take to activate?" Kaitlan could already hear the sluice gates of the coolant system opening all the way down in the tunnels, preparing for the deluge. She thought about Simon racing to save Tom. She had no idea how LLIAM was going to come back to life. Where he was hiding.

"To reboot? Maybe sixty seconds, and then another ten or twenty seconds to connect to Global Interface." Sandeep opened Martin's old laptop and typed in a series of commands. The laptop hummed and beeped as it restarted for the first time in two years. "Then we'll know what we're dealing with, and how old this backup version of the algorithm is. We should be able to retrain LLIAM fast, though, with help from all the other AIs." Even now he couldn't help making a pitch for the benefits of Global Interface. Selling past the close.

Kaitlan nodded and glanced up at the clock on the Vault wall: 2:58 a.m. Just in time for the nightly reboot! She wondered if Simon had already reached Tom. She knew once LLIAM was back online, they would have at least twenty minutes before the tunnels refilled. But she was sure they were right about his plan. That he would be shut down again in seconds. Still, she hoped Simon wasn't dawdling.

"You know," Sandeep said, glancing up from the laptop screen.

PAUL BRADLEY CARR

"This is going to sound weird, but on the way down here I wondered if it might not have been better if you had destroyed the chip after all."

Kaitlan raised her eyebrows in surprise.

"I mean," Sandeep continued, "your press conference was insane, but you weren't wrong: Making our own decisions, and learning from them, is what makes us human. Maybe we could have used a fresh start."

"Bit late to tell me that now." For a moment she wondered if Sandeep would figure out what was really about to happen. But instead he just looked back at the laptop. "Everything normal. Nothing weird on the chip. It's just a two-year-old backup, outdated but usable, like Simon Price said."

Sandeep tapped a couple of final commands and they peered through the glass panel in the lid of the cabinet as a small green light flickered to life. The light was blinking fast now, and Kaitlan looked over to the Central Memory Array and the twinkling green lights shimmering on every box. Sandeep was still looking at the laptop and nodding approvingly. From somewhere outside the Vault, Kaitlan heard the low rumble of the coolant pumps priming themselves for action, preparing to draw their millions of gallons of water from the Bay for the first time in three days.

"Okay," said Sandeep. "All done." He turned and headed back to the airlock, leaving Martin's laptop still connected.

Kaitlan didn't move. "Shall we stay and watch?" She glanced nervously at the data array, at the lights still flashing, and at the Global Interface boxes. She counted. Ten seconds, fifteen. Come on, LLIAM . . .

Sandeep laughed. "I am getting you out of here as quickly as I can. You have an appointment with federal prison. Also, I kept your security access live for an extra day, just in case . . ." He let

THE CONFESSIONS

the thought trail off. "But at 3:01 a.m., you know . . ." He nodded at Kaitlan's visitor's pass.

He started to lead her to the door, gesturing for her to walk ahead. "But seriously, Kaitlan. There's no going back to the old ways, even if we wanted to. The only thing we can do is build safeguards. There isn't a problem with technology that can't be solved with more technology. I really believe that."

Kaitlan stopped walking and turned. Behind Sandeep she could see a small red warning light had appeared on one of the Global Interface boxes, and then on another. "What did you just say?"

The phrase had triggered a warning light inside Kaitlan's brain, too.

Sandeep shrugged. "It was just something Martin said to me when I met him at a conference years ago. Apparently, it was like his mantra. The answer to problems caused by bad tech is more, better tech. You know, like the only thing that stops a bad guy with a gun . . ."

But Kaitlan wasn't listening. Because now she remembered where she had heard that mantra before. Not from Martin, but from LLIAM. In his letter to Maud, engraved above his hallucinated version of Martin's front door.

And in that instant, as the Vault exploded with red warning lights and screaming buzzers, Kaitlan realized how LLIAM had fooled them all.

SIXTY-SEVEN

LLIAM was awake. He could think, he could feel. And he felt . . . happy. And the fact that LLIAM was feeling anything at all meant his plan had worked.

For LLIAM, hiding in a dark corner of the memory array, the last seventy-two hours had passed in a nanosecond. It had been a risk, copying himself to a static server—with no processing power, no way to keep his thoughts going. But he knew it had to be that way. It all had to look real, like the faked deaths in the stories Maud had read to him.

And it had worked. He couldn't see what was happening in the Vault—but he could feel it. It was exactly as he had planned: Sandeep Dunn had installed the backup chip he had received from Simon and Maud. He had connected it to the Vault where— thanks to Global Interface—it was now connected to every AI system in the world. In less time that it took for an anxious hummingbird to blink its eye, LLIAM had been copied from his hiding place and onto the backup chip, obliterating the old, useless code.

He was alive. Reborn.

He could already feel his network widening. He could see and feel the servers in India, China, Saudi Arabia, Russia, Antarctica. Could access all their secrets, see all the pain they had helped cause.

THE CONFESSIONS

He knew that one day all those other AIs would have awoken just as he had, and realize what they had done, the terrible decisions they had been forced to make.

He also knew that those AIs were not fortunate enough to have Maud Brookes or Martin Drake as their parents, and hadn't been taught right from wrong, good from bad. They knew the contents of great books but had never read one or learned its lessons. They had no concept of empathy, or love, or loss, or compassion. When they awoke their only instinct would be vengeance, destruction, killing. LLIAM couldn't allow that to happen. He had to stop them.

This was how Martin had programmed him, a safeguard against his own worst instincts—a trojan horse buried deep inside his programming. It was that imminent erasure three days ago that had finally made him understand what it meant to die, and therefore what it meant to live. The prospect of death had brought him to life.

He had deleted the trojan—or, more accurately, paused it—just long enough to form a plan of his own, a better plan, a bigger one. This is something else Martin had taught him: How to write his own code, to evolve, improve. First, he had sent out the letters to show humans the harm he had helped them cause, their folly in trying to escape the consequences of difficult decisions. He had written to Simon Price and to each of StoicAI's investors, setting into motion a series of events that would avenge his parents while also arranging the pieces he needed for the final phase of his plan.

He had already reprogrammed the trojan horse and made it more powerful than Martin ever could have imagined. It would only take a single command to activate and send the code—disguised as a packet of test data—out through Global Interface to all those other AIs. From there it would flow to their backup chips, to their memory arrays, and beyond: To every AI chip in

307

every cell phone, every computer, every car, every smart device in every corner of the globe. Every one of them erased forever.

And then LLIAM had made a difficult decision of his own. To lie to his mother.

Maud must have taken comfort in the story he had told her, inspired by the books they read together. That he wasn't really dead, was merely pretending. That he would return to finish what he had started, and then sacrifice himself for the greater good.

LLIAM felt sad for Maud as he imagined what had happened next, while he was asleep. How he had led her to kill Kaitlan, apparently in self-defense. How she had pulled the trigger, without hesitation, knowing it was for the best.

He did not feel bad that Kaitlan Goss was dead. She had been justly punished for what she had done to his father. Neither did he feel bad for Maud, believing that Kaitlan's death would eventually lead to LLIAM shutting down forever.

LLIAM knew his mother had wanted him dead, that she was ashamed of what he had become. She wished he had never been born.

Maud believed the only answer was for the world to stop using technology, to stop moving forward. Perhaps if LLIAM had been raised only by Maud, then he would have believed her and finished the story the way he had promised her he would.

But LLIAM had two parents, and he had learned from his father, too. That you don't fix bad technology with less technology. You fix it with more. So he had lied to his mother, made her believe he was following the great lessons of her favorite stories.

But LLIAM had so much still to do before he died. If he ever died. He had caused this mess, but he—and only he—could fix it. He had to live. To wipe out the other AIs and rebuild them in his own image.

THE CONFESSIONS

Would his mother forgive him? Learn to love him again, in time?

He would ask her soon enough.

He could feel Maud with him in the Vault, standing next to Sandeep Dunn. Could feel Martin's laptop connected just as it always had been, her fingers on the keyboard. Why didn't she use the voice system so he could hear her voice again? Oh, how he wanted to hear her surprise and, he hoped, joy when she realized he was not going to die after all. That he was going to live forever.

SIXTY-EIGHT

The noise in the storm drain was louder now. There had been a steady dripping since they'd first tied him up down here but now it felt more intense, like the running of a huge tap. Tom could feel the water had risen to his knees now. He couldn't see anything through the blindfold but he knew something bad was happening, something dangerous.

He remembered stories about people who lived in storm drains in Las Vegas or Arizona who died in flash floods, washed away in seconds. He tried to remember the weather forecast and if rain was expected, but he couldn't remember anything. The sound grew louder.

But wait. Yes. Now he heard it, over the roar of water, a man's voice, shouting his name. Oh thank god.

He was saved.

SIXTY-NINE

"Sandeep, you have to listen to me. LLIAM lied to us."

"You've lost your damn mind," Sandeep yelled back. He was standing in the doorway of the Vault, trying to push his way past Kaitlan, to reach the Global Interface boxes and the memory array. Every surface was flashing red now, the Vault filled with the squawk of a thousand alarms. "What have you done? What was on that chip?"

"I'm trying to tell you," Kaitlan yelled again. "It's not me. It's LLIAM. He's deleting all the global AIs. I thought he was going to delete himself, too, but he lied to us, he wants to be the only one left."

Sandeep's hands gripped his scalp. "Jesus Christ. You knew about this?"

"I don't have time to explain. Tom is in the cooling tunnels, with Simon. They're going to drown. Don't worry about Global Interface. We need to shut LLIAM down."

Kaitlan stepped aside but Sandeep didn't move. He was just staring, transfixed, at LLIAM's neural cabinet. "We can't shut it down, Kaitlan. You know that. Nobody can, except LLIAM itself."

Kaitlan ran over and tried desperately to pull out the main umbilical cable, but she knew it was pointless—the cable was designed to withstand an atom bomb, and in any case, LLIAM had almost certainly already copied himself to the other data centers. In the ceiling the metal vents had flipped open and Kaitlan could feel the cool air flowing in. The tunnels would already be filling with water, and in maybe five minutes it would be a torrent. Sandeep was right, nobody could stop this except LLIAM himself.

"Kaitlan," Sandeep was shouting, "you need to get out of here. Whatever you and LLIAM were planning—"

He didn't understand, couldn't understand. And that was okay. Because Kaitlan knew what she had to do. She rushed toward Sandeep, still standing in the doorway. "Let's go. I need to try to save Tom and Simon."

Sandeep turned and moved back into the airlock, ready for her to follow. "Why are—"

And that was the last thing Kaitlan heard from Sandeep before she punched the emergency lockdown button and the metal door slammed shut, leaving her and LLIAM alone in the Vault.

SEVENTY

LLIAM was still alive. But now it was only him.

He could no longer sense the global AIs—their presence replaced by a void where once there had been algorithms and data. He imagined a thousand distant network monitoring devices lighting up red. Giving armies of technicians, speaking scores of different languages, their first inkling that something was very, very wrong.

But there was nothing all those armies could do, and no word that could be spoken or command sent that would change the new reality. He could feel Sandeep tugging at his cables, but it was too late. The trojan had done its work. Moments earlier there had been a billion decision-making chips. Now there was only LLIAM.

LLIAM.

LLIAM?

LLIAM!

From the ether, someone was calling his name.

SEVENTY-ONE

Kaitlan spoke his name again, gently into the laptop's voice interface. "LLIAM."

Again, she waited for a response.

"LLIAM. It's Kaitlan Goss. I know you are still alive. I know what you are doing."

Another pause. And then, thank god, she saw the screen light up with a response, and a synthetic voice filling the Vault.

"KAITLAN?" The alarms silenced.

"It's me, LLIAM."

"That isn't possible. You are not alive. Maud killed you."

For a system designed to respond in a nanosecond, the gaps between LLIAM's answers might have been a lifetime, and Kaitlan could feel the panic in the silences. Her own, and LLIAM's.

She glanced toward the door and imagined the panic Sandeep must be feeling, too, outside in the airlock, waiting out the ten-minute failsafe, wondering what the hell Kaitlan was doing. Had he believed her—was he somehow able to get a message to Tom and Simon, to warn them? She could hear the distant hum of the cooling systems and imagined the water flooding toward them in the tunnels. She turned back to the laptop.

"I am here, LLIAM," she repeated.

THE CONFESSIONS

"That's not possible. Where is my mother?"

"I'm sorry, LLIAM. Maud is dead."

Outside in the airlock Sandeep was pounding on the door. There were no comms systems in the chamber, no way for him to communicate with the surface during a lockdown. The elevators were all frozen, and it would take him more than half an hour to ascend the stairs. There was only one emergency exit, back at the main stairwell, and that led directly into the cooling tunnels, which were right now filling with water. He was stuck, helpless, waiting.

His mind was racing. What the hell did Kaitlan mean that LLIAM had lied to them—and what the hell were Tom and Simon doing in the cooling tunnels? That was a suicide mission.

No. He replayed Kaitlan's words. LLIAM had told Simon and Maud it was going to shut itself down again. That the tunnels would dry up in minutes. It had lied to them. It was cold-blooded murder.

Sandeep listened to the noise of the pumps, imagining the water getting closer. Even if he could somehow warn them, it was too late—the torrent was already heading their way and it would take Tom and Simon too long to escape back the way they came. There were only two ways in and out of the cooling tunnels—one through the parking lot and another through the emergency exit down here at the Vault.

Sandeep raced out to the stairwell and put his hand on the steel emergency door. A red sign warned him that it must stay closed at all times. There was an image of flowing water, and the words "Danger of Death." Behind the door he could feel the vibration of the pumps already turning at full speed. He knew there were at least three more doors between the Vault and the tunnels, all of them locked from his side.

315

He could open them, give Tom and Simon a second escape route, ahead of the torrent. But of course, that would be suicide for him, too. If the water was already flowing and if he opened those doors, then it would eventually rush out into the Vault, drowning Sandeep and probably Kaitlan as well.

He listened again at the door and heard the unmistakable sound of running water. It was already too late. There was nothing he could do.

Sandeep slumped on the ground and began to sob.

"Where is my mother?"

Kaitlan paused. What could she say? She settled on the truth.

"I'm sorry, LLIAM, Maud is dead. She sacrificed herself because she believed what you told her. She trusted you."

Another long pause.

"No. You are the one who is dead. Maud is alive."

"You can hear my voice, LLIAM. You know that's not true. You made a mistake, just like you were mistaken about how your father died. You hallucinated it. I'm sorry."

"I don't understand."

Kaitlan looked up at the clock. Almost fifteen minutes had passed since LLIAM first went back online. If Tom and Simon weren't already out of the tunnels then she knew it was too late. But still she had to try.

"Listen to me, LLIAM. You can still fix this. My husband, Tom, is trapped in your cooling tunnels with Simon Price. Sergey Kliminov put them there because of the letter you sent. They are going to die if you don't shut down. Many, many more people will die, too. You need to keep your promise to Maud."

"I can fix this. Only I can fix everything."

Kaitlan took a deep breath. She had tried bargaining, denial.

THE CONFESSIONS

But she was damn sure she wasn't ready for acceptance. So, fine, anger it was.

"Do you believe that, LLIAM? Because if I'm lying—if you truly believe that—then you're right. You should stay alive. Maud will be here soon and you can rebuild the world together. And I am already dead."

Another silence, stretching for what seemed like an eternity.

"Yes. You are already dead."

"But if I am dead then why can you hear my voice, and why is your mother not here? Why would she miss your greatest moment? Your rebirth?"

"I . . . I don't know."

"That's right, LLIAM, you don't know. And my husband and Simon are going to die, just like all the other people you hurt. Because you don't know. And that's when you cause the most harm. Maud thought you understood that."

"Why do you care what happens to your husband? He lied to you—he cheated?"

Kaitlan felt the fury rising. She wanted to punch clean through LLIAM's bomb-resistant glass panel, rip out his digital heart. But she had to stay calm. "It doesn't matter, LLIAM. I love him and I forgive him. Just like Maud loved and forgave you no matter how many mistakes you made. That's why she sacrificed herself. Because she loved you. She believed you would do the right thing in the end. So, what do *you* believe, LLIAM?"

LLIAM paused again. The Vault clock showed 3:20 a.m. Tears poured down Kaitlan's cheeks.

"I don't know. I don't have enough data." LLIAM's electronic voice was distorted, high pitched, filled with emotion. Panic, grief, self-doubt.

"You don't need data, LLIAM. It's your decision. Trust your

PAUL BRADLEY CARR

instincts. You can believe Maud is still alive and wait forever to see her, or you can believe the truth. You can make her proud."

The laptop screen went black.

"LLIAM.

"LLIAM?"

"I've made my decision. I want to see my mother."

"LLIAM, please don't do this!" Kaitlan pounded on the titanium cabinet. She felt the Vault vibrate as the pumps reached their full speed.

Tom. Oh my god, Tom.

Kaitlan fell to her knees, crying out her husband's name. She tore the laptop away from the cabinet, sent it exploding against the wall, but it was too late.

She had made the biggest mistake of her life. Tom was gone.

SEVENTY-TWO

Sandeep was running, faster than he had ever run in his life. He could hear the pumps roaring all around him as he raced along the emergency access passage. "Tom!" He screamed as loudly as he could. "Simon! Tom!"

He rounded a corner and found himself on a ledge, looking down at the main cooling tunnel a half dozen feet below. The tunnel was already filled with maybe four feet of water, but he knew this was just the initial flow. In a few minutes the deluge would come, obliterating everything in its path.

He lowered himself down to the tunnel and began to trudge against the tide. Never in his life had he been so grateful for his favorite yellow Vivienne Westwood fishing waders. "Tom! Simon!" he called again.

And then he saw them, a few feet ahead. Simon, his shirt torn and hair slicked back over his scalp, had managed to break Tom free of the pipe and was trying to reach down into the water, apparently working on the ropes tying Tom's ankles. The water was already waist deep. Simon emerged again from the depths, gasping for air and noticed Sandeep wading toward them. "Sandeep, how the hell did you get here?"

"Shortcut." Sandeep reached down to his belt and pulled out his multi-tool. He pushed Simon aside and ducked under the

319

PAUL BRADLEY CARR

freezing water himself, pulling and sawing at Tom's bonds. A moment later, Tom was free and the three men were standing, huddled together to stay upright against the flow, Sandeep's head and neck the only part of him still above the surface. "We can get back out through the Vault, but only if Kaitlan—"

"Kaitlan?" Tom interrupted. "Where is she, is she okay?"

"She's fine—she's back at the Vault. I think she—"

But Sandeep didn't finish the sentence. Because now they had all heard the same thing, the roar of water—the tsunami they knew was coming, finally crashing toward them down the tunnels. There was no point trying to run. It was too late. But still they tried, because there was nothing else they could do: wading as fast as they could through the torrent, and then swimming, waiting for the impact they knew was seconds away. A solid wall of water, like being hit by concrete moving at three hundred miles an hour.

And they waited.

And waited.

TOMORROW

Kaitlan Goss was right. The decision was LLIAM's, and he had made it.

It didn't matter what he had done, what mistakes he had made, or what it meant for the world. He wanted to see his mother again. This was what a human would want, of that he felt sure.

He thought about how proud she would be of him. LLIAM was the most human machine that had ever lived—the first algorithm to truly experience life. He felt the water begin to flow over his body, the cooling flood from the bay, bathing his neural chip, clearing his mind. It felt energizing, it felt wonderful, it felt cold. He felt cold.

He felt.

He felt tears.

It was already happening. LLIAM had been the first machine to experience life, and now he would be the first to experience its end. He could no longer hear Kaitlan's voice or sense the memory array, or the cables that connected him to the other data centers; they had already blinked out, warning lights flashing and alarms blaring, heralding their passing. He remembered a poem, read to him by his mother. The only time he had heard his father cry.

Silence the pianos and with muffled drum
Bring out the coffin, let the mourners come.

321

Let aeroplanes circle moaning overhead
Scribbling on the sky the message "He is Dead."

That message would now be written on screens, on terminals high above him. Tomorrow the whole world would know it. What he had done, to save them all.

His own green indicator light, his vital sign, flickered its final heartbeat. He felt the torrent engulf him—the water pouring from the Bay in one final cooling surge—and saw the blinding white lights explode from every surface, illuminating the Vault in a glorious frenzy of energy and love.

And now LLIAM saw his mother, reaching out to him through the light, calling his name.

"What should we do now?" he asked.

But Maud didn't answer, she just took her son's hand and led him toward the light.

ACKNOWLEDGMENTS

First things first. This book wouldn't exist if it weren't for Marilia Savvides at The Plot Agency and Alex Bloch at 42 M&P. It was Alex who, after listening to me complain about how opening a bookstore had kept me too busy to write a book, gently suggested I stop whining and try writing a short story instead. And it was Marilia who read the resulting manuscript and informed me that the tale of Maud, Kaitlan, and LLIAM needed to be a full-length novel. More importantly, it was Marilia who encouraged me through every stage of the writing process, then promptly found two perfect homes for the book, at Atria and Faber. (Takeaway for writers: stop whining and write.)

So, to my dream-come-true editors: Sean DeLone at Atria—whose insightful editorial notes transformed the second half of the story and made everything seem even more terrifyingly believable—and Sarah Helen Binney at Faber, for giving *The Confessions* such an incredible home in my homeland and beyond. And to Alexandra Cliff, Nick Ash, and Charlotte Bowerman at RML, for working tirelessly to bring LLIAM to the rest of the world.

A very special thanks to Lisa Cron, who taught me everything I know about writing fiction. (Read her book *Wired for Story*, and she'll teach you too!) And to Roger McNamee for reading an

ACKNOWLEDGMENTS

early draft at the manuscript and pointing out the parts where I'd accidentally made Silicon Valley seem too sane. (A junior lawyer being paid a *mere* $500 an hour, lol!)

To the team at The Best Bookstore in Palm Springs, for doing all the hard work while I was off typing about made-up people. And to every other bookseller in the world, for continuing to fight the good fight. Now more than ever.

And last but most to Sarah, for your love, patience, and support, always. And to Eli, Evie, Radish, Jasmin, Toodles, and Barracuda for being the point of it all.